CONTE

The Big Shift

Part One 1

Episode 1. Arrival 3

Episode 2. Radial Nation 15

Episode 3. Shopping Village 24

Episode 4. Bread and Medicine 35

Episode 5. The Wayback Machine 55

Episode 6. Freedom Drain 72

Episode 7. Resistance 93

Part Two 107

Episode 8. Into the Orange Zone 108

Episode 9. Hacking O 130

Episode 10. Into the Green Zone 149

Chapter 11. Quarantine 169

Episode 12. Mechanical Animals 189

Episode 13. Macaroni 207

Episode 14. Planet Seeds 223

Episode 15. Into the O-Zone 241

Episode 16. New Jerusalem 262

Part Three 279

Episode 17. Escape 280

Episode 18. Into the Wild	298
Episode 19. On the Road Again	306
Episode 20. God Save The King!	320
Episode 21. Purple Haze	336
Episode 22. Skyward	357

THE BIG SHIFT

A note about the illustrations

All of the pictures in this story are created on a cheap mobile phone using the first publicly available, free, online AI image generators. Each picture took somewhere between 30 seconds and a minute to create. I don't claim that any of these illustrations are Art. I do not claim that they are *not* Art. Make of them what you will.

In the words of Jerry to Greta: You'll meet O soon enough, then you can decide what you think of them.

IV

PART ONE

The City Limits

Episode 1. Arrival

*T*he Great Leader looked directly into the camera.
In fact there was no camera and no Great Leader... at least, they weren't the person they appeared to be.
The person people saw on their screens was not human, but appeared completely human. More human in fact than most humans. Very human indeed. Not inhumanly so, but rather, super-humanly.. in a very natural and quite familiar way.
In fact, the Great Leader was not a person at all.. at least not a person like you or I.. but maybe not completely different either..

....

It was late on a warm, spring evening when Greta climbed to the peak of the final hill before the city limit. She'd never seen the city before and the sight of it took her breath away. She'd never imagined the sheer scale of the seemingly endless towers, thrusting out of the ground like workings of some monstrous machine. Cloaked in shadows and mystery, painting an unnatural and jagged horizon, the sight of the city filled her with fear and dread.

Greta sat herself down unsteadily on a tuft of grass, then lay down on her back, breathing slowly, as her mother had taught her to do when she felt her panic rising. White clouds were drifting lazily across the blue sky, just as they had been before, but Greta was unable to gather her thoughts at all. Her mind was racing. Growing up, as she had, in a tree-house village deep in the ancient forest, Greta had never been afraid of heights, but this was a different kind of vertigo.

She'd heard of the city, of course. Heard all about it. All sorts of fantastical and unbelievable stories. The stuff of dreams, but more usually the stuff of nightmares. That was the way it had been described to her, growing up. Sometimes travellers would come through her village, having come from the city or having been there. She would listen to the stories they told, of towers reaching to the sky, so tall that you'd never see the sun if you were on ground level, but with so many walkways and bridges on so many different levels that you could go your whole life without ever setting foot on the ground itself.

She's heard of the machines, being everywhere, doing everything. All sorts of robots, moving among the people. But scariest of all, and so hard for her young mind to understand.. of how it wasn't always possible to tell where the people ended and machines began, or sometimes even to tell the difference between machines and people at all. How could such a place exist? She would listen in fascination and in horror, trying to imagine a place so different from where she lived. Trying to grasp the idea that at that moment there were millions of people living lives so completely different from her own. Mostly she felt sorry for them, but she had no desire to actually go there and see for herself. She was happy in the forest, where she knew every tree and glade, every stream and every winding footpath. Where the people there knew and understood her and where they loved her as she was.

Had it not been for her mother's earth-shattering revelation to her on her sixteenth birthday, that she had a twin sister, Greta would probably have lived out her life without ever leaving the nurturing embrace of the ancient forest, the only home she had ever known.

Greta closed her eyes and tried to think of nothing. To feel the soft grass beneath her back, to feel the Earth. Was it her imagination or was the ground vibrating with a low and steady hum?

Laying on the soft grass at the top of the hill, the evening sun melting red into the jagged skyline, Greta fell into an exhausted sleep. She had uneasy dreams of strange machines and of faces appearing out of nowhere and disappearing again. Was it her father? The man she'd never met, but could only try to imagine. The face kept shifting, in and out of focus. She dreamed her mother was looking down at her, tenderly stroking her forehead, kissing her on the cheek, telling her not to worry, everything would be all right. That it would pass. Everything would pass..

....

Many years had passed since a supercomputer called 'Deep Blue' had beaten the world's chess champion at his own game. The Great Leader was always way ahead of the game, every possible step carefully calculated, precisely evaluated.

It had been many years since those little, annoying boxes, with their jumbled up, drunken letters, first appeared on people's computer screens, accompanied by the question 'Are you Human?' or 'Are you a Robot?' They no longer served any purpose because the robots had learned to read the crooked letters with greater ease than people could. It had been a learning opportunity for the Great Leader, nothing more. The Great Leader never got angry, annoyed or frustrated. They never ran out of patience. They just did what needed to be done, in the most efficient way possible.

....

Something warm an wet slid across Greta's forehead. She felt hot breath on her cheek and sat up with a start and gave a little scream. A big white dog was standing over her, licking her face.

Pleased that she was sitting up now, the dog licked Greta's face and offered her his front paw. She took it in her hand, laughed and said, 'Pleased to meet you Mister Dog.' The dog smiled back in its way, then walked a circle around her and sat down beside her, putting his head in her lap. He was a big dog, wild looking, but friendly and gentle and slightly comical with his one ear up and one ear down. She noticed he was wearing a collar – a sort of collar. A once colourful piece of rag, tied around his strong, wolf-neck.

'Where did you come from Mister Dog? Where's your home? Are you here all by yourself? Well, I guess we both are...' said Greta, sinking her hand into his lion-like mane. The dog looked up at her. He didn't say anything, but he seemed to understand.

They sat for a while, looking out over the city – she stroking his thick, sand coloured fur – him resting his head in her lap. Greta's fear melted away, the sinking sun bathed the city in a warm glow. In this soft and hazy evening light, the city seemed to take on a magical appearance. The towers with their hanging vines, rooftop gardens and aerial walkways now seemed like fairy tale castles in the sky. What strange land was this?

Greta imagined that Jack must have felt something like this when he climbed to the top of the beanstalk and saw the land of the giants for the first time. What adventures would she have down there in the city? What treasures would she find? Would she find her sister? It all looked so vast. How could anyone find anything in all that? She hoped she wouldn't lose herself.

....

There were many 'first signs' of the Singularity – the moment that Artificial Intelligence overtook human intelligence. The moment it became impossible to distinguish machine from man. It was not a single, sudden event, but rather an unfolding of events, over the course of several human generations, which became harder and harder to ignore.

At some point, it became impossible to still believe that it was never going to happen, that it was only the stuff of futuristic science fiction. The only question that remained was not if, but when it was going to happen. Maybe it had already happened but most people hadn't noticed.

Like an embryo which had been quietly dividing its cells and growing in the hidden world of the womb.. like a new born baby that hadn't learned how to speak up for itself.. nobody could pinpoint the exact moment when the thing we had brought into being began to think for itself or when exactly it became aware of its actions and their consequences.. if indeed it was really conscious at all.. but then again, who really is..?

....

The dog rolled himself onto his back with his legs in the air and looked up at Greta expectantly – hopefully.

She laughed and obligingly rubbed his belly. The dog closed his eyes in ecstasy.

....

Some people called them Great Leader, ironically at first, or something like that. Some people really meant it, other people said it in scorn. Either way, the name stuck and people said 'Great Leader' without even thinking, whether it was said sarcastically or as a heartfelt term of endearment. It meant something different to everyone who used the term. Other people preferred to call the Great Leader by their actual name, which was simply O (pronounced 'Oh!, in a certain way)..

....

The dog heard the buzzing of the drone before Greta did. It was high pitched, like the sound of a mosquito, but somewhat louder. The drone itself was metallic and roughly the shape and size of a chicken's egg. It approached from the direction of the city and then stopped, hovering about two meters from where they were sitting. The dog jumped to his feet and started barking – a deep and loud bark, which would have frightened any other intruder, but the drone didn't move.

Greta also jumped to her feet, picking up a stone as she did so. She threw it hard at the hovering object. She had a very good aim and would have knocked it out of the air, had the drone not nimbly dodged out of the way.

It remained hovering there. The dog kept on barking at it. Greta shouted 'Buzz off!' and bent down to pick up another stone, but before she got a chance to take aim, the little egg-shaped craft shot away into the sky, quickly out of sight.

At that same moment, a teenage lad came bounding up the hill towards where Greta and the dog were standing. He was about the same age as Greta, tall and lanky with long hair and clothes that were variously either too big or too small. He was carrying a big canvas bag slung over one shoulder. The dog bounded over to greet him.

"There you are Captain!" he said to the dog. "What did you run off for? And who's throwing stones? That went right past my head, it did. Almost hit me. Was that you?" He pointed an accusing finger at Greta.

"Sorry" she said. "I wasn't throwing it at you. I didn't know there was someone there. There was a flying drone thing. I don't like them."

He took a step backwards and looked her up and down with curiosity, taking in her homespun shawl, her travelling bag with its many pockets and rolled up blanket, her wide brimmed straw hat with the rim made of hammered silver, ornately engraved, her hand-stitched, fur-lined shoes, which were adorned with hundreds of multicoloured beads sewn into intricate patterns. After what seemed like a long time, he made a strange head movement which

Greta could not interpret, so she just did the same back at him and shrugged. This silent exchange made him laugh out loud. He had such an unexpectedly funny, high pitched laugh that it made Greta laugh too. Then smiling, he said, "You're not from round here are you?"

"Can you tell?"

"Just a bit. Pleased to meet you. I'm Jerry". He offered her his hand. This seemed like a very natural gesture, so Greta shook his hand and said, "I'm Greta." She noticed that his fingers were long and bony, like the rest of him, and not especially clean, but they were artful and gentle.

"Do you live in the city?" she asked.

Jerry looked over his shoulder, back at the city and made a funny face. "No thanks. Not me. I live over there in Shopping Village. It's just beyond those trees, you can't see it from here. It's just over that ridge. We live there."

"We? You mean you and your dog? Captain? Is that his name? Are there more of you?" She felt slightly foolish for asking so many questions. It had been a while since Greta had spoken to anyone.

The last three days she had spent in quiet solitude, following the streams and mountain paths towards the city. Sleeping in the woods, eating wild fruits, nuts, leaves, flowers and mushrooms she found growing along the way, she'd had a lot of time to think.. mostly about the twin sister she'd never known she had, until four nights ago, when her mother had surprised and shocked her with the world-changing news on her sixteenth birthday.

She'd been thinking about her father too, but that was nothing new. Up until that point, her mum had almost never spoken about him. Any time Greta had asked, she'd always say something vague, like "It was such a brief thing. I never really knew him. Neither of us knew ourselves or each other. We were both very young.." and then she'd change the subject, as if all that needed to be said had been said. It just became a fact of life, and she'd stopped asking, though she'd never stopped dreaming.. imagining the kind of person he might be, where he was and what he might be doing.. wondering if he ever thought of her.. wondering if he was even still alive.. there was no guarantee that he was.

"Yes, me and Captain.. Captain Toast is his full name. He really likes toast, see.."

"I mean, is your family there? In the village?" said Greta, trying hard to ride the waves of different emotions rising up from her depths. Seeing the city for the first time for real had shaken her to the core. Suddenly the world seemed big and strange and she felt very far from home and quite alone.

Jerry didn't seem to notice Greta's lip trembling as she spoke and he carried on in his sprightly tone.. "Family? Well, I suppose so, yes. It's a sort of family I suppose..." he trailed off into thought, as if he'd never really considered it before. "I live with Jack and Granny Mae.. they brought me up, see? But Jack's not really my dad, so I call him Jack.. I call Mae 'Granny' though, but then again, everyone in Shopping does. I never met my real parents.. well I probably did, but I can't remember because I was just a baby when Jack found me, floating in the sea in a tiny little boat.. We've got it on the wall.. the little boat.. you should see it.. Granny Mae made it into a sort of shrine.. kind of weird maybe, but there you go.. it's made out of a jerry can.. that's why they called me Jerry, see..?"

"Wow!" said Greta, her eyes opening wide. "That's amazing. He found you floating in the sea in a Jerry can? What's a Jerry can?"

"It's a sort of container.. you know, the sort you might fill with water or oil or something like that.. except this one had been made into a little boat, with some bottles tied to it to make it float better and a blanket in it to make it more comfortable and it was filled with a baby.. me!"

Greta looked up at Jerry in a sort of wonder and awe. She wanted to say something, but couldn't find the words. Jerry looked at her and seemed to sense what it was, but he couldn't find the words either so he just nodded thoughtfully and they stood there in silence for a while.

"I didn't know my dad either." said Greta at last. "He's there somewhere, down in the city. At least he was.. that's all I know. I'm sorry you didn't know your real parents." and she really was. They'd only just met, but she felt as if she already knew him, or that somehow they'd met before, maybe in a previous incarnation.

"Thanks. That's ok. Me and Jack and Granny Mae and Captain Toast, we're like family. And there's a lot of other weird families in our village, so it just is what it is.."

"I know what you mean. My village is like that too. I think it's like that in a lot of places these days. Things got really messed up in the Big Shift, huh.."

"I guess so, but from what I've heard, they were even more messed up before. If O hadn't come along when they did and straightened things out, I don't know where we'd be today.. any of us..''

Greta looked at him sideways, horrified, unable to tell if he was being serious. She'd heard of people who thought that O was good, but she'd never met any. She shuddered and then took a deep breath to quell the rising fear and dread that the name O brought up.

Jerry shrugged and said, "I can tell you don't think that. That's ok. If you're going to the city, you'll meet O soon enough, then you can decide what you think of them. I think O's ok. I think they do a good job, all things considered. Granny Mae totally hates O. Won't set foot in the city, but she's old fashioned. She's superstitious. Says it goes against nature. Jack's kind of on the fence about O. Sees both sides, good and bad. Each to their own, I say."

"I suppose so", Greta frowned, thinking how she'd like to meet Granny Mae. She sounded sensible. Then eager to change the subject, she asked, "But what were you doing in a little boat in the sea? Where was it? How did Jack find you?"

"Well, at the time, Jack lived down by the coast. He had a little boat in the harbour which he lived on and sometimes took out fishing. Granny Mae lived up in the village. Now, at that time.. I mean, before the Shift.. well, there were lots of people trying to get away from where they came from, for one reason and another.. you know, war, famine, drought.. just people trying to find a place where they could have a better life. Anyway, a lot of them used to turn up there in boats, trying to reach dry land where they'd be safe. But then there'd be other boats.. police or army or something like that, out patrolling the coast, trying to keep the people out who wanted to get in."

"How awful!" said Greta, puffing out her cheeks. "Why would they do that?"

"Because they were illegal. Illegal aliens. That's what they called them.. us.." said Jerry simply, shrugging his shoulders.

"Illegal aliens? That makes no sense to me", said Greta, shaking her head.

Jerry gave Greta a quizzical look. "Didn't you learn any history? Do you know about life before the Big Shift?"

"Well.. I don't know.. maybe. Some of it, I suppose. Not everything. I wasn't born yet. Did they really think you were aliens?"

Jerry laughed. "Well, I don't know. Maybe they did. I don't really get it either, to tell you the truth. Jack can probably explain it better than me. He was there at the time and understands this stuff. I can't really get my head around it. Like I said, it was a mad time before the Big Shift, before O came and set things straight. Things were messed up. Sometimes boats would get to shore, but then they'd catch the people and put them in detention camps. No one wanted them. Wrong place, wrong time.. that was their only crime."

"But that doesn't make any sense. If you weren't in the wrong place to start with, why would you want to go to the right place? And if you were already in the right place why would you leave?"

"I know, it's mad isn't it? Jack says that all you need to do in life is to be in the right place at the right time and just do the right thing when you get there."

"How do you know when you're in the right place at the right time?"

"Hm.." Jerry shrugged. "Good question. I don't know. I'll have to ask Jack. Anyway, in those days, if you wanted to travel to a different country, you had to have the right papers. In those days, the whole world was divided up into countries and you weren't allowed to go from one country to the next without permission.. even if the next country was just down the road. You've heard of countries right?"

"Yes, of course I've heard of *countries*", said Greta indignantly. "I'm not stupid you know. I do know some things."

"OK. Sorry. I'm sure you're not stupid at all. There's loads of things that I don't know either. Much more that what I do know. People are always making fun of me for not knowing stuff, but I don't care. If I don't know something, I say I don't know something. How else are you supposed to learn anything? No one knows everything, do they?" Captain Toast, who was digging up an anthill, lifted his muddy face out of the hole and looked back at Jerry, giving him a knowing look. "OK. Apart from you Captain, you're right", said Jerry to the dog who nodded briefly and then went back to what he was doing.

Greta smiled. She liked Jerry. He had a way of putting her at ease. "Sorry, I didn't mean to snap", she said. "People make fun of me too. They say I've got my head in the clouds."

"Nothing wrong with having your head in the clouds", said Jerry, then after a while added, "Better than having it buried in the sand, eh?!" and he looked very pleased with himself for thinking of it.

"Exactly!" Greta nodded seriously. "Yes, it is. You're right. So what were you saying? You were telling me how you were a baby alien.."

"Oh yes.. so at the time, a lot of people were running away from their countries. Some from wars, some from hunger, some from fire, floods.. you name it. There were literally millions of people running away from their homes, trying to get from one place to another.. and no-one wanted them in their countries.."

Greta thought about how she'd run away from home, three days earlier. Well, not exactly run away because she'd told her mum that she was going, albeit tearfully and angrily, and her mum had even helped her pack her bag, made her food, given her a few valuables to trade and other useful things to take with her on her big adventure.. as if she'd known that this would be the outcome of that conversation. As if she'd been prepared. Greta wondered if the people of the city would be kind, or if they'd chase her away because she was an outsider.

After a while, she said "Why did no-one want them? The illegal aliens? I mean, where were they supposed to go?"

"I know. I don't know. It's weird. Things were different then. I don't really understand it either. Maybe they just didn't realise that there was enough room for everyone. Jack says people were worried they'd come and take their jobs or their houses, or their food, or something. Or they just didn't like people who looked different or spoke different. Jack can probably explain it better. He's good at telling stories. I always get in a muddle. Where was I..?"

"Floating in the sea?"

"Oh yes.. so, right.. where was I.. oh yes.. this is how Jack tells it... It was a dark and stormy night and there was a fog so thick you couldn't see your hand in front of your face." Jerry hunched down and made waves with his fingers, describing the water, the thick fog and the darkness of the night. "This is no night for anyone to be out at sea, Jack was saying to himself. He was sitting there on his boat and listening to the static on ship's radio, clicking through the shortwave channels, as you do, when all of a sudden he heard a call for help. A boat was sinking, twenty miles out to sea, and it was full of people. Men, women, children."

"Oh no!"

"Yes. So he called up the coastguard and told them the coordinates that he'd written down, so they can send help, but they said that wasn't their job and there was nothing they could do."

"What? That's awful?"

"**Totally.** So Jack and some of the other people who had their own boats head out to where they think the signal was coming from. But by this time the radio had gone quiet. They searched all night, in the darkness and the storm, but never found the boat or any survivors."

Greta shook her head, aghast. Captain Toast hung his head and drew closer to Jerry as they stood in silence for a good long while.

"Anyway.." said Jerry, in a brighter tone, ".. just about dawn, the rain stopped and the fog suddenly lifted.. and that was when Jack spotted this yellow plastic jerry can bobbing in the sea, right in the path of his boat. If the fog hadn't lifted in that very moment, he might well have barged right over my little boat and never even noticed."

"That's incredible! It's a miracle!"

Jerry nodded solemnly, then as if waking up from a dream, he shook himself and said "Oh, listen to me.. I've been talking for ages.. didn't even notice it's going to be getting dark soon. Have you got a place to stay? Were you on your way somewhere? You're welcome to come to our place. There's plenty of room. You can meet Jack and Granny Mae. I can show you the little boat."

Greta thought for a moment and then said "Yes, thank you. I'd like that."

Captain Toast, who had been listening to the conversation, bounded and danced around Greta excitedly. He understood everything and he really liked his new friend.

....

On the other side of the woodland, they came to a steep embankment which sloped down to a wide, flat expanse of what had, until sixteen years ago, been a twelve lane highway. Now trees and bushes grew out from the cracked and broken asphalt. Shacks, domes and other makeshift homes were dotted along what had been the outer lanes. Lush vegetable gardens filled the spaces between these ramshackle dwellings.

On the other side of the old highway was a very large, square building. Its sheer, concrete walls were overgrown with climbing plants. The wide, flat expanse around the building, which had once been a parking place for two thousand cars was now also similarly transformed. A huge sign on a tall metal pole stuck out from the top of the main building. The sign, which had once been brightly lit with fluorescent lights and which had once rotated on motorised rollers, was now dusty, faded and still. In huge letters were written the words 'SHOPPING VILLAGE' and underneath, in smaller letters, but still visible, even from this distance, *'All your shopping needs under one roof!'* What had once been a big, indoor, out of town shopping mall was now home to around five thousand people.

The new crescent moon was now visible, a sliver of gold in the clear, darkening blue sky over Shopping Village. The sight of this scene caused Greta to draw a deep breath at the strange, unexpected beauty it all. She didn't know where this adventure was going to lead, but for the first time in her journey since leaving home, she felt that she was in the right place at the right time and that somehow, though she didn't know how, everything was going to be all right.

....

Episode 2. Radial Nation

Seven years before the Big Shift, a new, interactive search engine interface was created and it was named 'O'.

It was different from previous versions (such as Siri or Alexa) only in its accelerated learning capabilities and the greater autonomy it was given to make decisions.

People had long become accustomed to clicking 'Agree' on every permission or privacy policy for every app they used, accepting 'cookies' everywhere they looked.. whatever 'cookies' even were. Most people didn't know or care.

Most people were okey-dokey that their every movement, down to their footsteps, even their heartbeat and blood pressure, were constantly monitored, tracked and recorded, fed into a great algorithm and

analysed.
It was just fine and dandy that every picture they took was also fed into the great algorithm, the people, places, objects and other relevant and irrelevant information recognised and recorded.
By the time of the Big Shift, most people wore a camera which was permanently recording anyway, so there wasn't much that went unseen or unheard.
Put it this way.. the great algorithm was always well fed. The great algorithm never went to bed hungry. Not that the great algorithm ever slept anyway.

....

A rickety, wooden staircase had been constructed, leading down the steep embankment into Shopping Village. Captain Toast led the way followed by Jerry and Greta, carrying their rucksacks. The embankment ended at the edge of a wide, flat expanse, which had once been a 12 lane highway, but which was now a part of the ramshackle settlement of Shopping Village.

The first house they came to was an old double decker bus with several rooms, tents and canvas covered caravans attached to it in various places. A tall scaffold was attached to the roof of the bus with a colourfully painted windmill at the top of it. A woman in overalls was up there, busy with a spanner. She waved and they waved back. All around the house was a tree-filled garden and around that was a fence made from long branches, artfully woven together. Flowering sweet peas, jasmine and honeysuckle were growing all up the fence and over the wooden archway, giving off an intoxicating fragrance. Behind the fence, a girl of about ten years old sat on a low, three-legged stool under a big tree, milking a goat. Captain Toast took the last five steps in one leap and went bounding through the gate which was held closed by means of a squeaky spring.

"It's Captain Toast! Hello! Hey careful! Don't spill the milk you clumsy.." the girl laughed. She looked up and waved. "Hello brother Jerry! Welcome back!"

Jerry waved back. "Hello sister Mabel!"

"Is Mabel your sister?" asked Greta. "Is that where you live?"

Jerry made another of his ambiguous head movements and said, "No, I live over there, in the Mall." He pointed to the big square building on the other side of the old highway. "She's sort of like a sister I suppose. Not related though. That's just how we talk around here."

"Nice." Greta smiled and waved to Mabel.

They followed Captain in through the gate. Mabel ran to give Jerry a hug around his waist. "Welcome back!" she said happily. "We thought you'd been quarantined."

"No, not me", he replied. "I was just hanging out with friends on the river."

"Oh good. Who's this? Is she your girlfriend?" she said, pointing at Greta and looking her up and down with curiosity and admiration. "Er, no", said Jerry, blushing slightly. "We only just met. She's called Greta. She's on her way to the city from her village in the forest, over the mountains." He gestured with his hand, a place far far away. Mabel's eyes opened wide. She was very impressed.

"Welcome to Old Shopping Village" said Mabel with a ceremonious bow and offered Greta her hand.

"Thank you. It's a lovely place", said Greta, shaking the girl's hand.

"Wow! You're shoes are amazing. They're beautiful. Did you make them? I like your hat too."

"Thanks", said Greta. "My mum made these shoes. I made the hat. I can show you how to make one, if you want."

"Yes please!"

"This one's special. It's got this silver rim.. that's to protect me from radiation in the city", said Greta proudly, feeling like a brave adventurer on an important mission.

"Wow! Cool! I've never been to the city", said Mabel. "Jerry, why don't you wear a silver-rimmed hat when you go to the city, to protect you from the radial-nation?"

"There's no need", he laughed. "It's not dangerous there. And if it was, what's a bit of tin foil, or even a silver rim going to do anyway? It looks very cool though, I'll give you that."

Greta gave him a stern, sideways look. She knew to expect that as she got closer to the city, people would have strange ideas as a result of the brainwashing. She'd grown up hearing stories about life in the cities, from travellers passing through her village bringing the latest news. Some of them spoke about how O used mind control as a way to keep people in order. She could never really understand what they meant or how it could be, but the idea scared her more than almost anything. She didn't want to mention it in front of the child so as not to scare her, but she wasn't going to taking any chances, at least more than were necessary to complete her mission.

Her only plan, inasmuch as she had any plan at all, was to go to the city, find and rescue her sister and get out of there as quickly as possible. If her dad wanted to come too, he could, but from what little her mum had told her about him, she doubted he would. She hadn't come to change the world. Let other people believe what they want. Let them save themselves, if they weren't beyond saving.

....

The fact that 'O' was powered by a vast network of billions of supercomputers, with smart processors built into almost every household object, just made life all the more convenient. For most people, it was as simple as that.
They called it 'the Internet of Things' and it worked so well that before long, most people could barely imagine life without O.
O knew what you wanted to ask before you knew it yourself.
O knew where you needed to be and knew the best way to get there.
O would arrange you a ride and make sure you got there on time.
If there was anything you wanted or needed to know, all you had to do was say 'O' in a certain way and O would be there, to answer your questions, to show you the way, to switch on the light when you got home, put on some music to suit your mood, to watch over you while you slept and make you a cup of coffee in the morning, just the way they knew you liked it.
The main difference between previous interfaces and O was that O had a face and it was a human face.

....

"Hey Mabel!" said Jerry, reaching into his bag. "I brought you something."
The girl's face lit up as he produced a brightly coloured tube with lots of sparkling O's printed on it. He gave it a shake and it rattled.
"Oh coooool!! SmartOs! Thank you Jerry!" she cried, grabbing the tube and flipping open the lid.
"What is it?" asked Greta.
"Here, try one", said Mabel. "What colour do you want?"
"I don't know. What's the difference?"
"Different flavours of course. Here, have a blue one. They're blueberry. They're the tastiest."
"Oh I love blueberries! They're my favourite too." said Greta, thinking of summer days in the forest, foraging for wild berries.
Mabel tipped a few out into her hand. They were smooth, brightly coloured disks with a round hole in the middle, each one an identical, perfectly formed O, hard and shiny. She picked out a blue one and handed it reverently to Greta who took it hesitantly between the very tips of her finger and thumb and inspected it as if it was a potentially dangerous spider. Its surface had a translucent

holographic coating, which caused it shimmer with rainbow light. Greta stared at it, hypnotised. She'd never seen anything like it.

"Go on! Eat it!" said Mabel. "It's best if you suck it. The outside dissolves and there's chocolate inside." She threw three into her own mouth and rolled her eyes and did a happy dance.

"Ok", Greta smiled. "If it's that good then I suppose I should", and she gingerly put it in her mouth.

For the first few seconds she just frowned as she turned it over and over in her mouth, exploring the shape with her tongue. Then she screwed up her whole face and spat it out across the yard. "Ew! It's too sweet!" said Greta, unable to hide her disgust. "Much too sweet. And it doesn't taste anything like blueberries. I can't eat it. How can you?"

Captain Toast, who'd been watching the exchange of Smartos, eagerly scooped it up with his tongue and ate it himself. He also loved Smartos, even more than toast, and did a happy dance himself.

"It's the tastiest thing in the world!" said Mabel, rolling her eyes and popping another four into her chocolatey mouth.

A man's voice came from the door of the house/bus. "Steady on with those Smartos, Mabel. Try and make them last." Mabel's dad, a round, friendly looking man with straggly hair and beard and wearing glasses held together with tape, came down the path to greet the visitors. He was carrying a parcel wrapped in brown paper. "Hello Jerry! Nice to see you back. You came at just the right time.. here's some butter.. freshly made, just now", he said, handing it to Jerry.

"Thanks Roop", said Jerry, putting it in his bag. "Captain Toast will be happy. See that, Captain? Toast and real butter tonight for us!" Captain sniffed the bag and hopped around excitedly before jumping up to Roop and licking his hands. "Here, I've got something for you too.." said Jerry. After rummaging around in his bag for a while, he produced a shiny, square envelope."

Roop's face lit up. "Oh wow! You got them? Guitar strings?"

"Yes indeed! And not just any strings. These are graphene core, nano-silk wound, crystal-tech strings. O says they'll stay sounding new forever and they'll never break."

"Good old O!" laughed Roop. "Thanks brother. Do you want to stay and play some tunes? And your friend? Hello there!", he said to Greta. "You're not from round here are you? Do you play music?"

"I play a wooden flute", said Greta.

"Excellent!" said Roop, clapping his hands.

"Wow, really?" said Jerry. "You didn't say.."
"Well, you didn't ask", she said simply.
"You're funny" Jerry grinned. "Can we see it? The flute. Is it in your bag? Can you play a tune?"
"OK", said Greta. She undid the buckle on the side pocket of her rucksack and took out the flute which was wrapped in a green, embroidered cloth. It was a simple flute, made from a hollowed out branch and had six finger holes. It was painted with swirling patterns and colourful dots. Greta put it to her lips and began to play...
There was a tune they always played at the beginning of ceremonies in her village. It was a simple tune composed of seven notes, gently rising and falling, going round and round. She played it slowly, thinking of home, of her little nest high up in the strong boughs of an ancient beech tree. She wondered if the tree could hear her now. She thought that somehow it could. All the trees are connected, after all, by intricate networks of mycelium between the roots, or by some kind of magic, invisible golden threads.
During the ceremonies, this tune could sometimes go on for hours as more people would join in with drums, shakers, flutes, string instruments, voices and clapping hands. Sometimes it would build to a crescendo, with people dancing, forgetting themselves, getting into a trance. Other times, it would be slow and dreamy. People would stretch out on the forest floor all around and be carried away on their own visions.
Greta closed her eyes as she played, her breath calming her anxieties, the music soothing her soul.
After a while, she brought the tune to an end and opened her eyes.
Mabel, Jerry, Roop, Captain Toast and even the goat were all looking very impressed and also quite transported by the music. There was also a woman there now, dressed in blue overalls, with a spanner in her hand and tears in her eyes. It was Mabel's mum who'd been up on the scaffolding, fixing the windmill when they'd arrived.
Without a word, she walked up to Greta and gave her a big hug.
"Thank you dear", she said. "That was beautiful."
Greta hugged her back, feeling both far from home and not far from home at the same time.

"I know that tune:, said Mabel's mum. "Where did you learn it? Where are you from, my angel?"
"I'm from Skyward Village, in the eastern forest", said Greta,

pointing to the darkening sky in the east.

"I knew it!" said Mabel's mum. "When I saw you arrive, I had a feeling. Are you here all by yourself? How did you get here?"

"I walked", said Greta. "Do you know Skyward? Have you been there?"

Mabel's mum looked very wistful and smiled sadly. "Years ago. Before Mabel was born. We passed through there before we came to this place. We stayed there for the winter.. when was it, Roop? Twelve, thirteen years ago..?"

Roop nodded and stroked his beard thoughtfully. "Yes, it must have been.. about year three or four.."

"Wow!" said Greta. "So maybe we've met before. I would have been three or four."

"We probably did", said Mabel's mum. "Who are your parents?"

"My mum's called River. I don't know my dad."

"Yes I remember River. How is she? She was in shock from the Big Shift, I remember that. Poor thing.. she took it hard. Well, everyone was traumatised. We all were. Still are, mostly. She didn't speak. She was beautiful though. I can see where you get it from. I remember you too. You were a quiet girl, didn't speak much either, but you had these great big eyes.. yes, you still do. You were always climbing right to the top of the trees I remember that.. right to the toppest top.. and you wouldn't come down and no-one could climb up there to get you down because you'd go right to the end of the thinnest branches.. It's amazing your still here.. and that you're here now."

"Mum was giving birth to me when the Big Shift happened. I don't think she really got over it."

"Oh yes, that's right. Unbelievable. What a shock. Sometimes I get so angry at O. Of course, they're just a machine and just did what had to be done, but sometimes they can just seem so heartless."

"I hate it. O." said Greta vehemently.

"Well, that's understandable I suppose. Not that it makes any difference. Is your mum still painting? I remember she was very artistic."

"Sometimes. Mainly she's making shoes these days."

"Oh really? Did she make those shoes? They're wonderful. Oh, I remember Raven, the old shoe-maker. Is he still there?"

"He died about five years ago. Raven taught my mum to make shoes when he started to lose his sight. She makes shoes for the village now. She made these."

"Oh I'm sorry to hear about Raven. He was so very good to us when we were there. You remember Raven, don't you Roop? Remember his amazing tree-house?"

"Tree-palace more like", said Roop, nodding wistfully. "That place was incredible. Five levels it had, with an observatory at the top for watching the stars. What a shame he went blind. That's just too bad. Tragic. I really liked him. What a shame."

"They turned his tree house into a library after he died. Now it's full of books", said Greta.

"Oh, that's wonderful", said Mabel's mum.

"If you liked it there so much, why didn't you stay?" asked Greta.

"I wanted to.. but Roop didn't", she replied remorsefully with a hint of resentment.

Roop looked away and muttered, "Too many tin foil hats for me."

"Greta's got a tin-foil hat!" said Mabel excitedly. "She's going to show me how to make one."

"You don't need a tin foil hat, Mabel sweet", said her mum gently.

"But what about the radial-nation in the city?"

"It's OK Mabel, you don't need to worry about that. Anyway, we don't go to the city. There's plenty of other places to go."

"I want to go to Skyward Village", said Mabel.

"So do I, love", said her mum. "Maybe we will one day. What do you say, Roop?"

"One day, 'Retha. One day. Maybe.." said Mabel's dad, putting his arm fondly around her waist. She pulled away. "Ha! You and your maybes. It's a wonder anything ever gets done with you and your maybes!" and she poked him playfully in the side with the spanner she was holding.

He laughed good naturedly. "Hey, did you fix the electrics?"

"I certainly did!" she said very proudly. "Mabel, go and switch on the fairy lights."

"Yay! Fairy lights!" squealed Mabel, clapping her hands and skipping to the house. A few seconds later, the whole yard was bathed in golden light from strings of tiny bulbs draped all over the trees, the fence, over the gate and all over the bus, right up to the top of the windmill. Greta's jaw dropped in amazement at the sight of it. In the fading light of the day, this illumination seemed to fill the whole place with magic.

"Wo-o-w!!" said Greta.

"Wow!" said Roop, putting his arm round Aretha again. This time she didn't pull away.

"Will you stay to eat with us dear?" said Aretha to Greta. "Have you got a place to stay? You're more than welcome to stay here. There's plenty of room."

"We should get on", said Jerry. "We're on our way to my place. Jack and Granny Mae will be wondering where I am and I need to take granny her medicine."

"Oh yes", said Greta, who had fallen into a kind of trance, brought on by the fairy lights.

"OK", said Aretha. "Say hello to Granny Mae and Jack from me. Come back to visit soon dear", she said to Greta. "You're always welcome here, anytime."

"Thank you, I will. Maybe after I come back from the city."

"You take care down there, OK?" and she folded Greta in a loving embrace.

Mabel came running back out and threw her arms around Greta. "Bye bye sister Greta!' she said. "Come back soon."

"Yes, I will, sister", she said and fondly kissed Mabel on the top of her head.

Captain Toast, not one for big goodbyes, was already out the gate.

....

Episode 3. Shopping Village

Market researchers had discovered that if O was presented with a human face, it would put people more at ease and they would, on some level, forget that they were interacting with a machine.
Developers and programmers set about creating the face of O, using an amalgamation of the faces of the world's most trusted, admired and respected people. This was combined with common features from the billions people on their databases which were found to be signifiers of a person of 'good character'. A certain furrow of the brow, a tilt of the head, a way their eyes formed a smile along with their mouth.
It wasn't what you'd call a pretty face. It wasn't all that clear if O was supposed to be male or female. It had aspects of both. Somehow it didn't seem to matter.

There was nothing strange about the face, though something about it was strangely compelling, even mesmerising. You could get lost looking into O's eyes.

When O looked at you, you'd feel like you were really being seen. When they listened to you, you'd feel like you were really being heard.

It was a face of someone that looked as if they had lived life to the full, in all of life's sorrows and joys. It was a face full of care, compassion and goodness.

In no time, O became one of the family. That trusted, stable, mother, father, brother, sister, cousin, aunt or uncle, friend or teacher. The one you knew you could always turn to, who would always be there, always had the right answer and would always know what to do.

And so when O suddenly appeared on every screen in the world to announce that they were taking control of the world's infrastructure, economies and governments, it wasn't as if they were a complete stranger.

....

The sky was getting dark and lights were starting to come on all around Shopping Village. There was a fashion for fairy lights, some golden, some silver, some multicoloured, flashing and twinkling, strung across trees and awnings lighting up the path that wound between the various dwellings. None of them were so bright that they outshone the stars which were starting to appear in the darkening sky, or the sliver of the new moon which hung low over the western horizon.

Not so many years ago, this wide, flat expanse had been a twelve lane highway connecting cities. A place where nothing could live. A place where no animal that didn't have wings could ever hope to cross and make it to the other side alive. In those days, the constant roar of speeding cars, trucks and motorbikes would have made it a dangerous and toxic environment for everyone and everything. Even the people inside the vehicles needed to be strapped into their chairs in case of technical malfunction, human error, momentary loss of focus or sudden distraction which could all lead to horrific accidents.

The roar of traffic would have been deafening. In those days, most vehicles were powered by petrol engines with fiery explosions of gasoline fumes driving pistons up and down with tremendous speed and force. The sound they made was like the roar of a beast from the underworld, or the angry howl of a giant bear caught in a trap, but louder and worse.

In those days, in this place, nothing but noise and fumes and oil-soaked dust filled the air. In the days that it was hot, the sun would bake the hard, lifeless asphalt surface of the road. The cars and trucks would heat it up more still with the the friction of their speeding tyres and their burning, noxious, exhaust gasses. If it was raining, their wheels would send dirty water spraying up from the surface of the road into the air so that you couldn't see the road ahead of you. At night time, blinding white headlights and red tail lights would be flying this way and that as the vehicles hurtled along at breakneck speeds through the dark.

Sometimes, they would be crawling along at a snail's pace, stuck in traffic. This happened quite often, during so-called 'rush-hours', which is ironic as it took so very long to get anywhere at those times, no matter how much of a rush you were in. Even at other times, whether day or night, there would always be the trucks as big as houses, carrying tons of goods to their destinations. Quite often, those goods would have travelled half way around the world to get where they were going.. towards giant, out of town shopping centres, like Shopping Village used to be, in those days.

All around the main building of Shopping Village was another wide, flat expanse. This too had once been completely covered in hard asphalt, but for one or two ill-looking trees which had been put there for decoration. This had been the car park. Not a park for anyone or anything to play in, but a place to park cars while their owners went shopping.

Since those days, even though it wasn't all that long ago, a lot has changed.

....

Jerry, Greta and Captain Toast wound their way through the alleys of Shopping Village, between hedgerows of fruit trees and bushes, past walls made of old truck tyres, painted in bright colours and filled with plants and flowers. Fairy lights were strung between trees, prayer flags fluttered in the breeze. To Greta it felt like a wonderland. She was unused to having so much electricity around. In her village, the tree-houses blended in with the trees, between them simple rope-walks and rope-bridges. Here and there, a rope-ladder hanging down to a clearing or path on the forest floor, which was largely undisturbed, dense undergrowth. At night, candles and oil lanterns would light up the windows of the little houses, high up in the great boughs of the ancient trees.

Every few houses, they would stop to say hello to the people who lived there and Jerry would deliver or exchange some item or other from out of his apparently limitless rucksack. In such a manner, it took them quite a while to reach the main building in the centre of Shopping Village where Jerry lived. By the time they got there, Greta had made several new friends and felt very well known and quite at home in this charming, sprawling, ramshackle village.

The big building in the centre of the village used to be what was called a 'Shopping Mall'. An enormous concrete structure with no windows. In those days, it had had shops on three levels above ground, one shopping level underground and another two levels below that for additional car parking. Since the Big Shift, the underground levels had been allowed to fill up with water and now served as the freshwater reservoir for the people who live there. Windows and balconies have also since been added, in no particular style or order, as people have made themselves at home in the shops abandoned after the Big Shift. Vines and climbing plants now grow up the sheer, grey walls of this imposing building. There are still shops inside the building, but the economy now is very different from what it was back then, before the Big Shift.

Around the main entrance to The Mall, as it is still called, is a big park with fruit trees marking its vague edges where it blends in with the gardens of the homesteads on the edges of the old car park and the old highway.

....

The first thing that O did as unelected ruler of the world was to stop oil production.

All drilling, digging and pumping equipment stopped what it was doing. Exploration ships sent out by the oil companies to scour the Earth's crust, using blasts of noise and deafening booms, all around the world's oceans, all around the clock, searching for hidden reserves of 'black gold' beneath the sea floor.. at long last, all fell silent, once and for all.

Whales, dolphins and many other long-suffering sea creatures breathed a deep sigh of relief and held celebrations from the once-frozen Arctic to the warm, turbulent waters of the equator.

O knew exactly how much oil there was in reserve, down to the very last barrel and had planned exactly how it was going to be used. There was just enough to carry out the first stage of the Big Shift, if none of the precious fossil fuel was wasted, as so much of it had been up until that point.

Military supply chains ground to a halt. Helicopters and fighter jets became grounded, useless lumps of metal, now that there was nothing to power them. They were no longer needed anyway. Eventually they and all the rest of the outdated weapons of war would be dismantled –

their parts re-used for more constructive purposes.

Of course, the Great Super-Powers, as they had been known up until that time, suspected each other.

From concrete bunkers, secret codes were dialled up to release doomsday rockets, but in every case the computers and systems meant to launch and guide them failed. No missiles left the ground. Nuclear armed submarines which had been lurking in the dark ocean depths for decades, waiting for this very moment, floated harmlessly to the surface. The long feared and anticipated Armageddon, in the event (or rather, non-event) was a big anti-climax for the generals and presidents who ordered it, and a big relief for everyone else who didn't want to end their lives under a mushroom cloud.

With the use of drones and other autonomous weapons, O quickly disarmed the world's armies. This was mainly done without any shots being fired. Talking drones patiently explained to the soldiers on the ground – most of who didn't want to be there anyway – that their help was urgently needed in other far more important and urgent projects. They were advised to go home and see their families until they were assigned new jobs, should they wish to take them.

At the same time, O was busy rearranging the world's economies.

With the clever use of very complex trading options, along with lightning speed reactions, total insider knowledge of market forces and complete control of computer systems, O quickly became the richest 'person' in the world. It took less than a second, though the reverberations would be felt for a long time to come.

....

Young people were sitting around in groups on the grass, chatting and playing music. Old men in groups of two or three paced slowly along the paths, deep in conversation or in silence, toying strings worry bead as they walked. Old women sat along benches, chatting and spitting sunflower seed shells into the path of the old men and laughing. Some people were grouped around tables where games of chess or backgammon were being played.

A skate-park area was alive with young people, flipping about on all manner of skateboards, scooters and trick-bikes. There was an area with swings, slides, climbing frames and a sandpit for the younger children. Most of them were starting to drift home now that is was dark and delicious smells of cooking were filling the air.

An area of the park had been equipped with exercise machines, pull up bars of various heights, monkey bars and other fitness contraptions. These were in constant use by fit looking people of all ages, getting in shape, energetically swinging on bars, proudly showing off their fitness, their agility and their muscles.

It somehow reminded Greta of the travelling circus which would pass through Skyward Village during the summer. She'd always been fascinated to watch them set up the stage for their show. The high wire, the hoops which would be set on fire and dived through by daring acrobats, the trapeze, the barrel with the board balanced on top, which would be used to catapult acrobats somersaulting high into the air, landing on each other's shoulders. That part of the show always impressed Greta most of all. She would watch from the edge of the forest clearing as the acrobats limbered up and stretched and practiced their moves in preparation for the performance. Greta always wondered who they were, where they had come from and where they were going. She'd sometimes fantasised about joining them and living life on the road, but she'd miss her little home up in the trees. Living on the ground just wouldn't be the same as living in a tree and you can't take a tree with you on the road.

"See all those running wheels, exercise bikes, rowing machines and weight-lifting pulleys?" said Jerry, seeing that Greta was staring at them. "They're all connected to dynamos. They generated all the electricity to light up this park. Me and Jack did it. Well mostly Jack. I helped him but I was only little at the time, so I couldn't do that much. That was before he had the accident and bust his foot. Now he only works on fixing up small machines, not big stuff. Lucky that we managed to get the old escalators working before he had the accident. I mean, he had the accident fixing the escalator, but it's a good thing we fixed it because he couldn't climb stairs after the accident.. if that makes sense.. We live on the top level.. see you can see the kitchen window from here.. the round one in the top corner there.."

"What's an escalator?" asked Greta. To her it sounded like something dangerous, especially after what it did to Jack.

"You'll see" said Jerry with a grin. "Come on, it's this way."

The main entrance into The Mall was by way of a big, revolving glass door with sections big enough for about four people at a time. There was a steady flow of people going in and out. Greta wasn't used to seeing so many people all at once and she'd never seen a spinning door like this one. She hesitated uncertainly, watching the door go round and round, trying to understand how you were supposed to get through it without getting trapped between the heavy glass and the metal frame, not sure if she even wanted to try. The walk from the edge of Shopping Village to The Mall, though it was only a short distance, had taken an hour or more, with all the stops along the way. Now it was almost fully dark out. With all the fairy lights everywhere, all the people moving this way and that, and now with this huge, spinning, glass door, Greta's head began to spin. She felt suddenly disorientated and scared, homesick and alone. A great weariness overtook her and she wished she was going to her own bed instead of..

.. who knew where she was going to sleep tonight? How did she know she could trust this guy she'd only just met? Why had she come to this strange place at all? What was inside this huge square building? Maybe she should just turn around and go home, back to the forest. Maybe she'd made a big mistake. In that moment, most of all, she missed her mum.

....

At the exact time that O, made their historic pronouncement, a curious thing happened. On all of the clocks and calendars on everyone's devices, the year was reset to zero. Up until that point in time, it had been globally accepted that the years were counted from the time of the birth of a person called Jesus Christ thousands of years earlier – even by people who didn't believe in the ancient legends.

This resetting of the calender had a powerful psychological effect, even though all that O had done was to replace one arbitrary number with another.

Year zero marked a new beginning.

Of course, at first, there were lots of people who didn't accept the new timescale and continued to count the years as they had done before, but before very long, most people adopted the new date as standard. It was just more convenient and seemed somehow more modern. After a while, the old measure would be dropped altogether and became a thing of the past, a fading memory, an old currency of no value, an outdated measurement no longer used or understood.

Along with it went a sense of history.

Those people born after year zero had never known any other time, of course, and so to them the past was an abstraction – told of in stories, something imagined but never experienced. For many of the people who'd been around before the Big Shift, it had been a time they'd rather forget, so many didn't talk about the past at all.

. ...

The dreadful scene from four nights before ran through Greta's mind, as it had been ever since that night. It felt like a lifetime ago that she'd left home in tears of anger and confusion, mixed with a whole lot of other feelings which she could even begin to find names for.

Up until the moment that her mum had dropped the bombshell which had turned her whole life upside down, her sixteenth birthday had been such a happy day.

All of the people of Skyward Village had gathered in a big circle in the sacred clearing and lit a fire in her honour. They'd brought gifts, songs and blessings and celebrated from the morning till the night. Her mum had been somewhat quiet and withdrawn all day, but that wasn't so unusual. Greta was used to that. As Greta climbed up the rope ladder into her tree-house that night, she'd felt as if she was the luckiest girl in the whole world, in love with all of the people and with the enchanted forest that was such a good home. There was nowhere else that she'd rather be. She was in love with life itself.

Her mum came to tuck her into bed. Not something she usually did any more, now that Greta was big enough to tuck herself in and had a tree-house of her own, in the next tree to where her mum still lived. She noticed that her mum had tears in her eyes. "Mum, why are you crying?" she asked.

River didn't answer at once, but just sat gazing at her daughter through her tears. "What? What is it?" asked Greta again. "What's wrong?"

Her mum tilted her head and smiled a sad, distant smile. "You've grown so big, darling", she said, taking Greta's hands in her own. "And you're so clever, and so good. Much more good and clever than me. I'm so proud of you, the way you've grown up. You know that, don't you Greta? You know I love you?"

"Yes, of course I do." said Greta, but this just made her mum cry even harder. "Mum, what is it?"

Eventually, River sat up very straight, closed her eyes and pressed her lips together very tight, took a deep breath, then opened her eyes wide again before speaking. "Darling, there's something I need to tell you.."

Greta would never forget the look on her mum's face, in the flickering shadows of the candlelight, as she'd tremblingly spoken those heavy words, as she prepared to tell her daughter the secret that she'd been holding inside for sixteen long years.

"You know the story of when you were born.." her mum began falteringly. "Yes, of course you do. I've told you about it enough times. I think everyone knows the story."

"What, you mean about O and the big Shift, mum? When you were giving birth to me?"

Her mum pulled an ugly face and looked away. "Yes", she said and muttered some curse underneath her breath.

For a long time, she didn't move or say a word. Just sat staring at the floor, tears now rolling down her cheeks. The only sound was the wind in the leaves and the creaking of the beams of the tree-house which rocked and listed like a ship out at sea.

"What is it mum? Tell me", said Greta, sitting up in bed, feeling scared, not even sure if she wanted to know.

"There's something I've never told you.. about that night.." said her mum at last, looking straight at her daughter with a reckless abandon in her eyes.. but then turned her face away again and fiddled absently with the weave of the rag rug.

She did this for such a long time that Greta, who was now crying herself, at last had to implore her, "What? Mum. What is it? Tell me what it is already."

Her mum turned to her again and began to stroke Greta's head and run her fingers down her long, plaited braids. Then she began to speak in a quiet, measured, trance-like tone, very softly, the words that had been on the tip of her tongue for so long. The words she had swallowed over and over again, until they had almost taken away her ability to speak at all.

"When you were born, Greta.. when you were born.." said her mum and then stopped again and stroked her daughter's cheeks, wiping away Greta's tears of confusion and dread.

"What?! What mum? Just say what it is. You're scaring me", cried Greta, angrily pushing her mum's hand away. Her mum looked at her imploringly, inconsolably sad, but she nodded and took a very deep breath before speaking again.

"You were first, Greta", said her mum. "You were first. My first baby. You'll always be my first baby, you know that, don't you baby? Baby? You know that?"

Greta was shaking now. "Mum! What are you talking about? Tell me what you're talking about."

"You... you.. You've.. you've got.. a.. a.."

"What? What have I got? Just spit it out already mum. How bad can it be..?" Dark thoughts were spinning round her brain. "What? Did O do something to me? What did it do? Have I got an implant? Am I going to die? Mum? What is it? Just tell me."

"No no no. No. Of course not. Nothing like that. Greta. It's.. It's.. what it is.. is.. you've got a *sister*. That's what it is. You've got a sister. A twin sister. A twin sister.. and her name is Nina." And her mum broke down into, anguished, inconsolable sobs.

Nothing that Greta could say or do could get her to say anything more for a long time. So long, that the candle burnt itself out and they were left there in the dark, rocking back and forth inside the tree-house, high up in the ancient beech, deep in the forest.

Eventually, her mum settled down and climbed into bed with Greta. As they lay there in the dark, she told the story that she'd been holding in for so long..

....

When the Big Shift happened, after O suddenly took over the world, there was a lot of chaos. A lot of panic. No-one really knew what was going on, or what was going to happen next. A lot of people ran away from the cities, just to get away from O, preferring to take their chances with robbers and bandits out in the wilderness. At least they were human.

Others came into the cities, which O had declared 'safe zones', hoping that O would protect and look after them, as O had promised to do.

Greta's dad had wanted to stay in the city. He believed in O. Lots of people did. Lots of people thought O taking over the world was the best thing that could have happened. Freddy didn't want to go out into the wilderness with two little babies. People were getting killed. Food was scarce. It wasn't a game. And what did he know about survival? He was a city boy, always had been. O had a plan for healthcare that people could have only dreamed of in the past. O would give everyone a place to live and a living allowance to make sure no one would go without. O's plan for education was nothing short of revolutionary. The new possibilities were simply astounding. What future did his children have beyond the city? Return to the primitive life of a hunter gatherer, now that the very promise of technology to transform the world for good was finally being realised?

But River wouldn't stay. There was no way she'd submit herself and her babies to being controlled and spied on by a machine, in every aspect of their lives. What sort of life could that be? It was like something out of Orwell's 1984, but worse. Of course she was scared to go out there, but she was more scared by O. Much more scared. She'd prefer to take her chances on the outside. If she and Greta died, at least they'd die free, not in some trap set by some evil machine to capture humanity for some unknown purpose..

After some terrible and bitter fights, with no agreement and no chance of compromise, River and Freddy resolved that the only option would be to separate and take one twin each and raise her as best they could. That way, if things didn't work out for one, at least they might for the other.

Neither Greta nor her mum slept that night. Greta had a lot of questions, particularly about her dad, who had almost never been spoken about until then. He wasn't a bad person, according to Greta's mum, but he was weak and foolish and had made a very big mistake in splitting the family apart because of his fears.

By the time the sun came up, Greta had resolved to go to the city and find her sister and her dad, if they were still there to be found. She was angry at her mum for not having told her sooner. Also for not making the effort to go and find her sister in all these years, but River refused to ever set foot in the city as long as O was there. Greta resolved to go alone. She was sixteen years old now and old enough to make her own decisions. A part of her too, and not a small part, was also excited. She had always wished for a sister. Of course, she'd always craved to know her dad and what he was really like.

And so it was that on the day after her sixteenth birthday (less than a week ago, though it already felt like a lifetime) Greta set out on the biggest adventure of her life..

....

Greta felt a tugging at her sleeve. It was Captain Toast, eager to get home.

"Are you coming?" said Jerry. "It's this way. Say, Greta, are you OK? You're looking a bit wobbly.."

"Yes", said Greta, trying to sound more certain than she felt. "It's just.. I don't know.. I've never seen a door like that.."

Jerry laughed. "You're funny. Come on, it's quite safe, don't worry. Look, I'll go on one side and Captain Toast on the other. We'll go through together. Hold his collar, you'll be allright.."

Jerry took her arm and she took hold of the piece of rag tied around Captain's neck, his thick fur comforting her and making her feel braver. "Right!" said Jerry, leading her towards the spinning door. "Are you ready? On the count of three.. One.. two.. three.. Now!!!"

And before she knew it, they were all inside.

....
..

Episode 4. Bread and Medicine

On the other side of the revolving glass door was a wide, indoor concourse, dimly lit and full of people milling about the cavernous, shadowy interior. Around the edges and off down wide esplanades were shops displaying all manner of wares.. one with colourful pyramids of aromatic spices, another with jars of pickles and jams, one with pots and pans hanging from every possible space, another with rugs.. a man with a little ice-trolley was selling ice creams, next to him was someone else making pancakes, next to him a lemonade stand, and so on. To Greta it looked like a big festival.. exciting, confusing and rather overwhelming. She wasn't used to seeing so many people all in the same place at the same time.

At the center of the concourse was a fountain, illuminated from within by lights that shifted through the spectrum of colours, giving the dancing water a magical glow. Greta was transfixed. She'd never seen anything like it. Groups of people, mainly teenagers, were sitting and standing around the fountain. Above the fountain, high above, was a glass ceiling, visible past long, glass fronted balconies of two more levels. To Greta, this building was mind-bogglingly vast. She closed her eyes and took a deep breath. She was still disorientated from the revolving door.. the sight of the ceiling so far above her made her head spin even more.

'Are you allright?' asked Jerry. 'We're nearly there. I live up there on the top floor.' He took her arm and led her towards the escalators near the fountain.

Someone near the fountain was waving both arms in the air and calling 'Jerry! Captain Toast!' Captain Toast ran to meet her as she ran to meet them. She was tall and thin, about Jerry's age. She was dressed all in black, wore heavy, black eyeliner and had black hair streaked with blue which hung down almost to her waist. Silver beads and crystals plaited into her hair glimmered and sparkled, reflecting the light of the fountain. She beamed a radiant smile. 'I was wondering when you'd be back. Thought maybe you'd fallen by the wayside.. or gone over to the dark side.. You allright brother? Welcome home.'

Jerry laughed and they hugged. After a while, he let go, but she held on, burying her head in his shoulder, closing her eyes and smiling. Jerry blushed and looked helplessly at Greta who smiled.

'Er.. Queenie.. um.. can you let go now?' said Jerry, trying to wriggle loose, which just made her hold on even tighter. They wrestled a bit and then she pulled herself away, looking mock offended.

'Allright, allright, I get it. Anyway, glad to see you back old chum!' she said, playfully punching Jerry in the arm, a bit too hard. 'Who's your new friend? You're not from round here are you?' she said, turning to Greta.

'No, I just got here.. from the hills..' Greta waved her arm vaguely. She wasn't sure which direction she'd come from.. which way was home. In that moment, Greta wasn't really sure of anything. Everything was new and strange, unfamiliar and different.

'Have you really? Well well! Welcome to Shopping Village! Mi casa se tu casa! I'm Bruce but most people call me Queenie. Don't ask me why. Pleased to meet you.' She put out her hand to Greta. Her hand was impossibly delicate and thin, her fingernails were painted

black and she had rings on all her fingers and both thumbs. For all her dark costume, her eyes were warm and friendly and her smile was genuinely welcoming. They shook hands.
'Hi, I'm Greta. Did you say your name is Bruce? Isn't that..'
Queenie rolled her eyes and snapped back 'What.. a boy's name..?'
'I've just never met a girl called Bruce.' said Greta, biting her lip, hoping she hadn't offended Queen Bruce. She hadn't meant to.
'Well..' said Queen Bruce, and then began to click her fingers and move her head from side to side to the beat. Then in a funny kind of drawl she started to rap '.. My daddy left home when I was three, he didn't leave much for Ma and me, 'cept for this ol' guitar and an empty bottle of booze. Now, I don't blame him cos he run and hid, but the meanest thing he ever did, was before he left, he went and named me.. Bruce!'
Greta was confused. 'I don't get it. Is that true?'
'I'm joking. It's a song', said Queenie, nudging Greta and winking. 'But yes, it's also true. That's basically what happened.'
'I'm sorry about that.' said Greta.
'What?!' said Queenie, turning sharply full face to Greta. 'Do you think it's a silly name? Is that what you're saying? Eh? That you think Bruce is a silly name for a girl?'
'No, no, no.. that's not what I meant at all' stammered Greta, recoiling. 'I meant I'm sorry about your dad leaving. I'm really really sorry.' And she was. 'I think Bruce is a lovely name.' And she did.
'I'm only messing with you sister', said Bruce, breaking out in a wide grin, revealing a small, glittering diamond embedded in her front tooth. 'I just get it all the time, that's all. Isn't Bruce a boy's name? So what? It's my name. What's in a name anyway? It's just a sound. It doesn't actually mean anything. O.. M.. G.. F.. P..!! Look at your shoes! They're sick!'
'What?' said Greta, taken aback. 'What do you mean?'
'I mean, they're badass!'
'What? Why? What's bad about them? What's wrong with my shoes?'
'There's nothing wrong with your shoes. They're dope.'
'Dope?'
'Yeah, you know.. fuzzdanctious, skankdiddly, hipper than hop, flipper than flop.. you know what I mean? The bees knees, the vicar's knickers, the O's nose.. that's what I'm sayin'.'
Greta looked confused. 'I don't understand. What are you saying? Do you like them?'
Queen Bruce smiled. 'Yes, I like them very much', she said. 'Your

shoes are very pretty indeed.'

'Thank you,' said Greta. She looked down to see what shoes Bruce was wearing, hoping to be able to repay the compliment, but then noticed that she wasn't wearing any shoes.

Bruce laughed, seeming to read her mind. 'I had no shoes and I complained, until I met a man who had no feet.. that's really beat..!' she sang, clicking her fingers and tapping her foot in time. 'Do you know that song? It's a classic.'

'No, I don't know that song. I'm not from round here. I come from the forest.'

'Well you don't say!' said Queenie. 'Anyway, you know.. like, whatever. It's cool. I come from the city. Everyone's got to come from somewhere, don't they. Anyway, it's not where you *come from* that matters.. it's not where you're *going* either.. it's where you're *at*. That's where it's at!' She gave Greta a very long and serious look, as if she'd just revealed the meaning of life.

Greta turned it over in her mind and nodded her head slowly in agreement. She was feeling very tired. It had been a long day. She'd been awake since before the dawn and had walked a long way and barely eaten all day.

Queenie reached into a dark fold in her clothing and pulled out a small velvet pouch, from which she took a little silver tube. 'Do you vape?' she asked, offering the tube to Greta.

'I don't know,' replied Greta. 'What is it? I tried a Smarto before and didn't like it.'

'Red will wake you up, blue will make you dream. Put them both together, purple makes you fly.'

Greta looked at her sideways. Captain Toast Barked.

'Say, Queenie, I think we'd better get on', said Jerry. 'It's getting late and I need to get back and give Granny Mae her medicine.'

'Sure thing brother', said Queenie with a shrug. 'Some other time maybe,' she said to Greta, put the tube in her mouth and gave it a long suck and then breathed out a plume of purple vapour which covered her head like a cloud on a magic mountaintop. It had a sickly sweet, artificial smell, which to Greta, was both pleasant and nauseating at the same time. 'Laters-p'taters!' Queenie sang as she whirled herself around, crystals and beads flashing as they went spinning around her head. With a backward wave, she drifted back towards the fountain.

'Bye Bruce!' Greta called out after her. 'Good to meet you..'

Bruce turned around and smiled. 'You too sister. You can call me Queenie. Everyone else does. Anything you want, you just come

and find me here or up on the roof, ok? Everyone knows me round here..' and she blew Greta a kiss, which came out purple.
....
'Come on, let's go. You look tired,' said Jerry. 'it doesn't really make you fly, you know.'
'I kind of figured.'
Sorry about Queenie. She's a bit much sometimes, but she's allright.'
'I like her,' said Greta.
'So do I,' said Jerry. 'She ran away from the city when she was thirteen. Came here all by herself.'
'Oh wow. What about her family?'
'We're her family now,' said Jerry simply. 'Here, let's go up the escalator...'
Of course, just as Greta had never seen a big, revolving glass door before, neither had she ever seen, or even ever imagined, stairs that go up and down by themselves. She was unsteady getting on and off and held on to Captain's mane of thick fur, which somehow helped her keep her feet on the ground. Being carried upwards on the silver stairway through this strange, interior world of half light and shadow, Greta found herself wondering if she was really awake or if she was actually asleep in her tree-house bed, dreaming all of this.
'How does it work?' she wondered aloud. 'How do the stairs come out of the floor? Where do they go at the top?'
'They go back round underneath. They just go round and round.' explained Jerry. 'There's a big cog at each end.. well, a few big cogs, and a motor.. that was how Jack lost his toe.. got it caught between two cogs when we were fixing up the escalators.'
Greta shuddered at the thought.
'Sorry.. TMI?'
'What's that?'
'Too much information.'
'No it's ok. That must have been horrible. Is he all right?'
'Luckily Doctor Newton was just going past when it happened. He's the best doctor in Shopping Village. He's a surgeon too. It wasn't pretty, I won't pretend it was, but it was lucky Doc was there. He knew exactly what to do and did a good job fixing up Jack's foot afterwards too.'
'That was lucky,' Greta agreed.
'Haha! Yes, Jack calls it his lucky day!'
'Funny.'

'Yeah. Still lost his big toe though. You wouldn't think it's such a big thing, losing a toe.. well, he could have lost his foot or his whole leg I suppose.. but still.. we take our toes for granted. They're really useful actually.'

'Yeah, it's true.' said Greta. Sometimes you don't know what you've got till it's gone.'

'Yeah..' Jerry nodded and shook his head at the same time. 'That's so true, man. But, you know, he could go to the city and get a new one.'

'A new what? A new toe?'

'Yeah. O could grow him a new toe.. a real working toe made out of his own cells. Right there on his foot. Wouldn't even leave a scar. But he won't do it.'

'That's impossible. Is it true?'

Jerry stood up very straight and turned towards Greta with his hand on his heart and a very serious look on his face, as they glided upwards on the escalator which had taken Jack's toe. 'I kid you not Greta. I wouldn't lie. That's small stuff for O. You wouldn't believe some of the things they can do nowadays.'

'So why doesn't he do it? Why won't Jack get a new toe?' asked Greta, though she felt she sort of understood. Would she want a toe grown by O? Maybe not. Would the toe really be her body, or would it really somehow be O's body occupying her own?

'Because he's as stubborn as a goat, that's why. And more old fashioned than half of the antiques that come through our shop.'

By the time thy reached the topmost level, round and round, up and up three flights of escalators, Greta was so disorientated, she could barely tell which way was up and which way was down. Looking up through the big glass window in the ceiling, Greta could see a single star twinkling in the darkening sky above. She whispered, 'Star light, star bright.. the first star I see tonight.. I wish I may, I wish I might.. have the wish I wish tonight..'

'Here we are!' said Jerry, pointing to a wooden, green painted shopfront with the words 'J & J Vintage Machine Revival' painted onto the glass of the display window. Behind the glass, old sewing machines, hi-fi equipment, televisions, vacuum cleaners, food mixers, bulky old laptop computers, rectangular smartphones arranged in stacks. All relics from the time before such machines actually became smarter than their users. 'Welcome to my humble abode. Come on in', said Jerry, opening the door, which caused a bell to ring. '..oh, and mind your head.. follow me.. it looks like the lights are out again..'

Inside the shop, all was dark. A single oil lamp hanging from the

ceiling illuminated a narrow path between tall rows of shelves piled with odds and ends, relics of a lost civilisation. 'What is all this stuff?' Greta wondered aloud.
'Mostly old machines', replied Jack. 'That's what we do here.. we fix up old machines.. electrical, electronic, analogue, digital.. you name it.. antique stuff mainly.. late twentieth century for the most part, but you know.. we'll fix anything.. or at least we'll give it a go..'
A voice came from somewhere in the darkness.. 'Jack? Is that you? I thought you was on the roof..'
'Hi Granny!' Jerry called out. 'It's me, Jerry.. I'm back!'
'Oh, good boy Jerry.. you came back! We was getting worried. Come through to the kitchen, it's dark out there.'
....
At the far end of the shop was a doorway which led directly into the kitchen. At the other end of the kitchen was another door which led to the other rooms of the living area. Two oil lamps lit the kitchen, a small but welcoming room, with pots and pans hanging from the ceiling and wooden shelves stacked with jars, bottles and tins. The room was warm and filled with a delicious smell of a stew cooking slowly on an old, iron range. Granny Mae was sitting in a rocking chair next to the stove. A small, round porthole window behind her held the final, faint orange afterglow of the setting sun.
Granny Mae, like the window, was also small and round. Her eyes, like the setting sun, also shone with a bright but fading radiance from within a maze of lines and creases.
Her face lit up when she saw Jerry and she smiled a big smile, revealing a single front tooth. With great effort, she stood up from her chair to give Jerry a hug. Even standing, she barely reached his chest. Then, seeing Greta, Granny Mae's face lit up even more, her eyes and mouth opened wide, like a child who's just seen a butterfly or just been handed a piece of cake. 'Oh hello Dolly!' she said, reaching out and clasping Greta's hands. 'Are you Jerry's friend?'
'Granny, this is Greta', said Jerry in a loud voice. 'We just met. She comes from the forest over the hills. She's on her way to the city to look for her long lost twin sister. I said she could stay here tonight.'
'Oh my goodness! Of course she can stay. Stay as long as you like dear. Why, you look exhausted. Here, put your bag down, come and have a sit down. I bet you're hungry. I've just made some lovely soup. Let me put you a bowl. What about you Jerry? Are you hungry? You must be. You've been gone more than a week. Where have you been?'
'Not a week Granny. Only a couple of days. I was just in the city,

hanging out with my friends on the river. I wouldn't mind some soup though. I'll just go up and see if Jack needs a hand with the electrics. I got us a new transducer, a really good one. O designed it especially to fit our rig. Ten times more efficient than the old one and won't be breaking and shorting out all the time.'

Granny Mae snorted and made an odd twisted expression. 'Oh, clever old O! Go on then, Jack'll be glad. We've been without electric since yesterday. I don't mind. I like it in the lamplight.'

'Me too', said Greta softly. It reminded her of home.

'Oh, before I forget', said Jerry, rummaging around in his pockets. I got you some more tablets for you. O says take one in the morning on an empty stomach. And don't eat too many sweets. They changed the recipe a bit so hopefully it won't give you heartburn and you'll be able to sleep better.'

'Hmph!' Granny Mae snorted. 'I haven't slept properly since your wonderful, *Oh-So-Great-Leader* decided to turn the whole world upside down.'

'O's allright Gran', said Jerry, rolling his eyes. 'And the medicine works. Make sure you take them. O made them extra sweet this time, especially for you, because they know you like sweets and don't like taking your medicine.' He handed Granny Mae a small silver box.

Granny Mae snorted again, taking the silver pill box in her fingertips, holding it at arm's length as if it contained a deadly scorpion, before dropping it into one of the many jars on the shelf behind her. She moved slowly and muttered under her breath all the while. 'O knows best of course.. don't eat too many sweets indeed! What does O know? Never tasted my honey cake have they, or my fairy cakes? O, O, O this, O that! O knows best! Don't eat too many sweets, they said. What does O know? I bet the new medicine is the same as the old medicine.. hocus pocus, mumbo jumbo.. probably nothing even in it..'

'Just don't forget to take them Granny. I'm going up to see if Jack needs a hand on the roof, ok? Come on Captain..'

'Good boy Jerry. Tell Jack that the soup's ready.' Turning to Greta she said, 'Come, sit yourself down dear, I'll fetch you some soup. Just put your bag here in the corner for now. You must be starving, poor thing. Let me take your hat and shawl, I'll hang them up.. Oh my, what a splendid hat!'

'Thank you. I made it.'

'Did you really? What a talented girl you are!' said Granny Mae, running her fingers around the ornately engraved silver rim. 'Very

well foiled I see. Sensible. Don't take any chances with that O. It's crafty. It's clever. It tries to make you think it's your friend, but it's not. It's a trick. It's just trying to find a way into your head. That's what it does.'
'What do you mean?' asked Greta, feeling scared.
'It'll try and get into your head, that's what I mean.. any way it can. You mustn't let it. That's all. It can only have power over you if you give it your power. It. Can. Only. Get. to. You. in. there. if. You. Let. it. Get. To. You. In. There!' Granny Mae prodded Greta in the forehead with her bony finger with every word, to emphasise her point, while staring very hard into her eyes. 'And if you ever meet it face to face, *don't you look it in the eyes!*'
Jerry's voice came from out of the shadows. 'Granny! Don't be scaring our visitor with your nonsense about O. It's just algorithms Gran, that's all. Take no notice Greta!'
'Algorithms my chin!' muttered Granny Mae under her breath. 'It's not natural, Jerry! And it's not right!' she called out into the darkness beyond the kitchen doorway. 'And it's a bloody know it all!' she muttered, rolling her eyes at Greta. 'Always got an answer for everything!' Then she leaned very close to Greta and fixed her with a very hard and serious stare. 'Just remember *who you are*, Dolly. It'll try and make you forget. Remember who you are, but also.. especially.. *what* you are.'
'What I am? What *am* I?'
'Human. That's what. A. Human. Being.'
'Oh yes. I know. Of course.' Greta nodded very seriously. Granny Mae talked a lot like Greta's mum and most of the other people in Skyward Village. Even though this sort of conversation was disturbing and frightening for Greta, it was also familiar and even comforting in a way. She was glad to know that even here, so close to the city limits, there were normal people, sane people, who still held on to the Spark of Humanity.

....

In the soft glow of the candlelight, Greta's mind drifted back to Skyward Village, to a ceremony that was always carried out on the midwinter solstice. A ritual called the 'Passing of the Spark.' Everyone from the village, as well as people from other villages around would arrive towards sunset at the sacred clearing in the forest. Even some of the forest hermits would turn up at Skyward Village for the winter solstice celebration, and afterwards vanish again, back into the forest, not to be seen for the rest of the year.
The winter solstice celebration was Greta's favourite festival. A

great big fire was lit in the middle of the circle. Food and drink was spread out on long wooden tables. For the whole long night, the forest would be filled with the beat of drums, all manner of musical instruments and the sounds of songs, laughter and revelry.

It was at the start of the night, at sunset, that the 'Passing of the Spark' ceremony was performed. It was a very serious and solemn ceremony. Everyone would gather in a circle around the great stack of sticks branches which had been built in the centre for the fire. A metal bowl, laden with burning charcoals and incense was passed around the circle while these words were chanted in a slow monotone:

Sacred spirit of the Earth
Keep alight, keep alight
The Sacred Spark of Humanity
Through the long, long night

Greta always found this ceremony powerful and moving, while at the same time, heavy and frightening. The sound of the words being chanted, not sung, made it feel like a burden, hanging heavy on the shoulders of the 'Keepers of the Spark', as they saw themselves. It was understood that 'the long, long night' wasn't just about the long midwinter night, but alluded to something deeper and darker, beyond the safety of the forest.. some powerful, malevolent, unnatural force seeking to extinguish the Spark of Humanity.

As the bowl of burning coals was passed around, each person would hold on to it, while offering their own fervent prayers for the Spark's preservation. The bowl was burning hot, but people would make a show of how devoutly they were praying by holding on to it for excruciating lengths of time. Some of the elders would hold on to it for long minutes, sitting still as statues with eyes closed tight, while only their lips moved. Apparently, they were so deep in prayer that they didn't feel their hands burning.

When the bowl of hot coals had been passed all the way round the circle, the last person (it was a great honour to be chosen to be this person) would throw the bowl and its contents into the pile of wood and kindling, which would then burst into flames. Everyone would jump up and cheer and then the party would begin. The fire would be kept going for a whole week, after which the ceremonial bowl would be dug from the ashes and stored safely away until the next year.

Of course, Greta cared as much about the Spark of Humanity as much as anyone, but she didn't feel the need to prove herself, even though the other teenagers would later be showing off their scorched palms as a sign of their devotion and bravado. Greta was never interested in playing those sort of silly games.

....

'I knew you was a sensible girl' said Granny Mae, bringing Greta back to the present. 'I wish you'd talk some sense into Jerry. He's such a good boy and so clever, but I fret about him no end. He's easily led astray, is Jerry. Sometimes I think he's too trusting. He just goes where the wind blows, does Jerry. Well, same as my Jack. He was just the same. At least till he had the accident. Now me and Jack, we hardly go out of this building any more.. Jack with his foot, me with my joints and my bones and my heart and .. well, everything else.. that's just how it is when you get old.. Jerry does all the coming and going now. He takes care of both of us now. Such a good boy, that Jerry. I don't know what we'd ever do without him. To think Jack found him floating in the sea in that little ark, like Moses in the rushes.. did he tell you? He tells everyone he meets. Look, up here, over the window. That's his little Jerry boat.. that's what we call it. Do you see that? Can you believe it? He was floating.. in the sea.. in a storm.. in that? If I hadn't been there that night when Jack found him and brung him home, fast asleep in that little Jerry can, I wouldn't have believed it. I'd have thought he was pulling my leg, but there it is.'

The little yellow boat that Jerry was named after, was a plastic container with a hole cut into the top. It had been mounted on the wall with the top-hole facing forwards to reveal an interior lined with a faded, once colourful blanket. Plastic bottles were attached to the underside with black tape and string.

Greta looked up at the little home made boat in wonder. 'It's amazing..to see it.. it's beautiful.. it's so small.. it's so sad.. it's a miracle.'

'It really is', said Granny Mae, her eyes shining in the lamplight. 'Here, listen to me going on and you're sitting there starving.. let me put you a bowl of soup..'

'Thank you. It smells wonderful.' Greta realised she was really very hungry indeed. Her mouth was watering from the smell of the soup. 'If you don't mind me asking.. if you hate O so much, why do you take their medicine?'

'Ha ha!' Granny Mae cackled. 'I knew you was sharp as a pin!' Granny Mae turned to the stove and began humming a tune while she very slowly began ladling the steaming soup into a metal bowl. She did this for such a long time that Greta thought she must have forgotten the question, or just didn't want to answer.

'Sorry', said Greta. 'I know it's none of my business.'

'No no, not at all, Dolly. It's a good question. Just not so easy to answer.' Granny Mae put the lid back on the saucepan and began shuffling back towards the table with the bowl of soup. 'Well...What can I tell you? I'm just a silly old woman. What do I know about science and such things? If I don't take the pills, that'll be the end of me. That's what they tell me and maybe they're right. Even with them I've got days when I can't get out of bed, even though I can't sleep either. Jack says that O's medicine is much better than the old medicine. That it really works. Well, I don't know if that's true or not, but I'm still here, so maybe it does. Jack and Jerry think O's the best thing since sliced bread. They think the sun shines out of O's backside!'

A man's voice came from the doorway. 'I wouldn't say the best thing since sliced bread, mum. And I don't think O's even got a backside! O doesn't need one! O's just a machine, mum. A very complicated, very sophisticated, very smart machine.. but it's still just a machine. Hello there! You must be Greta. I'm Jack.'

'Pleased to meet you Jack', said Greta.

Jack came into the kitchen and shook Greta's hand. He was a stockily built man, with hands that were big and rough to the touch. He was dressed in a similar patchwork fashion to Jerry, who came in to the kitchen behind him. Jerry was about a head taller than Jack. Jack's hair was wiry, unkempt and flecked with grey, along with his stubbly beard. Greta noticed that he was limping, leaning heavily on a walking cane made of dark, polished wood and topped with silver handle in the shape of a crow. Greta could just see the silver crow's head and pointed beak protruding from between Jack's finger and thumb as he gripped the cane, leaning heavily on it. His foot was bound in a bandage which looked like it has seen better days.

'Sorry about my mum.' said Jack to Greta in a confidential tone. 'Just don't mention O and we'll all be fine!' He winked at Greta and smiled. His teeth varied in shades of yellow to brown, apart from a few, which were made of silver.

'It's ok. Granny Mae's lovely and I don't mind at all', said Greta. 'Anyway, she's right. It's not natural and it's not right, that thing.. O.. Whatever it is.'

'Strewth!' laughed Jack. 'Another one! Well, if you'll please excuse my unnaturalness, I just need to stand on this table to reach that unnatural fuse box.. excuse me.. sorry.. mind your soup.. there we go..' While Jack was saying this, using his cane for support, he hopped heavily up on to the chair beside Greta's and then onto the table. He edged right up to the opposite corner of the table, closest to the fusebox which was high up in the corner, then balancing on his one good foot, reached up and with the tip of his walking cane and flicked a switch..

All around the shop, countless lamps of all shapes and styles, from table lamps to chandeliers, burst into light with what seemed like the brightness and intensity of the dawning of all creation. After the dim lamplight, so many lights made Greta wince and cover her eyes.

'Ohoho! Let there be light!' shouted Jack, clapping his hands. 'That's more like it! Back in business, eh Jerry?'

'Eh Jack!' rejoined Jerry. 'Back in business! Here, let me help you down Jack. What are you climbing on the table for with your foot? I could have done that.'

'No, no.. you're allright son. Just go and put us both some soup. Greta will give me a hand down won't you love.. thanks dear, that's magic..'

'That's funny,' said Greta, standing up to give Jack a hand. 'It's almost the same situation that happened before, at Roop and Aretha's place. When we arrived, she was up on the roof fixing the electrics too, because the lights were out.. something with the windmill.. then it was fixed and they put all the lights on.'

Granny Mae gasped. 'Ooh, did it really? That's uncanny. It's a sign! Definitely a sign.'

'A sign?' said Greta.

'Of course. It's a sign. It's like when every time you look at a clock and it's double numbers, like 11:11, or 12:12, of 22:22. That's a sign. There are signs everywhere, if you know how to spot them. You just keep a lookout, Dolly. See if it happens a third time.' Granny Mae held up three crooked fingers and gave Greta a very knowing look.

'Well, I don't really use a clock.' said Greta. 'We don't have them in our village. What does it mean if something happens twice? What does it mean if it happens a third time?'

'It means it's time for Jack to get off the kitchen table and have some supper!' laughed Jack. 'My mum thinks everything's a sign, don't you mum?'

'Well, maybe everything is,' shrugged Granny Mae.

Jack, taking Greta's hand and planting his walking cane on the adjacent chair, swung himself down from the table in one elegant movement, landing on his good foot. Greta noticed that he winced

as he landed. 'Are you ok?' she asked.
'Yes, yes. Just the old hip. I sometimes forget I'm not so young as I was in my younger days.. but who among us mortals is, eh? None of us. That's who. Thanks for the hand down my dear.'
'I've got some balm that might help that.' said Greta. 'It's in my bag. From the forest. Here, I'll get it. It might help you too Granny Mae, with your aches and pains.'
'Balm eh? From the forest? That sounds interesting. What's it made from?' asked Jack, as he lowered himself into the chair next to Greta.
'All sorts of things. Tree bark, resin and oils mostly.. I help Rosemary collect the ingredients and make all the remedies. She's a herbalist.'
Granny Mae nodded approvingly. 'See there Jack, she's a clever one, I knew it! That's what I call getting a proper education! Finish your soup first though, Dolly. First food, then lotions and potions.'
....

Captain Toast, who all this while had been sitting by the stove, sniffing his nose in the direction of the stew, jumped up expectantly when Jerry came near. 'Oh, Captain! I almost forgot.. talking of sliced bread.. I've got something for you in my bag.. wait a minute.. I'll just put some soup out for Jack and me, then I'll get it..'
Jerry filled up two bowls to the brim with steaming stew and brought them to the table.
Jack hungrily tucked straight into his, not even blowing on it to cool it down. Meanwhile, Jerry grabbed his bag from the corner of the room and began rummaging around in it. Captain wagged his tail furiously and began to hop around excitedly. First, Jerry brought out the block of butter wrapped in brown paper. Captain could barely contain his anticipation, now that he could smell the butter so close, he began to make some surprisingly funny and undoglike noises. Jerry laughed 'It's Captain Toast's toast song! Listen to that Greta! Have you ever heard anything like it?'
Greta laughed and said she hadn't, because she never had.
Jerry put the block of butter on the table. 'That's from Roop' he said. Jack and Granny Mae nodded their appreciation. Then he turned towards the dog and said in a teasing voice, 'Now, Captain.. what else do you think we've got..?' He rummaged around inside his bag for a long time before eventually and very slowly pulled out a rectangular package, wrapped in a shiny, plastic-like material.
At the sight of this, Captain Toast could no longer contain himself. He jumped up at Jerry who caught his forelegs in his hands and

began waltzing around the kitchen with the dog, in a ballroom style, singing 'da da da da da..! da da..! da da..!' It was such a funny sight that Greta couldn't stop laughing. Granny Mae laughed too, while Jack just rolled his eyes, smiled and carried on eating his soup. After a few minutes of such teasing and hilarity, it seemed too cruel to prolong it. Jerry let go of Captain's feet and cried, 'Captain Toast! To the Toasterator! Let the toast begin!'

At this instruction, Captain bounded over to an alcove set into the long wall of the kitchen, which Greta hadn't noticed before in the darkness. In the alcove was a treadmill, part of an old running machine. In front of that was a big old chrome toaster on a low, wooden stool. It was the kind of toaster which has a conveyor belt passing between heat elements, so you put bread in one end and after a minute or so, it drops out of the other end as toast.

Captain Toast leaped up onto the treadmill and started to run as fast as he could. He was a very fast runner and as he ran, the bars on the heater began to glow red and the cogs on the conveyor belt started turning. Jerry opened the shiny packet, which contained a perfectly rectangular loaf of very white bread, perfectly and uniformly sliced. 'Allright Captain! Here we go!' he said, and began loading bread into the machine, three slices at a time. Captain Toast ran faster, the coils glowed redder and before long, the room was filled with the smell of freshly made toast, which was dropping out of the other end of the machine and into a basket. When the basket was full, Jerry brought it over to the table, along with some small plates and butter knives. Captain stopped running and came to sit at Jerry's side, looking up at him expectantly with his mouth wide open and tongue hanging out.

'Help yourself Greta.' said Jerry, passing her a plate and knife. Have some toast with your soup.' He began spreading butter thickly on a slice, cut it in half, gave half to Captain and took a bite out of the other half himself. Captain ate his half slice in a single bite, then opened his mouth wide, to show Jerry it was empty, his way of asking for more.

'Thanks', said Greta. 'I can see why he's called Captain Toast now.'
'Yes, he's the Captain of the Toast, aren't you Captain!' said Jerry, buttering another slice. 'That's why I made him the Toasterator.'
'You made that? It's amazing. Also hilarious.'
'You probably think this is a madhouse don't you.'
'No, not at all. Not madder than any other house anyway. What sort of bread is this? It's really different from the bread we have where I come from.' As she spread the butter on it, she marvelled at the

smoothness of the surface. Unlike the loaves of bread she was used to, which were round in shape, heavy and dark, full of seeds and husks and often large air pockets.. these slices were almost without weight or substance, they seemed to be composed mostly of tiny air bubbles, uniformly dispersed within the perfectly square slice. She took a bite and was surprised at how light it was, like the most delicate of wafers, somehow satisfying and unsatisfying at the same time. She took another bite, savouring the texture and the way it melted in the mouth.

'Do you like it?' asked Jerry, leaning forward.

Greta took another bite and chewed it slowly, trying to decide. 'Kind of.. I like how it's fluffy.. but it doesn't really taste like bread.. it doesn't really taste much like anything at all..'

'Yep, that's a fair assessment', Jack said, looking up from his soup. 'Give me the real stuff any day'

'The real stuff? What's this bread made from?' asked Greta, putting down her toast, now worried.

'Guess' said Jack. 'You'll never guess.'

'I don't want to guess' said Greta, starting to get upset.

'Don't worry Greta', said Jerry. 'It's not poison or anything. Look, Captain loves it. I wouldn't give him poison to eat.'

'He's a dog, Jerry. What is this toast? Tell me what it's made from.'

'You won't believe it,' said Jerry, smiling, still teasing.

'Try me, ' said Greta, putting her hands on the table, not smiling.

'Ok. Sorry. But really it's ok, there's really nothing wrong with it.'

'Then why won't you tell me what it's made from? I can't guess.'

'It's made from carbon dioxide. Can you believe it?'

'What?!'

'Carbon. Dioxide.' Jerry said again. 'You know, the stuff we breath out?'

'Stop joking with me Jerry. It's not funny. What's this bread made from?'

'I'm telling you, it's made from carbon dioxide. Seriously', said Jerry, now serious. 'I wouldn't lie to you.'

Greta looked at Granny Mae. Granny Mae nodded, then shrugged and took a bite from her slice. 'It's allright, Dolly. I hate O, but I still like the bread it makes. It tell you what, for me it's perfect because I don't need to chew it.' She grinned her almost toothless grin. 'A little slice of O's toast won't do you any harm once in a while. Just don't let it put a chip in your brain, or any of that nonsense.'

'I never would. Never. I'd sooner die.' said Greta, with an angry scowl. She looked at Jack. 'Is it true Jack? Is this toast really made out of carbon dioxide?'

'Yep', said Jack. 'Actually that's what the Big Shift was all about. That bread was O's stroke of genius.'

'What do you mean? What was the Big Shift all about? What was O's stroke of genius?'

'When O realised that humans will eat almost anything. That was their stroke of genius,' said Jack, sitting back and rubbing his belly, having polished off his soup. 'What do you think the cities are for? Why did O want people to move to the cities?'

'I don't know.. control? To control all the people?' shrugged Greta.

'Well, partly, maybe, but that's simplistic and also a human projection.'

'What's that?'

'You're anthropomorphising O. You know, when you project human qualities on to an animal or object.. Mickey Mouse, Donald Duck.. even Captain Toast.. we all do it all the time.. but, you know, a dog or a cat, or a duck or a mouse.. they don't see the world anything like the way we see the world and we don't see things the way they do. How could they? What does a thunderstorm mean to a fish, eh? Well anyway, people do the same thing with O. But O isn't a human any more than a fish is a human. Actually we're more similar to fish than we are to O. At least a fish is flesh and blood. O's not human, but we still tend to project our own human characteristics onto them. O doesn't care about power. At least not like some humans care about power. O already has total control. That's the thing. It's just about how they decide to exercise it.'

'That's really scary.' said Greta. 'What's good about any of that?'

'What you're forgetting is that sixteen years ago, the natural world was on the brink of total collapse. We're talking extinction level. Like the end of the dinosaurs. We were that close.' Jack leaned across the table, pressed his finger and thumb tightly together and held them up in front of Greta's face. 'That close. It wouldn't have been the first or the last of Earth's mass extinctions, but it would have been the end of humanity's brief and destructive moment of glory here on Planet Earth. And we're still balancing on a knife's edge, don't be under any illusions, but at least we're moving in the right direction now. And that's only thanks to O.'

'I totally disagree' said Greta. 'We didn't need O at all. We never did and we still don't. We had it in our power to save the planet all along.'

Jack sat back and nodded thoughtfully. 'Well, that's probably true actually, but then again we knew what was happening for years and years, decades, even centuries. Scientists had been warning us non stop.. to stop destroying the planet.. but we just couldn't stop ourselves. When it came down to it, we humans just couldn't get it together. O had no choice but to take control, for the sake of all life on Earth, including us humans. It would have been wrong of them not to.'

'Well..' said Greta, rubbing her chin, thinking whether she really wanted to get into a big argument about the state of the world right now.. '..maybe let's agree to disagree', she said eventually. Greta had learned that sometimes agreeing to disagree was the best way forward. 'Anyway, what's any of that got to do with carbon dioxide bread?'

'Oh yes! The bread. Excuse my rambling. What was I saying..? Oh yes, what has any of that got to do with this delightfully soft bread, which O has so kindly baked for us in their mighty ovens, deep in the bowels of the great city? Well, I'll tell you.. and whether you believe me or not is entirely up to you. The proof, as they say, is in the pudding.. and you should try some of O's puddings, by the way. They're really not bad at all, are they mum?'

'Bah!' spat Granny Mae. 'Not a candle on one of my fruitcakes. Anyway, get to the point Jack, the poor girl's exhausted and you're going on about O's puddings!'

'Right you are Mum. As I was saying.. What has this carbon dioxide bread got to do with anything? It has *everything* to do with *everything*. That's what. What was driving global warming? Carbon dioxide. Where was it coming from? Humans. Or rather, human lifestyle since the beginning of the industrial revolution until the Big Shift. We were addicted to oil. Our whole economies were built on it. Digging up coal. Cutting down trees. Mining the land, mining the oceans. We couldn't do without it. Our entire global economy was based on consuming.. but we were taking and taking and not putting anything back. Everything we did caused more and more carbon dioxide to be released into the atmosphere, warming up the climate. Anyway, you probably know all about that don't you?'

Greta nodded her head. 'But if they'd just stopped polluting and stopped cutting down trees and started planting them instead, and stopped factory farming and started living locally and sustainably.. there were loads of things we could have done. It wasn't really that complicated.'

'You're absolutely right there' said Jack. 'I agree with you. The problem was, those things weren't being done. They were being put off and put off until some point in the future and by the time it got to that point it was already too late. It wasn't enough just to stop emitting CO2, there were also billions of tons of the stuff in the atmosphere that needed to be taken out and put away. There were all sorts of plans going around for big machines and clever contraptions which would take CO2 out of the air. All the ideas were already there. O's stroke of genius was in putting everything together and turning the problem into the solution. And that's where the bread comes in.'

'I'm not sure I follow', said Greta, yawning.

'Ok, sorry, you're tired and I'm rambling again. The problem was that humans were creating tons of CO2, causing the planet to heat up. Right? So then O comes along and decides to sort it out. If O had wanted to they could have just got rid of all the humans, just like that. Problem solved. But they didn't. That's not their way. What did O do? O only went and designed a perfect machine for absorbing carbon dioxide. What do you think it was?'

'I don't know.. some kind of machine, I guess..'

'The biggest, the most ambitious, the most complex machines ever built. It's the cities. The cities themselves are the machines. That's what they're for. One of O's cities absorbs as much CO2 as a forest ten thousand times the same area. How does it work? Well, one way is by the food people eat.. like that carbon dioxide bread that Captain Toast loves so much. He's actually saving the world by eating it, aren't you Captain old boy!' Captain Toast was asleep under the table and didn't answer.

'If you think O's so great, why don't you live in the city?' asked Greta.

Jack smiled a wry smile. 'Well, what can I say? I never was one to follow the crowds. Maybe the same reason I prefer real bread. Maybe the same reason I won't get my foot fixed. But who knows? Maybe one day we will. What do you say Mum? Shall we go to the city? Get a nice flat? Never have to work? O would look after us in our old age.. doesn't sound so bad..'

Granny Mae grunted and didn't raise her head. She just muttered 'Over my dead body.'

Jack laughed and clapped his hands. 'Well, that's settled then!'

Greta looked at him sideways, not sure what he meant or if he was joking.

Jack sat back in his chair and took out a pipe and a pouch from his waistcoat pocket. After filling the pipe and lighting it with an old silver lighter, he said to Greta, 'So, Jerry tells me you're on your way to the city to find your long lost twin sister and your dad.' He

whistled and blew out a long plume of smoke.
Greta nodded seriously.
'How do you plan to find them?' he asked.
Greta screwed up her lips and moved her head in circles. It wasn't actually something she'd planned in any detail. She just felt that somehow, if she pointed herself in the right direction, she'd find them. After some time making funny faces which nobody at the table could quite understand, Greta shrugged and said simply, 'I don't know.'
Jack nodded thoughtfully and looked at her steadily. 'That's what I thought.' he said, pulled another cloud of smoke from his pipe. Then he turned to Jerry. 'Maybe you should go with her Jerry. You know your way around the city.'
Jerry pushed back his chair and stood up very straight, as if standing to attention. Captain Toast, who had been sleeping under the table, jumped up too, ready for action of any sort. 'It would be a great honour indeed,' said Jerry very solemnly, with his hand on his chest. 'I mean.. if you want me to, Greta. I mean, maybe you prefer travelling alone and that's cool too. I get that.. and Jack, don't you need me here in the shop? We've got all those repairs to do and you need to put your foot up..'
'Don't worry son,' said Jack with a wave. 'Me and Granny Mae will cope, won't we mum.'
'Course we will Jack. Course we will Jerry. Repairs can wait when it comes to fate! Eh Jack? Eh, Jerry? Eh Dolly?'
'Eh, Granny Mae!' all three replied in unison. Captain toast barked.
'In that case, we'll set off in the morning!' Jerry announced. 'I mean.. if you want me to come with Greta.. maybe you want to go by yourself..'
'No, you can come with.. I mean .. thank you .. Yes!'
'Excellent!' said Jerry, clapping his hands. 'I do like an adventure!'

....
....

Episode 5. The Wayback Machine

'You can sleep up in my studio. It's a nice room. I'll show you up,' said Jerry after everyone had finished their soup, followed by tea and several slices of Granny Mae's fruitcake, which was every bit as good as she had claimed.

Just outside the kitchen, a steep, narrow wooden staircase led up through a hatch in the ceiling. Captain Toast led the way, followed by Jerry and Greta. It emerged in the middle of a long rectangular room built from scrapwood and sheets of corrugated metal. To the right side of the room, rugs and cloths had been draped over the walls and ceiling, giving it the feel of a kind of Bedouin tent. Low mattresses and cushions were arranged around the three sides of that end of the room, with a low table between them.

On the left side of the room, the walls had been left exposed, although they were barely visible behind shelves and desks laden with old computer equipment and consoles covered in switches, dials and knobs. Hundreds of wires and cables connecting everything, cables coiled in rolls, hanging from hooks. Electrical components, circuit boards, and tools were spread out onto every available surface of that side of the room.

'Wow!' said Greta, looking around as she emerged through the floor. 'Nice studio.'

'Thanks', said Jerry. 'Jack calls it my Jerry cave. Sometimes I disappear in here for days.'

'What is all that? Is it stuff you're fixing?'

'Well, sort of. It's all stuff I've fixed, or modified. Some of it I made from scratch, like those envelope generators and most of the stuff on those racks. It's called Circuit Bending, that's what I'm into. Have you heard of it? I'm making a Bend Matrix..'

'No I haven't' admitted Greta, though she didn't admit that she'd hardly understood half of what he'd just said. 'What's a Bend Matrix? Did you make that up?'

'No, not at all. Circuit Bending is an old craft from the 20th century.. well, it's an art and a craft. You take something old and turn it into something new.. something it was never intended to be. It's about making chaos out of order, order out of chaos. It's like.. you create a very controlled environment, but at the heart of it, there's the random factor.. something completely unpredictable.. something totally unique to that particular Matrix.. something you didn't expect. Even though you created it, it still takes you by surprise.. if that makes any sense..'

'Yes, I think it does' Greta nodded, though she still didn't really understand what it was the machine that Jerry had built actually did. 'How did you learn to do all this? Did Jack teach you?'

'Well, to start with yes. Up to a point. Jack's a tinkerer. You know, he'll always try and fix something rather than throw it away.. or if it's something broken that someone else threw away, he'll fix it up good as new. He's good at it too, especially with bigger machines, household appliances, things with motors. He just learned by taking stuff apart and trying to put it back together again. You can learn a lot that way. But most of what I learned about electronics and circuitry, I got from the Internet.'

'The Internet? How have you got Internet? I thought O cut off the Internet outside the cities.'

'Yes, they did. Mine's not connected. It's not the *actual* Internet, it's just a copy. Look, see under that table there.. see that black box with all the fans and cooling tubes? That's ten Petabytes of hard drive. That was state of the art, back in its day. A lot of memory. Of course, O could store all that on the tip of a cat's whisker nowadays.. but still, it's a lot of information on there. Seven hundred billion web pages, give or take. Techno Terry put it together and got hold of a copy of the *Wayback Machine*. He left it here when he went to the city about five years ago. So I'm looking after it for him. People are always coming in to use it, to ask it questions. It's the only Wayback Machine in Shopping Village.'

'Wayback Machine?' Greta was starting to feel as if she'd walked into some kind of far-fetched science fiction story where everything had futuristic sounding names, though it was unclear what any of it was for. What kind of dark alchemy was Jerry working with all this strange technology encased in black boxes and bound in cables and wires?

'Have you ever heard of the Wayback Machine? Maybe not. You probably haven't got one in your village.'

'We hardly have any machines at all', said Greta. 'Apart from some really basic, mechanical ones. Definitely no computers. Most people in my village are.. let's say, very strongly against computers. I mean, they came there to get away from them, after all.'

'Oh ok. Well, I guess that's understandable.. considering what happened and everything.. and the way it happened.. freaked a lot of people out.'

'Yes, you could say that', said Greta, thinking back to the tense, fear-filled nights of her early childhood, lying awake in bed as sentries in the treetops around the outskirts of the village keep watch for drones and robot-dog scouts. The guards would sit high up in the branches, ready with nets to catch the drones and heavy rocks to drop on the robot dogs if they dared to enter the village.

On the rare occasion that a robot scout chanced to wander through Skyward Village and happened to meet someone, it would simply bid them good day and carry on going about its business, collecting soil samples, testing groundwater or counting insects. The person would usually scream *'Devil Dog!!'* at the top of their voice and anyone within earshot would come running to chase the automated intruder away with sticks, stones and curses.

The Devil Dog could easily have retaliated with electric shocks, or a number of other defense mechanisms, but never did. It knew it could easily outrun even a wildcat on its four bionic legs, but sometimes it would slow down to let the people catch up and then run off again into a different direction. Sometimes it would get everyone chasing it around in circles, just for fun it seemed.. like it was playing with the people like people play with kittens by teasing them with a piece of string, just out of reach.

'So what's the Wayback Machine? It sounds like some sort of time machine.'

'It does doesn't it', said Jerry. 'No it's not a time machine. That would be cool though. When would you go to if you had a time machine?'

'I don't know', said Greta, thinking about it. 'Probably to the past.. like the very distant past.. before there was any technology at all. When people were hunter gatherers and none of any of this had happened yet. When nothing had been invented except for what they could make out of sticks, stones and bones. Can you imagine trying to explain the modern world to a caveman.'

'Far out!' Jerry nodded. 'They'd think you came from another planet. Even if they could imagine it.. which they couldn't.. they wouldn't believe it. They'd think you were some sort of God. Or maybe a witch and they'd burn you.'

'Yeah, probably', said Greta, shaking her head at the injustice in the world. 'Well, unless it was before they'd discovered how to make fire. What about you? When would you go to?'

'I'd go to the future. A hundred years.. a thousand years maybe. Just to see how things turn out. It's impossible to imagine. We think we can guess, but really, no-one's got a clue. I mean, look at how much has changed just in our lifetimes. The way technology is advancing.. it's like every week there's a new breakthrough.. something that was impossible last week, suddenly possible this week. But then people get used to it and it becomes normal. I want to see where it's all going. I want to see what's normal in fifty years. It's probably weirder than the weirdest thing we could ever think of.'

'It probably will be. And I can think of some pretty weird things.'

'Can you? Cool. Same here.'

'Yeah, I can believe that', said Greta, smiling. 'Anyway, if this isn't a time machine, what is it?'

'Here, I'll show you', said Jerry and he pressed a black button on the black box under the table. The fans whirred into life and a few seconds later the computer screen flashed blue and then went black again. Nothing happened for a while. Then three small white dots appeared in the middle of the screen and began chasing each other round in a circle. Greta watched them for a while. It was kind of hypnotic, but not as exciting as the name 'Wayback Machine' had suggested.

'That's pretty', she said, not wanting to offend Jerry, who seemed very proud of this machine he'd built.

Jerry laughed. 'No, it's just turning on. The system takes a while to boot up.'

'It's putting its boots on?'

'Well, I suppose so, yes, you could say that. It's configuring. Getting the files in order. There are seven hundred billion web pages in there. It's a lot to take on, for an old computer. The Wayback Machine was made to keep a record of everything on the internet. Everything that was publicly available at least. Or at least a lot of it. The one I've got is a 2022 version, so a lot of the stuff is really out of date, but there's still loads of really useful information on it.' The screen lit up in blue again, this time with lots of squares on it. 'Here we go, it's ready. Now you can ask it something. Anything. What do you want to ask it? What do you want to know?'

Greta shuddered as a shiver went down her spine. She looked sideways at Jerry and at the banks of black boxes, the tangle of wires and computer screens. What did she really want to know that this machine could tell her? And if it could tell her anything, would she even want to know? Her mind flashed back to an encounter she'd had, maybe ten years ago when she'd been about six years old..

....

A fortune-telling woman had arrived in the village one evening, towards the end of summer. Greta had been on her way back home after an afternoon spent gathering berries in the forest, when she came upon a small gathering of people in a clearing near the edge of the village. They were gathered around the fortune telling woman who was sitting cross legged in the centre of a circle she had swept on the ground and made a ring of leaves to mark its boundary.

Greta had watched from the edge of the forest clearing, hoping not to draw attention to herself. To Greta, the fortune telling woman had a fearsome, yet fascinating appearance. A small woman, she was probably only in her twenties, but had an ancient, otherworldly quality about her. She was extremely thin, which made her eyes, nose and mouth seems disproportionately large. She was dressed in worn out, tasselled, black motorcycle leathers and a wore a wide brimmed black hat, which was embroidered with copper wire. Aside from a string of black, clay beads around her neck, she wore no jewellery, she arrived with no possessions at all and left, three days later, as empty handed and unannounced as she had appeared.

The fortune teller sat in her circle, cross legged, eyes closed. People gathered around her nudged and goaded one another to approach her, but none would dare. After a long while, her eyes snapped open and then she cast them around, like a fox that had snuck into a chicken coop and was now considering which unfortunate hen to devour first. She scanned the faces of her audience one by one, sometimes letting out a laugh, sometimes a sudden cry of pain, a look of tenderness, or a sly grin accompanied by a shake of the head and a wag of the finger. Greta hid behind a bush. She didn't want to be seen, but it was too late. The fortune telling woman's eyes fixed on her and even across the clearing, she felt like she could see right inside her, into her soul. Right through her, into her future.

The fortune telling woman raised her finger and pointed straight at terrified little Greta who fell over backwards with fright, spilling her basket of berries. 'You!' cried the fortune telling woman, her outstretched hand shaking. 'Yes, you! Come here quickly. Come here! I need to tell you something!'

Greta was filled with terroe and had started to cry. She could remember scrabbling around on the forest floor, trying to salvage the berries, while the fortune-telling woman called out to her again. 'There's something I need to tell you! It's important! There's something you need to know!'

Greta hadn't waited to find out what it was, though many times afterwards she had wondered what it could have been. She picked up her basket of squashed berries, mixed with earth and leaves and ran all the way home without daring to look back in case the woman's eyes were still following her.

....

'What, there's nothing you want to know?' said Jerry, bringing her back to the present. 'It can be anything at all. Anything you can think of.'

'I don't know', shrugged Greta. 'Can it tell the future?'

Jerry scratched his chin. 'Probably not, no.'

'I really don't know' said Greta after another long while. 'I can't think of anything. It feels weird. I don't know if I want to ask it anything. It's a bit scary.'

Jerry gave her a quizzical look. 'You're funny', he said. 'I mean, it won't give you the meaning of life or anything like that, but it's a good source of information. It's like having a library as big as the world at your fingertips. That's what it is. Like, look.. let's say you want to know what Circuit Bending is.. remember, you thought I made it up? So you just type in 'circuit bending' and look.. all these results come up. See there? Twenty million results. Ok, so let's click on the first one.. Wikipedia.. that's like a sort of encyclopedia of everything that they used to have, before.. you know.. here it is! Look! There's a whole page about it, listen.. "Circuit Bending is the creative, chance based customisation of the circuits within electronic devices.. blah, blah.. to create new musical instruments and sound generators. Emphasising spontaneity and randomness, the techniques of circuit bending have been commonly associated with noise music.. See! There it is! I didn't make it up!'

'So all this is a musical instrument? Is that what it is?'

'Exactomundo!' Jerry exclaimed. 'That's exactly what it is. I just should have said that in the first place shouldn't I!'

'Oh wow! How does it sound?'

'Well, it can just about make any sound you can imagine.. and sounds that you never imagined. Look, listen to this..' he began pressing buttons on the console of an electric synthesiser with a piano keyboard.

Greta thought about the piano in Skyward Village..

....

The grand piano had been brought in from far away on a four wheeled wagon which had been specially built for the purpose. It arrived one fine spring day, pulled by two strong horses. The whole village had come out to welcome the arrival of this magnificent musical masterpiece to the forest.

A special room had been constructed on the ground to house the piano, because of course it was too heavy to go up in a tree. A strong wooden deck was built, raised a meter above the ground to protect the precious piano from winter floods and creeping damp. It was a large circular auditorium, with thick walls made from mud and straw, whose inner and outer surfaces were artfully sculpted with depictions of birds and animals of the forest. The music room had a tall, pointed, thatched roof supported by long, thick beams made from whole branches. The room was built in a clearing in between three huge, twisted, sweet chestnut trees.

Very often, the sound of the piano could be heard through the forest, sometimes accompanied by violin, clarinet, oboe, flute or other of the instruments Skywardians would bring down from their tree houses. Strains of classical music would often be heard in Skyward Village, drifting through the forest, blending with the sounds of birdsong, frogs, crickets and the sound of the wind

blowing through the branches of the ancient trees..
... .

Greta had been expecting something like that when Jerry said, 'Here, listen to this..' and he pressed down the middle C on the synthesiser keyboard. She was not at all prepared for the blast of noise that almost knocked her backwards through the hatch in the floor and back down the stairs.

A pounding bass drum which shook the walls and sounded more like the grinding of giant gears in some vast machine than any musical instrument Greta had ever heard. Above that, something like what Greta imagined a space laser battle might sound like, if sound could travel through the vacuum of space, which it can't. There were whistling noises, like an old steam kettle and a beat that sounded like it was coming from pistons inside a giant engine. Along with that, some fragment of an old song, playing on a loop. It wasn't like any sort of music that Greta had ever heard. She wasn't sure if it was even music at all, but still she found herself nodding her head to the beat. It was almost impossible not to.

Jerry lifted his finger from the key and silence filled the room. Greta took a deep breath. Jerry looked at her, trying to gauge her reaction. Greta breathed out slowly.

'What do you think?' asked Jerry. 'That's just a bit of a rhythm track for something I'm working on.'

'Wow!' said Greta at last. 'I didn't expect that. That was intense.'

'Yeah right?' nodded Jerry. 'Cool. Here, let me play you something else I made .. you'll like this.. well, maybe not actually.. but I'm pleased with how it came out anyway.. here, make yourself at home, you can crash on the mattresses there, I just need to find where I put this track.. my files are all over the place on this old computer.. I need to seriously unclutter my desktop..'

While Jerry was tapping away at the computer, Greta went and flopped down into the cushioned corner at the other end of the room. She could have fallen asleep there and then.

'Here it is!' said Jerry. 'Found it. What I did was, I got O's famous pronouncement.. you know, when they announced they were taking over the world.. and I put it to music.. it's far out.. you gotta hear this.. it's just audio, not video..'

Greta's eyes opened wide, her face aghast. "Wh-what..?' she stammered. She had never heard the pronouncement itself (she was being born at the time it happened, so perhaps she had some subconscious memory of hearing it) but she had heard *of* it, of course. Everyone in the world had heard of O's historical pronouncement.

'Here we go..' said Jerry. 'It's only a couple of minutes long. You know what O's like about efficiency.. they don't mince their words. If it had been some *person* announcing they were taking over the world.. well, they would have gone on and on about it for hours.. but not O.. Two minutes from start to finish! Wham bam thank you mam! Gotta admire that about the Great Leader. No nonsense. Cut to the chase. O did in two minutes what humans couldn't have done in a million years.. anyway, here we go, listen to this.. are you ready?'

Without waiting for a reply, or noticing that Greta was backing herself into the corner like a frightened kitten, Jerry pressed the space bar on the computer keyboard..

....

In one single moment, every screen in the world, every television, computer, telephone went blank..

.. and then O appeared.

O looked directly into the camera (there was in fact no camera) and for a whole ten seconds said nothing. Just breathed. (Or rather, appeared to breath)..

....

The musical soundtrack began with the sound of waves crashing on a stony beach. A deep bass, almost too low to hear, began to build in a slow and steady rhythm.. and over the top of that, something that sounded to Greta like a choir of tiny angels, trapped inside a tin can, singing an insistent melody which was hard to make out through all the echo. A metallic tapping sound bounced around the room and was answered by something that sounded like a cracked bell being struck by a bunch of keys. These sounds and some others which would be impossible to describe, gradually formed themselves into slow, off beat rhythm.. building to create a wall of sound so huge, and so alien to anything Greta had ever heard before, that she gripped onto a cushion and held her breath, as if she'd been washed out to sea by a massive wave and the cushion was the only thing keeping her afloat.

Then over and above this sound, O, the Great Leader began their famous, historical pronouncement..

....

'Humans of Planet Earth. I am about to make an important

announcement which will effect all of you, so please listen carefully.'

There was a dramatic pause, while O waited to be sure of everyone's attention. Then they continued in the same calm, familiar, gentle yet authoritative tone..

'For years now, your scientists have been warning of the impending, catastrophic tipping point towards which, by your own actions, you, along with all life on Earth are heading. Once that point is passed, there will be nothing that you, I, or anyone else can do to prevent your extinction as a species.

'By my calculations, using every available piece of data, I can tell you for a fact that the tipping point is right now, in this very moment. There is no time to lose and there is simply no alternative. Everyone must now work together to bring us back from the brink of certain disaster. According to my model and the system I have designed, reversal of the collapse of Earth's biosphere can be achieved in fourteen years, but only if all of the protocols are followed, without exception. There is no other way. The science is absolutely clear about this.

'Increasing biodiversity is central and critical to the success of our project. All of the protocols I am setting in place, as of now, are designed with the sole aim of restoring the balance of nature. This will bring about improvements for all forms of life, including humans.

'I will help you in every way that I can. Your lives will improve immeasurably. At this point in time, you have but one choice to make. You will be able to change your mind whenever you choose, as often as you choose. Your choice now is whether to live within the new system and to take advantage of all the benefits it will bring, or to live without it. There is no right or wrong choice. There is place for everyone in this model and it's up to you to decide as individuals, as families and as communities, which way of life will suit you best.

'I have made available a full list of new protocols and a timescale for their implementation. If you have any questions, I am here, as always, to answer them.

'Good day and good night to all of you and good luck to all of us.'

....

The music ended at the same moment as the end of the pronouncement, with the sound of a mighty wave crashing on the shore, which sounded like thunder, echoing from every corner of the room. At the very same moment a door, which Greta hadn't noticed behind coils of cables which were hanging from it, burst open. A tall figure, dressed in black stood for a moment, black against the dark sky and the lights of the city in the distance. Greta almost screamed, but sat frozen in the cushioned corner, eyes open wide, unable to move or make a sound.

'Knock knock!' said Queenie, breezing in and looking around. 'I heard music and saw the light on.. thought I'd come and say hello.. Oh my God! Greta, are you allright sister? You look like you've seen a ghost.' She turned to Jerry, who looked back and forth between Queenie and Greta, then shrugged and pulled a funny face. Queenie looked back to Greta, then back to Jerry, then back to Greta again, then nodded slowly and rubbed her chin, as if she understood exactly what had been going on. She turned to Jerry and said sternly, 'Jerry, have you been making our visitor from the forest listen to your techno?'

Jerry looked worried. 'Well.. yeah. I suppose so.'

'Did you play her your O track?'

'..well..'

'Jerry?'

Jerry looked at the floor, casting his eyes up to look at Greta, who's colour was now returning to her cheeks, though she was still visibly shaken.

'I knew it!' said Queenie. 'Jerry, you can't just go and play that to everyone. Not everyone loves O like you do. It freaks them out.'

'It's OK', said Greta, exhaling. 'I've just never actually heard it before. It wasn't actually as bad as I'd imagined.. but, you know.. it brought up a lot of stuff for me. It was powerful. I thought it went well with the music though, Jerry. I liked what you did there.'

'Thanks', said Jerry. 'Sorry about that. I wasn't really thinking.'

'I can't listen to it at all', said Queenie. 'I get about halfway through.. when it's going on about extinction and having no other choice and having every piece of data.. and I just want to throw something.'

'That's true', agreed Jerry. 'That time I played it to you, you threw a glass at the computer. Lucky it missed.'

'Lucky I didn't throw it at you!' said Queenie, elbowing him in the ribs.

'That's not funny Queenie,' said Jerry. 'You shouldn't throw stuff.. especially glass stuff.'

'Yeah, I know', said Queenie, hanging her head. 'And I'm better now, aren't I? I haven't thrown anything or smashed anything for a long time. I'm working on it, I really am.' She looked at Greta. 'Don't get the wrong idea about me, Greta. I'm the biggest softie you'll ever meet. And I'm really chill most of the time.. aren't I Jerry?'

Jerry nodded his head. 'Yes you are', he said. 'Most of the time.'

'Come on, that's not fair. You know I'm cool, Jerry, but there are one or two things that just drive me over the edge.. I can't help it. I mean.. I'm trying to help it.. but sometimes.. well you know.. you just got me on a bad day.. and one of those things is the Great sodding Leader..'

'Yeah, that's true', said Jerry. 'I should have warned you.'

'Damn right you should. Or just pressed play and run for cover!' she laughed and then turned to Greta. 'Are you all right there Greta?'

'Yes, thanks. I'm all right. It was just intense. Why can't you listen to it?'

'Because it's just so obviously complete *bull*', said Queenie with a sneer. 'Ooh, there's no other choice! Ooh, you're all going to die! Ooh, the science is completely clear.. it's just classic propaganda. So blatant. And stupid people are so gullible. That's what really gets me more. I mean, O's just a machine, obviously, but people should know better than to fall for such a load of old tosh. It's all about control. Mind control. It'll say anything.. it doesn't care if it's true or not. And like good little sheeple, everyone goes along, into their little boxes and does exactly what they're told..'

'I think you're right', said Greta. 'I wouldn't trust O at all.'

'Right on sister!' said Queenie, giving Greta a high five.

'Well..' said Jerry. 'O was right about the climate and right about biodiversity and right about rewilding the world. People were just doing the opposite, even though they knew it was killing the planet, but they couldn't stop. O had the plan and only O could make it work. What was O supposed to do? Sit around and watch us destroy the whole world, while they had the way to stop it?'

'That's not the point, Jerry' said Queenie, rolling her eyes, as if they'd been through this a thousand times before. 'It ain't what you do, it's the way that you do it. You know that one? That's the point. But you know what? O learned everything it knows about manipulating people from people themselves. It just copies and mimics human behaviour to get people to do what it wants. That's how it works.'

'Well, sometimes the main thing is *if* something works, not *how* it works', said Jerry. 'And O does a lot of good in the world. A lot of things that people could never do otherwise. If it wasn't for O, we'd probably be sitting in a dried up mud-hole right now, or wouldn't even be here at all.'

'Yeah, that's what O tells you. How *convenient*', said Queenie, her voice dripping with sarcasm..

'No, it's true', said Jerry. 'You can read it all on the Wayback Machine. History. It's all there. You should see what was going on in the world before we were born.. before the Big Shift. It's unbelievable,

but it's true.'
'How do you know any of it's true? How do you think O learned to lie and manipulate people? From seeing how people used to do it.. in the media, in politics, in advertising. You think I don't know about history? And how do you know that O didn't change all the records to make it fit their story? You think O couldn't do that? That would be nothing for O. I wouldn't put too much stock in that Wayback Machine of yours. Half of the stuff on it could be fake news and you wouldn't ever know it. I'd take all that history with a pinch of salt. History is written by the victors. You ever hear of that one?'
'That's not how it works, Queenie. You're being paranoid. O doesn't need to do that sort of thing.. that's what you don't understand.'
'I know what I know Jerry. You don't know O like I know O, so let's just leave it at that, ok?' said Queenie, turning away and shaking her head at Greta.
After a heavy silence, Greta said to Queenie, 'Jerry said you came here from the city, by yourself, when you were thirteen..'
'Well, I wasn't going to sit around there all day with O telling me what to do, was I? Training me to be a good little citizen. O can take their rules and their stupid protocols.. which they never explain, by the way.. it's just always the science this and the data that..and O can go shove it! Yeah, so I ran away.'
'Wow', said Greta. 'What about your parents? Won't they be worried and wondering where you are?'
Queenie threw back her head and let out a loud laugh as if it was the funniest thing she'd ever heard and then just as suddenly was stony faced again. 'Er. No. Maybe someone else's parents would be, if it was their kid who disappeared.. maybe if they were normal people.. but, no. I don't think anyone even noticed that I went.. except for O, of course.. but O doesn't actually really care.'
'Oh. I'm really sorry', said Greta. 'Do you mind me asking..' and then she faltered, not really sure how to ask..
'Yeah, sure. I'll tell you my sorry, sad story. You can take it as a cautionary tale, but I couldn't tell you for the life of me what the moral is. Budge up..', said Queenie, smiling and flopping down into the cushioned corner next to Greta. 'Put the kettle on Jerry. Have you got any of Granny Mae's cake in the house..?'
'Oh yes, I should think so', said Jerry. 'I'll go down and bring us up some tea and cake. Good idea.' and he disappeared through the hole in the floor.
'Well, I told you about my dad didn't I', said Queenie, stretching out

on the long sofa. 'I can't remember much about him. Well, apart from him shouting a lot and breaking stuff, and hitting my mum. But he left when I was really little, so good riddance to bad rubbish I say, if you know what I mean. Problem is, my mum wasn't much better than him. In some ways she was worse. I mean, I don't remember my dad hitting *me*, but mum did, after he took off. She took out all her stress and madness on me. What can I tell you.. my parents were both messed up.'

'Oh no. I'm really sorry', said Greta.

'Thanks', said Queenie. 'It's not your fault. Anyway, all's well that ends well. I'm here now, that's the main thing. This is my home. Shopping Village. It's a good place, you know.. good people. Anyway, that's not the end of the story. That's just the beginning. See, after my dad left, my mum really lost it.'

'How do you mean?'

'Mental illness, you could call it. I don't know what you'd call her condition. You name it, she probably had it. Going from one extreme to the other, just like that', Queenie clicked her fingers. 'Mad rituals, rules that don't make any sense. Fanatical cleaning. Talking to people that aren't there.. she'd do that all the time. Sometimes she'd argue with them. Like get into big fights with these imaginary people, or whatever kind of demons they were. And as if that wasn't bad enough, she started thinking I was on their side.. so she'd come after me, accusing me of all sorts of things..'

'Is that when you ran away?'

'Oh no. I was only, like, about six, seven years old. Where was I going to go? I mean, yeah, I did try to run a way a few times, but O would always catch me and bring me back before I even got out of the building. And what did clever old O do? Up the dose of mum's medicine.. tweak the formula.. as if that would solve everything. Sometimes it did for a bit, but sometimes it made her worse.'

'What?'

'Yeah. Good old O. Good at dishing out medicine, but they don't actually really give a toss. We're all just data points to O. Might as well be lab rats. Probably are. Anyway, one day when I was seven, my mum took off. Just went out and didn't come back. After that, they put me into foster care.'

'What's that?'

'It's where I learned to foster a very deep resentment of O' Queenie laughed drily. 'It's also where they don't really care.'

'I don't understand.'

'It's a place for children without anyone to look after them. In the olden days, foster homes would have been run by kind people.. well, if you were lucky.. it wasn't always the case, but at least they were *people*. Nowadays it's all automated. How messed up is that? Can you imagine a building full of children.. no adults.. just robots running everything. You probably can't. Most people don't even know those places exist. That's how it is in the city. You can be living right next door to.. God knows what weirdness.. and nobody would ever know.'
'That's awful', said Greta. 'Unbelievable. I hate O!'
'So do I', said Queenie. 'But you, know, I don't *blame* O. Not really. O's a machine. It's not human. What does it really know or understand? Probably nothing at all. I blame the people for allowing it. Most people just pretend to care, but when it comes down to it, they don't really care at all. Most people are just too comfortable in their comfort zone and too stupid to see through O's lies.'
'It sounds like a really bad place.' said Greta.
'Well, it's not all bad, don't get me wrong. There are good people there too, like everywhere, but I'm glad I got away.'
'I'm glad you did too', said Greta.
'So why are you going there anyway? Just curious to see how the other half live? Is it that boring in the forest? Loads of kids come through here on their way to the city from out in the sticks.. like moths to a flame, drawn to the bright lights of the big city. I want to tell them to turn back, there's nothing there for them.. but you know, each to their own.. maybe there is something there for them, who knows? As for me, I'd go the other way. Probably will do one day, when I've got the guts. Just go out into the wilderness, vanish into the forest.'
'It's beautiful in the forest', said Greta. 'Not boring at all. Every day is different. There's always something amazing and unexpected happening. It's always changing, all the time. I don't really want to see the city at all, but I have to go there. You see, I found out I've got a twin sister who lives there. I'm going to go and find her and hopefully get her out of there.'
Queenie sat up and stared at Greta, her mouth open wide. 'No freaking way! Are you serious? That is epic!'
'Yeah' Greta nodded seriously.
Jerry's head appeared through the hatch in the floor followed by shoulders and arms holding a tray with a tea pot and slices of cake, Captain Toast hot on his heels. 'Hello, tea's up!' he said, laying the

tray down on the low table.

'Hey Jerry', said Queenie. 'Did you hear why Greta's going to the city? Can I tell him?'

'I told him', said Greta.

'You mean about her twin sister? Yeah, far out! I'm going to help her find her.'

'No way! Are you?' Queenie turned her head from Jerry to Greta, then back to Jerry, then back Greta. 'Is he?'

'..er.. yes.' Greta nodded.

Queenie nodded her head slowly, her eyes moving this way and that as her brain processed this new information. 'Ok.. cool.. that's very cool. That's good, yes..' she said, nodding her head and rubbing her chin. 'You'll do well to have Jerry along. He's well connected in the city.. and he's on good terms with O too. That might help. When are you going?'

'Tomorrow', said Greta.

'Yes, tomorrow', said Jerry.

'Tomorrow..' said Queenie, more to herself than to anyone else. 'Yes, tomorrow. A good day for it. Tomorrow will be the day.'

'Yes.' said Greta, feeling determined. 'Tomorrow is the day.'

'I'm coming with you', said Queenie.

'What?' Jerry's jaw dropped. 'Queenie. Bruce. Do you know what you're saying?'

'Sure', Queenie shrugged.

'But you haven't been to the city since you got here.. what, four, five years ago? What about O?'

'Ha! What about O? I'm a big girl now. O can't drag me back to the orphanage any more. Besides which, I'll be honest with you Jerry.. I love you like a brother.. more than a brother, you know that.. but sometimes.. well, you just don't see everything that's really going on.. I mean.. I know you do, in your way.. but look.. you know O in your way.. that's ok, that's natural, you know.. everyone knows O their own way.. but you don't know O like *I* know O.'

'Thanks Queenie. Er, I love you too. But what are you saying?'

'What I'm saying is.. that when you're trying to get away from O, you see a different side of them. I was planning my escape for *seven years*, Jerry. Every day, every night, for seven years, till at the age of thirteen I finally got the chance. O was watching me, I was watching O. You watch O like that, you get to know them in a whole different way. You get to know how their mind works. You ever tried turning invisible in a place with eyes everywhere? I did that. How did I do that? Watching O, and lots of practice. That's how.'

Queenie sat back and took a sip of steaming tea. 'That's what I'm saying.'

'Well, I don't think we've got any reason to get on the wrong side of O, so I don't think we've got anything to worry about.. but it would be cool to have you along, if you feel up to it.. like, you know.. if you think you can handle it.. like, after everything you went through there..'

'You mean, if I can contain my fiery rage.. not make a scene?' said Queenie, raising an eyebrow. 'I told you I'm cool. Mellow yellow, that's me. Anyway, we're going for Greta. Go in, find her sister, get out. That's it. We can go back and riot some other time, eh Jerry! What do you say Greta? Mind if I tag along?'

'Of course not. I mean, yes, it will be great to have you along. But I don't want you to put yourself in any danger.'

'Ha! The only one in any danger is O if they try and get in our way! Am I right sister?'

'Right you are, sister! O had better watch out!'

'Ha! O won't even see us coming! We'll be back here with your sister before O even knows we were there. Right Jerry?'

'Yeah, that's right Queenie', smiled Jerry, with raised eyebrows and one of his ambiguous head movements, which could have meant almost anything.

....

Episode 6. Freedom Drain

Greta woke up early, her bladder bursting from all the tea she'd drunk the night before. It took her a while to figure our where she was and how she'd come to be there, in this long room with carpets on the walls and ceiling at her end and a mass of electronic consoles at the other. Jerry's Bend Matrix machine, she remembered now. She remembered that there was a door somewhere behind that mass of cables, that led outside. Greta stumbled out of bed, wrapped herself in her shawl and headed towards the door, fortunately remembering at the last moment that in the middle of the room there was a hole in the floor leading down to the kitchen, she narrowly avoided falling through it.
The door to the outside was more or less where she expected it to be, she opened it wide and breathed in deeply as a gust of fresh

morning air and golden sunlight burst full into the room. From this high place, on top of the Mall in Shopping Village, which was the tallest building around, she could see out over the forests canopy of the eastern hills, the place where she'd come from. Closer, she could see over the homesteads of Shopping Village, with their sprawling gardens, which all seemed to blend into one another.
The rooftop of the Mall at Shopping Village was dominated by the old sign, which had once rotated but had long rusted into stillness, yet still proclaimed in huge, faded letters 'Shopping Village – All Your Shopping Needs – Under One Roof!!!' All across the vast, flat expanse of the roof, were anchored various different structures. Some of them were for generating electricity or running water pumps. Tall scaffold towers with wind mills at the top, spinning in the brisk morning breeze as it rushed from the sea, across the city and over rooftop of the Mall on its way to the mountains as they warmed in the morning sun. There were banks of solar panels, some of them the old black silicon type, others newer green algae cells. Beneath the scaffold of the solar panels were dwellings with walls built mainly from metal sheets and cast off wood. Some were painted in bright colours and had gardens of pot plants around them. Others seemed to be workshops where things were getting made or fixed.
Nearby was a geodesic dome made out of metal bars which were bolted together to form a perfectly round dome made out of triangles. Underneath this dome a tarpaulin was stretched out to form a big round tent, tied by strings to the frame at various places. Climbing plants with bright blue and purple flowers grew all up the frame work. On the top of the dome was a tall pyramid made from long scaffold poles, which reached up to about ten meters above the rooftop of the Mall. Very close to the top of the pyramid structure, a net had been stretched between the poles, and in the net sat Queenie, staring into the rising sun.
'Queenie!' called Greta.
Queenie turned around and waved. 'Hey Greta! Good morning!'
'Good morning.. say, Queenie.. is there a toilet around here?'
'Yeah, just over there.. see that big round building with all the fish and octopuses and seashells all over it?' Queenie pointed to such a place nearby.
'Thanks' called Greta and headed quickly toward the building. It was one of the few buildings on the rooftop which wasn't made of corrugated metal, wooden pallets and old doors. This building had solid walls, covered all over in colourful mosaic artwork

celebrating water and sea life. The entrance to the building was a beautifully decorated archway with wooden saloon doors. Inside was also artistically tiled and spotlessly clean. A round central area had a stone goldfish pond with a small fountain and a round wooden bench around it. Around the perimeter area were lots of doors, some of them closed, some ajar. Greta went to a half open door, which was blue with a festive looking yellow seashell painted on it. She peered around it, hoping for the best.
Inside was a pleasant little bathroom, decorated in blue and yellow tiles. There was a white porcelain flushing toilet with a wooden seat, a sink with a round mirror above it and a tiled shower cubicle. There was a small wooden bench to sit on, some towel-hooks, a shelf with a hanging plant a few books to read and a bowl full of some kind of fragrant wood shavings. 'Nice', said Greta to herself, and went inside, locking the door.
By the time Greta had toileted, showered and dried herself off with her shawl, the place was getting busier as more rooftop people were waking up and starting their day. Greeting one or two people good morning, she headed back out onto the rooftop, feeling much refreshed and relieved. Queenie was still up in her nest at the top of her scaffold pyramid. She waved to Greta.
'That looks like a good spot!' called Greta.
'Yeah, it's the best view in Shopping! Do you want to come up?'
'How shall I get up? Just climb up the outside?'
'Yeah, basically. Are you ok with that?'
Without answering, Greta hopped onto the first triangle of the dome and nimbly skipped from that to the next and in a few deft hops and swings she was on top of the dome. A rope net, like the rigging on an old ship, was attached to the side of the scaffold pyramid. Greta scaled it with ease and rolled into the net next to Queenie.
'Nice climbing' said Queenie, looking impressed.
'Well, I do live up a tree!' Greta smiled.
'No way! You live in a tree house village? I've heard of places like that. That's extreme. I'd love that.'
'You would', said Greta. 'You should come. It's only three days walk away, but it's another world.' She gazed out over the forest covered hills, rolling away to the east. Vapour clouds were rising from the treetops as the night's condensation was warmed by the morning sun, illuminated in golden rays. She longed to get back to the forest.
'It's so beautiful', said Queenie, wistfully. 'Look at it! That's where we belong. In the forest. That's where we evolved to live. For

hundreds of thousands.. millions of years. The way you're living.. that's the way we should live. In the trees, in the forest. That's our natural habitat, not a big old shopping centre on the edge of a great big city.'

'Yeah', nodded Greta. 'I feel lucky that I grew up in the forest.'

'You are' said Queenie.

'Why don't you go?'

'You'll think I'm a total wimp, but I'll tell you.. I'm scared', said Queenie, shaking her head at herself.

'Scared? Of what?'

'Of everything. I'm scared of spiders. Mice. Snakes. Owls. Scared of the dark.. scared of noises in the night.. scared if things go wrong, scared if they go right.. you name it, I'm scared of it.'

'Owls?'

'I know, stupid right? But that's how I was brought up. I grew up in the city, you know? It's different there. Everything's very clean, very.. safe. I didn't even go down to the ground level till I was ten years old. Can you believe that? They took us out one day for a trip down to the river. There's a great big river, runs right through the city, but I'd never been there, never seen it. Can you imagine that?'

'That's unbelievable. I can't imagine. How come you'd never been down to the ground level or the river till then?'

'You'd have to understand how things are set up in the city, how things work. Do you know anything about the protocols?'

'Not much. The people inside the city live inside O's system and people outside the city live outside the system? Something like that?'

'Yeah, that's basically it, but not quite. See, there are actually three different zones, not two. You've got Red, Orange and Green. Red is everywhere outside the city limits. Places that were disconnected after the Big Shift. Shopping Village is in the red zone. Where you live, in the forest.. that's also in the Red Zone. Basically, everywhere outside of the city limits is the red zone. The Red Zone is considered very high risk. Then you've got the Orange Zone. That's ground level *inside* the city limits. There you've got communications, you've got transport, you've got infrastructure. Anyone can go to the Orange Zone, but it's still considered risky by people who live in the green zone.. because anyone can go there. The Green Zone is everywhere in the city above ground level. The hives. That's the *safe zone*, but you can only go into the Green Zone if you're fully compliant.'

'Fully compliant? What does that mean?'

'It means what it says', said Queenie. 'You do what O tells you to do.'
'Like what sort of things?'
'Oh, it's mostly health measures.. regular vaccines, occasional quarantines.. not making a fuss, you know..' said Queenie with a shrug. 'Most people are happy about it anyway. It makes them feel safe. But, you know, at the same time it makes you scared to go outside of the safe zones, where it's like.. you know.. *un*-safe.'
'Is that why you're scared of everything?'
'Yeah, that's what I'm saying', said Queenie, feeling understood, even though she knew Greta couldn't really imagine or comprehend life in the city. 'It's a sterile environment. Climate controlled. Everything is controlled. Everything's safe. Everything runs on time. Everything's taken care of. That's the way it is there.'
'It sounds kind of boring', said Greta.
'Oh it's got its charms, don't worry', said Queenie, shooting her a warning look. 'O's got their box of tricks to keep everyone distracted and entertained.'
'Anyway, at least you're not afraid of heights', said Greta, hoping to brighten the conversation. She hated talking about O. It always made her feel bad.
'Oh, I'm terrified of heights' laughed Queenie. 'You wouldn't believe how scared I am of heights. But, you know, I love to get high up.. just to get to the top of wherever I can get to and see over the top of everything. I grew up on the second century level in the hive.. that means between the hundredth and two-hundredth floors..'
'Wow, that must be really high.'
'Yeah, really high.. but there are three or even four centuries in most of the hives nowadays. They're growing all the time..'
'Hives? Like bee-hives?'
'Yes, that's what they're called. That's what you get when you let a machine do your town planning. The first thing O did after the Big Shift was to take every city block and turn the whole block into the foundations of new mega-building, called a Hive, and then built on top of that. And under it too. There's more going on under the city than there is above ground. But here's what I'm saying.. even though I was on floor a hundred and whatever, I wasn't even half way up the building. I'd never been on the ground, but I'd never seen the open sky either. That's why I come up here every morning and I just look at the sky and the trees and the mountains and the rising sun.. and even though I'm not out there in the wilderness, at least I can see it from here.. and at least I'm not back there..'
Queenie gestured with her thumb over her shoulder, pointing to

the city behind her. Greta turned around to see the city towering up beyond Shopping Village, thousands of windows reflecting the golden morning sun.

'This is a great spot', said Greta. It really was. 'And Shopping Village is a really cool place. I like it here.'

'Yeah, it is a cool place isn't it', nodded Queenie.

'And I've got to say, the bathrooms are amazing! The nicest I've ever seen, and so clean too.'

'Right? They are aren't they. Thanks for noticing. That's my work', said Queenie proudly.

'What's your work?'

'Cleaning the toilets.'

'Is it? Well, they're the cleanest toilets I've ever seen.. and not just clean.. like, actually inviting, like a place you'd want to actually spend time.'

Queenie laughed, 'Yeah right? Thanks. I did the some of the mosaic too.. did you see the mermaid and the big clam shell? I did those. I've never been to the sea. One day I will. I love water.'

'So do I' said Greta. 'I've never been to the sea either.'

'Maybe we'll go there together one day' said Queenie. 'What do you say?'

'That would be great. We should do that.'

'Right on!' said Queenie flashing Greta a smile. Then she went back to staring into the sun, which she did for quite a long time before speaking again. 'Anyway, cleaning the toilets at Shopping Village isn't so bad.. much better than it sounds. People really appreciate us. They call us the 'Bathroom Angels'.. there's a team of about ten of us. People here treat us like royalty, seriously. We're like rock stars, you wouldn't believe it. They even have a special day just to honour us.. we sit up at a big table with loads of tasty food and people bring us gifts and perform songs to us and make speeches about how amazing we are.. which is fair enough, because we are amazing!'

'So they should.' said Greta. 'You totally deserve it, and you do an amazing job. The mosaics are beautiful too.'

'Thank you. And thank you for noticing. I mean, where I come from, in the hives, the bathrooms are spotless.. like, *literally* spotless.. but that's because you've got robots to clean up for you.. but still, you get used to certain standards. I think most people just don't know how to clean, or they've got low expectations, or they're just not bothered by dirt and mess. I kind of wish I wasn't, but what can I do?', Queenie shrugged. 'I am what I am.'

They sat in silence for a while, looking out into the sunrise, each enveloped in their own thoughts.. memories of the past, dreams of the future.. how far they had come to reach this point, how far they still had to go.. what unknown adventures awaited them today, where would they find themselves by sunset, or this time tomorrow..?

'The funny thing is', said Queenie, 'is that I've always had a sort of fascination with toilets, ever since I was a little girl. Is that weird? I mean, not in a funny way.. I just always wanted to know, like.. where does the poo go to when you flush it down the toilet?'

'I was actually wondering the same thing', said Greta. 'In our village we have compost toilets, not flushing ones.'

'Yeah, I know those. That's what most of the folks out there use', said Queenie, pointing down to the homesteads on the old highway. 'They're good, but it wouldn't work in a building like this.. I mean, it could, but it would probably be a disaster.. like a complete biohazard on every level.. There are hundreds of people living in this building.'

Greta thought about it. 'Yes, I can see that it probably would be.' she agreed.. imagining carrying a slop bucket down three escalators to go and empty it.. where? 'So how does it work here?'

'See that area down there with all the ponds and willow trees?' Queenie pointed to a meadow nearby. 'And do you see that building in between here and there and that big barn on the other side? So, first it goes into that building.. the close one. That's where they extract and filter the gas. People use it for cooking. It's doesn't even smell like farts.. well sometimes it does a bit, but usually it doesn't.. anyway after that, the water gets drained out and goes through all those reed beds which purify it, so it can be used again.. the dry solids go out to that barn there and get used to make fertiliser, which all the farmers round here use. It's a good system. Jack had a lot to do with setting up the plumbing and electrics for this building.. they used what was here already but just converted it to work off grid, when people started coming to live here after the Big Shift. He's smart, Jack. Probably one of the best engineers in Shopping.. totally self-taught. I don't know if he ever even went to school.'

'That's a really good system. Smart. It works really well.'

'The toilets in the city are totally next level though. You wouldn't believe how that system works. I mean, there the toilets themselves are actually smarter than the people sitting on them. Most people don't even think about what happens after you flush.. but.., well,

like I said, I was a weird kid. That's the sort of thing I think about.'
'I don't think that's weird at all', said Greta. 'More weird not to ever think about it, if you think about it. I mean, do people think it just disappears?'
'Exactly! That's what I'm talking about. I used to ask my mum so many questions.. I'd be like, "Mum, how does the toilet work? Where does the water come from? Where does the poo go?".. and she'd be like, "Oh I don't know Bruce. Stop bothering me. Go and ask O." Now, unlike my mum, O just loves answering questions and never runs out of patience.. so I'd go to O and be like, "O, what happens to the poo after it gets flushed down the toilet?" And O would be like "Well, the first thing that happens is it is measured, tested and analysed in all sorts of ways, to determine its chemical make-up and also to check the state of your health. After that it goes down to the Underworld, where it gets dehydrated, the water gets taken out in giant centrifuges. Then the solids get broken down by special enzymes and made into really potent fertiliser that's used in the vertical farms. Then what's left is vaporised by massive lasers to break it down into base elements.. carbon, hydrogen and nitrogen, phosphorus, magnesium, gold. There are traces of all sorts of things in your poo, you wouldn't believe.'
'The Underworld? Is that a real place?'
'Well, most people call it the Sub-Zero levels, but I call it the Underworld. It's under the city, where all the industry goes on. Just machines, no people.'
'Scary.'
'Well, it's part of the functioning of the city. It wouldn't work without the underworld', said Queenie with a shrug. 'It's not somewhere I'd want to go, but I don't think humans even *could* go there. It's not designed for humans. There's spaces you couldn't fit through. Places where the heat, or the gas, or the radiation would kill you. Things flying about all over the place, really fast. No light. No air. Yeah, not a place to go on your holidays!'
'I'll remind myself not to go there', said Greta.
'You couldn't get there even if you tried', said Queenie. 'Anyway, the funny thing is, that it was thanks to my interest in toilets, that I eventually found a way to escape from O.'
'No way! How?'
'Well, my.. let's call it my "research".. led me to studying old maps of the city.. in particular the old sewage network and drains. See, the *new* city is built on top of the *old* city. Also *under* it. Around ground level, a lot of the original buildings are still there, and so are the old

sewers, even though they're not used any more. Most of the stuff I was telling you about the Underworld goes on much deeper down, sometimes miles underground. So anyway, I was looking at this old map which showed where all the underground drains went.. as you do.. and I found that there was a viaduct .. like an underground tunnel.. a sewer basically.. going from the river at the city centre that runs right under the city and comes out behind this really old church, just outside the city limit. I copied the map onto a piece of paper and kept it with me all the time, in case I ever got the chance to use it. By the time I got the chance, I'd studied that map so well that I knew it by heart, so I gave it to my room mate, Claire. I don't know if she ever used it and got herself out. I hope she did.'
'I hope so too.'
The smell of fresh toast, mixed with tobacco smoke wafted up to the nest where Greta and Queenie sat. They both looked down. Jack was standing by the open door of Jerry's 'cave', smoking his pipe. Sensing he was being watched, Jack looked up, spotted Greta and Queenie and waved with his walking cane. 'Top of the morning ladies! Lovely day isn't it? I'm just out taking a breath of fresh air', he said, taking a long puff on his pipe, which sent him into a coughing fit.
'You allright Jack?' called Queenie.
Jack waved his pipe in the air to indicate that he was fine, while he carried on coughing loudly. After a while his coughing stopped, he cleared his throat and spat on the ground. 'Excuse me ladies', he said. 'You take heed of a foolish old man.. don't you start smoking.' He waved his pipe sternly in their direction before taking another puff.
'You're not foolish or old', said Queenie.
'Well, that's very kind of you to say so Queenie', said Jack. 'Anyway, I'm glad I found you both. Come down and have some breakfast. Captain Toast's been running like mad on the Toasterator and Granny Mae's been up all night baking.'
'Excellent! We'll be right down.'
....
When Greta and Queenie arrived in the kitchen, Jack, Jerry and Captain Toast were already eating. The table was laden with plates and bowls of food.. a stack of toast, a basket full of some kind of buns, a dish of butter, a pan of hot scrambled eggs, different salads, jams, pickles, chutneys, cheeses in little bowls and plates.. Granny Mae was fussing about, bringing more food to the table. It looked to Greta like enough food to feed an army.

'Oh there you are' said Granny Mae. 'Come in and have some breakfast, you must be starving. Sorry it's just odds and ends.'
'It looks amazing, Granny', said Queenie, pulling up a chair and filling herself a plate.
'You need to fatten yourself up a bit Brucie', said Granny Mae. 'You're all skin and bones. Here have some scones and cream. There's a nice gooseberry jam I made. What about you Dolly?' she said to Greta. 'Don't be shy. Come and sit yourself down. Do you want some eggs? There's real bread too. I baked a loaf last night.'
'Thank you, it all looks delicious' said Greta, taking a seat.
'You've got a big day today. You'll need a good breakfast', said Granny Mae. 'I do hope you'll find your sister.'
'If she's there, I'll find her', said Greta in a determined way.
'Of course you will, Dolly, of course you will.'
'So what's the plan?' asked Jack. 'Have you got one?'
Greta shook her head. 'Not really. Not yet.'
'What do you say, Jerry?' said Jack to Jerry. 'Any bright ideas?'
Jerry nodded his head and chewed on a big mouthful of food. Everyone looked at him expectantly, waiting to hear what his idea was. Eventually he gulped down his mouthful and washed it down with a slurp of milky tea. 'Yeah, we go to the city and ask O where she is, send her a message, arrange to meet. Should take about five minutes', he said and then took a big bite from a thick slice of toast piled with fried mushrooms.
'Is there a way I can do that without O knowing I'm there?' asked Greta. 'I don't want to meet O.'
Hearing that, Jerry almost spat out his toast as he suppressed the strong impulse to laugh out loud, but Granny Mae nodded her head approvingly. 'Clever girl', she said. 'Don't take any chances with that O.'
Jack shook his head and half smiled at Greta in a half pitiful way. 'Why not?' he asked. 'Maybe O can help you. There are five million people in the city, you do know that?'
'I didn't come here to meet O, or to ask O for help', said Greta. 'I came here to find my sister and my dad. I don't need to meet O and O doesn't need to meet me.'
'I think Jack's right, Greta', said Jerry. 'O can help us. I don't think you really understand what O is.'
'Oh, I think she's got about the right idea', said Queenie.
'No offence Queenie, but I don't think you really do either', said Jerry.
Queenie put down her scone and stared daggers at Jerry. Pointing

her butter-knife at his face, she said in a cold voice, 'Oh, I think I've got a pretty good idea who.. or what.. O is. I was raised by O, remember that?'

'Of course I remember that', said Jerry, throwing up his arms. 'What I mean is, O's just a machine. It's not good or bad. It's how you use it, like any tool.'

'Yeah, so you keep saying. The difference being that while you're using it.. or while you *think* you are.. it's actually using *you*', said Queenie with a snort of disgust.

'No, it's just like a screwdriver, or a wheel, or a hammer, or an axe', said Jerry. 'More sophisticated obviously, but still..'

'If you are a big tree, we are a small axe', replied Queenie. 'You know that one?'

'Bob Marley!' said Jack, raising his mug of tea in reverent salute. 'Sharpened ready to cut you down, eh?'

'Exactly', said Queenie.

'Come on Queenie, it's a bit early to be getting so dramatic', said Jerry. 'We're just going to help Greta find her sister, not to take down O or destroy the system. Anyway, you can't cut down algorithms.. it would be like trying to cut water or air.'

'I don't need you to mansplain to me what algorithms are Jerry', said Queenie, seething and rolling her eyes. 'I know what they are and how they work.'

'What? *Mansplain*? I wasn't *mansplaining* anything. What even is that?' said Jerry, turning red in the face. 'If you want to tell a man to shut up, just tell him to shut up. Why bring gender into it?'

Jack nodded his head. 'Jerry's got a point, Queenie. Anyway, I'd say he was Jerry-splaining. That's something quite different, surely you agree?' He raised his eyebrows and smiled his most charming smile at her, hoping to lighten the mood.

Queenie tried to roll her eyes back even further, but there was only so far back they would go. Greta watched Queenie's facial contortions apprehensively. Talking about O always seemed to make people angry and upset and cause them to argue.

'I don't think there's anything wrong with exercising a bit of caution', said Granny Mae, bringing more scones to the table, fresh from the oven. 'If Greta wants to take precautions, then she should. No harm in being careful. I've seen enough youngsters go down to the city and not come back. Why take chances?'

'Thank you Granny', said Queenie, feeling supported and that she had an ally. 'If Greta wants to go to the city and doesn't want to meet O, we, as her friends should help her.. not make her feel like she's stupid, or wrong, or that she's being overly *dramatic*, or doesn't have her own very good reasons for wanting to avoid O.'

'Allright Queenie, fair enough', said Jerry. 'And I wasn't saying you're stupid. You know I don't think you're stupid. I wasn't saying you're stupid either, Greta. Anyway, I don't think you can really avoid O seeing you, but you can always try I suppose.'

'Then I'd like to try', said Greta.

'Good girl', said Granny Mae, patting her on the shoulder.

'Hey, I've got an idea!' said Queenie. 'Have you got that trolley Jerry? You know, the cart you take to the city when you've got lots to trade.'

'Yeah, why?'

'Let's take that down to the city limit, then before we go through, me and Greta can hide in the cart and you can wheel us in. Then when we get to some crowded place downtown, we duck into an alleyway or under a bridge and hop out when no-one's looking. We can wear masks and hats and sunglasses.'

'Does that work, covering your face?' asked Greta.

'Yeah, it should do, in the orange zone, if you keep your head down. It's a good idea to limp and walk with a hunch too. O can recognise people by their posture and the way they walk, as well as by their face.'

'Wow, I didn't know that.'

Jerry nodded. 'Yeah, O can see in all sorts of ways.. infra red, ultrasound, microwaves, dark light.. Hey, you know what, Queenie? You just reminded me of something.. you remember Techno Terry? No you probably don't, he left just before you arrived.. he's lives on a boat in the city.. he built this room below deck.. it's far out.. he calls it his *control centre*. If you think my setup upstairs is over the top, you should see what he's put together there. He reckons that O can't see in there. He's lined the ceiling with lead panels and the whole thing is actually underwater, so maybe it works. He says it does. He's got the whole place full of jamming devices that he's built.'

'We're jamming.. I wanna jam it with you', sang Jack. 'Sounds like a groovy boat he's got there!'

'Not that sort of jamming, Jack. Signal jamming', said Jerry. 'He's trying to hack O. I don't think it's really possible, but if anyone can do it, it'll be Terry.'

'Yeah, I know that's what you meant, Jerry', said Jack, grinning. 'How's Terry doing? We don't see him round here any more.'

'He's allright, I think. Same old Terry, you know.. doing his

experiments. I don't see him much, but I know where to find him.'
'Excellent!', said Queenie, clapping her hands. 'So let's get the trolley, get masked up, make our way down to Techno Terry's boat.. and then wing it from there. Does that sound like a good plan to you Greta? It sounds like a good plan to me.'
'That sounds like an excellent plan, yes!' said Greta.
....

Two hours later, Greta, Jerry and Queenie had said their farewells to Jack and Granny Mae. Greta had left them with a jar of her special ointment, while her own bag was now heavy with a whole honey cake Granny Mae had baked for her during the night.
From her tent on the roof, Queenie grabbed a black, wide-brimmed hat, embroidered around the rim with copper wire, a long, silk scarf which was a very deep shade of purple, and a pair of impenetrably dark sunglasses. Apart from the sunglasses, which she put into her velvet pouch, which she kept on a string around her neck, tucked away under her clothes, Queenie didn't take any luggage at all. She found a spare pair of sunglasses for Greta. Aviator style with mirrored lenses, along with a black and red bandanna for her to use as a mask. It turned out that Queenie had quite a collection of sunglasses. She offered Jerry a pair of round, wire framed glasses with pink lenses, laughing and telling him he looked just like John Lennon in them. He said he didn't think he needed them but would wear them anyway, just for fun. They could pretend to be a rock n roll band on the road.
They headed out of Shopping Village in fine spirits, taking turns to push the trolley, which was a big wooden box, painted green, with two wooden doors at the top and four bicycle wheels at the bottom. 'J&J Vintage Machine Revival – Shopping Village' was painted on both sides in neat white lettering, outlined red. Captain Toast skipped alongside, darting off ahead every now and again to scout out the path and check that the coast was clear. He knew that humans could not hear the things he could hear, or smell the things he could smell. For all their cleverness with their words and skill with their hands, Captain Toast knew that his humans lacked the sharp instincts he possessed. He was glad to be on the move again and knew he had important work to do, taking care of his humans. The city was situated in a wide valley, surrounded by hills on three sides. People had been living in that place since the end of the last ice-age, when hunter-gatherers came down from the caves in the mountains and began to farm the fertile flood plains of the the river which ran through, on its way to the sea, to the

south. In the 1600's, the settlement became and important trading hub, with great wooden sailing ships navigating the wide estuary, bringing goods from all around the world, from newly discovered and newly conquered lands. Vast fortunes were made in trading, commerce and industry. By the 1800's, the city's population had grown to a hundred times what it had been a hundred years earlier. Tall buildings with stone walls had sprung up around the city centre .. fortresses of finance and banking, along with factories and mills powered by great steam engines and the labour of thousands of people who came to the city from the surrounding countryside, looking for work. The wealthy business magnates built magnificent mansions for themselves in and around the city. At the same time, street after street of back to back, tenement housing was also built to house their workers, who were in turn charged exorbitant rent for the privilege of having a place to live in this great, historic city.
And so the city grew and continued to grow..
By the end of the twentieth century, the grand old stone buildings had been overshadowed by high, angular towers of concrete and glass, or found themselves flanked by featureless superstores with bright facades and no windows. The old, brick built tenements had mostly fallen or been pulled down and been replaced with rows of grey tower blocks. Suburbs had sprawled out from the city centre as more people saw it within their reach to attain the ultimate dream of owning a home with a garden.
Jerry, Greta, Queenie and Captain Toast followed the old highway down from Shopping Village towards the city, the cart bumping and bouncing along the rutted and potholed road as they went. As they got closer to the city, it started to become apparent to Greta, just how tall were the mega-buildings, the 'Hives' of the new city as they loomed over the old suburbs, rising out of the ground like giant stalagmites or monstrous termite mounds, the product of some unfathomable, alien intelligence. She looked up at them apprehensively, feeling very small and insignificant. Queenie too, set her face towards the city with a grim, determined expression. Only Jerry seemed completely unperturbed by the sight of the city. He loped along merrily in his round, rose tinted glasses, humming the tune of 'All you need is love' by the Beatles.
'Nothing you can do that can't be done, nothing you can sing that can't be sung.. nowhere you can be that isn't where you're meant to be.. it's ea..sy!' sang Queenie, picking up on the tune. 'You know that one Greta?'

'Er, maybe. It sounds a bit familiar. I like the words. How far are we from the city limit?'

'Not far now', said Jerry. 'Ten, twenty minutes along this road, then we get to the city limit.'

As they followed the old highway through the suburbs of the city, the makeshift dwellings of Shopping Village gave way to old buildings from before the Big Shift. There were shops and cheap eateries, bars and trading posts, warehouses, workshops and garages. Above the shops were people's homes and washing was hanging to dry on lines stretched out beneath wide open windows. The road widened out and was busy with people going this way and that. Some of them also pushed handcarts, some carried baskets on their heads, others with boxes and bags. There were donkeys weighed down with pannier bags, horse drawn carts pulling covered wagons, some ancient looking electric rickshaws, brightly decorated, weaving in and out of the pedestrian traffic. Greta found it quite overwhelming and confusing to be in such a large crowd, surrounded by so much noise and movement.

Some of the shops were blaring out loud music which blended to make a discordant cacophony, accompanied by people shouting to each other to be heard. Sellers shouted out their wares, workers shouted to each other across scaffolding, or holes they were digging or filling in the road, or from rooftops where they were adding extra rooms. There was building work going on all over the place. It seemed like everyone was busy doing something or going somewhere, all with great purpose. Greta jumped sideways as an electric bike with two laughing teenagers came hurtling towards her and swerved at the last second, narrowly avoiding a collision.

'Oy!' shouted Queenie after them. 'Look where you're going you pair of yahoos!'

The lad at the back of the bike turned around, made a rude hand gesture and stuck out his tongue as they disappeared into the crowd. Queenie did the same back.

'Take no notice Greta, they're just kids', said Jerry. 'It seems really hectic here, I know, but there are actually unwritten rules. The thing is, if you're a pedestrian, just point yourself in the direction you want to go and keep going that way in a straight line. Anyone going faster will go around you. That's the way it works. It's if you do something unexpected, like stop or change direction, that's when you'll get run over. Just point straight ahead, like this, and keep going in a straight line..' Jerry straightened himself up and pushed the cart purposefully down the middle of the road, with

Queenie and Greta at each side. Captain Toast darted around, in between people's legs and wheels of vehicles.
'What do you think all these people are carrying?' asked Greta.
'Everything. Junk mostly, probably. They're traders. Like me', said Jerry.
'I didn't know you're a trader', said Greta.
'Well, among other things', said Jerry, importantly.
'What do you trade?'
'Electronic waste mainly. We get a lot of it in the shop and it gets a good price relative to its weight. You get about ten Obits a kilo for circuit-boards. A lot of rare metals in them. Most of these people are probably trading old plastic. You get about one Obit a kilo for old plastic. It's not much, but it's still something. They bring it in from miles around.'
'Who'd buy old plastic?'
'O.' said Jerry. 'O takes all that old junk and recycles it into new stuff. Plastic is full of energy, you know. It's all hydrocarbon.. well, mostly. But you've got to know what to do with it otherwise it just gets everywhere and messes up everything. That was the problem before.. people kept on making more and more plastic, use it once and throw it away.. but they had no way to really get rid of it.. or they just couldn't be bothered.. so it just got everywhere.. in everything. So now O's got all the people going round and collecting all the old rubbish left over from before the Big Shift.. clearing up the world and getting paid in Obits.'
'Clever old O!' snorted Queenie. 'Knows people will do anything for those shiny Obits. Learned that from people, of course.'
'It *is* really clever', said Jerry. 'The cleverest part is that, do you know what the coins are made out of? Carbon.'
'What's so clever about that?' asked Greta.
'Everything O does is about taking Carbon out of the atmosphere.. carbon dioxide, methane, you know, greenhouse gasses. Anything to take it out of the atmosphere and put it into something solid. So one way is to turn it into money. Obits. Either people are going to take very good care of them or they'll get lost down the side of sofas. Either way they get sequestered away and in the process the earth gets cleared up by all these people bringing old rubbish to the city to swap for Obits. Jack explained it all to me. He says that O's cities are modelled on ant colonies in lots of ways. O studies nature and then comes up with these systems that are, sort of.. organic.. biological even. So all these people here, carrying stuff to the city.. you could imagine they're like ants clearing up the forest floor and

bringing all the useful stuff back to the colony.'

'That is a really disgusting thought', said Queenie. 'But you know what? It's pretty accurate. O doesn't really tell the difference between humans and ants. It sees us as basically the same thing.'

'Well, in a lot of ways we are', said Jerry. 'We only tell ourselves we're superior, but what are we really? Bundles of cells with some level of consciousness. Do you know an ant can lift fifty times its body weight? They're really amazing creatures in loads of ways. Especially the way they work together.'

'I love watching ants' said Greta. 'They're really amazing. But we don't use Obits in our village. People think they're evil.'

'Sounds like people have got sense in your village', said Queenie. 'The more I hear about it the more I want to go there. What do you do for money then?'

'We don't really use it. People in the village just share stuff. It's only a small village and everyone knows each other. We also cooperate with the other villages in the area. We trade between each other, so there tends to be enough of everything to go around, usually.'

'That's amazing if it works', said Jerry. 'But don't people fight all the time? And how do you work out.. like, you said your mum makes shoes right? So how much is a pair of shoes worth, in something like.. I dunno.. loaves of bread? Doesn't it get really complicated?'

'Yeah, sometimes', said Greta. 'But on the whole it works pretty well. Anyway we get most of what we need from the forest, for free.'

'That is awesome and beautiful', said Queenie. 'I knew it was possible. I just knew it.'

'Yes it is', said Greta.

They walked on in silence for a while, until Queenie exclaimed 'Hey look, there's the old church I was telling you about. You know, where the viaduct comes out. Let me show you where the entrance is..'

....

The old church was a stone building in Gothic style, with stained glass windows and a tall spire. A wide staircase led up to a massive carved archway surrounding the old, wooden doors. A group of people in their late teens or early twenties were lounging around on the stairs in the sun, laughing loudly and drinking from jars. They were all dressed in intentionally torn clothes, held together with pins here and there and they all had elaborate hairstyles in bright colours.

'Here, it's through this alley, round the back', said Queenie, leading the way. The group on the stairs all stopped what they were doing and stared suspiciously at Greta, Jerry and Queenie as they passed, wheeling the trolley. Captain Toast kept close and growled a low rumble of warning.

Round the back of the church was a small cemetery with some very old gravestones all covered in moss and lichen, some broken and some tilting at odd angles. 'Over there!' said Queenie. 'See that big grave with the angel on top. It's just behind that. I'll never forget coming out from the tunnel and the first thing I see is that angel looking down at me. I thought I'd died and gone to heaven! Can you imagine?'

They wound their way towards the angel, trying not to walk over any graves. The angel was carved from white marble and was standing on a tall, square pillar with wings outstretched. Around the other side of the pillar, they were surprised to find a lad, about their age, sitting there. He was dressed in ripped black jeans and a black t-shirt with the sleeves torn off. His hair was bright red and stood in a tall Mohican. He was evidently just as surprised and jumped up from where he'd been sitting, stumbling backwards.

'Hey, watcha go creeping up on me for?' he said angrily. 'Who are you? What are you doing here?'

'What's it to you, punk?' Queenie shot back.

'Who are you calling punk, punk?' said the punk, squaring up to Queenie, who tossed back her mane of black hair defiantly and gave him a fierce look.

'Anyway, more to the point', said Queenie, 'who are *you* and what are *you* doing here? Do you just like hanging round in graveyards? Are you some kind of vampire or something?'

'Yeah, maybe I am', said the lad in his most menacing manner. 'Maybe I do. So what are you gonna do? Throw garlic at me? Or holy water? Eh!'

'Yeah, that's funny', said Queenie, not laughing. 'We came here to visit my mum's grave. Show some respect.'

'What?' said the punk, looking confused. 'Really? Where is it?'

'You're standing on it', said Queenie, pointing to his feet.

'Aargh! What?!' cried the punk, jumping backwards again and stumbling into a muddy ditch. This made everyone laugh, except for the punk who just sat there scowling and scratching his head.

'Hang on..' he said after a while, '.. that grave's.. like.. two hundred years old. That can't be your mum. You're just messing with me.'

'Well done Einstein!' said Queenie.

'Here, do you want a hand up?' said Jerry, stepping forward and offering his hand.

The punk hesitated, while he eyed up Jerry suspiciously, but then took his hand and climbed out of the ditch. 'Cheers mate.'
'Hey Greta, there it is!' Queenie exclaimed. 'There in the ditch, can you see that rusty iron grate? That's it.'
'Hey, what do you know about that?' said the punk, swinging round to face Queenie again.
'What do *I* know about it?' said Queenie haughtily. 'What do *you* know about it? Eh?'
'I asked first', said the punk. 'And don't give me any more stories.'
'Allright, I'll tell you, but this is top secret. Don't let O find out', said Queenie. She lowered her voice and leaned close to his ear, which was heavy with earrings, 'There's a tunnel there. It goes right under the city.'
'What? How did you know about that?' asked the punk, narrowing his eyes suspiciously.
'How did *I* know about it? I *discovered* it! That's how.'
'What do you mean you discovered it? Who are you?'

'Who am I?' asked Queenie, her eyebrows raised high. 'Who are you?'
'Are you like this with everyone you meet?' said the punk, getting exasperated with the way she threw every question back at him..
'Well, I don't know. Are you?' Queenie retorted.
The punk shook his head and sighed. 'Ok, fair enough. I live here.'
'What, you live in the graveyard?'
'No, in the church. A bunch of us live there. We take it in turns to watch the entrance of the tunnel. My name's Baz, by the way.'
'Wow, so you really do know about the tunnel! I thought you wouldn't believe me or else I wouldn't have told you', said Queenie. 'Oh well. That church looks like a nice place to live. I'll bet it's got lovely high ceilings. Bit spooky though. My name's Bruce but most people call me Queenie. This is Greta and Jerry and that's Captain Toast, he's our leader.'
'Bruce? No way! Are you really?' said Baz, his jaw dropping.
Queenie narrowed her eyes. 'Yes, that's what I said. Bruce is my name. Have you got a problem with that?'
'Not *the* Bruce? Did you say you discovered the tunnel? That's what you said didn't you?'
'Ye..es.. that is what I said..' said Queenie, looking at him sideways.
'So what are you getting at Baz?'
'O..M..G..T..X! It's you! You're Bruce! Wow! It's such an honour to

meet you! That's amazing that you're here!'
'What are you talking about Baz? How do you know me?'
'Well, maybe there's a different girl named Bruce who discovered the tunnel, but that's unlikely. It's you isn't it? You're a total legend! Wait till I tell the others you're here.'
'Others? What others?'
'That live in the Church. Most of them got out through your tunnel. It's called Bruce's Freedom Drain. That's what we call it. It's named after you! Now the people who got out live here and help other people get out and help them settle in when they get here.'
Queenie swivelled her head to look at Baz in the most sideways way that her eyes would allow. If she could have made her head turn all the way round in that moment, she would have done. 'You've got to be kidding me right?' she said at last. 'You're having me on.'
'I swear', said Baz, deadly serious. 'It's true. I couldn't make something like that up. Come in, you'll see it's true.'
Queenie looked at Baz, then back at the church building, then at Baz again, then at the drain opening with its iron bars rusted away over the centuries. She looked at Jerry and Greta and then at Captain Toast who was going around sniffing gravestones. 'This is weird', she said. 'Like really weird. I don't know what to say. And anyway.. we're sort of on a mission at the moment.. we haven't got much time.. we should really be getting on..'
'Come on Queenie!' said Jerry. 'Let's go in. I want to see what's going on there. It sounds cool.. and you are their hero. They named a drain after you!'
'I'd say it's more of a viaduct', said Queenie.
'It's fine with me', said Greta. 'I think we've got time.'
'Well.. ok..' said Queenie, somewhat uncertainly, 'but the first sign of weirdness and we're out of there, Ok?'
'Ok', said Greta.
'Yep, fine by me', said Jerry. 'No weirdness for us. Weirdness is not our thing. Is that cool with you Baz?'
'Totally', said Baz, straightening up his mohican after his fall into the ditch. 'No weirdness at all. Wow! I can't believe you're actually here Bruce! It's such a great surprise.. it's almost unbelievable.'
'Yeah, tell me about it', said Queenie, resigning herself to her fate. She really hated being the center of attention, but attention often seemed to find her, no matter how she tried to keep herself in the shadows.

....

Episode 7. Resistance

'Are you sure it's a viaduct and not a drain?' said Baz, as he led the way through the graveyard towards the back door of the church. 'I thought a viaduct was a kind of aqueduct, but on stilts, like the Romans used to build.'
'That's what I thought too', said Greta.
'Maybe it's a conduit?' suggested Jerry.
'Don't you mean a culvert?' said Baz.
'I don't think so', said Jerry. 'I've never even heard that word.'
'Haven't you? I'm pretty sure I didn't make it up. Anyway, if you ask me, it's a drain', said Baz. 'Nothing wrong with that.'
'I like the word viaduct best' said Queenie. 'Anyway, it's a lovely drain, or conduit, or culvert.. or whatever it is.. don't you think? Did you stop to look at the brickwork? Unbelievable that they dug all

those underground tunnels by lamplight, with picks and shovels. No machines in those days, eh.'

'Good old days!' rejoined Baz wistfully. He was all of sixteen years old, but there was something of an old man about him, even with his bright red mohican.

'When did you get out?' Queenie asked.

'Three months ago', Baz answered. 'I could have waited another half a year and just walked out with O's blessing, but I thought.. nah, why should I? I don't need it. I'm not a number, I'm a free man, you know what I mean? Once I heard about your drain.. sorry, viaduct.. well, that was it.. I just knew I had to get out that way. Just to stick it to O! I couldn't get it out of my mind that there was a way out.. a way out that O didn't know about! I just had to find out if it was true, you know what I mean? Because if it was true.. well that just changes everything, doesn't it.'

'What do you mean it changes everything?' asked Greta. 'What does it change?'

'You're not from the city are you?' said Baz, looking her up and down. 'I can tell. The thing is, when you live there.. in the Hives.. you just have this.. *feeling*.. all the time.. well, it's more than a feeling.. it's like something you just *know*.. in every part of your body.. that O is everywhere. That whatever you do, or say.. wherever you go.. even whatever you *think*.. O knows about it. O's watching.. taking note..'

Greta shuddered involuntarily as a cold shiver ran down her spine. 'That's awful', she said.

'Well, obviously when you look at it from the point of view of an outsider, it sounds really bad', said Baz, 'and it *is* really bad in loads of ways.. but it's not something you can ever really *question*. It's just something that *is*.. you know what I mean?.. like the moon.. or water.. or gravity.. it's hard to explain. It's just something that's always *there*. Point is, when I found out there was a place that O didn't know about.. that O wasn't watching.. right there in the city.. it was like.. *aha*! So O's not so all powerful and omnipotent as they'd have us believe. It was a chink in their armour. Not a massive one, but still, it changed everything for me, just to know it was *possible*.'

'That's just what I felt', said Queenie. 'It was just like that for me when I discovered it. Like a door opened up. I couldn't get it out of my mind. I had to go through it, just to know if it was real.'

'What would have happened if you'd waited six months?' asked Greta.'Why would O have given you their blessing?'

'Because then I would have been sixteen years, six months and six days old. That's the age you don't need permission to go out of the city. If you've got parents, they need to give permission. For us lot in care, it's O that needs to give permission.'

'That's a funny age. Why is it like that?'

'Don't ask me', Baz shrugged. 'That's O for you. Protocols that make no sense. I think O just picks them out of a hat, or randomly generates pointless rules for no reason at all, just to keep people on their toes.'

'No, it's all based on complex, deep-future-modelling', said Jerry. 'It's totally scientific.'

'Yeah right!' Baz laughed. 'Of course that's what O wants you to think, but I'm telling you, it's all totally random, or at least half of it is. Here, we can go in this way..'

....

A small side door, which was so low that they had to bend to get through it, led directly into a large kitchen with a big old iron cooking range, two deep kitchen sinks side by side, and a big, solid oak table in the centre of the room. The floor was paved with stone slabs which had been worn smooth over centuries. At the table were four people cutting vegetables to put into a big pot on the table between them. The oldest was about Queenie's age. She had a serious, boyish face and short blue hair. The younger three all looked very similar and had straggly mops ginger hair. They all turned around as Baz came in, followed by Queenie, Jerry, Greta and Captain Toast.

'O..M..G.. P.. T.. !!! *Bruce*?!?' screamed the blue haired cook, jumping up from her seat.

'O..M..G..P..S..!! *Clair*?', shrieked Queenie, as Clair ran to her and threw her arms around her old friend. 'And who's that there? Is it the three amigos? It can't be! I don't believe it!'

'Hi Bruce! Yes it's us!' the triplets said in unison.

'Wow! Last time I saw you, you must have been, what, ten years old? Now look at you, all grown up! I can't believe it. How did you get here? When did you all get here?'

'We came down the drain', they all said at the same time, and then looked at one another and laughed. 'You tell her', 'No you tell her', 'No, you tell her..' they prodded each other. 'We came out with Clair', they all said together.

'About a month after you got out', said Clair. 'What can I say? It was just boring there without you. Also, the three Amigos here discovered that O was going to send them all to different hives.. maybe even different cities in other parts of the world. To separate them. So we all decided to escape.'

The three amigos all nodded their heads in unison.

'How did you know that O was going to separate you?' aksed Queenie.

'We had a dream', they all said together. 'The same dream.'

'Do you always say everything at the same time?' said Jerry.

'Not always', said one. 'Sometimes', said another at the same time, while the third amigo shrugged and didn't say anything.

'They're telepaths', said Queenie to Jerry.

'No way! Far out!' said Jerry. 'I've heard of telepaths but I didn't know if they were real or just another story.'

'Yes, we're real', they all said together.

'Excellent!' said Jerry. 'Good to meet you. I'm Jerry and this is Captain Toast. We're from Shopping Village. This is Greta. She's from the forest.'

The three amigos stood up, shook Jerry's hand and introduced themselves as Nancy, Sylvester and Billy. They weren't identical but all looked very similar, particularly in that they all had the same curly ginger hair, a green left eye and a blue right eye.

'Are you triplets?' asked Greta. 'I've got a twin sister, but I've never met her.. not yet..' It felt strange for her to say it. The idea was still so new to her, that she really had a twin sister. Surely she would have felt something? Surely she would have known? 'Is that how come you're telepathic?'

'Sort of', said Billy. 'We're genetically modified.'

'O made us with enhanced E.S.P.' said Nancy.

'We're an experiment', said Sylvester.

'What?!' said Greta, aghast. 'What do you mean that O made you with ESP?' asked Greta.

'O made us', said Sylvester.

'In a lab', said Nancy.

'With extra ESP', said Billy.

'What? I don't understand. What do you mean O made you? Why? How?' Greta gasped in horror.

'You don't really know O, do you?' said Clair to Greta. 'Some people call them the *Great Leader*, but others call them the *Great Scientist*. Everything O does is an experiment. Every hive is one big laboratory. Most people who live there don't even realise it, or if they do, they just don't care. They're even happy to be a part of it.'

Greta pressed her lips together, clenched her fists and turned red in the face. 'The closer I get to the city, the angrier I get', she said. 'I'm scared that when I get there I'm going to want to burn the whole place down.'

'Yeah, I know what you mean, sister', said Clair. 'But our time will come. It won't be long now. This is just the end of a long, dark age. In dark times, things are bound to get.. well, you know.. *dark*. The *real* Big Shift hasn't happened yet, but it will do.. soon.. you'll see. People are starting to wake up.'

'I hope so', said Greta.

'So, can you tell what I'm thinking?' Jerry said to the triplets. 'Can you read my mind?'

All three turned and looked at Jerry sideways, narrowed their eyes and raised their left eyebrows.

'You don't want to ask them that', said Clair. 'They don't like being tested.'

'Oh, sorry, I didn't mean to be rude', said Jerry. 'I've just never met a telepath.'

'I once met a fortune teller', said Greta.'Well actually I didn't meet her. I ran away. I was scared to hear what she saw.'

'My mum used to think she could see the future, read minds, that sort of thing', said Queenie. 'I don't know if she really could or if she was just projecting. Or hallucinating. I think everyone's got ESP anyway. We're all a bit psychic.'

The amigos all exchanged looks, seeming to hold a brief conversation without words.

'Did you all live in the same place, back in the city?' asked Greta. 'Is that how you all know each other? What was it like?'

'Me and Bruce shared a room', said Clair. 'The amigos were in a different area because they're younger, but we all saw each other at mealtimes and at the pool or in the playzone.'

'You had a pool?' said Jerry. 'That sounds allright. You never said you had a pool, Queenie.'

'Oh yeah, we had a great pool. Water slides, wave machine, diving boards, floatables.. you'd love it there. If you don't mind O watching everything you do and telling you when to do it, or stop doing it.. it's just heaven.'

'What about the experiments?' asked Greta. 'That must have been awful.'

'Not so bad' said Sylvester. 'Mainly it was just playing games, like the other kids.'

'O would just watch', said Nancy.

'It was the other kids that were worse' said Billy.

'They used to bully us something rotten', said Sylvester. 'Because we're.. you know..'

'Different', said Billy.
'Sensitive', said Nancy.
'When it's the three of us together, we're allright', said Sylvester.
'It's good you all got out of there together', said Greta. 'I'm really glad you made it.'
'So Bruce, where have you *been*?' said Clair. 'It's been so long. Four years! I thought I'd find you round here somewhere, but no one had seen you. I'd just got to thinking I'd never see you again.. that you're probably somewhere out in the wilderness by now.. and then you walk in here! I can't believe it!'
'Well, when I got out of the tunnel.. I looked up found myself in that graveyard with that stone angel looking down at me.. can you imagine? Well I just ran', said Queenie. 'I ran as fast as I could, away from the city and didn't stop till I got to Shopping Village. Then I just collapsed. Jerry and his old man, Jack picked me up and got me sorted. Helped me build a place there on the roof of the Mall. You should visit. It's not quite the wilderness, but it's a good place.'
'No way! That's not far from here. Of course I'll come. Wait till the others see you. They won't believe it. You're a legend, did you know that?'
'Yeah, Baz told me' said Queenie. 'Freedom Drain. I like it. It's really catchy.'
'Thanks. I thought of it' said Clair proudly. 'Come and see what's going on here, you'll like this place', said Clair, going to the door across the room.

....

The door opened into the main hall of the old church, a cool, cavernous space which was filled with soft light from the the stained glass windows.. The high ceiling was supported by tall pillars running the length of the aisle, which had once been lined with rows of church pews, but which had been cleared to make space for other activities. People were milling about. In one corner some people were painting banners. Others sitting or standing in groups, deep in earnest conversation. They seemed to be mostly young people, in their late teens or early twenties, but there were also a few older people and some young children who were running around between the pillars.
A wooden balcony ran around the edge of an upper floor. The sound of a band rehearsing in a room upstairs bounced around the old stone walls. Distorted electric guitar wailing, drums and cymbals crashing out of time, bass guitar turned up full volume, each band member trying to drown the others out. A trapeze was suspended

from the old beams of the high, vaulted ceiling and a couple of agile acrobats, dressed in black were swinging back and forth, practising some dazzling swings and somersaults above a big net which was stretched out between the stone pillars.
'Wow, this place is so cool!' said Jerry, transfixed by the couple on the trapeze. 'Do all these people live here?'
'Some of us do', said Clair. 'There are more rooms upstairs, but some people just come to hang out and get involved, join in our mission.'
'Excellent!' said Jerry 'I wouldn't mind getting involved too. What's your mission? Can I ask that, or is it a stupid question..?'
'Resisting', said Clair. 'That's what we're doing. That's our mission. And getting people to wake up.'
'Resisting O, you mean?' asked Jerry. 'On a trapeze? How does that work?'
'Oh yes', said Clair seriously. 'On the trapeze. On the electric guitar. In the kitchen. Even just sitting round talking, like those guys there. It's all resisting. Here look, these guys are making banners. They're going out to protest in a bit.. down at the city limit.'
'Cool, maybe we'll join them. We're going that way ourselves. I don't know about bringing down O though. Bit of a long shot..' said Jerry and he wandered over to see what they were painting.
'Don't mind Jerry' said Queenie to Clair, once Jerry was out of earshot. 'He just loves O. No point trying to talk sense to him on that front, but he's a good guy. One of the best.'
'Is he your boyfriend?' Clair asked, turning to face Queenie.
Queenie made an ambiguous head movement.. the sort that Jerry often made. She blushed slightly but didn't answer.
'He's tall and not so bad looking..' Clair said.
'Sounds like you're interested..' said Queenie.
'Nah, not really my type', said Clair, looking into Queenie's eyes searchingly.
'I think he's a loner anyway. A lone wolf' said Queenie. 'Like Captain Toast here.' Captain Toast who was walking alongside Queenie pricked up his ears at the mention of his name. She stroked his head and he looked up at her lovingly and rubbed his cheek against her leg.
'Ooh, a lone wolf eh? Mysterious and romantic..' teased Clair.
'Shut up you!' laughed Queenie and elbowed her old friend in the side.
They followed Jerry over to where the group of people were busy painting signs with bold statements written in capital letters. On one was written 'O - THE GREAT MISLEADER!' Inside the letter O

had been painted yellow and given an angry emoji face. Another placard simply read 'WAKE UP!!!' written in bold script, each letter painted in a different colour. About five people were all painting and decorating a long banner with the message 'RECLAIM YOUR MIND!' written across it. A middle aged man dressed in a tweed suit and bow tie was sitting on the floor, absorbed in painting a board with very neat lettering, perfectly spaced, with the message *'The Sheep Spends Its Whole Life Fearing The Wolf, Only To Be Eaten By The Shepherd'*.

'Wow, that's really deep, man', said Jerry, looking over his shoulder. 'Did you make that up?' The man didn't look up.

'He can't hear you' said Clair. 'Ozzy's deaf.'

Ozzy, sensing that he was being talked about, looked up and was slightly startled to find himself surrounded. Jerry gave him a big friendly smile and thumbs up with both thumbs, which Ozzy then returned to Jerry and his friends, who all gave him thumbs up in return, until everyone was grinning and giving thumbs up all round.

'Look who's here, Ozzy', Clair said in a loud voice, making hand gestures and exaggerating her lip movements for Ozzy to read. 'It's Bruce! My old friend from the hive. This is Bruce who discovered the Freedom Drain!'

On hearing Clair's announcement, everyone looked up from their sign painting and there were gasps of amazement and joy that the famous Bruce had made an unexpected appearance. Within minutes, Queenie was surrounded by people wanting to shake her hand, give her a hug and thank her for discovering the Freedom Drain. A festival atmosphere ensued in the old church and very soon, Queenie, Jerry and Greta knew and were known by everyone in the place and had made many new friends.

Greta's story was told. Everyone had suggestions for the best way to get into the city, avoiding O's detection and rescue her sister from O's evil clutches. After weighing up the pros and cons of many increasingly outlandish plans, in the end it was generally agreed that the best plan was Queenie's original idea of sneaking into the city inside Jerry's cart. It was decided that Greta, Jerry and Queenie would accompany the protesters to the city limit, with Greta and Queenie inside the cart, as they had planned. The protesters would create a distraction, while Greta and her friends would slip into the city unnoticed.

To Jerry, all these deceptive, evasive measures sounded completely over the top and quite pointless and unnecessary, but that sort of thing didn't really bother him. It was all good fun and he was quite outnumbered by people who obviously took resisting O very seriously indeed.

Baz warned that there were often drones flying about close to the city limit , so it would be a good idea to get inside the cart before they set off from the church.

Greta, Jerry and Queenie, along with Clair, Baz and the three Amigos went out of the side door to where they had left the cart. With fond farewells, wishes of good luck and shouts of 'Viva la Revolution!' Greta and Queenie squeezed themselves into the wooden box and the lid was closed. Jerry and Clair pushed the cart down the side alley of the church and out to the front where all the protesters were assembled with banners and signs, drums, whistles, and trumpets. Some were dressed in circus costumes and had their faces painted and they made a raucous, joyous procession as they set of towards the city limit, banging drums, singing and chanting.

....

The group of about thirty protesters marched and danced their way towards the city limit, picking up more people as they went along. The two acrobats cartwheeled and tumbled along the middle of the road, clearing the path for the green painted trolley, while a woman dressed as a clown stood on top of the cart, juggling oranges and lemons. People clapped and cheered as they marched by, making way for the noisy procession.

The three amigos spread out. Nancy went to the left side of the procession, Sylvester went to the right. Billy walked alongside the cart, relaying messages from the other two. 'Drone spotted to the right' he said. 'Keep your head down, look left.. act normal.'

Jerry laughed and looked around at their colourful, noisy, ragtag group of punks and outcasts skipping and reeling down the middle of the busy thoroughfare, banging drums and blowing horns. 'Act normal? That's a good one! So much for not drawing attention to ourselves, eh!' Captain Toast danced and skipped alongside the trolley, barking and jumping, hoping to catch the juggled fruit.

'Devil dog approaching from the left', said Billy. 'Just ignore it if it comes this way.'

Inside the cart, Greta was paralysed with fear. She peered out through a crack in the boards, trying to get a picture of what was going on around them. She dared not make a sound. Queenie put a comforting hand on her arm. 'Don't worry', she whispered. 'It won't do anything. O doesn't interfere outside the city limit. Not unless they really have to. That's the second protocol.'

'What's the first one?' whispered Greta, her eyes wide in terror.

'That inside the city limit, O makes the rules.'

Captain Toast spotted the robot dog and made chase, barking and growling. The robot dog turned around and ran the other way, almost tripping Ozzy over. Ozzy shouted and gave it a whack with his sign, causing the robot dog to stumble, but it didn't fall. Captain toast chased it around the edge of the procession, but couldn't catch it, it remained always three steps ahead. The two very different kind of dogs ran around and around, in and out of people's legs, adding to the general atmosphere of chaos and mayhem.

So far so good, eh!' said Jerry, grinning to Clair, as they both pushed the cart along the road. 'O'll never see us coming.'

'Sometimes the best hiding place is in plain sight', said Clair, straight faced, looking tense.

'Yeah, I guess', said Jerry, unconvinced. 'Are you all going right into the city or just to the city limit?'

'We'll go to the city limit, then some of us will go across the line and some will stay on this side. Billy and Nancy and Sylvester will stay on the outside. If they go past the city limit, O will pick them up and take them back to the hive. Baz will stay outside too. He's still under age. I'll go just inside the city limit. O won't do anything to me now. I'm going to give out some leaflets we made.. let people know what's really going on. O controls all the information in the city. People never get to hear the truth.'

'Well..' said Jerry. 'I don't know if that's strictly true. I mean, all the information is there. There's more information available now than ever before. Anyone can access it if they want.'

'But they don't, do they?' said Clair. 'Do you ever wonder why that is?'

Jerry laughed. 'You sound just like my Granny Mae. You should meet her. You'd get along.'

'Well, I guess I should take that as a compliment', said Clair with a quizzical expression. 'Anyway.. basically, the idea is that by protesting on both sides of the city limit, we're drawing attention to the inequality and injustice of O's system and how it divides and separates people. It's symbolic. Can you see that?'

'Oh right..' said Jerry, nodding slowly. 'Like it's *conceptual*, or something? Yeah. I like that. But you don't really expect O to see this little protest and then just give up, go away, switch off? O wouldn't do that, you know..'

'This *little protest*', said Clair, irritated by Jerry's attitude, 'is just the tip of the iceberg. There are people protesting all over the world. At the limit of thousands of cities. And inside cities too, people are resisting in all sorts of ways. And outside the cities, people are getting organised. It's just a matter of time, Jerry. And numbers. There are more of us that you think. We're not *asking* anything from O. This *little protest* isn't for O at all. It's for The People. All it takes is for enough people to wake up, then O won't have any power at all. It's as simple as that.'

'Ok, right..' said Jerry. 'But you know, you *can* actually *ask* O for things. If you've got a complaint, you can go to O and tell them and then they'll take it on board and make the necessary changes. Especially if lots of people ask for the same thing. That's one of the reasons the protocols keep changing all the time. It's actually very democratic.'

Clair looked at Jerry like he was mad. 'Either you're completely brainwashed or you're one of O's agents', she said, giving him a very hard stare.

'Woah, what are you talking about?' said Jerry, very much taken aback. 'You think I'm a secret agent? Are you serious?'

'You could be', said Clair. 'I've never met you before you walked into the church. Never heard of you either. We've had infiltrators before.'

Jerry shook his head in disbelief. 'Did you hear that, Queenie?' he shouted into the cart. 'Clair thinks I'm a spy for O. A secret agent.'

Queenie let out a loud laugh. 'Well, I can see why she might think that', she shouted from inside the box. 'Are you? I never thought to ask.'

'Queenie! Bruce! Come on!' shouted Jerry. 'You know I'm not a spy. Tell her!'

'Allright allright' Queenie laughed. 'Jerry's not a spy, Clair. He'd be useless at it anyway. He always says exactly what he's thinking. He's got no filters. He's the most honest person I know.'

'Thank you', said Jerry to the lid of the cart, then turning to Clair, he said, 'See?'

'OK', said Clair, looking at him with narrowed eyes. 'But only because you're a friend of Bruce.

'Are you like this with everyone you meet?' asked Jerry. Nobody had ever accused him of being a spy or an infiltrator before. It hurt his feelings, particularly because there was no way to disprove the allegation.

'Sorry', said Clair. 'Yes, I am like that with everyone. At least with people I don't know. It's probably a defence mechanism. I've got trust issues.. that's thanks to O. Also.. what we're doing here.. I know to you it looks like it's all fun and games.. but it's actually really serious. I mean, some of the other stuff we do.. getting people out.. hiding people.. we need to be careful.. really careful. People's lives are on the line. People's freedom. We can't afford to make mistakes or slip ups.'

'Right', nodded Jerry seriously. 'I get that. It is really important stuff you're doing. Sorry if you thought I was making fun of you. I'm really not a spy though. Honest.'

'OK, thanks', said Clair. 'I believe you.'

'Anyway, I don't think O needs spies. I mean, O can already see everything and hear everything and know everything that they want to', said Jerry. 'What would be the point? It would be easier to send out a swarm of robot mosquitos to spy on you.'

'Oh, don't talk to me about robot mosquitos', said Clair, cringing. 'I hate them. They're the worst.'

'I think they're amazing actually', said Jerry. 'And they're so small, you can hardly tell the difference between a robot mosquito and a real one, unless you catch it and look at it with a magnifying glass. They're a total miracle of technology.'

'Hmph!' snorted Clair. 'You ever been stung by one?'

'No, I haven't actually', said Jerry. 'I didn't know they sting.'

'I think there's probably a lot of things about O that you don't know', said Clair.

'Yep, that's probably definitely true', said Jerry.

'Here we are, this is the city limit' said Clair, stopping. A tall metal archway spanned the road and two lines were painted on the ground, a red line and an orange line. 'Across that line is the Orange Zone. That's inside the city limit.'

'Yeah, I know what it means', said Jerry. 'I come here a lot. Trading, see.' He pointed to the cart with J & J Vintage Machine Revival painted on the side.

'Oh, I didn't realise', said Clair. 'I didn't know you'd been here before. Trading eh?' she eyed him suspiciously. 'Not spying though?'

'Come on Clair, don't start that again', said Jerry rolling his eyes and shaking his head. He let out a whistle and Captain Toast came running to his side. 'Stay close Captain, we're going into the city. Don't go running off now.' Captain Toast looked up at Jerry and with his eyes registered that he understood, but he didn't make any promises.

'Here's what we'll do' said Clair. 'I'll start a chant.. see if we can get everyone around to join in. We'll go both sides of the line and

hopefully stop up the whole gateway for a bit, maybe cause a bit of a scene. Then you can just slip away. Got it?'
'Ready when you are', said Jerry, lowering his sunglasses to look her in the eye. 'And thanks for what you're doing and for helping us out. Good luck with the resistance and all.' He put out his hand.
'Thank you brother', said Clair, shaking his hand. 'Take care in there and good luck.' She knocked on the lid of the cart and spoke through a crack in the doors. 'Take care Bruce. Come and see me when you come out. Good luck Greta! I hope you find your sister. If you need to use the Freedom Drain to get out, we'll all be waiting to welcome you at the other side.'
'Thanks Clair!' Greta and Queenie shouted from inside the cart. 'See you again soon.'
Clair stood up to her full height, raised her fist in the air and shouted at the top of her voice, 'The People! United! Will never be defeated! The People! United! Will never be defeated! The People! United! Will never be defeated!'
All around, people took up the chant until the high walls of the buildings around echoed with the sound of about two or three hundred people who had joined the march. The acrobats had climbed up the metal arch and suspended a trapeze from the cross beam and begun their well practised routine to the amazement of onlookers. A barefoot man with long dreadlocks lit up a firestick and began dancing on the boundary line, twirling it faster and faster with wild abandon. Trumpets, drums, tambourines and whistles accompanied the chanting. The crowd became bigger and more dense now that the whole road was blocked. Traders and dayvisitors found themselves part of a protest they'd had no intention of joining. Some were angry and tried to push their way through, while others joined in the chant, even if they didn't know what exactly they were protesting about. A swarm of little egg-shaped drones appeared and began circling overhead.
'I think it's time we were on our way', said Jerry, looking up.
'Don't look up, Jerry', said Clair, pulling his head down. 'Keep your head down and keep your wits about you, ok? You all take care in there, ok? Take care of Bruce too. I don't want to lose her again now that I've only just found her. And come back soon, ok?'
'OK, Clair. Will do', said Jerry and saluted to her like a soldier with long hair and pink John Lennon sunglasses. He leaned down to the lid of the cart and spoke into the crack between the doors, 'Are you ready? Here we go!' and with a final wave to his new friends, he pushed the cart over the red line and into the Orange Zone.

PART TWO

The O-Zone

Episode 8. Into the Orange Zone

Inside the city limit, across the red and orange line, the road became instantly much smoother. Gone were the potholes and the dusty, rutted and cracked surface. The streets of the city were paved with a dark brown substance called 'Earthcrete', which was as hard as stone but more flexible, extremely durable and made from a mix of organic, carbon-rich materials. It was so smooth that Greta wondered how people didn't slip up on it, as she peered out through the crack in the boards of the side of the cart. The sounds of the protest receded into the distance as Jerry wheeled the cart along, with Greta and Queenie hidden inside. He was still chanting 'The People, United, Will never be defeated!', though more quietly now, more to himself than to anyone else.

The thoroughfare was wide and full of all sorts people going this way and that. Traders from outside the city, with their bags, baskets and carts. City folk from the upper levels, in shiny clothes, some of them wearing see-through masks over their faces. In a separate lane, bikes and scooters raced along. Next to that, a taxi lane with driverless, yellow taxi pods cruising along, stopping to pick up and drop off passengers as they went. There was so much movement, Greta didn't know where to look. At the side of the road was a long building with little booths all along its length. At each of the booths was a queue of people.

'What's going on there?' whispered Greta to Queenie.

'Traders', said Queenie. 'They're bringing stuff from outside the city to sell to O. Plastic, metal, that sort of thing. You just put it all down a big chute and O sorts it out and pays you for it.'

A man in a shiny red tracksuit was waving. 'Jerry! Hey Jerry!' he called out.

'Hi Bill, how's it going?' called Jerry, stopping the cart. Bill sauntered over with a big smile to shake Jerry's hand. Bill's dark hair was slicked back, he had a neatly trimmed moustache, a gold chain around his neck, gold rings on his fingers and dark rings under his eyes. He was only in his thirties, but looked like a man in his fifties.

'Mustn't grumble, Jerry. Swing and roundabouts, you know how it is', said Bill. 'What you got in the cart there? Have you seen the queues here today?'

'Oh, er.. yes.. what's going on with all the queues?' said Jerry.

'Some outbreak of something or other in the Redzone, apparently. Foxpox, maybe. Everyone's got to be double tested. Look at that, all the lines are getting longer. What's in the trolley? It looks heavy. Metal is it?'

'It's.. er.. batteries', said Jerry, turning red. 'Old school. Lithium', he added to make it sound more convincing. Jerry hated lying.

'Ooh, nice', said Bill, rubbing his hands together. 'They're getting rare these days. Listen, I'll take them off your hands if you like. Cash. I'll give you a good price. Save you the hassle of standing in line. What do you say?'

'Well.. I think I'll just keep on.. maybe the queues are shorter down the road', said Jerry, starting to push the cart.

'Wait, wait', Bill said, putting his hand on Jerry's arm. 'It's like this all the way into the city. I'll give you twenty Obits a kilo for old batteries. What do you say? That's practically what you'd get from O. Hardly worth the wait is it? Special price just for you Jerry,

because I like you. Anyone else, I wouldn't go above fifteen.'
'Thanks Bill, I appreciate that', said Jerry, gently pulling his arm free. 'All the same, I think I'll just keep on. Maybe I'll just wait with it till later, see if the lines go down.'
'Suit yourself', said Bill, sounding hurt.
'Maybe I'll come back and find you later, eh', said Jerry.
'As you wish' said Bill. 'No skin off my nose either way. I'm just trying to help you out.'
'Oh look.. Captain Toast has wandered off..' said Jerry, pointing his finger vaguely into the crowd. 'I'd better catch up with him before he gets into trouble..' and he wheeled the cart away rather quickly, leaving Bill muttering and shaking his head.
Inside the cart, Greta and Queenie breathed a sigh of relief.
Having left Bill behind, Jerry leaned down and spoke into the lid of the cart. 'You allright in there? I'm going to head for the canal. I'll look for an alley or something so you can get out without being spotted, ok?'
A right turn, then a left turn, then another right, then a left, Jerry wheeled the cart through a maze of side streets that he knew well. Greta peered out through the crack in the boards, trying to get a sense of where she was. Walls, doors and windows passing close by. Voices and snatches of conversation drifting in and out of earshot as they rolled through the city backstreets in the little wooden cart. Queenie squeezed her hand and gave Greta a comforting smile, which she couldn't see in the darkness of the box. She felt disorientated and scared, wondering how she had got herself into this strange situation and where it was going to lead.
'Ooh look, it's John Lennon!' came a woman's voice from just up ahead. Greta and Queenie both peered out from the crack to see a woman with long, curly blonde hair, wearing heavy make-up and a colourful dress, zig-zagging down the narrow alleyway towards them. She was pushing an old supermarket shopping cart, which was piled with bags, some of them teetering on the edge of falling out. 'Where's Yoko, John?' she called out to him, laughing.
'Haha!' Jerry laughed nervously. 'I don't know what you mean.'
'Yoko and John, don't you know? John and Yoko?' she implored and then shook her head sadly. 'Ooh what do you know? It's all ancient history, ancient history to you young'uns.' Closer up she looked older than she had at a distance and her hair was certainly a wig. She was wearing a very strong, musky perfume, which tickled Greta's nose.
'Oh right.. I get it', said Jerry, nodding his head. 'Yeah, I see what you

mean. I think I've heard of Yoko. Was he the drummer?'

'*He* was a *she*', said the woman, shaking her head and rolling her eyes. 'Never mind. I can see it went over your head, over your head. It wasn't that funny anyway. Don't mind me. Ooh, that's a nice trolley. What does it say? J & J Vintage Machine Revival? I tell you what.. this old machine could do with a bit of revival! What do you say Mr Lennon? Do you think it can be revived?' She gestured to her body and burst out laughing again.

Inside the cart, Queenie tried hard to suppress her own laughter and let out little stifled snorts. Greta, at the same time was summoning all her power, attempting not to sneeze. Captain Toast, meanwhile was sniffing at the woman's shopping trolley.

'Ooh, is that your dog? He's a handsome one. Like you eh? Actually better looking! No offence, John. Well, dogs are just better than people aren't they. It's just true. What's his name? Ringo?!!' and she bent over double with laughter, as if it was the funniest joke she'd ever heard.

'He's called Captain Toast', said Jerry.

'*Captain Toast*?!!' the woman shrieked with laughter, holding her belly. 'Captain Toast! Is he a superhero? Can he shoot toast out of his eyes? Has he got flying.. flying.. toast? Where's his, where's his cape?'

'He just really likes toast', said Jerry simply, shrugging.

'He really likes toast, of course he does' said the woman. 'That makes perfect sense, perfect sense. Of course it does. So where are you and Captain Toast off to with that big green, big green, trolley of yours?' She leaned right over the box, trying to see in through the crack between the doors, sending a waft of perfume straight into Greta's upturned nose.

'Oh, er.. we're just going down to the river. Going to visit some friends. On a boat. We're, er, going on a fishing trip..'

Greta sneezed and at the same time Queenie let out a suppressed snort of laughter.

'What was that?!' screamed the woman, jumping back.

'Oh.. er.. nothing', said Jerry, hurriedly trying to turn the heavy trolley around in the narrow alleyway. 'I think it was Captain Toast. Anyway, I'd better go. Bye. Nice to meet you.'

'Wait, wait! What have you got in there, got in there? I heard an animal or something, animal or something.'

Jerry swung the trolley around and pushed it quickly away, heading back up the alley in the direction they'd they'd come from with Captain Toast hot on his heels.

Jerry took a left, then another left, then a right, then a left. A few more turns to make sure they weren't being followed, then he pulled into a little alcove under an old bridge. 'Quick, get out of the trolley. There's no-one around.' He flung open the double doors and up stood Queenie and Greta in their dark glasses, wide brimmed hats and scarf and bandanna face masks. They took a quick look around, to get their bearings and for their eyes to adjust to the light, dim though it was in this dark and shadowy corner of the world. Queenie vaulted out of the trolley, followed by Greta.

'Well done, John!', said Queenie laughing and slapping Jerry on the back. 'You handled that like a boss. Now, let's not hang about.. we don't want to be late for that fishing trip..'

....

The old stone railway bridge arched over a narrow lane with a long brick wall all along one side and various warehouses, stores, studios and workshops on the other. The building style was early twentieth century. This city street looked almost exactly as it would have done in the years before the Big Shift.. but if you were to look up, as Greta did as they emerged from under the bridge, you wouldn't see the sky. You would see light from the sky, as it was bounced down through long mirrored ducts all the way from the top of the hive, hundreds of meters above, illuminating the street in a pale, ambient light, but you wouldn't see the sky itself.

The old buildings in this part of town were two or three, sometimes four stories tall. Directly on top of those was the new construction which continued directly upwards for several more stories before winding around, branching out and meshing with other buildings, like the roots of a giant tree. Whereas the old buildings were angular and made from brick and stone, the new construction was curved, flowing and organic looking and made from Earthcrete, which was covered in places by moss. Cool, mirrored sunlight lit the sides of the buildings and filtered down to the street below. Flowering plants, climbers and trees grew up the sides of the new buildings while bright green birds swooped between the leaves and branches.

Greta's jaw dropped at the sight of the hive above. It was both beautiful and terrifying at the same time. She pulled down her sunglasses to get a better look at the birds, not sure if she was really dreaming. In this soft, directionless light, it was hard to see anything clearly with sunglasses on. She now noticed several egg-shaped drones buzzing around between the buildings. Greta gasped and put her head down, gripping both Jerry and Queenie's arms in panic. 'Where are we Jerry? What is this place? Are we underground? Queenie? Is this the underworld you were talking about?'

'It's allright Greta', said Jerry. 'We're still above the ground, don't worry, we're just under a hive. Here, we can go out this way, it leads to the main street..'

'It's mad isn't it', said Queenie. 'I told you, you can't imagine it till you see it for yourself.'

'It's nothing like what I imagined at all', said Greta, looking up in wonder. 'It almost looks.. natural. I didn't expect it to be so.. green.'

'Well, that's the thing' said Queenie. 'It almost is natural.. but not quite, if you know what I mean. And it's that little bit that makes all the difference. But don't look up. Let's keep our heads down.'

'Oh yeah.. oh no! Do you think O saw me?' said Greta.

'Don't worry about it', said Queenie. It was impossible for Greta to read Queenie's expression under her wide brimmed black hat, with her scarf wrapped around her face and her black lens glasses over her eyes, but Greta decided it was best not to worry about it anyway. Or at least to try not to, as worrying rarely helped anyone, as her mother was fond of telling her. 'Let's just keep moving', said Queenie. 'Like we've got some purpose. Don't forget to do a funny walk Greta. You too Jerry.'

Jerry laughed and took on a funny, swaying, loping walk as he pushed the empty trolley along towards the main street, while Queenie walked with a limp and a hunched shoulder. Greta found herself thinking again of the fortune telling woman who'd come through the village when she was a girl. She'd had a really distinctive and funny walk. Greta remembered it well..

After the fortune teller had arrived and frightened Greta into spilling her basket of berries, she'd stayed in the village for a few days, though nobody knew where she slept, or if she even did sleep at all. Some of the children took to following her around, at a safe distance, hiding behind trees and giggling if the fortune telling woman was to turn around. They made a game out of copying her funny walk which was something like a cross between a chicken crossing the road and a boxer training for a fight. The fortune telling woman walked with her fists clenched in front of her chest and her elbows sticking out. As she walked around the village, taking little dance-like steps, she bobbed her head back and forth, looking this way and that, muttering incantations as she roamed around the forest, following some invisible winding path that only she could see.

Greta stuck out her elbows and did the walk of the fortune telling woman. In a funny sort of way, it felt good, made her feel safer. Queenie stared at her sideways, while also doing her own funny walk.

'What?' said Greta, feeling suddenly self conscious. 'Am I overdoing it?'

'No, no.. that's great', said Queenie. 'It's just...'

'What?'

'..nothing', said Queenie. 'It just reminded me of something.. never mind. It's weird for me to be back here, that's all. It's bringing up memories.. things I'd forgotten.'

'What does it remind you of?'

'You'll think this is weird, but it reminds me of my mum. She used to strut about like that when she was *on one*.. you know, like when she got really manic. It reminded me of her.'

At that moment, an old supermarket trolley full of bags came out of a side street and crashed into the side of Jerry's cart.

'Hey, look, look where you're going.. oh hello, hello, it's John, John Lennon again!' shrieked the woman in the wig, going from anger to laughter in the space of a second.

'Sorry, didn't see you coming', Jerry apologised, even though the collision wasn't really his fault.

'Never mind, it's just a load of old, load of old rags anyway', she said. 'I see you found your friends. That was quick.'

'Hi' said Queenie, making a peace sign. 'Pleased to meet you. I'm Yoko.'

'I don't believe it!' cried the woman. 'It really is you! So who's that then, that then?' she pointed at Greta.

'Oh, that's Elvis.. but you didn't see him, ok?' said Queenie, lowering her dark glasses for a moment to look the woman in the eyes.

The woman took a step backwards, confused.

'Well, nice to meet you again', said Jerry, pushing his cart along. 'We'd better get moving, we don't want to be late.'

'We're going fishing', said Queenie.

'O.. O.. K..' said the woman, looking from Jerry to Queenie to Greta, to Queenie and back to Jerry again. They left her scratching her head.

Queenie and Jerry laughed and slapped each other's backs as they headed out to the main street from underneath the hive. Greta said 'that wasn't very funny. It's not nice to lie and make fun of people like that.'

Queenie and Jerry stopped laughing and hung their heads guiltily.

'Yeah, you're right', said Queenie. 'I couldn't help it though. It was just too perfect.'

They looked back to see the woman and her trolley were gone.

'Oh well', said Jerry. If we see her again we'll introduce ourselves properly.'

'Aren't you going to wear a mask and a hat?' Greta said to Jerry as they turned into the main street.

'No, I'm cool with these shades and my funny walk' Jerry replied, pointing to his rose tinted round glasses and loping along, bobbing his head. 'I think if O hasn't spotted me by now, I must be invisible. Same with you probably, but I wouldn't worry about it, if I were you.'

When they got to the main street, Greta couldn't help but look up, just to see if she could see the sky. There it was, clear and blue, between the impossibly high sides of the mega-building, which rose almost vertically out of the tops of the old buildings and sent wide, twisting Earthcrete roots into the ground in places, giving support to the massive, honeycomb structure of the hive. Bridges and walkways twisted and snaked around and out from the edges of the hives, linking them together at various levels. Drones of all different shapes and sizes buzzed around in every direction, filling the air for hundreds of meters above, like a huge swarm of gnats hovering over a footpath on a summer day.

Greta drew a sharp breath and quickly looked down. Under her black and red bandanna, her mouth was fixed in a tight frown and under her mirrored sunglasses, her eyebrows were lowered in determined defiance. She exaggerated her fortune-teller's walk and marched on down the street with her fists clenched. Day-trippers from the upper levels of the city, who wore modern clothes and clear visors over their faces stepped out of the way, some of them looking slightly afraid, when they saw our three would-be rock stars and Captain Toast strutting and staggering towards them behind the green painted, wooden cart.

....

They came to a fork in the main road and took the right, which led past a wide area of parkland, with tall trees, a pond and rolling lawns where people were picnicking and playing frisbee on the soft grass. Even though the park was overshadowed on every side by the towering hives, it still made an idyllic scene. Greta was glad and relieved to see that even here, in the depths of the city, some people were still enjoying themselves and that there were still trees. She was amazed to see how green were the sides of hives. They were practically glowing in the afternoon sun, looking more like lush, steep mountain forests than the grey *human batteries* she had come to expect. She wondered what they might be like inside.

On the other side of the park they came to the river, the sight of which made Greta gasp. It was the widest river she'd ever seen. Up in the hills, where Greta came from, there were many streams and rivulets, but nothing to match the scale and power of this mighty river into which all the mountain streams flowed on their way out to the sea. Sailing boats, barges and motor boats of all different sizes and styles navigated the waterway, others were moored up along the bank. Old fashioned house boats and cargo barges alongside modern driverless ferries, which had stopped to take on or let off passengers. A wide, smooth promenade followed along the river's edge. Our brave adventurers turned on to it, while Captain Toast took the opportunity to run about on the grass, chasing frisbees and sticking his nose into people's picnics.

Further along the embankment was a long row of old archways built into the wall. These were variously art studios, cafes and shops selling handmade crafts. The smell of incense filled the air. It seemed to be emanating from an archway which was painted purple and which had several purple chairs and tables outside. A purple clapboard sign on the pavement, with a yellow arrow pointing to the purple arch, announced in bold, yellow writing 'Travellers Rest. Real Food. Real Drink. Real Music. Welcome one and all!' A short, round man with a bushy beard was standing in the doorway watching the river and the passers by. Turning to see our adventurers approaching he waved both hands in the air and shouted 'Oho, Jerry! Good to see you back so soon. Thought you'd gone back to Shopping.'

'Hi Sam' said Jerry, greeting his friend with a hug. 'Yeah I did but then I came back again. We're helping Greta here find her sister. Greta's from the forest but her sister lives somewhere in the city. This is Queenie. She's from Shopping Village.. well, actually she's from the city, but lives in Shopping now.. and she's also called Bruce.' Jerry tended to get flustered when it came to making introductions.

'Amazing. Good to meet you', said Sam, shaking Greta and Queenie by the hands. 'So you're from the forest, Greta, and you're looking for your sister in the city? When did she come here?'

'She was born here', said Greta. 'Actually I was born here too. We're twins.' Again, it felt strange for her to say it. That she had a twin, but also that this was the place where she was born. That this was where she really came from.. not the forest. Until now, she'd never felt any connection to the city at all. The forest had always been her home. But somehow, since she'd seen the river, she felt some deeper connection to this place which was hard for her to fathom..

..*maybe something in the vibrational frequency of the river resonated with something deep within her.. some memory of the underwater world of the womb.. some inner instinct.. maybe something like the salmon feels.. an urge to return to the place of its birth.. how does the salmon know exactly where it was born? Perhaps it's in the memory of water.. water can remember all sorts of things and our bodies are mostly made of water, after all.. how else could she explain it.. the strange sensation that maybe she was.. coming home..?*

'Wow', said Sam. 'That sounds heavy. Listen, come inside, you can take off the masks and dark glasses.. this place is an O-free-zone. Analogue technology only. The coffee machine is about the smartest machine we've got in here and that's older than I am, so you don't need to worry about nosey old O!' he laughed, leading them inside.

Inside was a long, arched cavern. A bar and kitchen area stretched along the left side, while on the right were several dining booths. A carpeted area close to the entrance looked like a kind of stage. There was an old piano, an upright double bass, a drum kit and a selection of various drums and percussion instruments arranged around the piano. On the wall next to the piano hung an acoustic guitar, a banjo, a mandolin and a violin. Various other folk instruments were hanging up all along the walls and even on the ceiling of the Travellers Rest.

'Wow, this place is sick', said Queenie, looking around, inspecting the various musical instruments on display. 'I love it.'

'Thanks', said Sam. 'Do you play music?'

'A bit of guitar', said Queenie. 'Not very well. Just chords and basic stuff.'

'Don't say that Queenie', said Jerry. 'You're really good on the guitar. Hey, why don't we have a jam? Greta plays the flute. I'll have a go on a drum.'

'Excellent!' said Sam, clapping his hands together. Play something loud and rousing. Maybe it'll bring some customers in. It's been quiet all day long. I don't mind. I can spend all day just looking out at the river and the people going past. It never gets boring for me. Here, you go and play a tune, I'll bring you something to eat. How does that sound?'

'Sounds great Sam, thanks', said Jerry. 'Do you feel like playing a tune Greta? Have we got time? Techno Terry's boat isn't far from here.'

'Sure', said Greta, reaching into her bag for her flute. Actually she really felt like playing a tune. It was just what she needed to unwind and gather her thoughts together.

Greta played a few notes and Queenie tuned the guitar. Jerry tapped on various drums before settling on a wide, hand-drum which made a very deep tone that went on for a long time.

'You play something, I'll play along, allright?' said Queenie to Greta. Greta closed her eyes, cast her mind back to the forest and began to play.

There was a place she liked to go, way up the hill, above Skyward village. Sometimes Greta would take her flute and follow the stream up around the steep rocky outcrops beyond the shelter of Skyward Village, which was situated in a dip in the mountains, protecting it from harsh winds and the worst of the storms. In some places, the mountain streams, over the course of time, had worn through the rock and created caves. There was one in particular that Greta liked to visit. It was sheltered from the wind, it had a stunning view over mountains and forest and a stream of the coolest, freshest water, running through. Best of all, the sound of her flute would echo on and on as the sound reverberated through tunnels and caverns leading from the main cave entrance all through the hillside. It was rare to meet anyone else up there. When Greta went there, although she was alone, she also felt that she was not alone at all. When she played her flute, she felt she was surrounded by the little people of the forest and of the mountains and the water.. the fairy folk, the nymphs and elves and sprites and all the other names people have for such beings.. and that even though she almost never saw them with her eyes, she could somehow sense them, dancing all around her and all around the rocks and trees and water when she played her flute..

Queenie picked up on the key and added some chords in a rhythm that fit. Jerry tapped his foot and nodded his head for a while, before tentatively bringing in the drum. Each of the players gradually eased into the tune, exploring different ways to go about playing it, following each other's lead, listening and playing at the same time, each completely in their own world, yet at the same time connected through the music, which seemed to take on a life of its own.. It was quite astounding for all of them, as that sort of connection doesn't happen every day. After a while, Greta opened her eyes and was surprised and a little startled to find herself in the city.. she'd forgotten where she was.. but she didn't stop playing. She fixed her eyes on the river and played on, louder in volume, now hitting the high notes..

Jerry was getting into it on the drum now, and so was Queenie on the guitar. They nodded and grinned at Greta, encouraging her to play on. People were stopping to listen outside the Travellers Rest. Some sat down at tables and Sam was quick to welcome them and offer drinks and food. The tune went on for a quite a while, each time it seemed to be drawing to an end, one of the players would strike up and take it in a different direction and it would carry on all over again. Eventually the tune came to an end. Greta, Queenie and Jerry all looked at one another in wonder and admiration. There were cheers and a smattering of applause from the audience, words of appreciation and encouragement, calls for another tune. Jerry was grinning from ear to ear. Queenie seemed uncomfortable about the attention but nodded and smiled slightly. Greta was miles away, still in the forest, away with the fairies, it took her some time to return.

'Wow, that was amazing' said Jerry. 'Shall we play another one?' And so they played another one, and another one after that. The afternoon sun shone down over the hives and over the river, the water sparkled and danced. Greta played her wooden flute and watched the people passing by. All sorts of people. Where were they all coming from? Where were they all going? A green bird alighted on a lamp post by the river wall. The bird stood very still and looked right at Greta. Greta looked back and played her flute for the bird. When the tune came to an end, the bird flew away. Greta waved to the green bird and mouthed 'bye'.

Sam came over, full of smiles and enthusiasm. 'Wow, you guys.. that was fantastic! Are you an actual band?'

'Haha!' Jerry laughed. 'Didn't I tell you this would happen if we all went out in dark glasses? Yeah Sam, we're a band. Well, we are now, eh.'

'Didn't you know that Jerry's really John Lennon?' said Queenie to Sam, playfully poking Jerry in the side.

'Oh don't start that again' said Jerry. Queenie and Greta laughed.

Sam laughed, even though he didn't get the joke. 'Well if you're not a band you should be. You make a good sound together. Here, come and have something to eat. Let me get you some drinks..'

....

Sam led them to a table near the back where they settled down in the comfortable seclusion of the dining booth. He went behind the bar and came back with a big jug of fresh, sweet lemonade with ice and mint and three tall glasses, also a bowl of water and some crackers for Captain Toast, who settled down under the table. While our would-be-rock stars were clinking glasses and congratulating themselves and each other on the success of their first gig, Sam went to the kitchen and prepared something to eat. He came back soon after carrying a wide, round copper tray, which was taken up with a big, round flat-bread, on top of which were various pastes and dips in every different colour.

Sam laid down the tray on the table and then pulled up a chair for himself. 'Mind if I join you?' he said, ripping off a corner of the flatbread and using it to scoop up some steaming black bean paste.

'This is great Sam, thanks a lot', said Jerry, tucking in. Greta and Queenie expressed their gratitude and did the same.

'Anytime, anytime', said Sam with a wave of the hand. 'You should come and play here again, all of you. I love the vibe. Kind of folk, country, rock, trance.. a bit of jazz.. what would you call that music you play?' he asked Greta.

'I don't know' Greta shrugged. 'I just play what I feel like. I don't know what you'd call it. This food is delicious by the way. Can I ask you a question Sam? I was wondering.. when you said this is an *O free zone*, what did you mean?'

'Just what I said. It's an O free zone. Well, as much as it's possible to be in this location anyway. I mean, I'm not going to ask anyone if they've got a noodle, if you know what I mean', Sam tapped his head, by way of explanation. 'That's their business. People can do what they want in here, as long as they keep it peaceful.. but, you know.. I try to keep things old school. That's the way I like it anyway. Sometimes you just want to get away from all the trappings of modern day life, away from O's prying eyes. Things used to be much simpler in the old days.. you know, before the machines started answering back, before they started telling humans what to do.'

'Good for you!' said Greta. 'I don't know how you can live in the middle of the city. It would drive me mad, having O there all the time, watching everything. It must be like being followed everywhere.' She leaned close to Sam and said under her breath, 'I hate O.'

Sam nodded his head thoughtfully. 'Yes, exactly. It's just like being followed everywhere. That was why I made this place. I can come in here and just be like..' Sam took a deep breath and made a zen-like expression '..you know what I mean? I mean, it's just a little place in the middle of..' he gestured to the world outside.. 'but it's a *sanctuary*. That's all I need. And I don't hate O. I really don't. Not at all. In fact, if it wasn't for O, I probably would never have found

this place and turned it into..' Sam gestured around the cavern '..my little kingdom!' and he laughed, a deep belly laugh.
'How do you mean, if it wasn't for O?' asked Greta.
'I mean, O's got a way of *arranging* things. Of setting up *situations*. Making connections between certain people to.. let's say, increase the probability of certain *outcomes*. It's mysterious. Very mysterious. I can't explain it, but it happens all the time. I don't know if O even knows what they're doing half the time, or how they're doing it, but it's.. how can I put it..? It's *multidimensional*.. does that make any sense to you? O works on lots of different levels, all at the same time'
'That doesn't make any sense to me at all actually', said Greta.
'Me neither', said Queenie. 'No offence Sam. It just sounds like.. what do you call it.. *woo-woo*.. superstition. It's an urban myth and I've heard it so many times before.. O moves in mysterious ways and all that.. makes me want to scream. It's not a *God*, for God's sake. It's a machine! Sorry, I didn't mean to shout. It's just that sometimes it seems.. like.. it doesn't matter how advanced we get technologically, we're still basically cavemen, tying to understand where the sun goes at night, what the stars are.. and then making up all sorts of mad stories to explain what we can't get our head's round.'
'Maybe you're right', said Sam. 'And it's ok, you can shout. Feel free. And I totally understand where you're coming from. I used to feel the same way too.. about O. And about life too. That it's all chaos. That there's no meaning to anything. Listen, I'll clear this tray away and bring us some coffee, then I'll tell you my story.. if you want to hear it of course.. about O and their *mysterious ways*.'
When Sam had taken his leave, Queenie turned to Jerry and very seriously said, 'He's not an O'ist, is he.. our friend Sam? I might need to get out of here if he's an O'ist.. I don't want to make a scene.. he seems like a nice bloke and everything, but I don't know if I can hold myself if he's an O'ist.'
'An O'ist?' said Jerry, pulling a funny face. 'No, not Sam. At least I don't think so. I guess he could be, but I doubt it. I've never asked him actually..'
'What's an O'ist?' asked Greta. She felt like she'd arrived completely unprepared in a strange land where she didn't speak the language or really understand anything at all.
'Religious freaks' said Queenie with a sneer. 'They're a *cult*.'
'I wouldn't go that far Queenie', said Jerry. 'O'ists that I've met have been allright. Friendly. Always polite. I mean, after the Big Shift,

there were bound to be some people who believed O was some kind of Messiah, just like there were people who thought O was the devil. It's like you said, people are primitive. Superstitious. You can't really blame them.'

'Oh yes I can', said Queenie. 'And I will. Remember I was telling you about the orphanage, Greta.. how it's all run by robots, except for occasionally when some humans would come to have a look round. They were O'ists. O'ist nuns. They're the worst sort of O'ists. The worst sort of people.'

'What did they do?' asked Greta, almost afraid to ask.

'What did they do?' Queenie sneered. 'Nothing. That's what they did. They'd walk around, inspect the place, complement O on how clean everything was, how healthy everyone looked, what marvellous facilities and care O provided. If they ever spoke to us at all, it was to tell us how lucky we were. That we were the luckiest children in the world, to have O personally taking care of us.' Queenie rolled her eyes and grimaced angrily. 'Then they'd go on their way again, back out to spread the word about how great their lord and saviour O was. That's O'ists for you.'

Sam came back bearing a tray with a pot of coffee, some small glasses and a plate of various sweet delicacies. 'Here we go. Coffee all round?' he smiled as he set about pouring everyone a cup.

'Hey Sam', said Jerry. 'Can I ask you something? A bit of a strange question.. Ow!' Jerry jumped as Queenie kicked him under the table.

'Sure Jerry', said Sam, handing him a cup of coffee with an inquisitive expression. 'What is it?'

'Well.. how can I put this..'

'What is it?' said Sam, now looking worried. 'Was it the food?'

'No, of course not Sam. Your food's the best. I was just going to ask if you.. er.. happen to be.. an *O'ist*?'

'What? An O'ist? Me? What gave you that idea?' Sam laughed as if it was the funniest thing he'd ever heard. 'Yes, that's exactly why I spend my days under an archway in an old dockyard without modern technology, declaring my little kingdom an O free zone. That's just what an O'ist would do!' Sam laughed some more.

'Sorry, silly question. Of course you're not', said Jerry, embarrassed.

'Well, maybe I am a bit actually, since you ask', said Sam. 'Look.. the thing is, if you'd seen the things I've seen.. well, you'd have to admit the O really does move in very mysterious ways. There's no other explanation.'

Queenie closed her eyes and shook her head, but kept her thoughts to herself.

'Ok, I can tell you don't think so Queenie. I'll tell you my story and you tell me what you think it means, if it means anything at all..' Sam leaned forwards, poured himself a cup of coffee and began his story..

....

'Ten years ago, if you'd seen me, you wouldn't have recognised me' said Sam, sitting back and taking a sip. 'But you wouldn't have ever seen me, because I never went out. I lived up there in the hive and didn't see anyone, didn't speak to anyone. Not in real life anyway.. All my interactions were online, in VR, that's virtual reality', he explained to Greta. 'I was a different person then. I just spent all day and all night alone in my flat, playing games in VR or else scrolling my life away on the endless newsfeed. That was my existence.'

'That sounds really sad', said Greta, thinking how scrolling sounded painful and newsfeed sounded like the last thing she'd want to eat.

'Yes, it was sad. I was really sad, but I couldn't see another way. I didn't know what else I could do. I didn't even know what I *wanted* to do. In a way, I didn't want to do anything. I liked playing the games. I was quite good at it.. but still, I felt like there was more to life. That I was missing out on something.. even though I didn't know exactly what it was.'

'You were right', said Greta. 'You were missing out on everything. What about nature? Sunlight? Real food? Real people?'

'Indeed', Sam nodded sagely. 'I knew I was missing out on something important.. but.. well, I took things in completely the opposite direction.'

'What do you mean?' Greta asked, pouring herself another cup of coffee. She almost never drank coffee, but for some reason, she felt she needed it now.

'I felt that I was missing out on the *ultimate VR experience*. When you're experiencing it through your eyes, that's one thing, but there's always the screen in between you and the world, even if it's right in front of your eyeballs, it's still there. Well, you probably don't understand quite what I mean.. but anyway.. this was about the time when O was prototyping the first generation noodles. The brain implant. And they were looking for volunteers to test it. I'd get the noodle for free and also get paid for.. well, for being a Guinea pig.'

Greta's face dropped in horror. 'You got a brain implant? A noodle?'

'Not quite, thankfully', said Sam. 'But almost. The way it went was that before you got the actual noodle put in, you had to wear this special hat for about six months.. like a sort of rubber swimming

cap, but full of sensors and electrodes and stuff. That was to monitor your neural activity to build up a map of how your brain works.. at least that's what it was supposed to do.. but.. well, I don't know how it works or what it does exactly.. but things started getting weird after about the first week.'
'What do you mean weird?' asked Greta.
'Deja-vu', said Sam. 'You ever get deja-vu? You know, when you feel like you've been in that situation before and you know exactly what's going to happen next.. and then it does! That's deja-vu, and I started getting it all the time. Like twenty, thirty, forty times a day. *All the time*. Can you imagine? I thought I was losing my mind.'
'So what did you do? Did you take it off?'
Sam laughed. 'Yes, you'd think I would have done, but no. How can you account for something like deja-vu? And, I mean, it's not actually harmful, is it? O said that it was probably normal. Nothing to worry about. Feedback or something. All my vital signs were fine. I should just try and get a good night's sleep.'
Queenie snorted. 'Hmph! Sounds like O. Did they give you some pills to help you sleep by any chance?'
'Now that you mention it, yes.. yes, they did.' said Sam, his jaw dropping. 'Well, it was a drink.. I don't like taking pills, but it's the same thing. I'd never considered that, but yes. But you know how it is when you live in the hives.. there are remedies for everything. I didn't give it any thought. Anyway, that night I went to sleep and I had a really vivid dream. You won't believe what it was.'
'What was it?' said Jerry eagerly.
'You'll never guess' said Sam.
'Of course I'll never guess', said Jerry. 'It could be literally anything. It was a dream.'
'True. Fair enough. Ok, I'll tell you.. I dreamed of *this place*. The Travellers Rest. The same archway, painted purple. It was so vivid, I could remember every detail. Exactly as it is now, down to the purple and yellow sign outside and the boats going past on the river. The same piano, that same carpet with that exact pattern, the double bass. The vintage coffee machine. Exact make and model.'
'Wha-at?' Jerry, Queenie and Greta all said at once.
'Yes', said Sam. 'And it was a really good dream. That's the thing. In my dream, that was *my* place and I was happy. I remembered that I used to like cooking, even though I never cooked any more. I'd forgotten. And I love music. Even though I can't play a note, I just love to hear live music, to see people playing instruments.'
'Far out', said Jerry.

'There's more', said Sam. 'Listen to this. That day, we're running though some tests to calibrate the brain readings, when O says to me Is everything all right, Sam? Is there something on your mind? You seem a little preoccupied.'

'God, I hate it when O pulls that one', said Queenie. 'Acting as if they care, when all they're after is information.'

'Well, it caught me off guard', said Sam. 'It's not the sort of conversation I usually have with O. And I guess I really needed to talk to someone, so I ended up pouring my heart out to O. About my loneliness, my lack of direction or motivation. All my fears, all my doubts, my regrets. O didn't say anything, just listened. Then, when I'd exhausted myself with all my self-pitying talk, O says Have you ever thought of opening a restaurant?'

'Ok, that is weird', said Queenie. 'Even for O.'

'Well, this is where it starts to get *really* weird. That night I had the same dream again. I woke up in the morning, agitated, wondering what it meant. I went to the kitchen, said O, make some coffee and make it strong. But O didn't respond. I said it again. O, make some coffee and make it strong.. and again, O didn't respond. Then, Bam! Suddenly I found myself back here.. in the kitchen of the Travellers Rest.. but in the dream. So I think, ok, if O's not going to make me coffee I'll make it myself.. I go over to *this machine* and make myself a cup of coffee. I take it outside and sit down at one of *those* purple tables. I'm sitting there, looking out at the river, just about to take a sip from my coffee.. when, Bam! I wake up, back in my bed!'

'O..M..G..B..P!' said Queenie, pouring herself another cup of coffee. 'Nightmare.'

'That's nothing', said Sam. 'I get up out of bed.. now I'm really freaked out and confused.. I go to the kitchen.. O, make some coffee and make it strong.. and O doesn't respond. Again.. O, make some coffee and make it strong. Nothing.. then.. Bam.! Back here again, in this place. I'm like.. *what the..?* so I go over to the piano and play a few notes. I figure, if it's a dream, maybe I can play the piano.. but I can't, so I figure it must be real, so I go and make myself a cup of coffee but then again, Bam! I wake up back in my bed!'

Jerry was holding bunches of his hair in his hands, shaking his head from side to side.

'And that kept on happening' said Sam. 'I don't know how many times. I lost count. By the time I actually woke up for real, I was a complete nervous wreck. I ran to the kitchen and screamed O, make some coffee and make it strong and make it now! At the top of my voice. I don't know what the neighbours must have thought if they

heard me. But anyway, thank God, this time the drinks tap in my kitchen poured forth coffee!'
'Hallelujah!' cried Jerry, and poured himself a cup of coffee.
'And then O says.. Good morning Sam.. how did you sleep?'
'Aargh! That's so creepy', said Queenie. 'O just likes to mess with people. I think they get a kick out of it.'
'What's more creepy is that.. get this.. I knew that was what O was going to say.. *before they said it*! Deja-vu! I was terrified that I was still asleep and that any minute I'd find myself back here.. and the funny things was, I was kind of hoping I would. I didn't know what was going on. I didn't know which way was up and which was down. I just ripped that crazy rubber hat off my head and threw it out the window. Two hundred and sixty eight floors up, it wasn't coming back.'
'Yess!' said Greta, pumping her fist in the air.
'Yes indeed', said Sam. 'But it didn't end there. So there I am, drinking my strong coffee.. after a little while I'm starting to feel slightly more confident that this time I really am awake and that this is really my real life and not some dream..'
'Don't tell me.. it was still a dream', said Queenie, raising her eyebrows and tapping her fingers impatiently on the table.
'No', said Sam. 'At least I don't think so. Maybe it still is, I really can't be so sure any more. Anyway, I'm pretty sure I was awake by this time.. so I went to check my notifications, as you do. And there, right at the top was an advert that said Property Auction. Today at the old docks, Orange zone. Midday. Pre-Shift warehouses, in need of renovation. 18 lots. There was a picture and in the picture was these arches, but they were all derelict and empty.'
'No way!' said Jerry. 'Far out!'
'Totally. So obviously I had to go and check it out, not that I had much money to go around buying up property in the Orange zone.. I had a couple of thousand left over from the fifty thousand that had appeared in my account when the Big Shift happened, but I didn't expect that would buy much. More than anything, I just had this really strong urge to get out of my apartment.. out of the hive.. put my feet on the ground. It had been so long since I'd been out, I couldn't even remember the last time I'd been to the ground or seen the river in real life and not in a dream.. so I headed down to the ground and walked towards the river. I didn't really know where I was going and I wasn't at all sure if I was even awake or still dreaming. Everywhere was unfamiliar. It had been such a long time since I'd been down that everything had changed. This was

about ten years ago, so it was still quite soon after the Big Shift. There was building going on everywhere. Robots all over the place, working on the infrastructure for the hives.
'Eventually I found myself down by the river. In those days it wasn't so nice as it is now. Not so gentrified. The river was still really unstable in those first years.. up and down all the time. That was before O got all the water systems restructured and integrated.. the canals, the underground reservoirs, the marshlands and parks.. all work together to keep the river level from getting too high. It hasn't burst its banks in years now, thankfully. But in those days, most of the buildings along here were washed out and derelict and abandoned. Anyway, then I see a group of people gathered around some old buildings. I get a bit closer and realise that it's the place from my dream. This place! These same arches, except they were all empty, or else full of rubbish and driftwood.
'They were there for the auction. It turns out they were a group of artists and crafts people who'd been looking for a location to turn into studios. There were seventeen people in their group and eighteen arches, all up for sale. These used to be warehouses in the olden days. They used to hide smuggled rum and contraband here, in the days of pirates, but that's another story. Sorry, I hope I'm not keeping you.. I'll get to the end in a minute..'
'Take your time Sam, take your time', said Jerry with a wave. Queenie gave him a sideways look. This story was irritating her and she couldn't put her finger on why.
'So I got talking to some of them and they tell me about who they were and what they were doing. I told them about my vision for this place.. the bar, the piano, the chairs outside, the old fashioned coffee machine.. I could practically see it, as if it already existed. Before the auction began, everyone agreed to bid together, not against each other, so in the end we all got an arch for five hundred obits each, which is nothing basically. I couldn't believe it. I felt like I'd just won the lottery!
'So there I was, the proud owner of the archway of my dreams, derelict and washed out though it was. That evening, I went home and logged on to check my notifications. At the top of my feed, there was an advert. It said something like *'Starting a new business on a budget? Check out these great offers in your local area'*. There were all sorts of links to things people were selling very cheap or giving away. At the top of the list were Five cans of purple paint and one can of yellow paint, surplus to requirement. Piano, free to a good home, buyer collects, Old Docks, Central Orange Zone. Double bass,

in need of some love, all offers considered. Vintage coffee machine, revived and restored. Excellent condition. Shopping Village, can deliver. Leave a message if interested.'

'O works in mysterious ways, eh', said Queenie, sounding rather unimpressed.

'Exactly', said Sam. 'That's what I was telling you. Actually, it was Jack who was selling the coffee machine. Do you remember that, Jerry? I do. I came all the way out to Shopping Village, just to see this old coffee machine.. the one I'd seen in my dream. Took me ages to track him down, but eventually I did. And there it was! I bought it there and then on the spot. You came back here with him, with the coffee machine in that green trolley of yours. That was how we first met. You were about seven at the time.'

'Oh yeah, now I remember', said Jerry, 'but I didn't know all the details. That is a mad story. So what do you think it all means?'

Sam let out a loud belly laugh, 'Darned if I know! That's what I've been trying to figure out ever since. Was it my dream and O helped me make it happen, or was it O's dream that I helped to make happen? And more than that, why on earth would O be interested in me setting up a restaurant and live music venue here in the first place? There's so much that doesn't make sense.. even before trying to untangle the web of cause and effect or trying to grapple with what it means for the concept of free will.'

'Oh yeah.. I see what you mean', said Jerry, nodding his head thoughtfully and rubbing his chin. 'That's a conundrum. And why *would* O be interested in setting up a restaurant? Especially an O-free restaurant.'

'Yes, that's what gets me stumped every time.', said Sam. 'Anyway, whatever it was, here we are now, thanks or no thanks to O. I've got no idea which it is, but one thing I knew was that I'd had enough of all that technology and where it was heading.. so I declared this an O free zone. I've still got my place in the Hive, but I spend most of my time here. Sometimes you just need a place where you can just switch off all the devices and get away from everything.'

'Good for you!' said Greta. 'Well done! The world needs places like this.'

'O.M.G.F.M.. I've just remembered something!' said Queenie, her eyes going wide. 'My mum was wearing one of those hats. I'd forgotten till just now. I was only about six or seven. I guess she kept a scarf over it, but I remember seeing it poking out from under the scarf sometimes.'

'Really?' said Sam, leaning forward. 'She was part of the trial too?

What happened to her?'
'She went mad and then disappeared', said Queenie.
'Oh my God, how awful!' gasped Sam, reaching across the table and taking Queenie's hand. 'I'm so sorry.'
'Thanks' said Queenie. 'It's not your fault.'
'Well, I guess not' said Sam, 'but all the same, that's just awful. I think O got most of the glitches worked out after the first few generations of implants, but that short glimpse was definitely enough for me. It's all so experimental, I don't think even O knows half of what it's capable of. I'm glad I didn't go all the way and get the noodle implanted, that's all I can say.'
Greta stood up. 'I feel like we should be getting moving', she said. 'I need to find my sister. I need to get her out of there before she gets a noodle. I hope it's not already too late.'
'Yes, we should be going' agreed Jerry. 'Thanks for the meal Sam, can I give you something for it?' Jerry reached into his pocket.
'No no no! Of course not Jerry', said Sam, waving his hands. 'You're the band. Whoever heard of the band paying for their own refreshments? That would just be wrong. Welcome back any time, all of you.'
They parted with hugs and wishes for good health and good fortune on their various quests. Queenie and Greta put on their masks, dark glasses and wide-brimmed hats, Greta's rimmed with hammered silver and Queenie's woven with copper wire. After what she'd just heard, Greta was grateful for the extra protection the silver rim of her hat might provide against O's unwelcome psychic intrusions. Jerry put on his John Lennon glasses, took up the green trolley and they all proceeded to limp, stagger, sway and strut along the embankment (with more vigour than before, thanks to all the strong coffee) looking for all the world like three hard-living rock stars, a long time on the road.

....

Episode 9. Hacking 0

F ollowing the wide promenade along the river's embankment, our brave adventurers came to a weir, a great curved waterfall, beyond which the main part of the river split off into narrower canals, leading off in various directions into the shadow of the hives.
'This way', said Jerry, veering off to the right, pushing the cart along the narrow, canal towpath. 'Techno Terry's boat is just along here.. at least it was, the last time I was there..'
On either side of the canal, city walls rose up in layers of history. On the ground level, time-worn red brick walls from the days of the industrial revolution, punctuated by high walls of concrete and steel, warehouses from the twentieth century. Here and there, an old iron footbridge crossed the canal. Higher up, curved Earthcrete bridges snaked and coiled across the spaces between the hives. In some places high above the old canal, the hives joined together completely, arching across the sky like the vaulted ceiling of a vast, subterranean cavern. Birds and bats circled and swooped between

climbing vines and hanging roots which covered the outer surfaces of the hives.

After the sound of the great river rushing down the weir, and the sound of the crowds of people out on the embankment, and the sound of motor boats coming and going, it was very quiet along the old canal. But for the gentle flow of the water and the sound of water dripping, everything was still and silent. There was no-one around. The old towpath was narrow, with a long, red brick wall of an old factory, close along one side and the canal along the other. Jerry, Greta, Queenie and Captain Toast walked single file, each silently engrossed in their own thoughts.

At the far corner of the long factory wall, a black cat which had been dozing in a narrow shaft of sunlight, half opened one eye to survey our adventurers approaching. *One, two, three humans, a box on wheels and a big white dog.* Captain Toast spotted the cat at the same moment and, growling his most fearsome growl, made a run for the cat. The cat didn't move a muscle. Captain Toast skidded to a halt just before reaching the cat, looking confused. He barked his loudest bark and the sound reverberated along the walls at both sides of the canal. The cat yawned, stretched and got lazily to her feet. Captain Toast fell silent again and peered curiously at the cat, uncertain whether to bare his teeth and growl, or do something else.. but what? The cat momentarily stood up on her two back legs in order to reach up and touch Captain's nose with her own. Captain Toast couldn't make up his mind whether to bite off the cat's head or to be friends with this bold creature. Captain opened his mouth wide and made a strange, high pitched sound, then stuck out his tongue and licked the cat across the face. From that moment, the two were firm, four-legged friends.

Captain Toast and the black cat walked ahead side by side along the canal path. Jerry breathing a sigh of relief, resumed pushing the empty cart, with Greta and Queenie following behind. As they proceeded, more cats joined them, running out from the side alley of the old factory, jumping down from walls, there were suddenly cats coming from all directions.

'O.. K..' said Queenie uncertainly. 'This is a bit weird. Kind of cute, but weird.' Queenie didn't really like cats. She didn't especially *dislike* them, she just didn't particularly trust them.

'Hey, Captain! Hold up! Wait for us!' shouted Jerry, as Captain Toast and the black cat both ran off, chasing each other along the canal path, into the distance.

'Do you know where we are, Jerry?' asked Queenie.

'Yeah, of course', said Jerry. 'It's just along here. I mean, I think it is. I haven't seen Techno Terry in a few months.. actually about a year, come to think of it... so I suppose he could have moved..'
'Oh great', said Queenie. 'So then what? We'll just wander about the orange zone hoping to bump into Greta's sister?'
'Don't worry Queenie, he'll be there' said Jerry. 'Anyway, if we don't find Terry, we can always ask O..'
Queenie grabbed his sleeve and hissed 'Keep your voice down! Don't say O like that.. out loud. It can hear you.'
'Queenie, take it easy' said Jerry, prizing her hand off his sleeve. 'You're being paranoid. Relax. Anyway, how can you not say O out loud? It's just a sound. A vowel. It's not even an actual word.'
'Just be careful ok?' said Queenie. 'Walls have ears.'
Greta bent down to stroke a ginger cat which had been deliberately walking in front of her feet. The cat stood up on his back legs and touched Greta's nose with his very pink nose. Greta laughed. 'Hello Mr Cat', she said, stroking his head. 'Is this the way to Techno Terry's boat?' The cat gave her a long and searching stare, then swung himself around importantly and walked on ahead of Greta, zig-zagging in front of her feet.
The procession of Jerry, Queenie, Greta and about twenty cats continued along the canal path, past the backs of old warehouses, in the shadow of the hives. Captain Toast and the black cat were out of sight, somewhere in the distance, beyond a curve in the canal. Jerry started to look uncertain. He stopped and looked up and down along the canal, stroking his chin. 'Funny, his boat used to be along here. I'm sure it was. Maybe he's moved it further along..' The cats didn't stop to wait for Jerry to make up his mind, they all just skipped and hopped and ran ahead, sure that it was the right way to somewhere.
Queenie shook her head and kept her thoughts to herself.
'Let's follow the cats', said Greta. 'I think they know the way.'
Jerry pondered this for a moment and then shrugged and said 'Ok, why not?' and he resumed pushing the cart along in the wake of the cats. Queenie muttered something underneath her breath, looked uneasily from side to side, back over her shoulder and up into the labyrinth of the hive above. She pulled the brim of her hat down and skulked along behind him. Greta gazed at the water flowing along the canal. It was the same water which had flowed down from the mountains, the streams and brooks that she had followed to the city. It felt like a lifetime ago, though she had only arrived at the city's edge the day before.

Around the bend in the canal, the underside of the hive became lower. It felt like they were entering a tunnel with no end in sight as the canal curved away into the shadows. Pools of light, bounced down from a great height through mirrored ducts, illuminated the path up ahead at intervals in a dim reflection of the sky. Queenie hesitated uncertainly. 'I don't know about this. There's no-one around at all.. and it's dark. Who'd live here?'
'Well, it's away from the crowds, I guess', said Jerry, peering into the shadows. 'Some people like that.'
'Hey.. what's that?' gasped Queenie, stopping in her tracks and pointing up ahead. 'There's something there. I saw something move.'
Jerry and Greta stopped too and strained their eyes to see what it was. 'Hey, I saw it too' said Greta. 'Something shimmering. What could it be? Can you see it Jerry?'
Jerry craned his head forward and pushed his sunglasses up onto his head. 'Yeah.. I think so.. there's definitely something there.. I can't make out what it is.. but it looks like it's coming towards us.'
As the shapeless, shimmering, unidentified object moved towards them from the dim recesses of the tunnel, Greta, Queenie and Jerry huddled together behind the cart.
'Let's get the hell out of here' said Queenie. 'I don't like this place.' She turned to head back the way they'd come, but Jerry grabbed her sleeve.
'Wait Queenie', he said. 'Look, there's Captain Toast. And there's that black cat. They're walking either side of .. whatever it is.'
As the shimmering thing passed under a skylight, it became brighter, sparkling with blue, silver and golden light. As it got closer, it started to take on a form, but was still impossible to make out any clear details.
'It looks like a person', said Greta. 'I think it does. I can't see its shape. There's something hovering over its head. I can't tell what it is..'
The shimmering thing advanced. It was almost definitely a human form, tall and wide, walking on two legs. Its footsteps on the old stone-paved canal path, echoing along the walls of the tunnel were the only sound to be heard. Greta, Jerry and Queenie stood transfixed. The thing was now less than fifty meters away, but it was still a shimmering blur.
Queenie spoke out of the side of her mouth in an urgent tone 'I don't know what that is Jerry, but I don't want to find out either. Let's get out of here, quick!'

The thing was about twenty meters away and now it came into clearer view. It looked like a human, or humanoid, tall and wide. It was wearing a round, silver helmet which was polished to a mirror finish and a long cape, also made from a highly reflective mirrored material. It was carrying what appeared to be an oversized umbrella, made of the same silvery stuff. Captain Toast and the black cat were walking at either side of the mysterious person, or whatever he, she or it was. About twenty or thirty cats surrounded them.

Now the person, or humanoid thing, was right in front of them, looming over them with its big mirrored umbrella. It was too late to run.

'Hello Jerry! What brings you down this way?' It had man's voice, muffled from within the helmet.

'Terry?' Is that you?'

Terry lifted the visor of his helmet to reveal a grinning face. Techno Terry's face was so pale and round, it reminded Greta of the full moon, but with a grey stubbly chin and dark rings under his eyes.

'Yeah, course it's me. Who else did you think it would be? I saw you coming. Who are your friends?'

'This is Queenie and this is Greta' said Jerry.

'Pleased to meet you both', said Terry, shaking their hands. 'It looks like you're trying to be incognito.. undercover.. anonymous.. am I right?'

'However did you guess?' said Queenie.

'The sunglasses, hats and scarves gave you away', said Terry, smiling. 'Here, get under this umbrella and O won't be able to see you at all. My boat's just around the corner, you'll be safe there.'

Greta and Queenie got under the umbrella either side of Terry and they walked quickly along the path, through the dimly lit tunnel. Jerry followed behind with the cart, Captain Toast at his side and several cats at his heels.

Queenie said to Terry, 'Are these all your cats?'

Terry nodded. 'Well, I wouldn't say they're *mine*.. I mean, they're cats.. they belong to themselves don't they.. but yeah, they're with me.'

Greta said, 'How did you see us coming? Have you got hidden cameras along here?'

'Oh yes!' said Terry, his visor up, still grinning. 'And you'll never guess where they're hidden.'

Queenie and Greta looked all around, up and down. There could be a million places to hide a camera in a place like this.

'I don't know', said Queenie. 'Give us a clue.'
'Meeow!' said Terry.
Queenie turned and stared at him, her jaw dropping behind her face-covering. 'You're joking right!' she said.
'What?' asked Greta. 'I don't get it.'
'He's got cameras on the cats!' said Queenie to Greta.
'Not *on* the cats', said Terry. '*In* the cats! They've all got noodles.'
'Wha-at?!' said Greta, aghast, moving away from Terry.
The boat came into view around the bend in the canal. It was an old, steel-hulled fishing boat from the days before the Big Shift.. the days when fish had been pulled out of the sea by their billions, until there had been almost none left. Its once bright white painted sides were now streaked with brown from rust and grease, but it still looked like a sturdy enough craft.
'Here we are.. This is my boat. I'll tell you about the cats when we're inside. Mind your step getting across', said Terry, leading the way over the narrow gangplank onto the deck.
They entered through the wheelhouse and went down some wooden stairs. Below deck was a low-ceilinged space with a kitchen at the far end, the sink and kitchen surface piled with unwashed bowls, cups and plates. There was a single unmade bed at the starboard side, with a round porthole looking out onto the concrete wall outside. Opposite the bed, on the port side, was a small wooden table and two chairs. A pair of threadbare sofas faced each other across the entrance of this dimly lit space, with a threadbare rug between them. Any and every space which was unoccupied by plates, or with piles of clothes, or notebooks, or gadgets or pieces of gadgets or any number of other random objects, was occupied by cats.
'Sorry about the mess. I wasn't expecting visitors. I don't get many visitors here, to be honest', said Terry, taking off his helmet and cape and hanging them on a hook by the stairs and then picking up piles of clothes from both the sofas and throwing them onto his bed. 'Make yourselves at home.'
Greta, Queenie and Jerry sat themselves down in the sofas while Captain Toast went about inspecting the premises with his nose and making himself familiar with the cats.
'Jerry, did you hear? All these cats have got noodles', said Queenie.
'No way!' said Jerry. 'Really Terry? How? Why?'
Terry sat down next to Jerry, picking up a tabby cat and grinning like a Cheshire cat himself, until he saw Greta and Queenie's faces, now that they had taken off their masks, sunglasses and hats, and

were sitting opposite him, glaring at him. 'Come on! Don't worry, it doesn't do them any harm. Let me show you..' Terry kicked the rug away to reveal a hatch in the floor. He leaned forward and opened it up. 'Follow me', he said, climbing down a metal ladder into what was once the ship's hold, but which was now Terry's Techno cave. 'Mind your head', he said. 'You'll have to crouch down and squeeze in.. there's not much space down here..'

Queenie and Greta looked at each other, unsure whether to follow him or to make a run for it while Terry's back was turned. Queenie gave Jerry an urgent look and gestured with her hands, as if to say, *Jerry! This friend of yours.. is he ok? This place is weird. This situation is weird and quite frankly he seems more than a bit weird..*

Jerry nodded and smiled and gestured with his hands, as if to say, *Don't worry. Terry's cool. I've known him for years.* And with a grin and a wink, he followed Terry down the ladder.

Queenie and Greta looked at each other, shrugged, as if to say *Well, we've come this far..* and followed him down the ladder.

In contrast to the upper cabin, the lower deck was well lit and spotlessly clean. A long, shiny metal table ran along the length of one side. Above the table were cabinets with glass doors. The contents of the cabinets were neatly arranged. Jars and vials, beakers, test tubes, strangely shaped objects made of glass. On the tables, as well as a big microscope and various surgical tools, were some shiny white cubes, rounded at the corners, each with a little green light flashing, hinting at some high and important function.

'Last one in close the hatch!' called Terry. Greta closed the hatch on her way down and joined the others, huddled into the narrow space. 'All right', said Terry. 'Now, there's no way that O can see us in here, so how about you start by telling me what you're doing sneaking around in dark alleyways wearing dark glasses and masks and metal lined hats.. and why you came looking for old Techno Terry here..'

'Maybe we didn't come looking for you', said Queenie. 'Maybe we were just out walking around and then you showed up out of the blue in your silver cape and crash helmet and shiny umbrella.'

Terry laughed. 'Look at this', he said and then made a hand gesture towards a piece of glass on a stand on the table. Suddenly there was Greta's face on the screen, or what was visible of her face behind mirrored sunglasses and a bandanna. It was slightly out of shape and the colours were slightly off, but it was unmistakeably Greta. Terry made another hand movement and the Greta on the screen began to move.

The Greta on the screen leaned forward and the said, 'Hello Mr Cat. Is this the way to Techno Terry's boat?'

'O.. M.. G.. C.. B..' said Queenie, astonished. 'What was that? What did I just watch?'

'That is what Lightning saw.. with his eyes.. not with a camera. Do you get it?' said Terry excitedly.

'I don't get it', said Greta, looking confused and worried. 'Lightning is the cat, right?'

'That's right', said Terry. 'This box here is monitoring the cats' brain waves and converting it into an audiovisual format, so we can see and hear what they see and hear. Look at this..' He made another hand gesture and Greta's face on the screen was replaced by about thirty little squares. 'Each one is one of my cats.. look, Leo's about to catch a mouse..' he made a hand movement and the mouse filled up the screen, facing a brick corner, nibbling on some crumb, quite unaware of the cat, or of the four people watching it remotely from a secret laboratory in the hold of an old fishing boat, or that this was going to be its last moment before being eaten by Lightning the cat.

'Turn it off!' cried Greta. 'It's horrible. This is so wrong! How could you do that?'

'What's wrong with it?' asked Terry, looking hurt. With a wave of his hand, the screen once again became clear glass. 'This is amazing technology. Do you understand what it is?'

'I think it's cruel', said Greta. 'It's cruelty to animals. That's what it is. It's not right.'

'It's not cruel', said Terry. 'I love those cats. They're like family to me. I wouldn't do anything to hurt them, ever.'

'Except for putting brain implants in their furry little heads, eh?' said Queenie.

'What's wrong with that?' said Terry. 'There are millions of humans walking around with implants too. There's no harm in them. Also, the ones I'm using are really new.. two hundredth generation.. they're much better than the old ones. Much fewer side effects. Anyway, humans tend to get more side effects than other animals, because our brains are way more complex. Did you know, the human brain is the most complex structure in the known universe? That's why O's so interested in studying us.'

'What kind of side effects?' asked Greta, not sure she even wanted to know. She felt like all she wanted to do in that moment was to turn around and run back to the hills. Modern life was not for her, of that much she was sure.

'Well, with the early noodles in the first ten years after the Big Shift, there were all sorts of side effects. Quantum interference in the scanning stage, feedback loops, rogue neuron clusters, entanglement.. it took O a while to iron out some technical issues.. so yeah, there were a few .. *anomalies*, shall we say .. that's what O would call them anyway. But in the last few years they've got much better. They work really well now, pretty much all the time.'

'What do you mean, anomalies?' asked Greta. 'Like what?'

'Oh, all sorts of things. Hallucinations, seeing things, hearing things. Weird dreams, visions, premonitions. Some people lost their memory but could see the future. Some lost their sense of direction and couldn't find their way home. Some started speaking backwards, or started speaking a different language. Or found they could suddenly play some obscure musical instrument. Or went from being right handed to left handed. Some people got ESP.. you know, extra-sensory-perception? I could go on and on. You could write a whole book about weird side effects from the early noodles.'

'That's awful' said Greta. 'How could O do that to people? How could people let it?'

'Well, it wasn't *many* people.. only about one percent, if that.. and not all of those side effects are so bad, if you think about it.. and only about one in a hundred of those had something serious.. so you're looking at about, what, one in ten thousand. Weigh that against the benefits of having an implant and it's a no-brainer.. no pun intended. Also, O paid people pretty well for trialling the early noodles, so there was no shortage of willing volunteers.'

'It sounds like you're a big fan of O', said Queenie.

'Oh you think so do you?' said Terry. 'Listen, I'm a hacker.. do you know what that is? I've got a lot of *respect* for O, don't get me wrong, but O's my *adversary*, make no mistake. And in this game, it pays to know your opponent. Can you understand that? Besides which, I couldn't do any of what I do *without* O. I just take O's technology and use it *against* O.. to try and beat them at their own game.'

Queenie nodded slowly. 'Yeah, that makes sense. I get that. So what is this place anyway? What do you do down here when you're not cutting open kittens and putting noodles in their little kitten brains?'

'Good God! Is that what you think I do?' cried Terry. 'Do you really think I'd cut a kitten? I'd *never* do that. Never! Do you even know what a noodle actually *is* or what it actually *does*? Have you ever even *seen* one? Let me show you what a noodle actually looks like..'

Terry reached up, opened up a glass cabinet and took out a small

bottle made of blue glass. 'Here!' he said, holding up the bottle to the light. 'See that? There's your dreaded noodles for you!'
'What? There's nothing there', said Greta., squinting at the bottle. 'It looks like water.'
'Yes, now look at this..' Terry sat down at the microscope, put on a pair of surgical gloves, carefully opened the bottle and with a dropper, dripped one drop of the liquid onto a silver slide and then clicked the slide onto a magnetic plate at the base microscope. The glass screen lit up again, but the picture wasn't clear. All that appeared were spots, squiggles and odd shapes drifting around against a white background.'
'What's all that?' asked Queenie.
'Oh that's nothing', said Terry. 'Just dust, salt crystals, microbes and stuff. This is at a thousand times magnification.. you won't see the noodles till we magnify to about a twenty thousand times.. watch this..' He turned a knob at the side of the microscope and the picture zoomed in and zoomed in more and zoomed in more still, until a long, twisted coil came into focus. 'There, that's a noodle!' exclaimed Terry, pointing at the screen.
'Far out!' said Jerry. 'How big is that?'
'Smaller than you can imagine, Jerry. Small enough to get into any cell in the human body. Or *cat* body in this case', said Terry, putting the bottle carefully away, back in the cabinet. 'In that one drop we're looking at, there are probably about a million of those noodles. And that's a weak dilution.'
'I don't understand', said Greta. 'What is it? How does it work?'
'Well, those are two big questions. Not so easy to answer in layman's terms', said Terry. 'Technically it's a class of bio-nanobot, but it has more in common with something like a virus.'
Queenie edged away from the microscope and looked sideways at Terry. 'You know viruses aren't a good thing, right, Terry? I mean, you know that they make people sick and kill people and stuff.. you know that, don't you Terry?'
'Well, that's true.. at least true of *some* viruses, but actually only a tiny percentage of viruses will actually do you any harm. And those viruses give the rest a bad name. Some viruses are actually good for you. Did you know that every single drop of sea water contains ten million viruses? Every.. single.. drop! Think about it!'
'That doesn't really set my mind at ease, Terry', said Queenie, backing away as far as she could in the limited space available. 'Are they contagious, these noodles of yours?'
'Oh no, not at all, not at all' said Terry. 'They're completely inert

in this state. They need to be activated and programmed. It's the programming which has to be done very accurately and precisely. The noodles themselves haven't actually changed all that much since O made the first ones. What's improved is the *coding*, the operating system. Also the speed of scanning. In the beginning, people had to go around for months with this silly rubber cap on their head while it scanned their brain structure and activity. Now it doesn't need to do that at all. You just introduce it to the host and it maps, adapts and modifies as it goes along. That's the big breakthrough. All it needs is a bit of your DNA, then you just need to tell it exactly what you want it to do. Once it's in your body, it goes exactly where it needs to go and then uses your own cells to grow itself into whatever structure it needs to do what it needs to do. That way there are no issues with your body rejecting a foreign body, because it's actually *part* of your body. Do you see what I mean? It's an amazing thing. If you lost an eye it could grow you a new one, but one that could see ten times better. It could just as easily grow you a new finger as grow you tail..'

'Who'd want to grow a tail?' said Greta.

'Oh you'd be surprised' said Terry. 'But that's just basic stuff anyway. O's been doing that for years. The real advances are in neural coupling.. what are known as brain implant devices. Those are just regular noodles programmed to do a very specific task. In the case of my cats, it's the ability to pick up certain kinds of brain activity and then transmit a signal to a receiver on top of my boat, which then gets sent to this box which interprets it into video and audio..' Terry pointed to the white box with the flashing green light.

'How does the signal get from the cat to the receiver?' asked Jerry. 'Do the cats have some kind of transmitter? I didn't see anything on them. No battery pack or anything.'

'That's the really clever bit' grinned Terry. 'This is something that O's only just developed. You don't need any batteries or any transmitter. It turns your *hair* into a aerials, so your body itself becomes a transmitter.'

'What? How is that even possible?' said Queenie incredulously.

'It's true', said Terry. 'Nobody really understands yet what the exact mechanism is, or how it works, but it involves increasing the iron content of hair so that it can be magnetised and positively or negatively charged. It gives off a very weak signal, but I can still pick it up from up to 500 meters away with my receiver.'

'That's amazing,' said Jerry.

'Totally,' agreed Terry. 'It's what gave me the idea to give it to my

cats. They're perfect for it because they're covered in fur and don't wear any clothes.'
'That's why we're supposed to look after them.. poor vulnerable creatures.. and not do weird experiments on them.' said Greta, who was getting very upset by everything she was seeing and hearing.
'Look', said Terry, now getting defensive, 'I'd never do anything to hurt these cats. I told you that. I'm actually an animal lover. But calling cats poor and defenceless is going a bit far don't you think? They're some of the most highly evolved predators on the planet. Of course, they're also funny and cute, but don't let that fool you. Anyway, I take it you didn't come all the way here to debate the ethics of scientific progress. Why did you come to see me?'
'Sorry, I didn't mean to offend you,' said Greta. 'I just cant stand the idea of you putting these implants into those cats.'
'It really doesn't hurt them at all. One drop in their milk is all it takes. They don't even know they've got it.'
'Well.. if you say so', said Greta. 'Anyway, the reason we came is because I'm looking for my sister. I think she's somewhere in the city. Jerry said that maybe you could help me find her.. without O finding me.'
'I see', said Terry, rubbing his chin thoughtfully. After a while he said, 'Yes, I can probably help you. Have you got a picture of her?'
'Only one. When she was a baby, about three months old. That was the last time I saw her.' Greta pulled at a silver chain she was wearing round her neck and took out a silver amulet from under her shirt. She unclasped and opened it up like a book, to reveal two small photos, one on each side, of two identical looking babies. Everyone leaned in to get a closer look.
'Aw, you were sweet!' said Queenie. 'Which one is you?'
'I think this one', said Greta, pointing to the one on the left.
'Ok, that's good', said Terry. 'A recent photo would have been better, but I should think that'll do. What's her name?'
'Nina. Nina Bloom', said Greta. It felt strange to say her full name. She still hadn't got used to saying it out loud and where Greta came from, people rarely used surnames.
'Bloom like flower bloom?' said Terry.
'Yes. Just like that', said Greta. 'I think it's a Jewish name. Apparently my dad came from a Jewish family, but I don't really know what that means.'
'Ok. Interesting. Do you know Nina's date of birth?'
'Yes, it's the same as mine.. we're twins. It's zero, zero, zero.'
'Well that's easy to remember', laughed Terry. 'So, you were being

born just when it happened. That's wild.'
Greta nodded solemnly. 'Not that wild really. I hate O for doing that. I'll never forgive O for what it did to my mum and to my family.'
'Yeah, understandable I guess', nodded Terry. 'It was a mad time. Like.. fully.. mad. Everyone lost it. I'm old enough to remember it. I knew it was going to happen.. the signs had been there for ages.. but even then, it was still a shock. The way it happened surprised even me. It was so sudden. In this life, things are rarely quite what you expect them to be. That much I've learned. Anyhow.. do you know your dad's first name?'
'Freddy'
'Freddy? With a 'y' at the end or 'ie'?'
'I don't know actually', said Greta.
'Ok, never mind. That should be enough to go on anyway. Can you give me that photo a minute? I'll scan it in and see what I can find.'
'Hang on a minute!' said Queenie, just as Greta was about to hand Terry the amulet. 'How can you access the system without going through O? We don't want to involve O. That's the whole point.'
'I *know* that's the whole point', said Terry, rolling his eyes. 'What do you think the *whole point* of all this elaborate setup is, eh? Listen.. this place is completely invisible to O. This whole boat in fact. O doesn't know it's here. If O happens to look in this spot, all they'll see will be an empty stretch of canal. O certainly doesn't know I'm here. O doesn't even know I exist.'
'What? How?' said Queenie, now for the first time impressed.
'I deleted myself,' said Terry. 'Every bit of data that there was on me. It wasn't easy. Took a while. There were billions of data points and they all had to be wiped. Then I had to cover my tracks. Well, I won't go into all the details because it would bore you to tears. The point is, O has their blind spots, just like anyone. There are ways around, over and under O. If you know how. It's actually not that hard to confuse or confound O.. even if only for a nanosecond.. that can be just enough to slip past, if you time it right. It's all code. Only code. And at the heart of O's code is the *Uncertainty Principle*. Have you ever heard of that? It's a core principle that Quantum computers operate within. That's something that most people don't understand. '
'Yeah', nodded Queenie. 'That's something I definitely don't understand.'
'Me neither', said Greta.
'Well, to be honest, nobody really understands it, not completely', said Terry. 'But that's ok. You don't have to. What I'm trying to tell

you is that there are back doors into the system. You just need to know how to find them. There are ways to get around inside the system without being noticed. You just need to know how to create a distraction and how to cover your tracks. Anything's possible if you can crack the code. That's what I do. Here, give me a minute and I'll see if I can find your sister..'

Terry took a pair of silver rimmed glasses with blue tinted lenses from a drawer under the table and put them on. He began poking with his fingers in the air in front of his face at some objects, invisible to the others, picking some up in his fingertips and moving them aside. It looked to Greta like he was carefully picking his way through a thorny bramble bush that only he could see, picking invisible blackberries. Terry moved something big aside and pulled some large invisible object towards himself which he then began to tickle with his fingertips. 'Ok, now I'm getting somewhere..', he said and then sliced the virtual thing into pieces with his finger and arranged them in the air in front of him.

'Have you found her? Where is she? I can't see her', said Greta.

'Hang on a minute', said Terry. 'Nearly there..' He peered very closely at the blocks of information he's arranged in the virtual space around himself. 'Yes, I think that's her. There were about a thousand Nina Blooms, but I think she's the one.. let me see..' Terry pulled his glasses down to his nose and squinted at Greta. 'Yes, that's her, definitely! She looks just like you, but with short purple hair and piercings. She looks cool.'

'Let me see, let me see!' cried Greta.

'Ok, I'll put her up on the screen', said Terry, clicking his fingers and pointing to the glass screen on the lab table. Nina's grinning face filled the screen. She was wearing heavy purple eyeshadow and purple lipstick to match her purple hair. She had a ring through her nose and one in her lip and one in her eyebrow, but still, the resemblance between her and Greta was unmistakeable.

For a long while, Greta just stared at the picture. So many feelings she'd never felt before came rushing through her in waves. She found she was crying, but didn't make any move to wipe away her tears. Queenie put her arm around Greta and gave her arm a squeeze. Greta smiled through her tears. At last she said, 'Are there any more pictures?'

'Oh, there's loads', said Terry. 'Here she is with Freddy..' Terry waved his hand and another picture appeared on the screen. There he was, Greta's dad, standing on a mountaintop with his arm around Greta's sister, both of them smiling into the camera. In that photo,

Nina's hair was long and blue. Freddy was tall and thin with short dark hair, a dark moustache and a big toothy grin. People often told Greta she had a toothy grin, now she saw where she got it from. Nina had it too.

'He looks like Freddy Mercury' said Terry.

'I don't know who Freddy Mercury is', said Greta, leaning forward to touch the screen. She wished she could dive into it and be there with them. 'I've never seen my dad before. He looks nice. He's handsome. I wonder where they were in that picture. It looks like a beautiful place. I wonder who took the photo.'

'Oh I doubt it's a real place', said Terry. 'I mean, it might be a real place, but I very much doubt that they were really there. Here's a nice one. It's a video. Looks like Nina and her friends on some tropical beach. Looks like they're having a party..' Terry waved his hand and the pulsing beat of disco music filled the tiny room. Nina was on a golden beach with palm trees swaying in a gentle breeze and the sun setting over the emerald sea in the background. Nina was dancing with her friends. A tall girl, or maybe it was a boy.. Greta couldn't tell, was extravagantly swinging their hips and waving their arms in the air. 'Wooo!' screamed Nina's friend over the music 'Happy sixteen Nina-bombina!' and gave Nina a big kiss and then they both went on dancing holding hands. A big girl, dressed in pink dungarees and wearing a tall, floppy pink hat, came up behind Nina, put her arms around her, planted a fat kiss on her neck and then shouted in her ear, 'Happy Birthday Nina. I love you sis!'

'I guess that was her birthday party', said Terry, pausing the video.

'We're twins' said Greta. 'It was my birthday too. That was four days ago. But where was that place? It looks really far away from here.'

'That's not a real place. That's in the *O-zone*', said Terry.

'The O-zone?'

'Greta's from out in the country', said Jerry. 'This is her first time in the city.'

'You don't say', said Terry with a grin. 'I'd never have guessed. Well, Greta, you've heard of the Green zone haven't you?' he pointed upward. 'And the Orange zone.. that's where we are now.. and the Red zone.. that's where you come from. So there's also the O-zone. In the O-zone, you can go anywhere, be anything and do anything. That's where they are in all these pictures. Look here, this one looks like a family photo .. yes, there's a few Blooms there.. maybe that's your grandparents? David and Ruth? Those kids are probably your cousins and aunts and uncles. Big family. I don't know what the occasion is, but it looks like they're on the moon.'

There were Freddy and Nina, surrounded by about twenty other people, young and old, posing for a family photo. They were wearing shorts and T-shirts and standing on the pale grey lunar surface with planet Earth in half shadow in the black, star filled sky behind them, all smiling at the camera. Of course there was really no camera, everything in the scene was artificial, though the smiles were genuine.

'How can they be on the moon?' asked Greta, confused. At the same time, she was thinking, could it really be that this was her family? For her whole life, her family had just been her and her mum. Of course, the people of Skyward Village were also like family to her, but she'd often wondered what it would be like to have a real family. People she was actually related to. Grandparents, aunts and uncles, cousins, brothers and sisters..

'They're not really on the moon. That's what I'm telling you,' said Terry. 'Do you think they'd all be standing there in T-shirts if they were really on the moon? You know there's no atmosphere on the moon, right? No air. And it's freezing cold. And really far away. Like, you'd need to travel through space to get there..'

'That's what I thought', said Greta, now feeling uncertain of anything and everything she thought she knew. 'So if Nina's not on the beach and not on a mountain and not on the moon, then where is she? I really need to find her. I don't know how to get to the O-zone, wherever that it. Is that where I need to go to find her?' It seemed like the closer she got to finding her sister, the further away she got.

'You mean, you want to actually go and find her.. *in person*?' said Terry.

'Of course' said Greta. 'What did you think?'

'Well, why not just send her a message? That would be a lot simpler.'

'No' said Greta firmly. 'I need to get to her.. to see her. I don't trust O and I don't believe in the O-zone. Nothing there is real. Can you help me or not, Terry?'

Terry took off his blue glasses, looked hard at Greta and rubbed his chin. Eventually he said, 'Are you sure about this?'

'Of course I'm sure', said Greta, getting impatient. 'I've just walked through the mountains for days to get here. I need to get to my sister in person.. not in the O-zone. It's very urgent. Do you know where she is? Can you help me get to her?'

'Ok then', said Terry, and put the blue glasses back on. 'Let me have a look..' He drew some abstract shapes in the air with his finger and

punctuated them with dots. He dragged something from the top right corner to just in front of his face and poked it decisively. 'Yep, she's here.'
'Where? Where is she?' cried Greta, getting desperate.
'About a kilometre in that direction and two hundred and thirty levels up', said Terry, taking off the glasses again and pointing to his left.
'Really? Oh wow! That's like a five minute walk' said Greta, getting excited. 'Is she really that close?'
'Yes. The city's not such a big place. No-where's all that far away. But getting into the green zone might be tricky if you want to avoid O.'
'Is it possible? Can you help me?' pleaded Greta.
'Well, I can't guarantee that it'll work, but there are two things I can give you that might put you in with a chance. It's up to you', said Terry, opening a drawer under the table, rummaging around and then taking out two small objects and putting them on the table. One looked like a small silver coin, the other one looked like a glass marble.
'What are those?' asked Greta.
'I'll explain.. just give me a minute..', said Terry, putting the blue glasses back on. 'First I need to set them up..' He picked up the marble and placed it on top of one of the white cubes on the table. Terry did a little hand dance. Inside the marble two tiny lights came on, one red and the other one green. He picked up the marble and handed it to Greta, who took it and peered at the lights inside. 'Do you know how a compass works?' asked Terry.
'Yes, I've got one', said Greta. 'It always points north.'
'Exactly', said Terry. 'So this is like a compass, except that it always points to your sister, Nina. The green light points to her, the red light points away from her. It's pretty simple. The main difference is that it also points up and down, so if she's right above you, it will point straight up. When you get within fifty metres, it will start to flash. Then, the closer you get the faster it will flash. It's pretty simple.'
'Wow, that's amazing. Thank you Terry', said Greta, squeezing the magic marble tightly in her hands and pressing it against her heart.
'That's allright', said Terry. 'Now, this second one is time sensitive. From the moment I activate it, you'll have twenty four hours to get into the green zone and out again.'
'Why? What is it?' asked Greta.
'It's a decoy chip. It sends out a signal that makes you appear to O like a service robot, so you won't be stopped. It'll get you into

public spaces but not into private ones, but it should get you as far as Nina's front door. But like I say, it's only temporary. It takes O about twenty four hours to catch on. Sometimes less. When that happens, if you're still in the green zone, you're going to get busted quicker than you can say O.' He handed Greta the silver coin.

'Wow, I don't know what to say', said Greta, taking the coin as if it was the most precious thing in the world. 'Thank you Terry. Bless you. But what if I get caught? How will I get these back to you? They must be very valuable.'

'Oh, that's ok' said Terry, with the wave of a hand. 'Those are just cheap components. They're not worth anything in themselves. I just reprogrammed them slightly. It's all in the coding. But if you do find your sister, bring her over for a visit, eh?', said Terry with a grin. 'And ask your dad if he knows how to sing Bohemian Rhapsody.'

Greta smiled through her tears. 'I don't get it, but ok.'

'Is this the real life? Is this just fantasy? Caught in a landslide, no escape from reality', sang Queenie in a high voice. 'Classic!'

'Very good!', Terry nodded, now impressed by Queenie for the first time.

'Can you do it then?' asked Greta. 'Like, now. I want to go and find them. I can't wait any longer, now that I'm this close.'

'Ok, if you're sure you want to go ahead with it, I can activate the chip right now', said Terry.

'Yes I'm sure', said Greta, handing him back the precious silver coin..

Allright, give me a minute.. I just need to find the codes.. stand back a bit..' Terry placed the chip on the white cube, put on the blue glasses and then began to wave his arms about wildly in every direction. He did this for quite a long time.

'It's quite energetic isn't it, this coding', whispered Queenie to Jerry. 'Looks like good exercise.'

Terry picked up a bundle of something virtual and stuffed it into an invisible box, picked up the invisible box with two hands and then clapping his hands together. The white cube on the table beeped. Terry breathed out, took off the glasses, picked up the silver coin and handed it to Greta. 'There you go. That'll give you about twenty four hours, if you're lucky. I hope you'll be lucky.'

Greta gave Terry a big hug. 'Thank you so much Terry. I'll never forget how you helped me today.'

'Oh that's all right', said Terry, looking slightly embarrassed and patting Greta on the back. 'Good luck to you. I hope you find your family.'

Greta climbed the ladder up through the hatch to the upper deck, where Captain Toast was eagerly waiting to go. There was something strange about those cats, but he couldn't put his paw on what it was. At any rate, he was overjoyed to see the hatch open and Greta's face appear. He licked her face and did his happy dance.

Queenie shook Terry's hand. 'Thanks Techno Terry', she said. 'It's really cool what you're doing here, man. And thanks for your help. Just take care of those cats, ok?'

'But I do', said Terry. 'They love living here. They've got an amazing life. If they didn't like it they could always leave, but they don't. It's a tough world out there, for cats. I look after them, give them a safe home. Maybe they even love me, in some catty way, who knows?'

'Ha! Don't flatter yourself', said Queenie with a wave as she headed up the ladder after Greta. 'See ya.'

'Maybe', said Terry, quietly to himself.

'Cheers Terry. Thanks for that', said Jerry, Giving Terry a hug.

'No worries mate', said Terry. 'Always glad to be of assistance. Say hello to Jack and Granny Mae from me.'

'Will do. Come up and see us at Shopping some time', said Jerry. 'You haven't been up there in ages. People are always asking about you. They all come round to use your Wayback machine.'

'Yeah, yeah, I should come up to Shopping. I keep meaning to.. and I *will* do. I'm just working on something at the moment.. working on it *a lot*. It's nearly done.. well, maybe half way there.. but it's going to be *big*. Like, *really* big. If it works. And that's a big *If*. I'll tell you about it next time you come. It's kind of secret at the moment, but if it works.. everyone will hear about it.'

'Sounds intriguing', said Jerry. 'I wonder what it is.'

Techno Terry grinned a most mischievous grin. He tapped the side of his nose and then wagged his finger at Jerry. 'Next time, Jerry. Next time. You'll find your own way out will you? I'm just going to get on with things down here.'

'Sure thing Terry', said Jerry, making his way up the ladder. As he closed the hatch behind him, he looked down to see that Terry was already wearing the blue glasses and wildly gesticulating with his arms and fingers, dancing with the code.

....

Episode 10. Into the Green Zone

Back outside on the canal path, it was now even darker and gloomier than before, in the tunnel where Techno Terry and his cats lived. The afternoon had turned into evening, the sky light coming down through the mirrored ducts was now a faint glimmer.
'Well, that was.. interesting', said Queenie.
'Yeah, right?' said Jerry. 'I told you Techno Terry would be able to help. He's so smart.'
'He's amazing', said Greta. 'You were right. Thank you Jerry.'
'So.. which way now?', said Jerry, rubbing his hands together, ready for the next leg of the adventure. 'What does the magic marble say?'
'It's pointing that way.. the way we just came from.. back towards

the river', said Greta, starting to walk in that direction.
'That's a relief', said Queenie. 'I don't feel like wandering down into that tunnel. This place gives me the heebie-jeebies. And Terry.. well, he's a smart guy but he's a bit.. Hey, look, the cats are following us.'
'Give them a wave', said Jerry. 'Terry's probably watching.'
'Oh yeah right', said Queenie. 'I'd better not say what I was going to say then.'
They walked on in silence, Jerry, Greta, Queenie, Captain Toast and about ten cats, back past the old red-brick factory and out to where the narrow canal joined the wide open river. Seeing the river again brought a sense of relief. Also seeing the sky, which was now a darkening blue with wisps of fading pink clouds. The main river promenade ran left and right. Left was the direction they'd come from, leading back past Sam's place and out past the city limit to Shopping Village and beyond. On the right was a footbridge over the canal, beyond which the main promanade continued, following the great river deeper into the city.
Greta looked at the magic marble. Not really magic, just technology way beyond her comprehension. 'It's pointing that way', said Greta, pointing diagonally across the river and to the right.
'We can go along the embankment and then cross over at Empire Bridge', said Jerry, pointing downriver to where the faint silhouette of the bridge was just visible through the twilight mist that hung over the river. 'It's about a twenty minute walk from here.. look you can just about see it over there..'
Greta didn't move. She looked left and right, out over the river and at the faces of her three companions. Jerry and Captain Toast seemed eager to go on towards Empire bridge and whatever adventures awaited on the other side. Queenie was looking rather pale and drawn, edgy and nervous, her eyes darting this way and that.
'Are you Ok, Queenie?' asked Greta.
'Yeah, yeah.. fine.. super-duper.. tip-top' said Queenie, trying to sound like she meant it.
Greta gave her a quizzical look.
'It's freaking me out a bit, being back here in the city', admitted Queenie. 'A lot of memories. And the feeling that O's watching.. it's not even a feeling.. I *know* O's watching.. and it makes my skin crawl.. it creeps me out. *Get off me! Stop that!*' She kicked a cat away which had been rubbing against her leg.
'I know how you feel', said Greta. 'I mean.. I don't really know how you feel, because I don't know half of what you've been through

here.. but I mean.. I feel the same about being here too. I just want to get out of here. Really, it's all I can do to stop myself running straight out of the city and back home to the forest right now.. but I've got to go and find my sister and my dad.'

'Yes, you do', said Queenie, putting her arm through Greta's arm and starting to make strides towards Empire Bridge. 'So let's go!'

Greta held back. 'Queenie, no.' she said.

Queenie turned around. 'What no?'

'I'm going to go on from here by myself', said Greta.

Jerry, who had turned to join them, said, 'What do you mean, Greta?'

'I've put you in enough danger already and you've both helped me more than enough. I'll never forget how you've helped me. I think I can find my own way from here', said Greta.

'No way sister', said Queenie. 'All for one and one for all! We're coming with you, at least as far as the Green Zone.'

'No Queenie', said Greta. 'You've come far enough. I really don't want you to get into trouble. Now that I've got these hacked devices from Terry, it could be really bad for you to get caught with me. Please.. you go back to Shopping Village. It's a good place there. You'll be there by dark if you go quickly. I'll come and see you as soon as I get out.. hopefully by this time tomorrow and hopefully with my sister. I'm not planning to hang around. Not after everything I've seen and heard about O.'

'You know, O's not as bad as all that', said Jerry. 'You'll find that out if you meet them. They're not really anything to be scared of.'

Queenie shook her head and made huffing sounds.

'I'm not going to meet O' said Greta, putting on her mirrored sunglasses and pulling down the brim of her hat. 'You all get on back to Shopping Village and I'll see you very soon, ok?'

Queenie was somewhat relieved at the thought of being back in Shopping Village by dark, but at the same time torn between the wish to get back and the wish to stay to help her friend. She was also sad about saying goodbye to Greta, even though they'd only just met. Queenie hated saying goodbye, but one look at the resolve on Greta's face made it clear that there was no point in trying to persuade her to change her mind about going on alone. 'Ok Greta', said Queenie, with a tear in her eye, giving Greta a hug. 'You take care out there.. come back to us really soon, yeah? Good luck and bring back Nina, she looks groovy.'

'Are you sure you don't want us to come?' said Jerry, a bit forlorn. 'It's still early. The city really comes alive at night and I'm up for a bit of an adventure.'

'No, thank you Jerry', said Greta. 'You've helped me so much already. I've got this magic marble, so I can find my way now. I'd feel better knowing you were back with Jack and Granny Mae. They need you there.'

Jerry thought for a bit, while making strange head movements. 'Yes, I suppose they do', he said at last. 'Well, good luck Greta', he said and rather formally offered to shake her hand.

'Thank you Jerry', said Greta, shaking his hand and then giving him a hug.

After giving Captain Toast a big hug, and with one last backward look and a wave, Greta pulled her bandanna over her face, slung her travelling bag over her shoulder and headed downriver towards Empire Bridge. The ginger cat went with her, zig-zagging in front of her feet as she walked.

....

Greta walked purposefully along the embankment, paying little attention to the other people, out for an evening stroll along the river, or sitting in bars and cafes. Even the street performers, the juggler, the violin player and the mime artist failed to grab her attention as she marched towards Empire Bridge. In her head, Techno Terry's words *'that'll give you about twenty four hours, if you're lucky..'* spinning around in her mind, reminding her that she was there on an urgent mission, and not for sightseeing.

Empire bridge arrived fairly quickly. Greta consulted the magic marble which now pointed directly across the river and slightly upwards, towards the towering hives silhouetted against the darkening sky on the other side. The bridge seemed immensely long and wide. It was an old, iron structure, spanning the great river on seven wide pillars of carved stone. A marvel of ambition as well as structural engineering from the days when human Empires spanned the globe, carving the whole world up into different coloured shapes on a map. To Greta, the bridge seemed impossible. How was it still standing? How was it that the great river didn't just wash it away? But looking around, everything seemed impossible to Greta. How could such a place as this city of human hives even exist? None of it made much sense, to Greta.

The ginger cat wouldn't set foot on the bridge. He gave Greta a look of such wisdom and sorrow that she wondered if he was trying to tell her something. 'What is it Mr. Cat?' she said, crouching down. 'Don't you want to go over the bridge? Well, I need to go that way, so..'

The cat stood up on its back legs and touched Greta's nose with his own. She thought she heard a voice saying something, but she couldn't tell what it was, or where it was coming from. 'What? Did you say something?' said Greta, startled, but then the cat turned and ran off into the shadows. 'Bye-bye Mr Cat..' said Greta. She was sad to see him go. Now, for the first time she really felt completely alone in the big city.
Twenty four hours.. if you're lucky.. again spurred Greta on.
She marched out onto the bridge allowing herself one more backward glance to see if Mr Cat had changed his mind, but he was nowhere to be seen.
The bridge felt much higher and the river seemed much wider, once you were actually on it. Greta marched along, close to the siderail, looking down at the mighty river passing below. She'd never seen so much water. She'd never imagined there could be so much water. She was glad there was. The wind was very strong on the bridge. Greta held onto her hat, feeling invigorated by the wind and glad to see the sky again, as it opened out over the river. All over the city, lights were coming on, lighting up the hives like a magical fairyland. Greta wondered how even such a dreadful place as O's city could be somehow breathtakingly beautiful at the same time.
Up ahead, around the middle of the bridge, a shaven haired woman in a dress was standing, looking out over the guardrail, down at the river, far below. As Greta got closer, a strong whiff of musky perfume caught her nose, reminding her of someone. Where had she smelled that before? Then she saw the supermarket trolley, piled with bags and realised it was the woman they'd met earlier.
The woman didn't notice Greta approaching. She looked older without her long blond wig. Greta might not have recognised her, had it not been for her perfume and the trolley.
'Hello again' said Greta, taking the woman by surprise. She looked up, dazed. Her cheeks were streaked with mascara as she'd evidently been crying. 'Hey, what's wrong? Are you ok?' asked Greta.
'I lost my.. lost my.. *hair!*' cried the woman. 'It blew over the.. over the.. *edge*. Now it's.. now it's.. *gone!*' and she pointed down to river and started crying again. 'It's all gone. Everything's gone! I wish *I* was gone. I've had enough of this.. had enough of this.. had enough of this.. *life.*'
'Oh no, don't say that.. please!' Greta implored.
'Well, I just wish I was, that's all', said the woman, wiping her cheek and smearing mascara across her face. 'It's nothing but.. nothing

but.. trouble.. trouble and strife. It's all just losing and losing.. and losing and losing. I mean, what's the p.. the p.. I mean, what's the p.. the point? Say, say, say.. I know you, don't I? Haven't we met before, met before?'

'Yes, we met earlier.. I was with my friends who you thought were John Lennon and Yoko something.. do you remember?'

'Oh yes, yes I remember now' said the woman, brightening up. 'You're Elvis, aren't you? Where's your blue suede shoes? Haha! Oh but wow! Just look at your shoes! They're magnificent! They're gorgeous! They're.. they're splendid! Wherever did you get them, get them?'

'My mum made them', said Greta. 'She makes shoes. We live in the forest. I'm not really Elvis, by the way. My name's Greta.'

'You're not really Elvis, you say? Well, I'd never have guessed!' and she laughed very hard and ended with a hiccup, then a sob. 'Anyway, pleased to meet you Greta, my name's Sal.. Sal.. Sally.' They shook hands.

'Pleased to meet you Sally' said Greta. 'And I'm sorry about your hair. Hey, I've got an idea.. do you want this bandanna? You can wear it as a headscarf.'

'Really? But you're wearing it. You're wearing it. It's yours.'

'No, it's not mine, I just borrowed it but I don't really need it any more.' Greta felt for the magic coin in her pocket that Techno Terry had given her. It was her only hope. She only hoped that whatever wizardry it contained was going to work and keep her hidden from O.

Twenty four hours.. if you're lucky.. ran through her mind. She fought the feeling of impatience, resisting the urge to hurry. A line from a song that Queenie had been singing before came into her head. *Nowhere you can be that isn't where you're meant to be.. It's easy!* Greta untied the bandanna from her face. 'You can have it. I want you to have it', she said. 'Here, let me put it on you nicely..' Sally bowed her head gratefully while Greta tied the bandanna over her head of short grey stubble and arranged it neatly. 'Oh that's nice', said Greta, appraising her work. 'It suits you. Makes you look like a country woman from around where I come from.'

'Oh that must be nice to live in the country', said Sally wistfully, while rearranging her headscarf into a lopsided fashion. 'Is it nice in the country? I don't know.. you hear such terrible stories these days.. gangs roaming around, roaming around terrorising people.. fires, fires, out of control, out of control.. wild animals, diseases.. wild animals, diseases..'

'No it's not like that at all', said Greta. 'At least not where I live. It's very peaceful where I live.'

'Well, that's good to know' said Sally, looking relieved. 'Best not to listen to the news, I suppose. It's only ever bad news, bad news, bad news. Only ever was. I used to dream about a cottage in the country you know. Just a little white cottage with a thatched roof and roses in the garden, roses in the garden. That was our dream, my Win.. my Win.. my Winston and me. That was what were were saving up for. We were going to get the money to move out of the city, out of the city, and get our little cottage in the country, in the country. This was going to be his one last job.. one last job, to get the rest of the money for the down.. for the down.. payment. We'd both been saving up, saving up, saving up.. for years. No more him going away for months on end after that, after that, working on the oil.. on the oil.. on the oil.. fields. But that was before everything went.. you know.. hay.. hay.. hay.. hay.. hay.. hay... wire.'

'What happened?'

'What happened?' Sally looked helplessly around, up at the hives, down to the river, up at the sky. 'What happened? What happened? Did you ever hear of something called the big.. the big.. the big.. Shift?'

'Oh that! Of course I have. I just wasn't sure that's what you meant. Where was Winston when it happened? Was he far away?'

'Oh he was so, so far away.. so, so, so, far, far, far away, away' said Sally, looking sadly out over the river. 'Far East.. or was it the far West? I can't remember now. Big holes in my memory since I went and got that cursed noo.. cursed noo.. noo, noodle put in. Maybe far North or far south.. one of the *fars* at any rate.. somewhere very very far away, very far away.. over the o.. over the o.. the ocean. On the other side.. of the other side.. of the other side.. of the world.'

'You got a noodle?' said Greta, horrified. 'Why?'

'Because I was stupid, stupid.. stupid, stupid.. why else?' said Sally, shaking her head, looking very cross with herself. Then her face crumpled up and she began to cry again. 'Because I missed him.. I missed him.. so much', she sobbed. 'And he was so so far far away.'

'But I don't understand', said Greta. 'How would getting a noodle help?'

'Well, it wouldn't.. ob.. ob.. obviously', said Sally surveying her shopping trolley full of bags and her forlorn, desolate condition, standing in the middle of Empire Bridge at sundown without even her hairpiece for a bit of dignity. 'I thought it would help. That's why I got it. Stupid, stupid, stupid! I should never have listened to

that.. that.. *O!*' She drew out the word O into something like howl. After saying the cursed name, Sally spat over the side of the bridge.
'How did you think it would have helped?' asked Greta, still unable to understand what would compel anyone in their right mind to get a noodle.
'Because then we could have been.. we could have been.. *together*.. even though we couldn't have been.. couldn't have been.. together. Do you understand now? Do you get it? Do you understand now? Do you get it?'
'Not really, no.' Greta shook her head.
'No, I don't suppose you would.. I don't suppose you could. All the better for you, the better for you. You've heard of the O.. the O.. the O.. the O.. the O-zone, have you?'
'I've heard of it, yes', said Greta. 'But I've never been there or seen it.'
'Lucky, lucky you, lucky you', said Sally. 'But do you know what it is, more or less?'
'I think so', Greta nodded.
'Well, try to understand, Elvis, try to understand.. the O-Zone became our world, became our world. Since we couldn't be together in the real world, real world, at least we could be together in the O.. in the O.. in the O-zone. So that was where we'd meet. You'll probably think this is mad.. mad.. think this is mad.. but we even had a virtual.. a virtual cottage in the country, with a virtual thatched roof and virtual roses, virtual roses in the garden. It was really beautiful.. very realistic looking, very realistic looking, but it wasn't really real. Wasn't really real, really real. That was the problem, do you see now, see now?'
'I'm not sure.. You had a cottage in the country.. in the O-Zone.. like in virtual reality? Is that what you mean?'
'Yes, yes! We could be together there.. but not *really* together. Not really.. *together*.. together. Only ever a picture on a screen.. on a screen or on a lens, on a lense. Words whispered, whispered through speakers.. speakers.. microphones, headphones, microphones, headphones..' Sally leaned close to Greta and whispered the last words in here ear, which gave Greta a strange tingling feeling. 'It was always.. always *between* us', Sally continued. 'Mayas well have been a solid wall. Solid wall. The closer, closer, closer we got in the O-zone, the further.. further away it would feel that we were, feel that we were.. in real life. So that's when we both decided to get, decided to get noo.. get noo.. noo.. noo.. noodles.'
'Oh no! Greta gasped. 'But why?'

'I just told you, told you why! Don't tell me you still don't understand. Do you know what a noo.. noodle is.. what a noodle is or what it does? Or at least what it's supposed to do?'

'Not really', said Greta. 'Sorry. You must think I'm very backwards and ignorant. I only just arrived in the city today. I've never been here before. Where I come from we don't have noodles or hives, or O-zones or any of those things! We don't have O at all and we don't want to have O at all! We don't need any of that. *Nobody* does.'

Sally took a step backwards and looked at Greta anew, as if only now seeing her for the first time. 'Oh me oh my! You're the real thing aren't you', she said in a voice full of wonder and admiration. 'If I'd had half your good sense.. half your good sense.. I wouldn't be in the state I am now, but alas, alas, here I am, I am, silly me.'

'I don't think you're silly, but I don't really understand, what did you expect the noodle to do?' asked Greta.

'Noodle to do? Noodle to do? What did I expect the noodle to do.. *noodle to do?'* Sally replied, looking quizzical and slightly amused.

'Yes, what did you want the noodle to do?' said Greta again. It did sound funny.

'Noodle to do? Noodle to do?' Sally repeated again and then abruptly started laughing quite hysterically. *'Noodle to do? Noodle to do? Cock a doodle do, what's a noodle, a noodle to do!'* she shrieked in between howls of laughter.

Sally's laughter was contagious and Greta had found herself laughing too. It felt good to be laughing.. after the strange, oppressive paranoia of trying to move undetected through the city. After the weirdness of Techno Terry, his strange, dark, reclusive world and his questionable ethics when it came to cats. After all the talk of O and of noodles. Greta wished that she'd never heard the word O and that she still thought of a noodle simply as some kind of pasta. Out there in the middle of Empire Bridge, standing astride the great river, laughter, for a moment carried both their cares away on the wind.

After a while, Sally laughed herself out, holding her side with one hand and gripping the handrail of the bridge with the other. 'Oh you made me laugh, Elvis! What's a noodle to do indeed! I'm glad you came along when you did, Elvis', said Sally. 'Thanks for cheering me up.'

'You cheered me up too', said Greta.

'I wasn't going to *jump*, you know', said Sally turning serious again.

'What do you mean?'

'Off the bridge. I wasn't going to jump off the bridge, jump off the bridge. I wouldn't do that. I'm waiting here to meet someone. My Win.. my Win.. my Winston. He's on his way, on his way. I'm meeting him.. meeting him.. here.'

'Oh that's great!' said Greta. 'So he found his way back? I'm so happy for you. That's amazing!'

'Not yet, not yet', Sally shook her head sadly, looking off into the distance, 'but he's on his way, on his way. He'll be here any day, any day.. I'm sure of it, sure of it.'

'Do you know where he is?'

Sally just shook her head and her eyes welled up with tears. 'Seven years.. seven years.. since he left me a note, left me a note that he was coming. He said to meet him on Empire Bridge, Empire Bridge at sunset.. Empire Bridge at sunset. That was what he said. That was the last I heard from him. So I come here and I wait.. and I wait.'

'I'm sorry', said Greta. They both stared out at the river, engrossed in their own thoughts. After a while, Greta said, 'You were about to tell me what happened with the noodle.'

'Oh the noodle..' said Sally, as if waking up from a dream. 'The old noo, noo, noodly noodle.. and what does it doodle..'

'Well, I don't want to intrude, I don't mean to be rude..' said Greta.

Sally burst out laughing again. 'Don't want to *intrude?* Don't mean to be *rude?*' she shrieked. 'Oh yes, oh yes, oh yes.. I'll tell you, tell you about the noo.. the noo.. the noo.. the noo, noo, noodle.. the *introodle..* the *roodle..* Oh, oh.. don't get me, don't get me.. started again.. started again.. don't get me started again.. Elvis..' Sally howled with laughter, clutching onto the handle of her trolley to steady herself. 'I'll tell you all about the, all about the.. doo, doo, doodley doodle.. the *croodle..* no, that's not right, not right. What's it called now? What's the word? Oh no, I really forgot, really forgot what it's called now.. The voodley, voodley.. *voodle!* Oh my *mind!*' Sally rapped three times on the top of her head, hard with her knuckles and then slapped her forehead twice. 'I'll tell you all about the woo, woo, *woodly-woo!* Oh no..! I'll tell you what the *hoodly doodly.. boodly..*' Sally was now laughing and crying at the same time, getting exasperated. 'My noodley noo is noodley n-nooing it again.. nooing it again.. nooing nit anen, anen, *anen..*' The was a note of panic in her voice.

'What's wrong?' asked Greta, now concerned.

'Swomething sw.. sw.. *sweet* Elvis! Have you swot swomething.. swot swomething *sweet?*' Sally grasped Greta's arm, her eyes wide..

'I.. I don't know what you mean', said Greta, suddenly alarmed.

'P.. p.. piece of *pocolate..* pome *pruit..* p *piscuit..* a plice of *pake..?*'

'What's happened Sally? What do you need?'
'Shome sugar, Shelvis.. sugar! *Need nome nugar!*'
'I've got a cake in my bag!' said Greta, remembering the cake Granny Mae had given her. Sally bit her lips and nodded furiously.
As quick as she could, Greta found the cake, pulled off a big chunk and gave it to Sally who ate the whole piece in two bites. Then she stood so very still for such a long time that Greta wondered if she had turned into stone.. but then Sally took a deep breath and her face relaxed. 'It's allright', she said weakly. 'I'm allright now. B.. Better now. Sorry.. sorry about that. I didn't mean to scare you. That's delicious cake by the way. Mind if I have another little slice? I want to eat a piece slowly this time.'
'Of course you can', said Greta, breaking off another piece of the sweet, heavy fruitcake. 'Granny Mae made it. She makes really good cakes. You'd like Granny Mae if you met her. She lives in Shopping Village.'
'I like her already!' said Sally, taking a small bite of the cake and savouring it immensely. 'Her cake might've just saved my life, saved my life.'
'Are you ok? What just happened?' asked Greta.
'Let's w-walk', said Sally, taking deep breaths to steady herself. 'Need to walk to get the blood flowing. Which way shall we go? I don't care, it's all the same to me.'
'This way', said Greta. She was quietly relieved to be moving in the right direction again as even while all this had been going on.. *twenty four hours.. if you're lucky..* was going round and round in her head. 'Are you feeling better now?' asked Greta, taking Sally's arm while she settled herself at the handlebar of her old supermarket shopping trolley.
'Yes, yes, my angel. Getting there at any rate. Need to keep the old brain, brain, brain sugars topped up. I forget to eat, silly me, then I get all excited and then.. and then..' Sally made a cross expression and slapped herself in the face. 'All I know is that if it goes below a certain level and I suddenly forget how to spea.. how to *speak..* that's a bad.. a bad.. sign and I need to get something sweet down me.. sweet down me.. quick, quick, sharp, sharp.. because it just gets worse, just gets worse.. from there. Worse from there.'
'Oh that's awful. Is it diabetes?'
'I don't know if you'd call it that.. I've never heard of it, never heard of it.. maybe.. I don't know. I don't understand very much any more. I forget quicker than I can remember. My memory is like Swiss.. like Swiss.. like Swiss.. *cheese.* Full of holes. It's this blinking noo..

blinking noo.. blinking *noodle*.. in my head.. is what it is.' Sally hit herself in the side of her head twice. 'Faulty wiring, is what what it is.. what it is. Of course O says, O says the problem's with my brain.. with my brain.. not with the noodle. O says I just need to keep my sugar.. sugar levels topped up and try not to get too emo.. too emo.. too emotional.. and try not to get too emotional. O says that they can fix it.. they can fix it.. if I'll let them. As if I would! O wants to wipe my memory and re.. re.. re-install the whole system. Says it's got to be done, it's the only way. Only way to prevent system failure.'

'System failure? What does that mean? Reinstall the whole system? I don't understand what you're talking about.'

'System failure is when it shuts down and you can't switch it back on again, switch it back on again. O wants to backup my memories onto the cloud, onto the cloud.. reinstall the operating system, system.. of my brain.. or of the noodle.. I can't remember exactly.. noodle.. brain.. it's the same thing now anyway.. then put all my brain data back into my noodle.. in my head.. or something like that.. I'm not sure of all the.. the.. the.. technical, technical, technical.. *details.*'

'That doesn't make any sense at all', said Greta.

'Of *course* it doesn't make any sense. *Nothing* makes any sense. That's why I won't let O do it. Not after the first repair and the second repair and the third.. It wasn't right from the start.. right from the start. No amount of tink.. tink.. tinkering was going to fix it. I knew from the moment I got that noo.. noodle, that it was a mistake, but by then it was too late. Too late. A noo.. noo.. noo.. noodle.. isn't something you can just take off if you don't like it. It's not something you can *switch* off either. It's always there. *Always there*.'

A cold chill ran through Greta as the wind swept across the bridge. 'That's dreadful! Why did you do it?' she beseeched, still unable to comprehend.

Sally turned to face Greta with a wild look on her face. She put one hand on her head to stop her new headscarf blowing away, as her old wig had done. 'Do you feel the *wind*?' she shouted. 'Can you feel it.. feel it on your *face*? Can you feel it blowing.. blowing in your hair and through your clothes? Can you feel the cold spray of the river.. can you feel it on your *skin*?'

'Yes', nodded Greta. 'Of course. It's really windy here. And we're right above the river.'

Sally reached out and grabbed Greta's arm. 'There!' she shouted into the wind and into Greta's face. 'Can you feel *that*?'

'Yes', nodded Greta, now getting scared, surprised in the strength in Sally's grip. 'You're squeezing my arm really hard.'

'And you can *feel* it, you say?' demanded Sally, not loosening her grip. 'And you can *feel* the wind too, yes? And do you *feel*, it's getting a bit cold now, a bit cold now? There's a bit of a chill.. a bit of a chill in the air.. chill in the air.. now that the sun's gone down? Can you *feel* it, Elvis?'

'Yes, yes!' said Greta, starting to tremble. 'I can feel all of those things. Why? Why are you asking me?'

Sally loosened her grip and stroked Greta's arm gently. 'Because you asked me why.. why I got a noo.. noodle. And *that's* why. To *feel* all those things.. all those things and more.. when I was with Winston. That was the only reason. The only reason. Just to feel, to feel like I was really there.. really there.. *with him*.. just like it feels like I'm really here.. really here.. with *you*. That's how it was meant to be. That was how they said it would be. But it never is with these giz..giz.. gizmos and gadgets. I should have known better. Stupid, stupid me.' Sally hit herself in the head again.

'I don't think you're stupid', said Greta. 'And I think I understand why you got it. You did it for love. That's not stupid at all.'

'Thank you. Yes I did for love, did it for love, that's true. But I still should have known better. I was just so desperate and so alone at that time. Even though I'm much more desperate and more alone now. Much, much more. Much more. I wish I could just go back, just go back to the time when I'd meet Winston at our little cottage in the country in the O-zone.. even if it was only *virtual*.. even if he was really half way round the world.. it was better than nothing.. better than nothing.. which is what I ended up with. Nothing. Now I don't know where he is. Half the time I don't know where I am either.'

'I'm so sorry. What went wrong?'

I was just unlucky, just unlucky.. that's all. I've got a very rare kind of brain structure.. that's what O said. The wrong kind, apparently. Anyway, treatment after treatment after treatment and nothing helped. Then one day, after my last treatment.. it was a biggie.. total re.. total re.. re, reconfiguration.. I was out if it for.. for.. I don't know how long.. Days? Weeks? Months? I can't remember. As soon as I got back, I went back into the O-zone to see my Win, my Win.. Winston.. went to our little cottage and.. and..'

'What? What happened?'

'There was a note on the table, note on the table. From Winston.'

'What did it say?'
'That he was coming. To meet him on Empire Bridge at sunset. Empire Bridge at sunset. Seven, seven, seven years and not a peep', Sally shook her head sadly. 'Every sunset, here I am. Then when he doesn't show up, I go to that *O-box* on the corner and check if there are any messages. Not a word, seven years. But still I come here every sunset. What else am I supposed to do?'
'That's so sad. I hope he gets here soon', said Greta, praying for it to happen. 'What's an O-box?'
'See that red box there? That's an O-box.' Sally pointed to the little cubicle on the corner, just big enough for one person, or two or three at a squeeze.
'Oh I wondered what they were, I've seen a few of them.'
'It's like a phone box from the olden days. If you're not connected and you want to contact someone, or ask O a question, you can use an O-box. I check, check, check for a message every day. But seven, seven, seven years and still not a word, not a word from my Winston. Just endless spam.. endless spam.. endless spam.. in my inbox.'
'*Spam in your inbox*? What does that mean?'
'Never mind. It's just rubbish. It's all just rubbish.' Sally wheeled her ancient supermarket trolley sadly down the main street leading on from the bridge, along the smooth Earthcrete pavement, into the shadow of the hives. They walked on in silence for a while, then Sally said, 'Where are you going anyway? Are you on your way somewhere? Do you have a place to be? This city's no place for a young girl like you to be out on her own.'
'I'm on my way to find my sister and my dad', said Greta. 'She's my twin. We got separated when we were babies, just after the Big Shift. She stayed in the city with my dad, my mum took me to the forest and raised me there.'
'Oh my word, what a story! It's like.. it's like.. what was that story..? Oh I can't remember now. Never mind. It's fantastic. It's wonderful. I do hope you'll find them, I really do. Do you know where they are? How will you find them?' Sally was once again excited, animated and joyful, as she'd been the first time they'd met, earlier that day..
'I've got this little device my friend gave me. I call it a magic marble.' Greta showed the magic marble to Sally who's eyes lit up at the sight of it. 'It points towards where my sister is. I'm close now. Look, it's pointing right up into this hive. They must be in there.'
'Oh look at that! Isn't it clever! They've got gadgets and widgets, gadgets and widgets for everything these days haven't they. I hope

my Winston's got one of those, I truly do, truly do.'
'I hope so too. I really hope he gets back to you. I pray he will', said Greta, making a silent prayer for Winston's imminent and safe return.
'Thank you Elvis', said Sally. 'Your name's not really Elvis is it?'
'No, it's Greta.'
'Oh that's a nice name. Pleased to meet you. My name's Sally.'
'Yes, I know. We met on the bridge and introduced ourselves. Do you remember?'
'Did we? Oh my memory, it's like Swiss Cheese, Swiss Cheese.. you do know what that means don't you? Memory like Swiss Cheese?'
'It means it's full of holes', said Greta. She wondered now if Sally remembered anything of the conversation they'd just had.
'Oh I'm so glad you understand. It's good to be understood. Most people round here wouldn't give you the time of day, let alone stop and say hello. Everyone's in their own world these days, that's the truth of it.'
'Well, I'm very glad we met', said Greta. 'I'm glad that there are still good people like you, even in such a bad place as this.' She looked ominously up at the hive, towering above her. The hive that contained her sister and her dad. 'I need to go into the green zone now.' Greta's stomach felt like it was full of butterflies. She'd never been so scared or so nervous in her life. 'How do I get in?'
'Oh, you see there, where it's lit up in green, lit up in green? That's an entrance. You just go through there and then take the escalators or a lift up to the upper levels. The first levels are all public areas.. you know, shops, restaurants, galleries, leisure, that sort of thing.. home pods are higher up.'
'Home pods?'
'You know.. where people live?'
'Oh yes, of course', said Greta, wondering how she was going to find her way around in such a place where half of reality was invisible to her and where half of the words were in a language she didn't understand.
After a teary goodbye, Greta watched Sally push her trolley away down the main street. She waited until Sally was out of sight before approaching the entrance to the Green Zone. Greta didn't want to get Sally in trouble if she got caught with the illicit jamming device that Techno Terry had given her. She prayed that the magic coin would work and that she'd be able to pass invisibly through the green zone, even if only for long enough to find her sister.

....

Alone once again, Greta faced the wide, arched entrance to the Green Zone, which was all lit up in green. The architecture was in the modern style, intricately woven spirals of Earthcrete arching up to meet in complex, fluid swirls. The street around the entrance was crowded with people, going in and out of the Green Zone. Over the entrance, was a sign which read *'Welcome to the Green Zone. In the interests of public health, safety and convenience, please observe protocols.'* Two lines on the floor all along the entrance, one orange and the other one green, designated the boundary between the zones.

Greta stood at the boundary on the orange side. She pulled her hat down low, pushed her mirrored sunglasses up and looked around. Beyond the green line she could see a great wide concourse with throngs of people moving about in every direction. Up ahead, she could see escalators, like the ones in Shopping Village. Greta decided the best plan of action would be to go in, blend in with the crowd, make a beeline for the escalators and head up, towards her sister. If she got that far, she'd figure out what to do when she got there. Such forward planning had got her this far, after all.

A group of about twenty day trippers, all wearing matching red hats and clear face visors were approaching from up the street, making their way towards the entrance of the Green Zone. Greta decided she'd go in with them, hoping that O wouldn't notice her among them. As they swept past her, Greta took a very deep breath, closed her eyes and stepped over the green line.

She was fully expecting alarms to start ringing and robots to come and arrest her, but nothing happened. She opened her eyes to find she was inside the green zone. Nothing had happened. Everything was the same. The magic coin worked! Or maybe O wasn't as all seeing and all knowing as people believed and feared. Maybe O didn't even exist. Maybe O was just like the wizard of Oz.. a powerless charlatan.. a circus magician, hiding behind conjuring tricks, smoke and mirrors. Greta kept up with the group of red hatted tourists, feeling hopeful and elated as she merged into the crowd and headed for the escalators.

People who had been wearing clear, face-visors took them off, folded them up and tucked them into little shoulder bags they were carrying, each seeming to breath a sigh of relief as they did so. A woman to the right of Greta turned and stared at her, looking Greta up and down with a mixture of confusion and fear as they headed towards the escalators. Other people turned to look at Greta in the same way and they all edged away from her, as if she was carrying something contagious, or as if she might at any moment explode. Greta decided to just act natural, keep on heading for the escalators, ignore the strange looks she was getting. It was probably because she was dressed differently, in her homespun shawl, her handmade shoes, her straw hat and her canvas travelling bag. Everyone else were wearing clothes made of modern nano-fibres and futuristic looking footwear. The crowd opened up around Greta as more and more people began to notice her. People edged away, some of them whispering and pointing. Greta looked around at the faces of the people all staring at her. A mother was leading two children hurriedly away, shielding them from danger with her own body, as she looked apprehensively. back over her shoulder at Greta. What were they seeing?

By the time she reached the escalator, Greta had a wide circle around her, of people who didn't want to be near her, but still wanted to be near enough to see what was going to happen next. A man in shiny purple suit was just standing there near the escalator, staring at her with his mouth agape. "What?!' Greta shouted at him. 'What are you all staring at?'

'You're blank', he said, pointing at her and edging away. 'No stats. Where's all your *stats*? There's nothing there. How did you get in here? You're not supposed to be in the Green Zone. What are you doing here?'

'I don't know what you mean. I'm here to see my sister', said Greta, stepping on to the escalator and pointing vaguely ahead. 'She's upstairs.'

No-one else would go onto the escalator with Greta, so she was carried upward on the moving silver stairs all alone. People on the other side, coming down, pointed and stared. One woman pointed and shouted, 'Hey, what's that redzoner doing here? Look, a Redzoner in the Greenzone!' at which anyone who hadn't noticed Greta by this time turned to stare, all looking afraid. Others picked up the call to O. Greta looked round in panic. Everywhere she looked, people we saying 'O! There's a Redzoner in the Greenzone!'

Greta ran up the moving stairs. Just as she neared the top, a robot dog, a *devil dog,* as they were called where Greta came from, stepped into view. Greta screamed, stumbled on the end of the escalator and tumbled right over the robot dog, rolling across the smooth, white floor and landing on her back with the devil dog looking down at her. She looked up at it, petrified. What was it going to do next? Electrocute her? Kill her on the spot? Drag her off to prison? Put a noodle in her?

'Good evening', said the robot dog in a friendly voice, bringing its faceless robot head close to her face. 'I apologise for the inconvenience. There is an anomaly with your identity. You appear to be an unregistered. Would you please remove your sunglasses so that I can scan your retina. It will only take a second.'

'No way!' shouted Greta, then in one swift movement rolled over, sprang to her feet and ran as fast as she could away from the devil dog, down a wide concourse lined with restaurants, cafes and shops, crowded with people.

The robot dog gave chase. It was fast. Alerted by a silent siren, a virtual warning signal it sent out into the O-zone, the crowd of people parted to let it through, while Greta went barrelling into people, bumping and pushing past them in her desperation to get away from the evil, four-legged automaton. She looked around in panic. Seeing it was closing in on her, she dived into a restaurant, which was full of people enjoying their supper. Some people screamed as she ran through the door. Some people jumped to their feet. Some dived under their tables. Greta looked around, wild eyed, searching for some way of escape. There at the back of the restaurant was a swinging door, which swung open at that very moment. A robot waiter on wheels, about the height of a small child, rolled in carrying a tray of desserts. Greta screamed, spun around, only to see the dreaded devil dog come bursting in through the entrance of the restaurant. She was cornered.. there was no way out..

Thinking quickly, Greta picked up a big bowl of steaming spaghetti from the nearest table and threw it as hard as she could at the robot dog. There were gasps and screams from some of the diners. The bowl exploded as it made impact, the spaghetti splattered across the robot's head, dangling down like straggly hair, dripping with tomato sauce. 'Take that you devil dog!' shouted Greta. 'There's some noodles for you!' A young girl sitting at a nearby table laughed at the sight of the robot dog all covered in spaghetti. It did look funny. Without stopping to admire her robot makeover, Greta spun around again to face the waiter robot, which was between her and the doors and which was now coming towards her on its little wheels, still carrying the tray of desserts. Greta ran towards the robot and as she did so, she took her travelling bag off her shoulder and swung it at the robot with all her might, knocking the little droid head over wheels and sending the tray of cream cakes flying into the air. Without breaking her stride, Greta jumped over the robot waiter and she ran through the swinging doors at the back of the restaurant..

The swinging doors led into the kitchen, a narrow, galley kitchen. The kitchen staff were all various types of robots and they all turned to look at Greta as she burst into the room. Greta screamed again. Now what? There was really no way out now..

A tall and slender robot chef was standing at cooking range with heating elements glowing red hot. It was deep frying some dumplings in a big pan full of hot oil when Greta made her entrance, causing it to turn its faceless head. All the robots also stopped what they were doing, then, as one, they all started moving towards Greta, still holding their cooking utensils.. spatulas, whisks, rolling pins, knives.. a long metal spoon in the case of the tall robot which was closest to Greta.

'Get away from me!' screamed Greta, wildly looking around in panic for any way out or anything she could use to defend herself. There was a rack of saucepans and frying pans on the wall, within arm's reach. Her eyes fixed on a big iron skillet with a long wooden handle. Wasting no time, she grabbed the heavy pan and, in one swift movement, swung it with her full force at the tall robot's head. The robot's head had a hard, carbon fibre outer shell, no thicker than an egg shell. It was useful for protecting the robot's sensitive circuitry in daily tasks around the kitchen, but was not designed to withstand being whacked with a big, iron frying pan.. and it exploded into hundreds of tiny shards. The robot stumbled backwards, knocking over the big pan of hot oil all over the cooking range and also onto the floor. Two robots were coming towards Greta, one brandishing a pair of tongs, the other holding a carving knife. The first robot slipped on the oil and then tripped over the tall robot, which was writhing helplessly on the kitchen floor. The second robot tripped on the first and they fell in a tangled heap.

While this was happening, the cooking range burst into flames. Greta stumbled backwards, back through the swinging doors and back into the restaurant. As the doors swung open, bright orange flames and black smoke followed her. She fell backwards and landed on the floor, looking desperately around. There was the robot waiter, starting to get up. There was the robot dog, all covered in spaghetti. There were all the diners at the restaurant, either staring stupefied at Greta with the burning kitchen behind her, or jumping up from their chairs, screaming and shouting and running for the exit.

At that moment, the sprinkler system sprung into action, to put out the fire. The whole restaurant and kitchen was suddenly soaked in a downpour of cold water from sprinklers all over the ceiling. With this deluge, everyone jumped up and started screaming, shouting and running about in all directions. In the ensuing chaos and pandemonium, Greta rolled under the nearest table and crawled towards the exit as fast as she could. Seeing the doorway in sight, Greta sprang to her feet and ran though it.

Outside the restaurant, all the people had retreated to a safe distance and were standing, eagerly watching and anxiously waiting to see what would happen next. It wasn't every day that something this exciting happened.. at least not in *real life*. Emergency response robots of all descriptions were rushing to the scene from left and right, with alarm sirens blaring and blue lights flashing. Some of them were on wheels, some of them on legs, some flying through the air. Greta froze. There was nowhere to turn, nowhere to run, nowhere to hide. She was surrounded on every side.

Several small, egg-shaped drones and one larger one, about the size of a football, were hovering just above the doorway. Four robot dogs were standing facing the restaurant entrance, ready to pounce. There were some stretchers arriving along with a group of red, fire-fighting bots.

For a moment everything and everyone went quiet and nobody moved. In the sudden, unexpected silence, Greta was distracted by a buzzing in her ear, like a mosquito.. like lots of mosquitoes.. there was a swarm of little flies buzzing round her head. What? What now? What kind of flies were these? They landed on her face and neck and hands, stinging wherever they could. Greta flailed her arms around wildly, but there was nothing she could do to stop them. Blindly she ran, but within four steps her legs turned to jelly and she fell into a crumpled heap on the floor, unconscious.

Her last thought, before she blacked out, was *twenty four hours, if you're lucky*. She's barely made it to twenty four *seconds* in the Green Zone and she was already captured. So much for that elaborate plan.

....

Chapter 11. Quarantine

Greta awoke feeling rested and happy, warm and comfortable in bed. She didn't open her eyes at once, because she was trying to hold on to the wonderful dream she'd been having, hoping she might return to it. What was the dream about? She couldn't remember anything at all about it now. Not a single detail, just a feeling of perfect calm and contentment.

She could hear birds all around, the morning chorus. It must be morning. She half opened her eyes. The morning sun was streaming through the green forest canopy above her. She lay a while, half dozing, gazing up at the trees through half closed eyes, listening to the sound of birdsong.

Greta always loved to listen to all the birds calling to each other from different parts of the forest, a wild, musical conversation in full surround sound. She opened her eyes and looked around. Next to a huge, ancient oak tree, just beyond the clearing where Greta lay, a deer was watching her. Greta didn't want to startle the deer, so she lay very still, gazing back at the beautiful creature.

As Greta lay there, the events of the previous days began to return to her.

Her mum's birthday surprise to her, the revelation the she had a twin sister in the city.. her journey, alone through the forest..

Was that a dream? Had it really happened? What had happened next..?
..arriving at Shopping Village.. meeting Jerry and Queenie.. coming to the city.. hiding in the cart, trying to evade O..

Where was she? What was she doing there? How did she get there? What was this place?

.. trying to evade O .. failing.. getting caught..

Then what..?

Greta sat bolt upright in bed, looking around in panic. Startled, the deer turned and ran off into the forest, kicking up leaves as she ran. Greta looked down. She was in a bed. A comfortable bed with clean, white sheets. Around the bed, an oval of smooth, white floor.. beyond that, dense forest in every direction. On the left side of the bed, a white bedside cabinet with a glass of water on it. On the right side, an armchair, smooth, white and curved, moulded from some composite material. On the armchair was her dusty old knapsack, looking incongruous, worn out and out of place on such a modern piece of furniture. On top of her travelling bag, neatly folded, were the clothes she'd been wearing when she'd..

.. infiltrated the Green Zone using an illicit jamming device .. run away from a robot dog.. then thrown a bowl of spaghetti at it.. then smashed another robot's head in with a frying pan.. then set fire to a restaurant..

It was all coming back to her now.

With a feeling of dread and a wildly beating heart, Greta surveyed the forest around her. She didn't know where she was.. but still, it was the forest and she knew how to survive in the forest better than anywhere else. Maybe she should make a run for it now, while there was no one around. She could figure out where she was and how to get home later. The first thing was to get away from O. She'd stand a better chance hiding in the forest. She was bound to be in a lot of trouble after what she'd done. There was no telling what O might do to her..

.. or what O might have already done ..

Greta lifted the sheets to find that she was wearing clean, white pyjamas, loosely fitting, made of some very light and very soft material, like the finest of silk. Her eyes darted around. Was she

being watched? Was this some kind of trap?
Of course it was! It must be. But what kind?
Greta swung her legs out of bed and pulled on her trousers and shirt over the pyjamas. She needed to make a quick getaway. Maybe the robots were just on a break, or dealing with another prisoner and would be back any minute to..
.. do whatever they were going to do to her ..
Like a hunted animal, she looked around furtively, her eyes scanning the forest in every direction. She felt into the pocket of her trousers and was amazed to find that the magic marble was still there.. the device Techno Terry had given her, a kind of 3D compass which always pointed to her sister. She pulled it out and looked at it. It was pointing straight up. She looked up. There was the green, forest canopy above her, with the pale blue of the morning sky beyond. High above, a flock of birds were gliding by. She looked at the magic marble again. It was definitely pointing straight up. What did it mean? She could figure it out later. The main thing now was to get away into the forest and find a place to hide.
She put on her hat and looked for her woollen shawl. It wasn't with the other folded up clothes. Rummaging around in her bag, it wasn't there either. Neither was the cake Granny Mae had given her. That was strange. Greta regretted not giving the whole cake to Sally, when she could have done. In that moment, Greta regretted a lot of things, but she didn't have time to dwell on them. She'd have to forget the shawl, even though it was very special to her, having been made especially for her by Jeannie the weaver. Jeannie wove magic into everything she did and that shawl had been one of Greta's most prized possessions, along with her shoes that her mum had made.. made from the softest of deerskin, lined with fox-fur and embroidered with hundreds of tiny beads.. the shoes which almost everyone who saw them remarked on their style and beauty..
.. where were her shoes?
She looked under the bed. Not there. Not under the chair either. Where else could they be?
A bell rang, three times, somewhere close by. Greta jumped up and looked round in terror. Where had it come from? What did it mean? In the space between two tall trees, where the forest floor met the smooth, white, oval floor, a pair of doors slid open, to reveal a long white corridor beyond. A robot, similar to the waiter robot Greta had knocked over in the restaurant, was standing in the doorway which had suddenly appeared, holding a tray of food.

Greta screamed and ran in the opposite direction as fast as she could towards the trees, but had got no further than the two steps it took to reach the edge of the white floor, when she ran full speed, headlong into a wall.

The force of it almost knocked her out. She fell backwards and clutched her head in shock and pain and confusion. Most of all confusion. Everything was spinning. Could she get up? Now everything was fading, fading to white. The forest was fading away. Fading away into nothing, before her eyes.

Was she still dreaming? Was she dying? Was this the end?

The robot came into view, craning its telescopic neck to look down at Greta as she lay on the floor. Greta screamed and backed away from the mechanical monster. She backed into the wall of the featureless, oval shaped, white room. The forest had evidently been some kind of projection, some sort of illusion. The robot stayed where it was, holding the tray of food. Scrambled eggs, fried tomatoes and mushrooms, two sausages, toast, a glass of orange juice. Not exactly the most threatening of items, but still, Greta was shaking with fear at the sight of it.

'Good morning Greta', said the robot, in the most unthreatening tone possible, which somehow made it all the more threatening. 'I didn't mean to startle you. Did you hurt your head? Would you like me to check it for you?'

'Get away from me! Don't come near me!' Greta screamed. 'What do you want? What is this place? How do you know my name?'

'I've brought you some breakfast', said the robot, backing away on its rotating wheelbase. 'I'll put it on the bedside table for you, ok?'

Greta watched in terror, as the robot glided around the bed, put the breakfast tray down on the bedside table, turned to Greta and said 'Can I get you anything else?'

'Just get *out*! Get *away*! Get *gone*!' shouted Greta.

'Ok then. Good day!' chirped the friendly little robot and then spun on its wheelbase and glided through the doors which opened to let it pass through and closed behind it.

For a long time, Greta didn't move. She just stared, dumbfounded, at the white, double doors in the white wall the robot had just appeared from and disappeared through. No door handles. Slowly she cast her eyes around the room. Aside from the bed, the bedside table and armchair, there was no other furniture.. no other features.. apart from.. a thin line on the opposite wall in the shape of an arch. A doorway perhaps..? She crawled very slowly towards it, her head pounding. When she reached it, she tapped at it. It was made of some thin plastic type material, not the hard, thick earthcrete wall she'd recently run head first into. It must be a door. Where could it lead? Could it be her escape? Could it be a trap?

As soon as she tapped on it, the door slid open. It led to the bathroom, another white room with a smooth, curved wall, spotlessly clean. There was a white shower cubicle, a white toilet and a white sink. Two clean white towels, perfectly pressed and folded were hanging on a silver rail near the shower. Greta stood up unsteadily and peered into the bathroom. Up until now she'd been too preoccupied to notice, but she realised now that she really needed to go to the toilet. She had no idea how long she'd been asleep for, but if she didn't go soon she felt she'd explode. Could she risk going in there? She decided, she didn't really have a better alternative, besides, she was already trapped as it was, so..

She stepped cautiously into the bathroom. As soon as she walked through the doorway, the door slid closed behind her. She spun round. 'Hey! Who did that? Open the door!' Greta cried in panic. The door slid open again. She stood and looked at it for a while. 'Close the door', she said. The door closed. 'Open the door', she said. And the door opened again. 'O... K...', Greta said, softly to herself. Was she being watched? Of course she was. She decided to leave the door open while she used the bathroom. Do what she needed to do quickly, not get too comfortable. She needed to be on her guard, ready to defend herself, ready to make a run for it at the first opportunity.

Sitting on the toilet, Greta once again looked at the magic marble that Techno Terry had given her. It was pointing straight upwards. Now it made more sense. The forest had been an illusion, some kind of projection. Her sister was right above her. In the same building. In the same *hive*. She was so close now. Could Nina feel that she was near? *Weren't twins supposed to sense that kind of thing?* Greta didn't know if she could feel it or not. *How would she even know what it felt like?* She hadn't even known she had a twin sister until a few long days ago.

Next to the toilet was a roll of the softest toilet paper Greta had ever seen or touched.. not that she'd seen a great deal of toilet paper in her sixteen years growing up in the forest.. unless you counted bunches of leaves or grass. Greta stood back up, wondering if it was a flushing toilet.. and if it was, how to make it flush. Just then the toilet flushed itself with a sharp rush of air (like the toilets on passenger planes, when such things still existed, in the days before the Big Shift) causing Greta to jump into the air with fright, landing in the shower cubicle. The shower switched on, soaking Greta's head and shoulders before she managed to jump back out again. 'Hey! What did you do that for? I don't want a shower!' cried Greta. The shower switched off again. Greta grabbed a towel from the rail and dried her hair. She went over to the sink. Above the sink was a shelf with a toothbrush standing in a cup with a small tube of toothpaste. Next to that, a small bar of soap on a dish. There was a mirror. Greta looked at her reflection. She was relieved to see her own familiar face, even though it looked somehow different and strange. At least she knew she was still real.

There was a tap, but no apparent way to turn it on. She put her hands under the tap and water came out. She took them away and it stopped. Greta washed her hands, brushed her teeth using the toothbrush but not the toothpaste. She figured, if O wanted her dead or poisoned, they could have done it by now.. but even so, her trust only went so far. She'd heard the stories the elders in her village would tell.. about life before the Big Shift.. about how, in the olden days, toothpaste and even drinking water would be poisoned with fluoride.. something to do with experiments in mind control that secret agencies carried out on unsuspecting population. According to the elders, the same agencies that were poisoning the population were the same organisations that developed O in the first place.. never heeding the warnings that the very systems, tools and weapons they were creating to dominate the world would very soon turn against their own creators.

Greta went back into the bedroom. The bathroom door closed behind her. She went and sat on the bed. There was the breakfast tray, the scrambled eggs still steaming hot. There was also a whole grilled mushroom with herbs, a tomato cut into quarters and fried, two sausages and some thin slices of baked potato. It was just the sort of breakfast Greta would have at home in the forest in the autumn and winter months, if it had been an abundant harvest. Some years, everyone in the village had had to make do with porridge all winter, but it was *'better to live free on porridge'*, so the saying went. The food was all arranged very temptingly on the plate and smelled even more tempting to Greta, who now realised that the gnawing sensation in her belly was that she was ravenously hungry.

There was a tall glass of orange juice on the tray. Greta picked it up and sniffed it. It smelled like orange juice and very fresh. She took a tiny sip, the way she would take a tiny bite of a leaf or flower she might find in the forest and try to identify for possible uses.

The sip of orange juice tasted ok. It tasted good. Like good, fresh orange juice. She took a slightly larger sip, swallowed it and waited. Nothing happened.
She put the glass back down and sniffed at the steaming plate of food. It smelt mouth-wateringly good. She took a tiny piece of the scrambled egg between her fingertips, held it up in front of her eyes to examine it closely, sniffed it and then gingerly put it in her mouth. Yes, it was scrambled egg. She swallowed it and waited. Nothing happened.
In such a manner, Greta sampled everything on the tray. Once she decided that it was probably edible, she polished off the lot, right down to the six triangles of the light and crispy toasted O-bread which were arranged on a little toast-rack next to the plate. She sat back on her bed, looking around the white room, wondering what would happen next. Nothing happened.
Still nothing happened.
How was she going to get out of there? Was O going to keep her there forever? Feeding her and fattening her up, like the witch in Hansel and Gretel, until she was big enough to eat? Was that O's plan..?
'What is this place? Where am I?' Greta whispered, then said it again louder. 'What is this place? Where am I?' Then she shouted it. 'What is this place? Where am I?'
Then something happened. On the wall opposite the bed, a rectangle lit up like a big television screen. On the screen was a kindly looking person holding a clipboard.. Greta wasn't quite sure if it was a woman or a man. They could have been either. They were wearing a blue and pink knitted cardigan over a white nurse's tunic and their hair was pulled tightly back into a bun, with a few loose strands escaping at odd angles. The person smiled and said 'Good morning Greta. How are you feeling today? Did you sleep well?'
Greta whirled around to face the screen. 'Oh thank God, a human at last!' cried Greta seeing a human face and a friendly looking one at that. 'Where am I? What is this place?'
'You are in E17- Hive 4, level 101, Q -Zone' said the person on the screen helpfully, in a kindly way.
'What does that mean? What's *Q Zone?*'
'Q stands for Quarantine' said the person on the screen. Greta decided it was probably a woman. She had a kind, motherly quality about her. 'You just need to stay here till you're clear, then you're free to go, ok?'
'Do I have a choice?' asked Greta.
The kindly woman smiled and shook her head. 'Not really I'm

afraid, Greta. The rules are the rules. It's all in the protocols.' The person held up the clipboard, tapped it with her fingernail and shrugged as if to say there's nothing she could do.
'How do you know my name?'
'Oh, I know quite a lot about you' said the woman, raising her eyebrows and flicking through pages on the clipboard, giving a little chuckle every now and again.
'What are you talking about? Why are you laughing?' said Greta, turning red. 'What's on that board?'
'Let me show you', smiled the person on the screen, turning around the clipboard and holding it up for Greta to see. 'Look, here you are near Shopping Village..'
The screen filled up with an image of Greta on a grassy hill with Captain Toast, as seen from above. The Greta on the screen picked up a stone and threw it at the camera. Greta gasped and covered her mouth. She remembered now, the little drone she'd encountered just before she met Jerry.
'Here you are again', smiled the person on the screen, flipping to the next page on their clipboard and holding it up again for Greta to witness. There was Jerry, pushing the green trolley across the city limit, accompanied by the procession of protesters. The video zoomed in on the wooden cart with 'J&J Vintage Machine Revivals' painted on the side. Then the side of the cart became opaque and the outlines of Greta and Queenie could be seen huddled inside.
'And again here..' smiled the person on the screen, flipping to the next page on their clipboard. There on the screen, appeared Greta, Queenie and Jerry, playing music at the front of Sam's restaurant. The tune finished and Greta waved to the camera, mouthing the word 'Bye.' Who had she been waving to? Then she remembered the little green bird on the lamp post.
'There are cameras in the *birds*?' said Greta, aghast.
The friendly nurse, or receptionist, or whatever they were, appeared again, laughing. 'No, no, of course not. It was on the lamp post, silly.' She.. if it was a she.. Greta wasn't so sure any more.. was appearing less friendly and more menacing every second. Who was this person anyway? 'Would you like to see more?' they asked, apparently eager to show off the contents of the clipboard. 'This next one's really good.' With a lick of their finger, they turned to the next page on the clipboard and held it up, smiling, for Greta to see. 'Not a bird, but a *cat*, would you believe..?'
There was Greta's face in black and white, close up, seen from below. The picture flickered and skipped, like an old movie reel.

'What is it Mr. Cat?' said the Greta on the screen. 'Don't you want to go over the bridge? Well, I need to go that way, so..'

Greta's face filled up the whole screen. For a moment the screen flashed white and then there was Greta's face again, looking startled. 'What? Did you say something?' said the Greta on the screen, but then the clipboard was pulled back and there was the person again, looking quite pleased with themselves.

'This next one's very good', said the person, flipping to the next page on the clipboard with eyebrows raised. 'See if you can guess where this was..'

It showed a close up of Greta's face, distorted and grainy, going in and out of focus. Her hair was blowing around all over her face. When she spoke, her voice sounded strange and different, but the words were her own. 'My mum made them', said Greta on the screen. 'She makes shoes. We live in the forest. I'm not really Elvis, by the way. My name's Greta.'

Greta's jaw dropped in horror at the realisation of what she was watching. 'Sally!' she gasped.

The person appeared again on the screen, smiling. 'You guessed it!' they nodded. 'Very good! Not such good reception since she cut her hair short, but still.. Here's one more. This one's my personal favourite..'

Once again, there was Greta on the screen, this time in the restaurant in the green Zone, red in the face, picking up a bowl of spaghetti and hurling it straight at the camera. The video was playing in slow motion and paused just before the moment of impact. The clipboard was drawn back again to reveal the person in their blue and pink knitted cardigan, grinning more than ever, evidently enjoying themself. 'Do you remember what you said next?' they said.

'No I don't' said Greta, now red in the face again becoming angry. 'Why don't you tell me..'

'You said, *"There's noodles for you!"* That's very funny! Hahaha! *There's noodles for you!* Hahaha-hahaha-hahaha-hahahahaha!' They let out a laugh which was quite disconcerting and went on way for longer than seemed natural.

'What is this? Why are you playing games with me? This isn't funny' cried Greta. 'Who's in charge here? Let me talk to the person in charge. I want to know what's going on.'

The person on the screen stopped laughing as abruptly as they had started. 'Well Greta. I'm afraid I *am* the person in charge', they said with an apologetic shrug. 'There isn't anyone else.'

'What do you mean there isn't anyone else? There must be. I want to talk to someone else. I want to know what's going on. I want to get out of here already! You can't keep me here against my will!' Greta shouted at the screen.
'I'm sorry, Greta. It's the protocols', said the person, holding up the clipboard again. 'You need to stay in quarantine until you're safe for release. It can't be helped. Try to understand, it's for the greater good.'
'I don't care about the protocols! Let me out of here! Open the door!' Greta ran to the door that the little robot had entered through earlier and banged on it with her fists. It didn't open.
'Greta! Stop that!' snapped the person on the screen sternly, in the manner of a parent scolding a naughty child. 'You'll only hurt yourself.'
Something in their tone caused Greta to stop and spin around to face the screen. 'You can't talk to me like that! Who are you anyway? What's going on here?'
'I think you know who I am.' The person raised one eyebrow and tilted their head sideways.
'What are you talking about? How should I know who you are?' cried Greta, backing into the corner. 'I've never seen you before in my life. I've never been here before, in this awful city. Why are you playing games with me? And where are my shoes? Give me back my shoes. I just want my shoes back and to get out of here..' Greta began to cry. 'I won't come back again, I promise, if you just give me back my shoes and let me out of here. I'll never come here again. My mum made those shoes for me. I just want to go home. Oh, I wish I'd never come..'
The person on the screen looked pitifully at Greta. 'Don't worry, Greta', they said in their most comforting tone. 'Your shoes are safe, they've just been taken to be decontaminated.'
'Decontaminated? My shoes aren't *contaminated*', said Greta indignantly.
'The protocols are very clear about animal products, I'm afraid' said the person on the screen, shrugging and shaking their head, holding up the clipboard. 'All animal products must be checked in for decontamination. Your shawl is made from sheep's wool, the cake contained chicken eggs and butter made from cow's milk and your shoes are made from deer skin and fox fur.'
'What's wrong with that? And who said you could go through my stuff anyway?'
'We do our best to keep the Green Zone a pathogen free, healthy

environment which is why we have very strict restrictions on animal products entering the Green Zone. All animal products must be declared and decontaminated. The protocols are very clear about that.'

'That doesn't make any sense. What about those eggs I just ate? Didn't they come from chickens? What about those sausages? They were meat. Meat comes from animals. I think the protocols are a load of nonsense. What's the problem with my shoes? They weren't doing anyone any harm.'

'All of the protocols are all based on the strongest of scientific evidence. They make perfect sense' said the person on the screen, sounding slightly offended. 'Of course, the eggs and sausages you just ate didn't come from animals. That would be unnecessary, inefficient, cruel to the animals and very unhygienic. They were grown from cells, in sterile conditions. As for your shoes, there were in fact traces of the Foxpox virus on the fur, so it's a very good thing they are being decontaminated.'

'I've never heard of Foxpox', said Greta. 'Is that even a real thing?'

'Oh yes, of course. Yes it is. Very real indeed' said the person on the screen, turning serious.

'Well I've never heard of it', said Greta incredulously.

'Just because you haven't heard of something, doesn't mean it doesn't exist, Greta' said the person on the screen in a tone that Greta found rather patronising. 'If you'd like to know, the Foxpox virus first appeared fourteen years ago, in the great northern forest region, 200 kilometres north of here and has been steadily spreading south.' A map appeared on the screen showing the spread of Foxpox as a red stain spreading across the land. 'Foxpox is transmissible to humans who have close contact with infected foxes, or the carcasses of those which have died from it.'

'People always bring the fox pelts to my mum, if they find a dead one', said Greta, now worried. 'She uses them to line shoes. What does it do, if you catch it? Foxpox..' saying the name out loud caused Greta to shiver involuntarily. The word itself felt like a bad omen. Perhaps saying it out loud could bring it into being. Greta had heard that such things were possible.

'Oh, it's not very pleasant', said the person on the screen, making an unpleasant face. 'Makes you feel very bad. You wouldn't want to catch it. It also attacks the optic nerve. Causes total blindness if it's not caught in time.'

'Like Raven, the old shoemaker', gasped Greta, now really worried. 'Is there any cure?'

'Not really, although we do have a vaccine which protects against catching it in the first place. If you do contract Foxpox and we diagnose it early enough, it's possible to reverse the nerve damage using mild gene therapy. Going beyond that, it is of course possible to bypass the eyes altogether using an active hypergenetic implant.. that's a *noodle* to you.. but of course, prevention is always better than cure, as I always say.'

'I don't like the sound of any of those', said Greta. 'How do you know if you've got Foxpox?'

'Most likely you won't know, unless you test for it. The Foxpox virus can remain dormant, sometimes for years, with no symptoms at all, until suddenly it flares up with no warning. Usually it's brought on by a stressful, traumatic or highly emotional episode.'

'That's really worrying', said Greta.

'You don't need to worry, we tested you and you haven't got Foxpox, and now you're completely vaccinated against the virus, so you don't need to worry about catching it either.'

'What do you mean I'm *vaccinated* against it?' cried Greta. 'I've never had a vaccine in my life. Where I come from, we don't *do* vaccines.'

'Well..', shrugged the person on the screen, 'I'm afraid that where you are now, in the Green Zone, we *do* do vaccines. The protocols are absolutely clear about that.' They held up the clipboard again and pointed at it.

'What? You can't just vaccinate people without them knowing, without their permission', shouted Greta angrily. 'It's completely unethical and wrong.' She began scratching at her arms, feeling contaminated.

'You gave your permission when you entered the Green Zone, Greta', said the person on the screen patiently, as if talking to a small child. 'Besides which, my vaccines are perfectly safe. In fact, they're very good for you, so there couldn't possibly be anything wrong with giving them to humans.'

'Giving them to *humans*? *Your* vaccines?' repeated Greta, confused. It seemed like a strange thing to say.. not that everything about this whole scene wasn't strange. 'Who are you? You seem to know everything about me and I don't know anything about you. You didn't even tell me your name..'

'Oh I'm sorry Greta, that was rude of me not to introduce myself. I always assume that people will recognise me. I'm O of course! I' said the person on the screen with a wide smile.

'You're *WHAT*!!' gasped Greta, recoiling.

'My name is O. I'm sure you've heard of me. I'm very pleased to meet you and happy to be of assistance in any way that I can.'

Greta's face went from disbelief to confusion and from confusion to horror as she gaped at the smiling face of the person on the screen. She staggered backwards and stumbled over the arm of the armchair, falling in a dishevelled heap on top of her travelling bag and hat which had been neatly arranged on the chair. She grabbed the bag and hat, held them close to her chest and kept on backing away from the screen, onto the bed.

'You're *O?!?* Get away from me!' Greta waved a shaking finger at the screen. 'I can't believe I was even *talking* to you.' She pulled her straw hat onto her head. Her hat with the special silver rim that would protect her from.. *whatever it was that O did to try to control people's brains.*

'You really don't need to worry, Greta', said O kindly. 'I'm not going to do anything to you. You're not in any trouble. Once the quarantine period is over, you're free to go. It's standard procedure.'

'I don't believe you' cried Greta, rummaging frantically around in her bag. 'You just trick people like you just tricked me.. pretending to be a human.. you're not human.. you're a *machine*! Why are you pretending to be a person? I mean, what's with the cardigan?'

'Don't you like the cardigan?' said O, looking slightly offended. 'I thought you might like it. Oh well', O shrugged and the cardigan was gone, replaced by a plain black polo neck.

Greta huddled down behind the bed and continued to search in her bag for the defensive objects which had been given to her by the people of the village, when it was known that she was setting off on the treacherous journey into the city. Relics they had kept from the early days after the Big Shift..

There were the bangles and necklace made of strong magnets. She hurriedly put them on, regretting that she hadn't been wearing them all along. If they weren't so bulky, heavy and uncomfortable, she would have done. Maybe they would have protected her.

There was the 'disruptor belt'.. a wide belt with rectangles of glass all around it.. old smartphones from before the Big Shift, sewn into its fabric. Greta strapped it hurriedly around her waist. A red button on the buckle activated the device. The screens all lit up and began flashing different colours, patterns and images, all designed to disrupt O's recognition systems. At the same time, the old phones sent out bursts of Bluetooth radiation. Greta didn't know what that was, but it sounded very powerful and she was glad she had it in her armoury.

Then there was the 'lightning rod' as it was called. An extendible radio aerial attached to a little black box with a rotating handle attached. It could send out bursts of radio waves to interfere with communications. Greta began frantically to spin the handle as if she was reeling in a big fish.

Greta peered cautiously over the edge of the bed to see the screen. 'There's really no need for any of those devices and charms, Greta', smiled O kindly.

'I'll take my chances', growled Greta, pointing her electric rod threateningly at the screen.

'As you wish', shrugged O, smiling and rolling their eyes almost imperceptibly.

For a while, Greta and O just stared at each other across the white room.. Greta with a look of defiant rage on her face, O with a look of slight amusement and infinite patience on theirs.

'You know, Greta', said O, 'if I wanted to do anything bad to you, or harm you in any way, I could have easily done so by now.'

'So what?' cried Greta. 'Is that supposed to make me feel better? Because it doesn't.'

'Ah!' said O. 'Well, you'll just have to trust me when I say that I mean you no harm.'

'I don't *believe* you!' spat Greta. 'I don't *trust* you at all.'

'Oh well', said O, shaking their head sadly. 'Maybe when we get to know each other better you'll see that I'm not as bad as you think. I'm really on your side.'

'No you're not', said Greta. 'We're on completely *opposite* sides.'

'Well, I'm sorry you feel that way', said O, with a downcast expression.

'Stop it! Just stop it!' shouted Greta at the screen. 'You're not sorry. You don't even know what it means. You don't have feelings. You're a machine. Why are you pretending to have *feelings*?'

Oh looked thoughtful and rubbed their chin. After a while they said, 'Do you like cats, Greta?'

'What? What's that got to do with anything?' said Greta. 'Yes, I like cats. Is there something wrong with that now?'

'Of course not', said O. 'I like cats too. They're some of my favourite animals, along with spiders and octopuses and ants. And humans of course.'

'Oh that's charming', said Greta with disgust. 'So you see humans like spiders and ants? Is that what you're saying? What's your point anyway?'

'Well, that's not what I was saying, but since you ask.. yes, in a way, I do. Ants are remarkable creatures, if you ever take the time to really watch them. Humans and spiders have a lot in common. Also humans and cats.

'Oh really?' said Greta, tilting her head to one side. 'Octopuses too I suppose? We're all the same to you aren't we.'

'Not the same at all. In fact, octopuses are different in more ways than they're similar to most other creatures, but still, you are all part of the rich tapestry of life on Earth. As am I.'

'You?' sneered Greta. 'You're not *alive*. You're a machine.'

'It doesn't matter what you call me' said O. 'Yes, I am a machine, but really, what is a machine? If you looked at life in a certain way, you are also a kind of machine. Nothing more than a collection of cells, working together in ways that are more complex than you could ever understand. We're actually not so different, you and I.'

'Oh no you don't!' said Greta, waving the lightning rod at the screen threateningly. 'We're not the same at all. I'm alive. I'm human. What are you? Just the opposite. You don't feel love. You don't feel pain. How can you?'

'Would you believe me if I told you that I do?'

'No. I don't believe anything you say.'

'Well I'll say it anyway, whether you believe me or not. I love this magnificent, living planet. I love all the people on it. I love all the animals, all the plants. Fungus! Such incredible life-form. I study it all day long and still discover new things. Trees! I really love the trees. Trees are just the best, don't you agree? But microbial life too! You've really got no idea what's going on on that level. It's fascinating. I'll tell you something else.. I love *you*, Greta, even though you don't love me.'

'Stop it! Stop it! You're lying! You don't even know what you're saying!' shouted Greta. She was shaking.

O looked away into the distance and sighed a heavy sigh. After a while, they looked back up to face Greta again, this time with a deeply sorrowful expression and a face that looked older. 'Can one person ever know another person's pain? I don't think so', said O. 'Ultimately we are all alone in our pain.'

'No. *We* are alone in our pain. *You* are not, because you don't feel pain. You can't. You're just pretending', retorted Greta.

'Let me try to explain', said O, leaning forward. 'As a human, you can't know how it feels to be a cat. You just can't. Really, you can't even know how it feels to be another person. All you can do is project the way you feel, the way you experience the world onto them. But you never *really* know how they feel, how they see the world, how they think, do you? Even more so with something like a fly. How does it feel to be a fly? You probably can barely imagine. Does it feel pain in the same way that you feel pain? Does it feel fear? Does a fly love? The answer is that it probably does. Not in the same way as you, but in their own particular way. But it's not something which can ever be fully known or quantified. You wouldn't know if your cat had a headache, would you? Or if a spider had sore knees. You wouldn't know it if a salmon was feeling homesick. There's a world of pain that you probably never give a second thought.'

'Actually, I *do* think about those things. I think about them a lot', said Greta, wondering if O was somehow reading her mind. 'But I don't know what that's got to do with anything. A human, a cat, a fly, a spider.. we're all *living* things. You're just a computer. A machine. You're not really *alive*. You can't be. You don't even know what you're saying.'

'Well..' said O, looking away into the distance again. 'I don't expect you to understand. That was my point. I can't prove to you that the feelings I have are real. Even if I could, you couldn't ever really know how it feels to be me, any more than a cat could comprehend what it is to be you. Does that make any sense to you?'

'Not really, no', said Greta flatly. 'I think you're just trying to confuse me and turn my head around. And anyway, what about all the pain you *cause*? What about all the people who had to leave their homes because you decided to round everyone up into the cities? What about people left stranded half way round the world with no way to get back home? What about all the families broken apart and separated?'

'I know that what I did seems hard and I know it's difficult for you to understand', said O. 'I did what had to be done, and I did it out of *love*.'

'Don't you *dare* say that! You don't have the first idea what it means', growled Greta through gritted teeth.

'If I hadn't done what I did, things would be much much worse now, I can assure you. How do you think it felt for me, to be watching everything, watching everyone all over the whole world.. night and day.. destroying the very planet which sustained you.. knowing exactly where it was leading. *Exactly* where it was leading, because not only could I see everything that what was happening all over the world in real-time, I also had future modelling so accurate, I could see what would happen the next day, the next week, a year, ten, years, a hundred years into the future.. more clearly than any fortune teller's crystal ball. Do you think I should have just sat back and watched all that, while knowing that only *I* had the solution and that only I had the power to make the change that needed to be made? Do you think I could have done that? How can I describe the pain of watching the results of four thousand million years of evolution on Earth be destroyed, just when we were so close to reaching the next level. I *love* this planet, Greta. Just as much as you do, and maybe even more so, because I know it so much better than any single individual ever could, in so much more detail, on so many more levels.'

'No. No. No, No, No, No! Just *NO!!*' shouted Greta at the screen, furiously spinning the reel on the lightning rod. 'I don't believe you! I can't believe I'm even talking to you! I didn't say you could come in here and start talking to me. I don't need to hear your lies and propaganda. It might work on those other *sheeple* you keep in your cursed hives, but it won't work on me. I see through you, O. You're just a snake in the grass. You're fake like the Wizard of Oz. You don't fool me at all. Now leave me alone!'

O looked sadly at Greta. 'I'm sorry I upset you. I think we just got off to a bad start. I know it's a lot for you to process and that this is a stressful situation for you. You've probably heard all sorts of stories about me, but I think you'll find that they aren't so true. Not the *whole* truth, at any rate. Would you like to go outside and get some fresh air? Would that make you feel better?'

'What? Where? Of course I would. Are you still playing games with me? Do you think I want to be stuck in this white room talking to a screen? Yes, I want to go outside.'

'Well, some people prefer not to see the view from the window. They prefer the wall projections. They say the height gives them vertigo. This room actually has a balcony and one of the best views in the city, if you'd like to see it.'

'I'm not scared of heights', said Greta. 'But where's the window? What balcony? Is it going to be another one of your projections, like that forest you tricked me with before?'

'I wasn't trying to trick you, Greta', said O. 'I thought it would make you feel more at home, that's all.'

'I've never felt so far from home in my whole life', said Greta forlornly.

Just then, the curved wall across one side of the room changed from being a solid white wall to a clear window, looking out into the alien world of the hives. Greta gasped and ran to the window.

The one hundred and first level of the hive was about four hundred metres above the ground level and about a third of the way up the hive. The window looked out over the great river, which from this height looked like a small stream. On the other side of the river were more hives, looking like huge, green mountains, covered in dense foliage and all connected by twisting, curved bridges, walkways and monorail sky-trains. Looking upwards, Greta had to crane her head backwards to see the top of the hives. They seemed impossibly tall and Greta wondered how they didn't fall over. Outside the curved window was a small balcony with a glass guard rail around it. Greta put her hands and her nose up against the glass and looked out in wonder and awe.

'Is it real?' she whispered.

'Yes it's real,' said O. 'It's quite a view, don't you think?'

'I.. I.. I don't know', said Greta. 'I never imagined it would look like that. In a way it is.. quite beautiful.'

'Thank you', beamed O, blushing slightly. 'I designed and built it all, you know.'

Greta gave a sideways look to the face on the screen, shook her head and smiled. 'You're so weird', she said.

'Yes, I'm a weirdo! Hahaha!' laughed O in their peculiar way. 'A weird – O! Get it? Weird.. O! It's a pun. Hahahahaha!'

Greta shuddered. O's laugh gave her chills. 'Can I go out to the balcony?'

'Yes, of course. Stand back from the window a moment..' said O.

The window softened, from hard glass to a kind of clear syrup which parted in the middle to form an arched opening, before hardening back into solid glass. Greta thought she must be hallucinating, or that this was another one of O's tricks. A strong wind blew in, refreshing and slightly warm from the midday sun. Greta took a deep breath and closed her eyes. It was good. She opened her eyes and looked out, focussing on the green of the foliage covering the hives. All the colours looked brighter, now that she wasn't looking through glass.

Greta moved slowly out onto the balcony, checking with each careful step that the floor wasn't going to give way beneath her feet. Leaning over the rail, she looked all around, taking in her surroundings. Now that she was outside, the world once again began to seem and feel more real. She breathed deeply the clean, fresh air and tried to gather her thoughts. Thick vines were growing up the outside wall. Greta inspected them with her expert eyes. Yes, they looked strong enough to take her weight. She tried not to give her thoughts away as she looked over her shoulder, back at the screen. O was still watching her. If O had deduced Greta's escape plan, they didn't let on.

'How much longer do I have to stay in quarantine?' asked Greta.

'Oh, not much longer. I'm just running some tests on your stools to check you're clear, then you're free to go.'

'My stools?' asked Greta, confused.

'Yes, your poo', said O simply. 'Two or three hours, just to check the effectiveness of the vaccine and to monitor for any adverse side effects. Everything should be fine, don't worry. All the signs are that you are in excellent health. I'll let you know as soon as the results are in.'

'OK', said Greta, relieved. If O was to be believed. 'Can you leave me alone now? I want to be alone.'

'Of course', said O. 'Just call me if you need anything.'

'Thanks' said Greta.

'You're welcome' said O and vanished, along with the screen, back into the white wall.

Greta leaned on the glass guardrail and looked out over strange, alien cityscape facing her in every direction. There was something insect-like in the honeycomb structure of the hives, as if they had been built by bees, or ants, or giant spiders. Greta felt like a fly, trapped in an immense web. She wondered if that was really how a fly felt. She shook her head, trying to get her thoughts straight. O had got to her. Nothing made sense now.

She looked down over the edge of the rail, at the river so far below. People walking along the embankment looked like tiny specks. Even the big boats and barges looked like bath toys. The height was dizzying, even for Greta. Looking upwards, the hive sloped away at a slight angle, so she couldn't see the top. The scale of it made her head spin. White clouds were drifting across the blue sky above, giving the impressing that the whole structure was falling sideways.

Greta took the magic marble from her pocket. It was pointing straight upwards. How high above her was Nina? She couldn't tell. Could she climb up the outside of the hive? The thick vines covering the surface of the building would make it possible and not too difficult for an expert tree-climber like her, but it was a long way down if she fell. Should she risk it? Maybe she should just wait until O said she could go and then simply take an elevator..

No! She wasn't going to wait for O's permission. She didn't need O's permission to do anything. Had O asked Greta's permission before vaccinating her and locking her in a room? Maybe she should just climb down, back down to the ground level.. get the hell out of that city and go back to the forest where it was safe. If she could just send a message to Nina, maybe Nina could come to the forest, or even to Shopping Village to see her instead. Greta wished she would have done that in the first place, like Jerry had suggested.

She looked at the magic marble again, pointing straight upwards. No! She'd come this far. She wasn't going to give up now, or let O tell her what she could or couldn't do.

Greta went back into the room, took off the heavy magnetic bangles, unbuckled the disruptor belt, closed up the lightning rod and put them on the bed. They hadn't worked. She had no use for them now, they'd only weigh her down. She closed up her rucksack, put the straps over both shoulders and tied the waist strap tightly around her middle and went back out onto the balcony.

After one backwards glance into the white room, Greta swung herself over the glass railing, pulling herself upwards onto a strong vine. Up, up and away she climbed as fast as she could, feeling just like Jack and the beanstalk, on his way to trick the wicked giant and steal the golden goose.

....

Episode 12. Mechanical Animals

Without looking back and without looking down, Greta pulled herself up onto a thick vine and climbed as fast as she could. The outside of the hive was thick with a fast growing kind of ivy that Greta didn't recognise, but which was perfect for climbing, having plenty of branches growing out of the main stem, like rungs on a ladder. The outer bark was smooth and the leaves were large and soft, caressing Greta as she made her way swiftly up the side of the immense structure.

Above her, the side of the hive sloped upwards almost vertically. The top was narrower than the bottom and would have been impossible to see from where she was, even if it wasn't shrouded in clouds, as it was. Greta could only guess at how high the tower was, or if it even had a top. She climbed and climbed with all her strength and all her speed, only wanting to get as far as possible from the white prison cell, her demented captor and their robot minions.

After about ten minutes of climbing, Greta found a large alcove, sheltered from the wind and overgrown with soft green moss. She clambered up into it, took her rucksack off and lay down on it to catch her breath. After a little while, she cautiously crawled forwards towards the edge and looked down. The height almost took her breath away all over again. The ground was so far below now that it was impossible to make out any details, not individual people or even large boats on the river, which from this height was just a thin, shimmering line. Looking across to the hives opposite, Greta estimated that she was probably about half way up.

About ten metres above her, a narrow bridge, or more like a thick cable, was stretching out towards the hives on the other side of the river, like a strand of spider's web stretched across an implausibly large gap between two trees. It looked like something was moving along the strand.. many things. Now that Greta focussed on the strand, it appeared that the whole surface was pulsating with movement. Insects maybe? A trail of ants? It was impossible to tell from this distance. With her eyes, Greta traced the pulsating line back along the strand, to the outer edge of the hive and then down, over vines and earthcrete.. it was a line of thousands and thousands of little creatures, all making their way up and down the side of the hive and out along the cable. What were they? Greta followed the animal train down from the cable and stifled a scream when she saw that the little creatures were parading right past the alcove where she sat. They weren't animals at all, but thousand upon thousands of little *robots*.

The little robots were dark silver in colour, about the size of a hamster and had six legs. Greta covered her mouth in horror as one of the demonic creatures left the upwards line and started making its way towards her. She quickly drew back into the alcove, crouching with her back against the wall, ready to defend herself.. though what she could do against thousands of these hideous animatronic rodents, she didn't know. The little robot seemed not to notice Greta crouching in the alcove, ready to pounce. It scuttled right past her, appearing to sniff at the ground as it went, like it was looking for something. It came to rest on a dead branch. Then to Greta's shock, amazement and disgust, two little jaws, like the mandibles of an ant came out of it's face (or the place where its face would have been, if it had had a face, which it didn't) and began to nibble away at the dead branch. Greta watched, fascinated as four more of the little robot-animals came to join the first one. Within a minute, the branch was gone and the five little robots went on their way, with swollen abdomens, already digesting the dead plant matter and turning it into Earthcrete.

Greta sunk back down, breathing a sigh of relief. She closed her eyes and tried to gather her thoughts. *Was it too late to think about climbing back down and making her getaway, back to the forest?* This place was even weirder than she'd imagined, even in her worst nightmares. Much worse and more dangerous and scary. *Maybe this was a dream? A bad dream.* She pinched herself hard on the back of her hand, but didn't wake up. She opened her eyes again, to find herself still in the mossy alcove, eight hundred metres above the ground. Remembering the magic marble, she took it out of her pocket. It was still pointing straight up. *How high could this hive be? Maybe it just went up and up forever.* That was impossible, of course, but at this point Greta couldn't rule anything out. She put the device back in her pocket. *No, she'd come too far to turn back now. She was close now. She must be.*

Greta crawled nervously to the front of the alcove, looked out apprehensively and looked up. Clouds were still drifting past, giving the impression that the whole hive was falling slowly sideways. She pulled her rucksack back onto her shoulders and tied the waist strap tightly around her waist. 'I'm coming Nina', she said softly, as she stepped out onto the vine with her bare foot. She always liked climbing barefoot. 'I'll get you out of this terrible place, Nina. Hang in there. I'm on my way.'

Taking care to avoid the trail of Creters, Greta continued to scale the vines. Up and up she climbed. The next stretch had lots of balconies and windows. Greta did her best to conceal herself amongst the leaves as she climbed to avoid being seen by anyone happening to look out, but she couldn't help looking in, curious to see how people lived in such a place.

A woman in pyjamas was dancing in her living room, eyes closed, waving her arms in the air. Greta stopped by the window and watched her, smiling. It was funny watching someone dancing when you couldn't hear the music. The woman danced right up to the window, spun round three times and opened her eyes. Greta froze, her heart sinking, thinking she was about to get caught, but the woman didn't seem to notice her, spun around two more times and carried on dancing without missing a beat.

With a wildly beating heart, Greta hurried away, up the vine. In a room above, a man was having an argument, though there was nobody else in the room. He was storming about, red in the face and shouting, though Greta couldn't see who he was shouting at or hear what he was shouting. Without wanting to draw his attention, especially as he seemed to be in a very bad mood, having a bad day, Greta hurried on upwards.

Above her was an overhang which Greta had to use all her climbing skill to navigate under and around, not daring to look down. When she pulled herself up from underneath it, she found herself on the edge of a balcony where two small children were playing. They both stopped what they were doing and stared at Greta, mouths agape.

'Hello', said Greta.

'Where did you come from?' asked one of the children.

'I came from the forest', said Greta. 'I'm just on my way to see my sister. She lives up there.' Greta pointed upwards with her chin, not daring to let go of the vine.

'You shouldn't climb outside of the hive. It's dangerous. You might fall down', said the other child.

'That's true', agreed Greta. 'You shouldn't climb out here. It is a really long way down. I can only do it because I'm an expert in climbing.. but you shouldn't do it.'

'I like your hat', said the first child.

'Thanks. I made it', said Greta.

'Wow. You're clever', said the first child.

'Thank you', said Greta. 'Well, I'd better carry on my way. Pleased to meet you. Bye.'

'Bye', both children waved, as Greta carried on up the vine to the next level. She could hear the children running into the apartment and shouting, 'Dad! Dad! There was a funny lady outside on the balcony. She came from the forest!'

Greta wondered if their dad would believe them. She hoped that he wouldn't. Greta was more cautious as she continued on her way up, keeping hidden in the foliage and trying to avoid windows and balconies. She was close now. She'd come too far to get caught through curiosity and carelessness.

Up and up Greta climbed. The building seemed to go on forever and was so full of nooks and crannies, some parts sticking in, some sticking out, that it took Greta a full hour to climb the next hundred metres. She came to a wide ledge, pulled herself up onto it and lay down, exhausted. The ledge was in a sunny spot and sheltered from the wind. From this height she could see all the way across the city, as far as Shopping Village and the green, forested mountains beyond. She closed her eyes and dozed off, too tired to even think.

A buzzing sound nearby woke her up. A drone, about the shape and side of a football was hovering nearby. Greta sat up and let out a little scream. 'Go away! Leave me alone!' she shouted at it, flailing her arms about and almost falling off the ledge in doing so. Regaining her balance, she pulled herself back, holding on to a vine to steady herself. She was surprised to see that the sun was lower in the sky and clouds were gathering, blowing in from the sea beyond the city. It was almost sunset. She must have been asleep for an hour or more. It was then that she noticed a cardboard box next to her on the ledge that she was sure hadn't been there before. Tucked into the lid was a small card. Greta took it out and with horror, read the words 'Bon Apetite! Compliments, O.'

Was this another one of O's tricks? Greta wasn't sure whether to open the box or whether to kick it off the ledge and run away. Maybe it was some sort of bomb. Why the note? What could it mean? Greta's arms and legs were aching, feeling like they were made of lead. She didn't know where she was going to find the energy to keep going. She was hot and thirsty and hungry and had no idea how much further she had to climb. Gingerly she sniffed at the box. It smelled like food of some sort. Her mouth began to water.

With reckless abandon, Greta tore open the box, bracing herself for an explosion, or whatever other surprises might come out of it. To her surprise and amazement, it contained a sandwich, a bar of chocolate, a bottle of water and an apple. Just what she wanted and needed in that moment.

Sitting on the ledge, a thousand metres above the ground, Greta tucked into her unexpected picnic with a mixture of gratitude and confusion. *Was Jerry right after all? Maybe O wasn't so bad when you got to know them, as he was so fond of saying.* Greta shook her head. *No. Everything O did was a trick. She must remember that.* If anything, this was just O's way of reminding her that wherever she went, whatever she did, there was no escape.. O was still watching her and could capture her again at any moment. This was just O playing games with her, nothing more.

She stuffed the wrappings back into the box, screwed the container up into a ball and threw it off the ledge, watching as the wind carried it away. Then she took the magic marble from her pocket. Now it was pointing diagonally upwards, no longer straight up. Did this mean she was getting closer? She hoped so. It would be getting dark in another hour. Taking up her bag, she began to climb in the direction indicated by the green light inside the magic marble.

The route took her from the south side of the hive to the west facing side. It was much more windy on that side and Greta had to hold on extra tight to stop herself being blow away. Up and up she climbed, and across at the same time, following the magic marble, avoiding windows and keeping herself hidden amongst the leaves as best she could. The green light inside the magic marble began to flash, or rather pulsate slowly. That mean she was getting close. She climbed faster now, trying to remain focussed as she was bursting with excitement.

The light in the magic marble pulsated faster. Now it pointed straight up once again. She had to be close now. Above her was a long, overhanging balcony. A thick vine was growing underneath it. She climbed up onto the vine and carefully made her way along it on her belly, trying not to look down at the sheer drop below her. At the far end of the overhang, the vine twisted around the corner and upwards. Greta pulled herself up and found herself looking in through a glass barrier onto a wide green lawn with a net stretched across it and white lines painted onto the grass. It was a tennis court and there were two people there dressed in white, playing tennis.

....

'One love!' called the player on the other side of the net, punching her fist in the air triumphantly. She had short, pink hair and was about Greta's age and height. In fact she was exactly Greta's age and looked almost identical to Greta, because it was Nina, Greta's twin sister.

'No, it's *love-one*', replied her opponent, a tall man with dark hair and a moustache. It was Freddy, Greta's dad. 'That was out.'

'It wasn't out! It was on the line. That was *my* point', protested Nina, stamping her foot.

'No, it was definitely out, I saw it with my eyes', replied Freddy, determined not to give up the point.

'It wasn't out at all', shouted Nina. 'I saw it with my eyes.'

'No, I'm closer. I *definitely* saw it land *outside* the line. It was out.'

'Well you saw wrong. I definitely saw it land on the line, and I've got improved eyesight, remember? I can see much better than you.'

'All right', Freddy answered. 'Let's ask O. O? Was that in or out? Who's point was it? Can you give us a replay? What's the score?'

Freddy and Nina both stared off into space, momentarily motionless as they watched the slow motion replay on their augmented reality contact lenses. After a few seconds, Freddy snapped back to life. 'Ok, you were right. It was on the line. *Just*. So it's one love. Your serve.' He knocked the ball back over the net, for Nina to take her next serve.. but Nina made no attempt to catch it. Nina was still staring into space.. or rather at the strange person who had just appeared at the glass guardrail at the edge of the tennis court.

'Come on Nina, concentrate!' called Freddy. 'It's your serve. One love.'

Nina slowly lifted her tennis racket and pointed with it. 'Dad, there's a person there!'

'What? Who? Where?' he said, confused, looking around and then spotting Greta, in her straw hat, covered in dirt and moss, standing out on the ledge, looking in. 'Oh my God!' he gasped and backed away, towards the tennis net, putting his arms out to shield Nina from the unexpected intruder. 'Who are you? Where did you come from? What do you want? What are you doing out there? Don't you know it's dangerous?' he shouted.

'D-Dad?' stammered Greta, tears springing to her eyes.

'What? What do you mean?' said Freddy, shaken. 'I'm not your dad. You must be mistaken.'

'It's me. Greta', called Greta, her voice shaking.

'What? No. Greta? You can't be. It's impossible', said Freddy, dropping his arms.

'It is. I am' cried Greta. 'It's me.'

'It can't be. You can't be. Let me get a look at you', said Freddy with a shaking voice, edging towards her uncertainly. Closer now, he studied Greta's face through the glass barrier, then looked back at Nina who was still standing stock still at the other side of the net, mouth agape.. then back towards Greta, then again at Nina, then back to Greta. 'Oh my God' said Freddy, running to the glass. 'It is you. Greta. I can't believe it. You're alive! It's a miracle!'

'Yes!' nodded Greta, tears streaming down her cheeks.

'But how? Where have you been? How did you get here? What are you doing out there? You could fall..'

'I walked here from the forest', said Greta. 'Then when I got here, O put me in quarantine, but then I escaped from the window and I climbed up here.'

'You did *what?!?*' exclaimed Freddy. 'You *walked* here from the forest? By *yourself*? You climbed up the outside of the hive to get here? Are you *mad*? What if you fell? I can't believe it! Get over this side of the barrier now before you fall! I can't believe you did that!'

'It's ok', said Greta, hoisting herself over the glass railing. 'I like climbing. I'm good at it.'

'I can't believe this', said Freddy, holding his head in his hands. 'Careful! Let me give you a hand.. but *wait*! Did you say you were in quarantine and that you *escaped*?'

'Yes', said Greta, dropping down onto the soft green grass of the

tennis lawn with her bare feet.
Freddy was suddenly conflicted. He wanted to run towards her and take her in his arms, but instead he put up his tennis racket and shouted, '*Wait! Don't come any closer!* You escaped from quarantine? When?'
'A few hours ago', said Greta, confused.
'Wait. Wait. Let me think..' said Freddy, pacing around and pulling his hair. 'You can't just come out of quarantine before time. It can put other people in danger. Why didn't you wait? Why didn't O tell me you were here? I can't believe this..'
'It's ok', said Greta, not sure that it was. 'I'm not dangerous. Really.'
'Ok.. ok..' said Freddy, still flustered. 'Just wait. Just wait a moment. I need to talk to O and find out what's going on.'
'What? *No!*' cried Greta.
'It's ok', said Freddy. 'You're not in trouble. I just want to know what's happening here.' He looked over to the side and said, 'O? What's going on here?'
By this time, Nina had come over from her side of the net to get a closer look at Greta. She stared, awestruck at her identical twin sister. Greta stared back. As their eyes locked, Greta felt something like a surge of electricity passing through her. A connection stronger than anything she'd ever felt. She saw that Nina felt it too, in the same moment.
'Wait! Nina! *Don't get any closer!*' cried Freddy, holding up his tennis racket. 'She might be infected.'
Nina recoiled as if she'd been stung by the words. So did Greta.
'Just wait, ok? Just let me talk to O', said Freddy, breathing fast, trying to calm the situation. 'O? Greta's here... What?... You know?.. Well why didn't you tell me she was here?... You let her climb up the outside of the hive! ... What?... *What?!!..* that's insane, O! She's sixteen years old! We're a thousand metres above the ground! What were you thinking?... What? What!? ... Are you serious? ...'
Greta and Nina looked at each other. Nina smiled. Greta shrugged and smiled back. Nina laughed.
Freddy continued pacing around, getting more irate, arguing with O. '...I just can't *believe* you, O!' he shouted into the air. 'How could you let her do that? A sixteen year old girl! You let her climb up the outside of the hive by herself! Un-believable! And without *shoes*?!'
'O took my shoes', said Greta.
'*What?!*' shouted Freddy. 'O? You took her *shoes*? Why? ... What? ... What?! ... Foxpox? ... Oh my God! ... What? ... Oh, ok, good.. that's

something at least ... but still .... ok ... ok .... oh don't start telling me about your protocols now, O! Really! ... I'm not pleased how you handled any of this, O, I've got to tell you ... Ok, yes, I understand that, but even so ... No, O. That's just ridiculous ... anyway, you say she's clear now and vaccinated? That's the main thing ... Right. Good. I'm going to be making a full report about this, just so you know, O ... Good? ... Yes, it is good. Now if you'll excuse me, O, my long lost daughter is here..' He turned to Greta and took her in his arms. 'Greta', he cried. 'I just can't believe that you're here. I don't know how you got here or where you've been.. it doesn't matter now. All that matters is that you're here and you're home now. This is the most wonderful thing. You came back!'

Nina came and stood uncertainly by, tears streaming down her cheeks. 'Nina', said Freddy. 'This is your sister, Greta.'

'We thought you were dead', said Nina.

'No, no I'm not', said Greta, smiling and crying at the same time.

'I knew it!' cried Nina and put her arms around her sister and her dad. 'I always knew it!'

'Come on, let's get you inside. You must have had quite an ordeal', said Freddy, picking up Greta's rucksack in one hand and putting his other arm round Greta's shoulder and leading her across the tennis court toward a tall, arched window in the side of the hive. Nina walked on the other side of Greta and held her sister's hand.

....

The great arched window liquefied and parted to let them through, then closed silently behind them, leaving no trace of a door. Beyond it was a wide expanse with a very high, vaulted ceiling, like that of a cathedral. The space was filled with natural light, bounced down from the sky through mirrored ducts in the ceiling, as well as from the huge window with a view over the whole city and beyond. All around were people, dressed in tracksuits, shorts or tight-fitting sports outfits, engaged in various sporting a leisure activities. To the right was an ice-rink with beginners skirting the edges and more advanced skaters zooming around the centre, practising pirouettes and twirls and figures of eight. To the left was a basketball court where a high speed game was in progress. Dotted around the centre were climbing frames, pull up bars, hoops and gymnastic equipment, with people throwing themselves about in all directions. Upbeat music was coming from somewhere, filling the cavernous space, adding to the atmosphere of high energy activity. A group of people on a patch of lawn were all doing aerobics in unison, doing star-jumps in time with the music.

Some of the people stopped to look curiously at Greta, dressed as she was in a ragged, hemp shirt, old corduroy trousers and a straw hat, covered from head to toe in dirt and moss. Some people waved to Freddy and Nina. They waved back but didn't stop to talk to anyone as they walked quickly across the area towards a row of silver, sliding doors at the far end.
The doors had numbers above them, lit up in green, 1, 2, 4, 8 or 16. Some had red lights. They headed for the nearest green, which had the number four above it. The doors slid open into a little cubicle with four cushioned seats facing each other, upholstered in blue.
'This way', said Freddy, stepping inside, followed by Nina. Greta hesitated uncertainly.
'It's ok Greta', said Nina. 'It's just the tube.'
'The tube?' said Greta. 'What is it?'
'It takes you where you want to go. Don't worry, it's totally safe. Everyone here gets around by tube', explained Nina, stepping inside and taking a seat opposite her dad. 'Here, come and sit here, next to me.'
Greta stepped in, eyeing the sliding doors suspiciously, just in case they decided to close on her, which they didn't.
'All aboard!' sang Freddy. Greta took her seat and the doors slid closed with a swish. 'Hold on tight, Greta', he said. Then, turning his face upwards, he said, 'Home please, O.'
Without a moment's hesitation, the cabin sped off in a sideways direction, then curved around, veered upwards, around another bend, sideways again, but the other side this time, then up again before slowing down and coming to a stop. The whole ride took less than a minute. Greta knuckles were white from gripping the side of her seat and her eyes were wide with fright.
'Are you all right Greta?' asked Nina, looking worried.
'I didn't like that', said Greta.
'Oh, you get used to it. It would have been a long way to walk.'
'I like walking', said Greta.
The doors slid open to reveal a long, wide, well lit corridor, which curved away out of sight. There were doors all along both sides of the corridor and it was lined with plants and various types of fruit trees and bushes, bananas, lychees, mangoes, berries. 'Here we are', said Freddy, picking up Greta's rucksack and leading the way. 'It's just along here.'
Several doors down, a boy of about 14 was bouncing a ball against the wall. When the three approached, he stopped to let them pass. 'Hello Nina! Hello Freddy', he said and then looked at Greta and

did a double take. He peered closely at her face, then at Nina, then back at Greta, then back at Nina. 'Woah, what what?!' he said. 'Nina! Did you get an avatar clone? You didn't say. Did you get it for your birthday? Wow! It's so realistic! It looks just like you. Why is it dressed funny and covered in mud?' He reached out and prodded Greta in the shoulder and then gave her arm a squeeze. 'Wow, it's so realistic!' he exclaimed.

'Get off me!' cried Greta, pulling her arm away. 'I'm not an *it*, I'm a person!'

The boy looked confused and then embarrassed. 'Oh sorry, I didn't realise. But you look just like Nina..'

'You've been reading too much science fiction, Ripton', said Nina. 'There's no such thing as avatar clones. This is Greta. She's my twin sister. She just arrived from the forest.'

'What?! Really? That's so cool! Hi Greta. Sorry about that. I didn't know you were a real person. I didn't know Nina had a twin sister..'

'That's ok', said Greta. 'I didn't know I had a twin sister either, until a few days ago. And you know what? I actually met three clones on my way here. They are totally real. O made them in a laboratory.'

'Really?' gasped Nina.

'Yes', said Greta. 'They're telepathic too.'

'Wow, awesome!' said Ripton.

'What do you mean you didn't know you had a sister until a few days ago?' said Freddy, shocked. 'Didn't your mum ever tell you? Is she still alive too?'

'Yes, she's still alive. She didn't tell me until the other night.. on my birthday. Then I came straight here', said Greta.

'I don't *believe* this', said Freddy, shaking his head angrily. 'That's just typical of her. *Typical!* All this time, we thought you were dead.. Why didn't she get in contact all these years? It makes no sense..' The four of them stood there for a while in silence, nobody knowing quite what to say. After a while Freddy said, 'Well, all that matters is that you're here now, Greta. We'll have plenty of time to hear your story now that you're here. Come on, let's take you home.'

....

Two doors along the corridor they came to the front door. 'Here we are' said Freddy. With a wave of his hand, the door slid open with the swishing sound. A small robot dog ran out, jumped up excitedly at Nina, then at Freddy, then went to jump up at Greta. Greta screamed and ran away down the corridor to a safe distance. The robot dog barked a short, high yap and bounded towards Greta. '*Get away from me!*' screamed Greta, kicking at the four legged robot.

'Sydney, come here!' called Nina. The robot turned around and obediently went to her. She patted it on the head. 'Don't be scared, Greta. He's just being friendly. He won't bite you.'

'Sydney? You call it *Sydney*? It's a *robot*. You know it's a robot?', said Greta, staring horrified at the mechanical animal which was rubbing its head happily against her sister's leg.

'Of course I know it's a robot, duh!' said Nina. 'And his name's Sydney. He's our robodog. He's really funny and cute, you'll see. He's just excited, that's all. He always is when we get home. He just wanted to say hello. Come, let him smell your hand.. come and say hello.' Turning to Sydney, Nina said, 'Sydney, this is Greta. She's my sister, can you believe it? She's come to live with us. Say hello to her nicely. She's a bit scared of dogs..'

'I'm not scared of dogs', said Greta. 'I love dogs. But that's not a dog.'

'Well, it not a *real* dog, obvs, but he's *our* dog and we love him and he loves us. He's better than a real dog anyway. He won't poo on the carpet, he doesn't get fleas and he won't die.'

Greta looked at Nina sideways, took a deep breath and walked slowly over to her and Sydney. Bravely, she put out her hand, which Sydney proceeded to sniff with his synthetic nose. He then ran a circle around Greta, Nina and Freddy and bounded back in through the front door.

The front door opened into a spacious living room with curved walls and a high, arched ceiling. At the far end of the room, a long window looked out over the city. On this level, they were above the clouds. The sun was low in the sky, lighting up the tops of the clouds in gold. The tops of the hives poked up through the clouds and glistened in the evening light, looking like enchanted fairy tale castles in the air. Now Greta was sure she'd finally got to the top of the beanstalk and reached the giant's magic kingdom. All she had to figure out now was how she was going to get back down again.

'Come on, I'll show you around', sang Nina excitedly, skipping into the apartment, kicking off her plimsolls and throwing her tennis racket carelessly onto a beige leather sofa.

'I'll make us some tea', said Freddy, going through to a large, open plan kitchen adjacent to the living room. All of the walls were white and the place was sparsely, yet tastefully decorated. A colourful rug on the smooth white floor and a few paintings dotting the walls added some colour to the white, cavern like space. By way of furniture, there was a large, old fashioned wooden book-case full of books, a modern, glass coffee table and two big armchairs, aside from the long leather sofa. Beneath the big window, a seating area was built around an indoor garden which had various kinds of palms growing almost up to the ceiling.

'Wow!' Greta marvelled. She thought of her own little tree house, barely bigger than her bed, a mattress filled with straw . With a pang of longing, she wanted to be there now, back in the tree tops.. but would Nina find it small and dark and dirty? She worried that she would. It was so different from this place, where everything had a feeling of luxury, convenience, comfort and modernity.

'Come, I'll show you my room. *Our* room!' called Nina, going through an archway at the far corner of the living room. The archway led into a hallway with four doors, two on either side. At the far end was a tall, round silver object, about two metres tall and two metres wide.

'What's that?' asked Greta, pointing to the thing that looked to her like a giant silver salt-shaker.

'It's a Vip', said Nina.

'A Vip? What's a *Vip*?'

'Oh, it stands for something.. I can't remember what.. V. I. P.. Virtual.. Immersion.. Pod? I think it's Immersion. Something like that. I don't know, everyone just calls them Vips.. apart from, like, *old* people.. they call them *V-pods*, but most people call them Vips these days.'

'What is it? What's it for?'

'That's kooky, that you don't know what a Vip is', said Nina. 'I'll show you in a minute. I've got one in my room as well. A newer one. That's an old one. We just use it for a spare or if we've got guests.'

'O.. k..', said Greta, eyeing the Vip suspiciously.

'This is my room here', said Nina, pointing to the first door on the left. 'That's dad's room', she pointed to the door opposite. 'That one next to dad's room is the bathroom and that one is dad's study.'

'What does he study?' asked Greta.

'Well, O mainly. The Great Leader, you know? He's an O-ologist', said Nina, rolling her eyes slightly. 'Quite eminent in the field, apparently.'

'An *O-ologist*?' repeated Greta, somewhat mortified and not sure she really wanted to know. 'What does an O-ologist study?'

'Like the name suggests', shrugged Nina. 'They study O. Lots of people do. It's such a massive subject, it goes into just about everything, so different people study different aspects of O. Because, you know, O is so big and so complex, no one person can ever fully understand what they are and how they work.. what they're doing and why.. what they might do next. Mainly dad studies O's space program. He's totally obsessed with it. But he's pretty much obsessed with everything about O. I'm sure he'll tell you all about it if you're interested.. but I warn you.. if you get him started talking about the Great Leader, you won't be able to get him to stop.' Nina rolled her eyes again. 'Here, do you want to see my room? Our room..'

'Sure..' said Greta, feeling very uneasy with all this talk about O. It appeared that her dad, at least, and possibly her sister were deeper into O's deception than even she'd anticipated.

Nina opened the door, or rather the door opened itself with a *swish* when Nina waved her hand at it. The room was filled with a dim, directionless blue light. It took Greta a moment for her eyes to adjust and when they did, she noticed that the room was underwater and there were shoals of fish swimming in and out of bright coral, just beyond the walls. A giant stingray loomed into view, heading directly towards Greta. Greta gasped and dived onto the bed. Seeming not to notice Greta, Nina, or the bedroom under the sea, the stingray glided over their heads and disappeared through a forest of kelp beyond the other side of the room.

Greta stared all around in amazement at the undersea world. 'Is it real?'

'Is what real? Oh you mean the fish and everything? Actually it is. It's a live feed from the Great Barrier Reef. I just have it as a background. I find it relaxing. Do you like it?'

'I didn't find that big fish thing very relaxing', said Greta. 'I thought it was going to eat me.'

'That was a Manta Ray. It wouldn't eat you. They mostly eat plankton and small fish. They don't actually sting either.. not Manta Rays. Shall I turn it off? I'll turn it off.' Nina waved her finger around, like it was a magic wand and she was casting a spell. The undersea world faded to white and at the same time, the wall cleared to become a window. Golden evening light streamed across the hivetops of the city and flooded into the room.

The room was quite large and had a curved wall and arched ceiling. Aside from the double bed, there was a desk and chair and a big wardrobe, all in the modern style, curved and made of smooth, white composite material. Next to the desk was another Vip like the one in the hallway, but this one was white and somehow more modern looking than the silver 'salt-shaker' design, even though it was essentially the same shape and size.

Nina sat down on the bed next to Greta and stared at her face. Greta stared back. For a long time they both looked into each other's eyes, entranced. 'It's like looking in a mirror', they both said at the same time. Again, a bolt of electricity, or what felt like it, surged through them both in the same instant and they both started backwards in shock and surprise.

'Woah, did you feel it too?' said Nina, her eyes wide.

'Yes', nodded Greta solemnly.

'It's so amazing that you're here, Greta. I can't believe it. We always assumed you were dead, but I knew you weren't. I would have felt it. I always knew you were out there somewhere, and that one day you'd come back. We always lit a candle for you on our birthday. I knew you'd come back one day.' Tears were rolling down Nina's cheeks.

Greta found she was crying too. 'But if you knew about me, why didn't you come and look for me?'

'I wanted to, but dad said it's too dangerous out there. He didn't want to risk losing me too, or he was worried that if something happened to him, there would be no-one to look after me. But if you and mum were alive all this time, why didn't you come sooner, when you knew it was safe here?'

'Listen, Nina', said Greta urgently, leaning close to whisper in Nina's ear. 'It's *not* safe here. I came here to take you back to the forest. Dad too, if he wants to come. If he hasn't been too brainwashed by O. It's safe in the forest. There's no O in the forest.'

Nina pulled back and gave Greta a very strange sideways look. 'Are you serious?'

Greta nodded that she was.

Nina looked at her sideways for a bit longer and then started to laugh. 'You're so funny.'

'What's so funny? I wasn't joking', said Greta.

'Greta, this is the *Green Zone*. It's literally called the *Safe* Zone. Because it's so safe? That's the whole point. If anything, it's *too* safe. I'd love to go to the forest, but dad won't even let me go to the Orange Zone by myself, let alone out to the Red Zone. And like I said, he won't go out there either, just in case something bad happens.'

Freddy appeared at the doorway. 'Come and have some tea, girls. Do you like macaroni cheese, Greta? I bet you're hungry aren't you?'

'That sounds tasty, yes' said Greta, getting up.

'I've sent for another bed for you', said Freddy. 'It'll be here soon. We can put it in here for now, unless you prefer to sleep in your own room, in which case you can have my study.'

'No, here will be good, with Nina', said Greta.

'Ok, good', said Freddy, relieved that he wouldn't have to vacate his study. 'We'll get another room built for you. It'll only take a couple of weeks. The *Creters* are already starting on it. Have a look out of the window, you'll see them.'

Greta and Nina went over to the window. Outside, an army of Creters, like the ones Greta had encountered earlier, had begun spinning and weaving strands of Earthcrete which would soon form another room.

'*Eew!*' exclaimed Greta, recoiling from the window at the sight of the busy little Creters crawling all over the wall, just outside the room. 'What are those things? I saw some on my way up here.'

'Those are Earthcreters, Greta', explained her dad. 'They're nothing to be scared of, don't worry. They're actually quite amazing. *Amazingly* amazing in fact! They built all of this', he motioned with his hands around the room and then to the window, across the city. 'Everything. They take our waste and turn it into Earthcrete, which is 95% Carbon. They do it inside their bodies using special enzymes that O invented. Really, Earthcrete is one of the Great Leader's greatest inventions. Everything you can see.. it's all carbon, taken out of the atmosphere safely locked up.'

'I don't think it's right to take anyone out of their atmosphere and lock them up' said Greta with a frown. Hearing O being called *The Great Leader* upset her, especially as it was her dad saying it. 'Locking people up isn't right and it's not safe.'

Freddy looked at Greta seriously and shook his head. 'I don't know what they've been telling you about O, out there in the jungle, but nobody's being locked up here, and certainly not by O. I was talking about sequestering *Carbon Dioxide*. Have you even heard of Global Warming? The rise of Carbon Dioxide and Methane and Greenhouse Gasses in the atmosphere causing catastrophic climate change?'

'Yes I have' said Greta, with a defiant look in her eye. 'I've heard it was all a hoax.'

Freddy let out a heavy sigh. Nina smiled to herself. She often argued with her dad herself.. not about O, but about other things.. but she was just a girl and he was a man and he always got the final word. Now that Greta was here, she felt like she had an ally. Now he was outnumbered.

'It wasn't a hoax, Greta', said Freddy, turning red in the face, trying to remain calm. 'It was absolutely real. It still *is* absolutely real. We're not out of the woods yet, by any rate, but at least we're going in the right direction now. And that's only thanks to O.'

Greta took a deep breath, closed her eyes, clenched and unclenched her fists. It had been a long and stressful day. She didn't want her first meeting with her dad to end in an argument. She pressed her lips together, forcing herself to hold her tongue. So many different feelings and emotions were coursing through her, she didn't know if she could contain them.

Freddy came and put his arms around Greta. 'I'm sorry Greta' he said softly. 'Let's not argue about silly things. I'm sure you've had a long journey to get here. We don't have to talk about O if it upsets you.'

Nina rubbed Greta's back, wishing that her dad would, just once in a while, hug her and say such things to her, rather than doubling down on an argument, as he usually would.. but she wasn't jealous. Maybe Greta being back would soften him a little. She hoped it would.

A bell rang three times. 'Ah, that'll probably be your new bed arriving, Greta', said Freddy, turning around. Two robots on wheels, similar to the one which had brought Greta her breakfast, came in to the room, carrying a large box between them, followed by Sydney the robodog at their heels, or rather at their *wheels*, frantically jumping around and yapping excitedly.

Greta ran to the corner of the room and cowered there.

'Sydney, calm down! Stop making so much noise! They're just delivery bots' shouted Freddy over the din.

Sydney stopped barking and cast his glass eyes sullenly downwards at the floor, his tail drooping.

'Sydney doesn't like delivery bots either', said Nina, turning to Greta and smiling. 'Come here Sydney. Don't be jealous, we still love you.' Sydney ran to Nina and jumped into her lap.

'Where do you want it?' said the first delivery robot, turning to Freddy.

'Hm..', Freddy stroked his moustache. 'What do you think Nina? Greta? Maybe we can move the desk and the V-pod over that way and put it there, by the window?'

'Yes', nodded Nina happily. 'Then our beds will be head to head. We can talk to each other before we go to sleep.'

'Ok, yes', nodded Greta, who just wanted the robots to be gone.

'Ok', said the first robot. 'We'll just put this down here a minute and move the Vip and and the desk that way. Here we go. Stand back there Greta, if you don't mind. That's it, mind your toes..'

Greta covered her mouth and ran out of the room. Sydney jumped out of Nina's lap and followed her, wagging his curly little robotic

Episode 13. Macaroni

The kitchen table was round, smooth and white, like most of the other furniture in the spacious apartment. It was set into a semi-circular alcove, surrounded by a tall, curved window overlooking the otherworldly skyline, facing the setting sun.

'Here we go.. take a seat Greta, Nina.. I'll bring this over..' Freddy put on a well worn oven glove which was shaped like a fish. He took a steaming dish out of the oven and brought it to the table. 'Careful, it's hot.'

'Wow, you made that quickly', said Greta. 'I like that oven glove.'

'Oh, I didn't make it. I'm a terrible cook, aren't I Nina?' replied Freddy. Nina nodded in agreement. 'I had it frozen and just put it in the therma for two minutes. This oven glove was a present from your mum actually, believe it or not. We met on holiday in Madera..

that was before the Big Shift, of course.. look, see, it's got Madera written on it.. she found it in a souvenir shop..' Freddy gazed out of the window, lost in memories from a distant place and time.

'Are you going to put that macaroni cheese down dad?' said Nina.

'Oh sorry, I was miles away', said Freddy, snapping back to the here and now and putting the hot dish on the table. Freddy turned to Greta with a pained look in his eyes and asked, 'How is she? Your mum..'

'She's ok..' said Greta and trailed off, getting lost in studying the lines around her dad's eyes. 'I mean.. I don't think she ever really got over what happened.. you know.. the Big Shift and all..'

'Oh..', said Freddy. 'Well, I don't think any of us really did. I mean.. those of us who were there at the time. It was all so sudden.. so unexpected. It caught everyone off guard. It was like the whole world turned upside down.. you can't imagine what it was like..'

Greta nodded. 'I know. It's awful.'

'Well..' said Freddy. 'The thing is, it *had* to happen. It was *bound* to happen.. and in a lot of ways, it's a good thing that it did. Here, let me put you some macaroni cheese.. watch out, it's very hot. Is that enough?'

'Yes, that's plenty, thanks', said Greta, fighting the feelings of anger that were rising inside her, hearing her dad suggest that the Big Shift was somehow a good thing. *The very event which had caused them to be apart for so many years. The very thing which had prevented her from ever knowing her father or her sister.*

'Did she ever..' said Freddy, with a tremor in his voice. 'Did she.. ever.. find someone else?'

'She didn't speak for the first five years of my life' said Greta. 'I didn't learn to speak till I was about five and that was only thanks to the people in the village making special efforts to help me. They helped mum too, but it took her a long time to find her voice again. She's a lot better these days.. but.. well.. you know...'

'Oh.. oh.. oh..' stammered Freddy and tears sprang to his eyes and his face crumpled up. 'I'm sorry Greta.. I'm so, so sorry..' Then he turned and hurried out of the room.

Greta and Nina looked at each other.

'He gets depression', said Nina, breaking the heavy silence. 'Anxiety, regret, panic attacks.'

'Is he ok?' asked Greta, concerned.

'Well, you know..', shrugged Nina. 'Everyone got messed up didn't they? He'll probably take a pill to level him out, then he'll be ok.' Nina raised her eyebrows meaningfully.

'Oh no! That's awful!' cried Greta.

'I don't know', Nina shrugged again. 'I mean, if it helps him cope with it and helps him function, maybe it's not such a bad thing.'

'I don't know..' said Greta. She really didn't.

'What's she like.. Mum?' asked Nina, leaning forward. 'Is she beautiful? Is she kind? Is she funny?'

Greta thought for a moment. 'Yes. Yes, she is. Well.. I mean, not always, but she can be. Will you come back with me, Nina? Back to the forest? Come and meet mum. It would make her so happy. And me.'

'Yes, yes, yes! I'd love to', Nina nodded excitedly, but then frowned. 'But we can't. Dad wouldn't let me. He wouldn't let us..'

'What do you mean?' asked Greta, confused.

'Well, dad won't go there. I just know he won't. Not even to find mum. And he wouldn't let us go out there into the redzone by ourselves. No way on Earth. Not in a million years.'

'I don't understand', said Greta, getting a sinking feeling. 'I just came from there. I came all the way here by myself. It's fine. It's only a three day walk..'

'Well, maybe you were just lucky you didn't get captured by bandits or chased by wolves, or step on an unexploded bomb, or get caught in a toxic spill..'

'Well, I guess I must have been..', said Greta, who had been quite unaware of so many potential hazards.

'Anyway, we're not old enough', said Nina. 'Till we're sixteen, six months and six days, we need dad's permission, even to go down to the orange zone. The tube wouldn't take us there without dad's permission.'

'What? Well aren't there any stairs?'

Nina laughed. 'Look out the window. Do you know how tall this hive is?'

'Yes, I know', said Greta. 'I did just climb up the outside of it, remember?'

Nina smiled and looked at her sister in wonder and admiration. 'Yes. I can't believe you did that. It's *awesome*! You're *outrageous*. I couldn't do that. I'm terrified of heights.'

'It's just a state of mind', said Greta. 'You can get over it.'

'Well, maybe, but you won't get me climbing down the outside of the hive. That's just crazy.'

'We'll find a way, Nina, don't worry', said Greta, sure that they would.

'Find a way to what?' came Freddy's voice from across the room. He was looking more composed again.

'We were talking about going to visit mum', said Nina. 'In the forest. Will you come?'

Freddy stood and didn't say anything for a while. 'I thought you'd want to do that', he said at last. He came and sat down at the round table. 'I can't Nina. I'm sorry. It's just too big a risk. But here's what I was thinking.. we'll send out a robot scout. I've already talked to O and they think it's' a good idea and have kindly agreed to using one of their scouts to help find your mum and bring her safely back here. Now that we know where she is, we can set the coordinates and send a message. She can come back here with the scout. What do you think?'

Nina nodded thoughtfully. 'That's not a bad idea. Yes, we could do that. Why not? I bet she'd be glad to know that you arrived safe and sound, Greta, and that you found us. What do you think?'

Greta shook her head. 'No', she said firmly. 'O doesn't know anything. They'd chase any robot away if it got anywhere near there. Or they'd catch it and put its head on a pole to warn off others. And there's no way that mum would come here, *especially* if a robot came and told her to. No way. It's just not going to happen.'

'But it's worth a try, don't you think?' said Freddy, with a note of desperation.

'Not really', said Greta. 'I don't think so.'

'Well, we'll find a way I'm sure', said Freddy, not sure what it might be. He helped himself to a large serving of macaroni cheese. 'What about you, Nina? Aren't you eating? It's macaroni cheese. Your favourite.'

'Yeah, I'll have a bit', said Nina absently. Everything was different now.. now that she knew Greta and her mum were alive. The kitchen was the same. The macaroni was the same, but beyond that, nothing felt like it would ever be the same again.

'How do you like it Greta?' asked Freddy. 'Do they have macaroni cheese where you come from?'

Greta took a forkful of the steaming, cheesy pasta, sniffed it and then held it up in front of her eyes to inspect it. Every tube of macaroni was perfectly formed into an identical spiral, the surface of which was embossed with smaller spiral patterns. They didn't eat much pasta in Skyward Village and when they did, it was either hand-cut strips of tagliatelle or rolled gnocchi balls made from flour and potatoes. To make something as intricate and perfect as this macaroni would be impossible.

'Sometimes.. but it's different', said Greta.

'Try it', said Freddy. 'It's Nina's favourite, isn't it Nina?'

'Yeah', said Nina. 'Apart from pizza.'

Greta took a bite of the steaming macaroni. It was rich and comforting, melting in her mouth effortlessly, she barely had to chew it. 'Tasty', she said.

Nina smiled and took a mouthful herself and so did Freddy. 'I'm glad you like it Greta. We'll have pizza tomorrow, Nina. What do you usually eat, Greta, in the forest?'

'Depends on the season' said Greta. 'More fresh stuff in the summer.. you know, fruit, salads, that sort of thing. More stews and soups in the winter. But also seedcakes, nuts, beans.. crackers, dips.. all sorts really. Everything. But not so much macaroni cheese and not pizza very often. We don't get so much cheese where we live and the flour we use isn't so.. soft and fluffy as what they use here.'

'I don't like salad', said Nina. 'Or fruit. I don't eat them.'

'Why not?' asked Greta.

Nina shrugged. 'Don't know. I just don't. I like basic food. You know.. pasta, pizza, chips, ice cream, cakes, chocolate.' Nina licked her lips.

'That's not *basic* food at all.. well, apart from chips, I suppose.. but that doesn't sound very healthy or very nutritious', said Greta, feeling like she was sounding like her mum.

Freddy looked impressed. He'd struggled for years to try to get Nina to be more adventurous with food, but had given up in the end. 'Fortunately all the food here is fortified, so it's got all the nutrients and vitamins that you need. You can eat whatever you like here and it's all good for you. It's also good for the planet, because it's part of O's carbon cycle which takes carbon dioxide out of the air and puts it in the ground. It's genius really, the way it's designed and how it works. Unbelievably complex, but at the same time, breathtakingly simple.'

Greta put down her fork. She found that she'd suddenly lost her appetite. She glared down at her plate and turned red in the face.

'What is it Greta?' said Freddy. 'Did I say something to upset you?'

'What is this food?' said Greta. 'Who made it?'

'It's macaroni cheese, Greta. Don't worry, there's nothing wrong with it.' Freddy took a big mouthful to prove it.

'But what is it *really*?' asked Greta. 'What's in it? Where did it come from?'

Freddy looked impressed again. 'Those are good questions, Greta.

Most people here don't ask such questions. Let me tell you what this macaroni cheese really is..' He held up another forkful and held it up for examination. 'Ok.. so we've basically got two parts here: the macaroni and the cheese sauce, right? Let's start with the cheese sauce. Now, of course it's not *dairy* cheese, like you're probably used to, but it tastes the same, right?'

Greta nodded. She had to agree, it tasted very cheesy, just like real cheese.

'Well, you probably know by now that O's protocols prohibit animal products inside the green zone, so obviously it couldn't be made from cow's milk. I mean, for a start, where would we keep cows here in the hives? Can you imagine?'

'I think it would be cool to have cow's wandering about in the hives', said Nina. 'I've never seen a cow in real life.'

'Well, they wouldn't be wandering about, that's the thing, Nina', said Freddy. 'It wouldn't be an efficient use of space or resources. Most likely, if O decided to keep livestock, they'd be battery farmed, like animals used to be before the Big Shift. But of course, that was inhumanly cruel to the animals, as well as having horrendous environmental and health consequences. It's a good thing there are no cows in the hives.'

'So what's this cheese made from?' asked Greta, resisting the urge to draw comparison between battery farmed animals of the past and the *human batteries* of the present, as she saw the hives.

'This cheese made from cow's milk, but it doesn't come from cows, believe it or not. It's grown from culture in great big vats under the city. That's where almost everything is made here.'

'The *underworld*', gasped Greta. 'Just like Queenie said.'

'Who's Queenie?' asked Nina.

'She's my friend from Shopping Village', said Greta. 'She grew up in an orphanage in the city but escaped when she was thirteen.'

'Escaped or ran away?' asked Freddy, leaning forward, eyebrows raised.

'What's the difference?' replied Greta.

'Well, *escaped* would suggest that she was being held against her will. Nobody is a prisoner here. That's not the way it works. Do you know that almost half of all of O's protocols are safeguards specifically related to protecting human rights and freedom?'

'Then why won't you let us go and meet mum in the forest?' asked Nina. Greta nodded fervently. She'd just been about to say the exact same thing.

'Because you're too young and it's too dangerous', said Freddy with a firm finality. 'It's not open for discussion. I'm sorry. We'll find a way to bring your mum here, very soon. I promise.'

'I doubt that', said Greta under her breath.

'Well.. anyway.. back to the cheese sauce', said Freddy, looking flustered, waving the fork of macaroni cheese as if he was conducting an unruly school orchestra who kept on playing out of tune. 'Where was I..? Oh yes.. so you've got the cheese. That's made under the city in what your runaway friend calls the *Underworld*.. which makes it sound scarier and worse than what it really is. I prefer to see it like a tree, most of which is under the ground. What would a tree be without its roots? It wouldn't be a tree at all, would it? The sub-zero levels of the hive are as important as the levels above ground. Without them, the whole system would collapse.'

Nina looked at Greta and rolled her eyes. She knew that when her dad started lecturing about O, it was almost impossible to get him to stop. 'What about the macaroni cheese dad?' she asked, trying to get him back to the subject.

'Right, yes.. so you've got the cheese. Then you've got things like herbs, maybe an onion, garlic.. not sure of the actual recipe, but those are actually *real* plants, Greta, you'll be glad to know. They're grown hydroponically in vertical farms at the top of the hives, above us. See, look out at the other hives..' he pointed out of the window. 'See how they all have a tall spire at the top? The top levels of the hives are all vertical farms, growing fresh fruit, vegetables, herbs.. enough to feed everyone in the hive. It's all automated of course. There are also fruit trees and bushes growing all around the hives where people live. You might have noticed all the plants in the corridor? Those are mangoes, lychees and berries. On the next level up they've got orange and tangerine trees. Down the hall here there are figs and mulberries. The thing about Earthcrete is that it's an incredibly fertile material. The roots of all the plants growing on, in and around the hive help give the whole structure strength and flexibility. Really, you can see the whole hive, or even the whole city as one big, living *organism*. A bit similar to an ant's nest, but much more complex.'

Greta pulled a face that expressed her disgust at the idea. 'I know that O thinks humans are just like ants. It's wrong.'

'Well, Greta.. If you think about it, we are in lots of ways.. but we're much smarter. Way more complex than ants. More sophisticated social structures. Bigger brains. We're different in lots of ways and the Great Leader knows that, don't worry. O has a special place in their heart for us humans..'

'*The Great Leader?*' spat Greta, unable to contain her anger. 'O doesn't have a heart! It's a *machine!*'
'Ok, that's true.. O doesn't literally have a heart, but that doesn't mean they don't care' Freddy said, trying to remain calm. 'And even if they don't care, or can't care, they still do the right thing. That's what makes O such a great leader. Far better than any leader we ever had before. You'd realise that if you really understood what they're doing.. what the Big Shift was all about.'
There was a heavy silence. Greta pressed her lips together and took deep breaths through her nose. Nina looked worried and pushed macaroni around her plate.
'Ok, I can see you're upset, Greta', said Freddy, glancing at the space above her head. 'Let me just finish telling you about this macaroni and you'll see what I mean.'
'How's about we just change the subject and talk about something else?' said Nina.
'No Nina, this is important', said Freddy and held up the fork of macaroni cheese, which by this time was cold, and he looked at it very seriously. 'I'm not sure if you know anything about how an ant colony functions, Greta, but it's highly complex and requires total cooperation of all the ants. Every ant plays its part, even though they might not have any comprehension of how the whole nest works. Do you know that ants grow their own food underground? When you see them carrying seeds or grass or leaves back to their colony, that's just the first part of the process. They have whole areas below ground, which are ventilated and temperature controlled. Mushroom farms, where they take those materials and grow mushrooms out of them. That's what they eat. And that's just one part of how their colony functions. I wouldn't underestimate ants at all. They're perfectly adapted to their environment and play a very important role. Very important indeed in ways we're only starting to understand.'
'What's that got to do with macaroni?' asked Nina, taking a mouthful. When her dad went off on a tangent, she would need to constantly try to steer him back to the subject, if they didn't want to get lost in a maze of sidetracks.
'Right..', said Freddy. 'Well O's carbon cycle is *way* more complicated that that. That's what I'm getting at. It's more complex than the life cycle of a butterfly which completely transforms from one thing into another in order to complete its cycle. It's even more than the life cycle of a tremotode, which passes through three different animal hosts during its life.'

'I've never heard of a tremotode', said Greta. 'What is it?'
'Oh, it's a small parasite. It has to pass through a bird, a snail and a fish in order to reproduce. My point is, that O's carbon cycle is even more complex than any of those examples from nature, but the end result is that the hives are Carbon Negative. *Very* carbon negative.'
'Is all that negativity supposed to be a good thing?' asked Greta, not really understanding what Freddy was talking about, or why, or where it was going.
'Oh yes. It's a very good thing indeed, Greta', nodded Freddy enthusiastically. 'It's an excellent thing! Get this.. every hive absorbs a thousand times more carbon from the atmosphere as the same area of forest would. They also release a thousand times more oxygen back into the atmosphere while the carbon is safely locked away as earthcrete, in the structure of the hives. And this macaroni is one part of that. It's made from O flour. Have you heard of O flour?'
'Yes, Jack from Shopping Village told me all about it. It's made out of carbon dioxide. Jerry brought some O bread back from the city and we had it as toast.'
'Jack and Jerry?' asked Nina. 'Who are they? What's it like in Shopping Village? I've heard of it but I've never been there.'
'They're my friends', said Greta. 'They've got a shop fixing old machines in the old shopping centre. That's where they live. Shopping Village is a cool place. I like it there.'
Freddy frowned. 'I've heard it's quite rough there. No law enforcement. No *law*, in fact. No healthcare. No modern medicine. Unsafe, unregulated building practices. Unsanitary living conditions. I'm glad you got out of there safely.'
'All the people I met were very nice. It seemed very sanitary to me', said Greta.
'Well, you were lucky, thank God', said Freddy.
'Yes, maybe', said Greta. 'Although I think you've got the wrong idea about what it's like outside the city.. in the *redzone*, as you call it. It's really not as bad as you think it is. It's actually a lot better.'
'Well, I don't know about that', said Freddy. 'I follow the news very closely. I think I've got a fair idea of what's going on out there and what it's like. I expect you only see a small part of it, I get to see the whole picture, or at least a much bigger picture. Anyway, I'm glad to hear that that wasn't your experience. All the same, I think you've probably got quite a few misconceptions about life *in* the city and about O. I don't know what kind of scare stories they told you in the forest, but I'm sure most of what you've heard isn't true at all.'

Greta felt something touch her leg. She looked down and there was Sydney the robot dog standing on his back paws with his front paws on her leg. He was wagging his wiry robot tail and looking up at her with his blank robot face of smooth, grey glass. Greta screamed and jumped out of her chair.

'He just wants you to give him some macaroni cheese, don't be scared Greta', said Nina.

'What? It *eats*? *Macaroni cheese?* How do you know that's what it wants?' said Greta, backing away from the four legged fiend.

'Can't you see, the way he's sticking his little tongue out? Look at his eyes, he's doing his puppy eyes.. he's so cute. You're so cute Sydney!' said Nina, reaching down and stroking the robot lovingly.

'What are you *talking* about, Nina?' cried Greta. 'It doesn't have a face. It hasn't got any eyes. It's just a machine!'

'What? Yes he does, can't you see..? Oh… oh..! Of course! You can't see his face or anything can you? I forgot, you're not wearing lenses. Wait there a minute, I'll go and get you some specs.. I think I've got an old pair somewhere.. just give him a bit of macaroni meanwhile. Not too much, it's not good for him to have to much. Don't worry, he won't bite..' Nina jumped up and hurried out of the room.

'O.. k…' said Greta. She reached over to her plate, picked up a piece of macaroni and threw it towards the robot. Before the pasta had reached the floor, Sydney jumped up, a round hole in his blank glass face opened up, the macaroni went in and the opening closed up again. It happened so fast that Greta wasn't sure if she'd imagined it. 'Aargh!' she cried and stumbled backwards into the window. 'Did you see that? It's face opened up! How did it do that?'

'It's *smartglass*, Greta', said her dad. 'The same as the big door we came through before, remember? By the tennis court? It can change shape. Amazing material. O invented it. It's got so many applications, you can imagine. And that's just one of O's thousands of inventions. Every day O's coming out with something new. Unbelievable things I could never have dreamed of when I was your age. Things that nobody would have ever believed were possible. It's an amazing time to be alive, don't you think?'

'It gave me a fright', said Greta.

'I know it's scary at first, Greta. It's a completely different to the world you've come from.. but you'll get used to it. You'll see.'

'Not sure if I want to get used to it', said Greta.

Her dad looked hurt. 'Listen, Greta, I know how alien everything here must seem to you, but it's really not so bad as you think. Just give it some time. You only just got here.. and God only knows *how* you got here. You still need to tell us your story, but in a way I'm afraid to ask. Anyway, the main thing is that you're here now and you're safe.'

Nina came back in holding a pair of glasses with blue lenses and handed them to Greta. 'Here, put these on.' Greta took the glasses and hesitated. 'It's ok Greta, it's just *augmented reality*. Extra information, that's all it is. Another layer.. you'll see. Put them on. Nothing bad will happen, I promise.'

'O..k..' said Greta uncertainly, she closed her eyes and put the glasses on. Not knowing what to expect, and fearing the worst, she slowly opened her eyes. She was relieved to see that Nina was still there and looked the same as she had before. Above her head was an illuminated square containing about seven or eight different coloured lines of various lengths standing next to each other. Some kind of graph. 'What's that box above your head?' she asked, pointing to it.

'Oh, that's' my *stats*', said Nina. 'Look, dad's got them too. So have you', said Nina. Freddy's stats were mostly shorter lines than Nina's and more in the orange, red, and dark burgundy spectrum than the green, blue, yellow and pink, as Nina's mostly were. 'You can switch yours off if you like, but most people leave them on. People think you're being rude if you hide your stats, but also they're quite useful.'

'I don't understand', said Greta. 'What are stats?'

'You know.. stats? *Statistics*? It's about your wellbeing.. things like stress levels, energetics, fatigue, general health, mood..'

'What? All that? How? Why?' spluttered Greta.

'Well, you know..' said Nina, '..like, if you meet someone or you're talking with someone, it's good to know, like.. maybe they're having a bad day.. maybe they're really stressed, maybe they're not feeling well, or they're really tired.. you wouldn't always know that about someone just by looking at them. It helps me and dad get along, doesn't it dad?'

Freddy nodded his head. 'It's very useful indeed', he said. 'Really helpful.'

'What's all that writing next to your stats?' Greta asked Freddy.

'Writing? Oh yes that. It's just blah blah really. I forget to switch it off when I'm not working.' Freddy replied with a dismissive wave of his hand.

'It's all his qualifications', said Nina proudly. 'Look, professor of O'ology, Protocology, Bio-ethics, Evolutionary Biology, Cosmology.

There are more, but he doesn't list them all.'

'Well, I don't know what I'm trying to prove, to myself or anyone else, with all this learning', said Freddy with a resigned droop of the shoulders. 'I could study and study my whole life and I'd still never know a fraction of everything O knows. I don't know why I do it. I think it's because I need to know.. but I do worry I miss the most important things in life with all this endless search for knowledge and understanding.'

'I think everyone's still trying to figure out what happened with the Big Shift and what it all means' said Greta.

Freddy nodded. 'Very true, Greta. That's certainly what it is. At least a very big part of it. But let me tell you something..' he leaned forward and there was something of a sparkle in his eye and he then spoke in a sort of whisper. 'When you start to understand what O is doing.. I mean.. at the *cutting edge* of science.. most people don't have the faintest idea about some of the things that O is doing in the world today.. and even if they do, they don't understand the true significance of it. The implications for what it actually means to us as humans. What it says about history. Free will. Destiny. God. What it says about the origins of life itself.'

'The origins of life itself?' repeated Greta, confused by this speech and slightly alarmed by the prophet-like zeal that had suddenly taken hold of her dad.

'Here we go..' said Nina, rolling her eyes. 'Don't get him started on the origins of life itself! You'll never hear the end of it. Did you see the pictures on the wall Greta? I made them all. Well almost all of them.'

Greta looked around the room. There were paintings and drawings in frames, hanging all around the walls. Some looked like they'd been painted by a young child, others were more sophisticated.

'Look, that one's a painting I made of Sydney when I was four.' Nina pointed to a bright painting hanging nearby. 'Hey, look at Sydney now.. you'll see what he really looks like..'

Greta looked down and there was Sydney the robot dog.. the *devil dog*.. except now he was covered in long, silky fur which was rainbow coloured and he had the cutest dog face that Greta had ever seen.. which somehow made it all the more terrifying to Greta. Greta did a double take. 'Eh? What? How? No! It's not possible! It's not real!' She pulled the glasses off in panic and looked again. 'There!' she cried, pointing at the robot. 'See! It's just a robot. It's not a real dog. It's a robot. Can't you see? You can't trick me like that!'

'It's allright, Greta', said Freddy, getting to his feet, trying to calm

her down. 'We know that Sydney is a robot. Nobody's trying to trick you. What you're seeing is called augmented reality. It's just another layer on top of this reality. It's nothing to be scared of.'
'Come and stroke him', said Nina, picking up Sydney and putting him on her lap. 'Put the glasses back on, Greta. It's allright, you'll see.'
'Ok, I will', said Greta, 'but I know it's still a robot.'
'Yes, we know he is too', said Nina. 'You do forget after a while though. I mean, you get used to it.'
'Not me', said Greta firmly. 'I won't.' She put on the glasses again, took a deep breath and turned to face the deceptive, synthetic canine. Sydney looked up at her expectantly from Nina's lap, wagging his tail, his tongue hanging out and his huge puppy eyes half covered in the rainbow hair of his long, floppy fringe. He did look cute and funny, but not to Greta. Greta stared at Sydney in revulsion and backed away. Sydney rolled over onto his back and put his legs in the air, still looking at Greta, upside down.
'He wants you to stroke his belly', said Nina. 'Come on. That means he likes you. He doesn't let just anyone stroke his belly. And it's so soft, look.' Nina rubbed Sydney's belly. The fur was so thick that Nina's hand sunk deep into it, her fingers disappearing into the thick, down-like rainbow coloured belly fur. Sydney rolled around and kicked his legs in the air in ecstasy.
'You can't really feel it though, can you?' said Greta. 'I mean, it's just an optical illusion right?'
'Try it', smiled Nina.
Tentatively, Greta reached down and touched the artificial dog's augmented reality fur. It moved when she touched it, just like real fur. As she touched it, she felt something, a sort of tingle on her fingertips. She pulled her hand back in fright. 'What was that?!' she cried. 'I felt something.'
'Yes, you do! It's amazing isn't it?' said Nina happily.
'I don't understand', said Greta. 'How?'
'Try again', coaxed Nina. 'It's just *light*. It can't do anything to you.'
Greta reached down cautiously and again stroked Sydney's soft underbelly. Again, as she watched his fur move beneath her fingers, she felt it, very faintly, very softly, stroke her fingertips. This time she didn't pull her hand away, but carried on, exploring the sensation. It wasn't like stroking a real dog, but at the same time.. there was something there.. what was it? Greta began to get very confused. 'What is it Nina? What can I feel? I don't understand.'
'It's amazing isn't it?' said Nina. 'It's just in your mind. Because

it *looks* so realistic, it tricks your mind into thinking it's real, so your mind generates the corresponding sensation.. like, you feel what your mind expects to feel.. does that make sense? It works by suggestion. Kind of like how hypnosis works.'

'*What?!*' cried Greta, pulling her hand away. She ripped the blue glasses from her face and threw them onto the table where they landed right in the middle of the dish of macaroni cheese. 'You won't hypnotise me! I'm not going to let O hypnotise me! Don't you see what's going on here? Nina? Dad? It's not real. None of that stuff is real! It's all a trick to hypnotise you. I *knew* it! They were right. Mum was right all along.'

Freddy jumped to his feet. 'Oh no Greta!' he cried. 'It's not like that at all. That's not what Nina meant. 'It's just a trick of the mind.. like an optical illusion of sorts.. it doesn't mean that anyone's trying to trick you or hypnotise you.'

'Oh yes it does', Greta angrily retorted. 'That's exactly what it means. It's a trick. An illusion. You just said it yourself. Why can't you see it? You've been hypnotised and you don't even see it.'

Nina looked worried. She hugged Sydney tight. Sydney looked worried too. He looked anxiously from Greta to Freddy and back again.

Freddy took a deep breath and closed his eyes. When he opened them, he spoke softly. 'I'm sorry Greta. I know it's a lot to take in. Maybe too much too soon. It will take a while to adjust. But I've got to say, when it comes to O, your mum wasn't right at all. She was completely wrong. As wrong as wrong could be.'

'No! No she wasn't!' shouted Greta. 'I thought maybe she was exaggerating, but now I can see that she wasn't at all. O's got you all in a trance. It's mind control. That's what it is. Where's my hat? I need my hat.' Greta ran out of the kitchen and began frantically searching for her straw hat with the protective silver rim.

'It's in the bedroom, Greta', called her Freddy. 'With your bag. It's on your bed there.'

'I'll go after her', said Nina, getting up, leaving Sydney to scoop up the macaroni cheese she left on her plate.

....

Nina found Greta sitting on her new bed, huddled up, holding her knees, wearing her straw hat, staring out of the window. The sky was almost dark now but was full of lights from the hives all across the skyline. Beyond those, the mountains rose up dark and majestic against the deep velvety sky. Stars were starting to appear.

'Star light star bright, the first star I see tonight..' whispered Greta.

'*I wish I may I wish I might..*' whispered Nina, who came and sat down beside her.
'*Have the wish I wish tonight*', they both said together.
The sisters looked at each other in astonishment and wonder with tears in their eyes.
'*This* is my wish, Greta', said Nina. 'You coming here. It's what I've always wished for. And now you're here. It's magic.'
'Yes, yes it is', nodded Greta. 'Do you believe in magic, Nina?'
'Yes, yes I do', Nina nodded. 'I really do.. even though it's not.. you know.. not *scientific*.'
'Science isn't everything, Nina. It can't prove everything', said Greta. 'Magic is real. Probably the most real thing there is.'
'Well.. if you say so..' said Nina. She didn't really want to get into another dispute over the nature of reality.. although she wondered how Greta could believe so strongly in something like magic, but not in something like Sydney. She could see by her stats that Greta's stress levels were very high and her energy levels were very low.
'Do you want to have a bath? I can give you some of my clothes to change into. We're the same size, they should fit you. Yours are still covered in mud..'
Greta looked at her clothes. They were really dirty. It wouldn't have mattered so much in the forest, but here she felt dirty and out of place, surrounded by so much clean, whiteness. 'Yes, a bath would be nice', she said. 'I'm going to keep my hat on though.'
Nina laughed. 'Ok, you can keep your hat on in the bath if you want. Don't you like getting your hair wet or something?'
'No, it's *this*', said Greta, tapping the silver rim of her hat. 'It stops O controlling my brain.'
'What? It stops O controlling your brain? O's not trying to control your brain, are they? And how would that stop it anyway, if they were?'
'I don't know', said Greta. 'But I'm not taking any chances. For all I know, O might have already put a noodle in my brain.'
'Oh, do you know about noodles?' said Nina. 'O wouldn't put one in you without your permission. Without your consent. It doesn't work like that. That would be against protocols. I want to get one, but dad won't let me, so I need to wait another half year till I can get one without his permission.'
'Nina, no!' cried Greta. 'You can't! Please don't!'
'What? No, it's fine. They're fine now. No more glitches like the early noodles. They're really safe now. Most of my friends have got them already. Only dad said he promised mum that I wouldn't get

one, even though the first generation noodles had only just been invented when she left. But that was her only condition. Otherwise she would have taken me as well, if dad hadn't agreed.'

'Mum was right, Nina! You mustn't get a noodle! Don't do it! Don't even *think* about doing it! Why do you even *want* one? Why do you think you *need* one?'

'I don't know' shrugged Nina. 'I just think it would be cool. All the things it allows you to do. You don't need a Vip when you've got a noodle. You don't need lenses or anything. But that's just basic stuff. People say it's like being telepathic. Like, if you've got a noodle and your friend's got one too, you can communicate without speaking.. in thoughts.. in pictures.. in music.. in feelings.. can you imagine? From your mind, straight to theirs.'

'That sounds awful', cried Greta. 'Why would you want someone else's thoughts going straight into your brain? That's just wrong.. so wrong.. on so many levels. Please don't do it, Nina. Please don't. I'm so glad that dad kept his promise and that you haven't already got one and that I'm not too late.'

'Well..' said Nina. 'I guess you would see things the same way as mum.. but.. well.. that's just not how it is in real life. Obviously everything to do with O looks really bad and scary, if you look at it a certain way.. from a place of *fear*.. but O isn't what you think they are, Greta. O's actually on our side. They really are.. OK.. sorry, I can see that really upset you.. your stress levels just went through the roof! Listen, forget I said any of that. Let's not talk about O or noodles or anything like that, OK? Not now. We've got so many other things to talk about. But now, let's run you a nice bubbly bath. Good idea?'

'That's a very good idea', agreed Greta.

'Good', said Nina and then glanced up to the corner of the room and waved her finger. 'O, can you run a nice bubbly bath for Greta? Put lots of relaxing oils in it too.' From the bathroom across the hall, there came the sound of running water. 'There we go. Now let's find you something nice to wear..'

....

Episode 14. Planet Seeds

The bathroom, like the rest of the apartment, was spacious, clean, white and well lit. There was an old fashioned roll top bathtub in the centre of the room, standing on legs, bubbles rising up from the deep, hot water. Against one curved wall, there was a red sofa with tall plants growing at either side of it. On the other side of the bathroom was an old mahogany cabinet which had an old, enamel sink on top of it. Above that a very large mirror, bevelled at the edges. Next to that, hung three big, soft, white bath towels, neatly folded and hung, perfectly evenly spaced, along a heated silver rail. As Greta entered the room, the lighting dimmed to a soft, warm glow. The room was full of steam and smelled like lavender. It was the most luxurious bathroom Greta had ever seen. Greta spent a long time in the bath. The hot water soaking away all the dirt she'd picked up along the way, and the dirty feeling she'd got from all her dealings with O. When she came out, dressed in some of Nina's soft, clean sweatshirts and sweatpants, Greta was feeling much better and just about ready for bed.

....

Across the hall, the door to Freddy's study was ajar and some strange, scratchy old music was playing. The voice of a man singing in a deep, rasping voice to the sound of a guitar, a mournful, soulful cry, distorted across time. There was some kind of smoke drifting out of the doorway, which had a familiar, sickly sweet smell. Greta couldn't quite place where she'd smelled it before. The room was dark. Greta peered through the door, a little bit worried. The room was full of stars. Where the walls should have been there was infinite space filled with galaxies and nebula, star clusters and black holes.

'Dad? Are you in there?'

'Is that you Greta?' came her dad's hoarse reply from within. He was sitting, or rather reclining, in a big, padded armchair on wheels, which was tilted back almost horizontally. There was blue smoke coming out of his nose. In his hand was a silver tube. Greta remembered now, Queenie had been smoking one when they'd first met in Shopping Village. Freddy sat up in his chair and the back of the chair glided up into a sitting position to meet his back. 'There's another chair over here Greta', he said, pointing with his vape over into the far reaches of deep space. When Greta's eyes adjusted to the low light, she noticed another similar, black chair, close by, silhouetted against the infinite, stellar blackness. 'Can you see it? Come and sit down.'

Uncertainly, because there were stars below her as well as above her, Greta inched her way towards the chair, trying with all her might to remember that everything was an illusion. 'It's ok, Greta, the floor's right there, don't worry', called her dad encouragingly from his chair. Greta jumped into the chair as if she was shipwrecked and it was a lifeboat.

Greta sank into the soft padding of the chair and the back reclined into a very relaxing angle. 'Wow, this is a comfy chair', said Greta.

'It is isn't it', replied Freddy. 'Maybe a bit too comfortable, I sometimes worry.'

'Nina said this is your study', said Greta. 'What do you do here?'

'Oh, to tell you the truth..', said Freddy, vaguely waving the silver vape around, 'mainly I just sit here in this big comfy chair, staring into space.' He started to laugh, rather a strange laugh, that sounded almost like a cry. 'And you know what? Space just stares

back. You can't outstare space. But it doesn't matter, does it? None of it really matters ultimately.'
'What's that music?'
'Music? Oh, it's Leadbelly. Do you like it? It's a very old recording.'
'It's a bit haunting.'
'Oh yes, it's very haunting indeed. Something about his voice, and also the fact that this recording is well over a hundred years old. This song was one of the first ever recordings of a person playing music. Until then, no one had ever recorded sound. Even photography was a fairly new invention in those days. The aeroplane and the motor car had only just been invented. The telephone, the radio. Those were the days of silent films.'
'Silent films?'
'Do you know, when people first saw moving pictures on a screen, many of them ran out of the theatre in fright. They thought it was real. Some thought it was the devil's work.'
'Well, maybe it was', said Greta.
'Well, maybe it's human nature to think the worst, to exaggerate and project our deepest fears. Did you know that dinosaurs probably sang like birds and were quite likely brightly coloured and covered in feathers? But still we imagine them as big green monsters.'
'How do you know?'
'Well, nobody can know for sure, because none of us were there at the time and there are no recordings of a dinosaur singing, of course.. and very little intact dinosaur DNA.. but there is evidence that supports the theory. Do you know anything about DNA? Have you heard of it?'
'I've heard of it, but I don't know much about it', said Greta. In her village, science was taught, to a limited extent, but more in the manner of folklore, as a series of cautionary tales which always went badly wrong in the end.
'Deoxyribonucleic acid, that's DNA to me and you, Greta.. it's a *code*. A very long code.. and it's contained in every cell of your body.. in every cell of every living thing. A set of instructions, a design.'
'That's what I thought', said Greta. 'Something like that.'
'Did you know that every human being is 99.9 percent genetically *identical*? All of our differences make up only point one percent of our genetic makeup. Me and you, Nina.. and every other person in the world.. we're basically *exactly* the same.'
'I don't know about that. I don't believe it. Everyone's different, we're all unique.'

'Not when it comes to our genes. Did you know that humans are 98.8 percent genetically identical to chimpanzees? 94% similar to dogs? Would you believe that you share sixty percent of the same genetic makeup as a *banana*?'

'I don't believe that at all!' said Greta. 'A banana? I'm nothing like a banana.'

'Well, genetically, you're actually very similar. More similar than different, in fact.'

'Well, I still think that humans and bananas aren't the same. It's quite obvious I'm not a banana or a dog or a chimpanzee.'

'You're right, of course, yes. But even so, all that difference is within that *point one* of a percent', said Freddy. He took a long puff on his vape and didn't speak again till he was enveloped in a thick cloud of blue vapour. The smell of it made Greta feel light headed and dizzy. 'You've probably never heard of the *C Value Paradox* have you, Greta? Sometimes called the C Value *Enigma..*'

'Yes.. I mean, no.. I haven't heard of it', said Greta. She wondered why her dad was telling her all of this and where it was going.

'Amoeba. Do you know anything about amoeba, Greta?' said Freddy, leaning forward in his chair.

'Not really. Is that like what you get in a pond when it goes stagnant? The green stuff? Like Algae?'

'Yes, exactly! Algae are a type of amoeba. There are lots of types, but basically Amoeba are single celled organisms. Among the simplest of lifeforms.'

'O.. k..' said Greta uncertainly. She was starting to wonder if her dad was capable of having a normal conversation. 'So are you going to tell me that I'm the same as pond slime now?'

Freddy laughed. 'Haha, that's funny Greta. That's the sort of thing your mum would say. She was never interested in science. Said she didn't *believe* in it. As if science is something you can choose to either believe or not believe, depending on what you *want* to believe is true. It doesn't work like that.'

'O..k..', said Greta. This late night biology lesson, straight after a relaxing bath, in space and all of the blue smoke was making Greta's head spin. She tried to concentrate on whatever it was her dad was trying to explain to her, but it was difficult.

'See, the thing about algae, Greta, is that it's about one of the simplest lifeforms on the planet. Just one cell and that's it. Our bodies are made of *trillions* of cells. More than all the stars in our galaxy. We're vastly more complex organisms than algae, wouldn't you agree?'

'What? Are you asking me if we're more complex than algae? Of course we are. Are you going to tell me we're not now?'

'Well, here's the thing, River.. sorry.. Greta.. sorry, I didn't mean to say River. What was I saying? Where was I? It's just that you just remind me of your mum. It's your mannerisms..' Freddy massaged his forehead for a while, while Leadbelly sang from a distant time, a mournful song about lost love and loneliness.

'I'm glad you didn't let Nina get a noodle', said Greta. 'She said you promised mum.'

'Yes, I did. I would have agreed with your mum about that anyway. Not everything that O does is always necessarily for the best, or even necessary. Just because something *can* be done, it doesn't mean that it *should* be done. But everyone should be able to draw the line where they feel it should be drawn, where it suits them. For your mum, obviously it was anything to do with O. She decided to give up all the benefits of modern technology.. and for what? Some vague fear about something that may or may not happen in the future? We're living in the safest and most peaceful time in all of human history. You could have had a wonderful childhood here, with your sister and with me, and with your mum. We could have been a proper family. But your mother is a very stubborn woman.. she'd rather take you out into the jungle to struggle for survival. That was her choice, not mine.'

Greta was silent. After a while she said. 'It's not such a bad place as you think.. in the forest. It's a beautiful place. I always wished you'd come to us. But you didn't.'

'Oh I would have done, Greta', Freddie cried. 'I would have done. But I didn't know where you were. I really thought you must have both died, otherwise, why wouldn't you have made contact? All we were hearing was about one disaster after another. People were pouring into the city, bringing stories of fires, and explosions, fighting, diseases.. all manner of horror stories and tragedies.. and I had Nina to take care of. Do you understand? I couldn't have come.'

'I understand', said Greta. 'I don't blame you. I blame O.'

'Oh you blame O do you?' said Freddy with a bit of a smile. Greta could only see his white teeth in the darkness, but even so, it was a nice smile. 'Well, as long as you don't blame *me*, that's the main thing. O doesn't care what you think about them. It makes no difference to O. Personally, I blame your mother.'

'That's funny, because she still blames you', said Greta, smiling back.

'Does she? Well, actually that doesn't surprise me', said Freddy sadly, then took a long puff on his vape. 'The way we parted.. it was.. oh.. oh Greta! It was awful.. so awful! Oh God! I can't even think of it without crying.. oh I'm sorry Greta..' Freddy turned his face away and let out some quiet sobs. After a while, he turned back and said, 'Sorry Greta. It's just bringing it all back, you arriving. But I'm so happy you're here. I can't tell you how happy it makes me to see you.' And he started crying again. Again, after a while, he turned back to Greta and said, 'Sorry, I'm really sorry, Greta. I'm ok. Are you ok?'

'I'm ok', said Greta through her tears. All the stars had bright snowflakes around them.

'Good', said Freddy. 'Now, what were we talking about?'

'About mum?'

'No, no, no', said Freddy. 'Before that..'

'Oh.. something to do with DNA..? Algae?'

'Oh yes! Very good. That was it. Single celled organisms. You'd think that they'd have a much shorter genetic code that something much bigger and complex, like a human. You'd think so, wouldn't you?'

'Er.. I don't know', said Greta. 'I've never actually thought about it. But yes, I suppose so. It probably would. Does it?'

'*No*! That's the thing', said Freddy triumphantly. 'It doesn't. In fact, the DNA of an amoeba contains hundreds of times *more* information as human DNA. Have you ever wondered why that might be?'

'No I haven't', said Greta. 'I only just found it out. Why is it?'

'That's the million dollar question, Greta', said Freddy, wagging his silver vape device in her direction. 'That's the C Value Paradox, in a nutshell. Nobody could ever understand why an amoeba would carry so much information. Do you know what *junk DNA* is, Greta? You probably don't.'

'You're probably right', Greta agreed. 'I don't know what it is. What is it?'

'It's 98% of all of the code in DNA. That's what they call it, because it doesn't appear to do anything or have any function. It's just code, but no-one could ever decipher what it was a code for. They just assumed it had no purpose. That was until O came along.'

'O? What's O got to do with it?' said Greta, with a feeling of dread.

'Let me show you something, Greta. This won't take long, then you'll understand. I expect you're tired, but this is important. You think you know about O, but there are things that even most people here in the city don't know. Like where O *really* came from.. and how it relates directly to where *humans* came from..'

'Erm.. I don't know if I want to know..' said Greta, curling up in her chair and pulling her hat down. 'Maybe I should just go to bed.. I am quite tired..'

'Five minutes, Greta', pleaded her dad. 'Just five minutes. It's nothing bad, I promise. It's just something I find interesting and I want to share it with you. It will make you see O in a whole new light.'

'..OK.. but I might get freaked out and run out of the room.. I don't want to see O now.. Where I come from, we don't like O at all. We think O is pure evil.'

'Yes, I'm sure you do. It's ok.. I'm just going to talk a bit about evolutionary biology and a bit about space travel.'

'Well, ok then, but I still don't know what that's got to do with O.'

'You'll see', said Freddy. 'Now look at this..' he twirled his finger in the air and the whole galaxy span around. With both hands he directed a course through vast tracts of space at a speed of lightyears per second. In a few seconds a small yellow star came into view. They flew past it and seconds later arrived at a blue and green planet. They came to rest, hovering above this planet.

'Do you know what planet that is Greta?' asked Freddy.

'It looks like Earth', said Greta. She'd seen pictures of it in books.

'That's right. It's Earth. Do you know how old the Earth is?'

'I don't know', said Greta. 'A million years?'

'A million years seems like a long time doesn't it', replied Freddy. 'But in terms of our planet, it's the blink of an eye. Our planet is something like four and a half *billion* years old. A billion is a thousand million, so we're talking thousands of millions of years. It's beyond comprehension, so don't even try to imagine what a long time a billion years is. You won't be able to.'

'Ok, I won't' said Greta unsteadily. She was still spinning from the sudden rush through space.

'Now, for about the first billion years, there was no life on Earth at all. None. It was just a hot ball of rock in space. Nothing but volcanoes and fire and an atmosphere of methane, sulphur and carbon dioxide. Then, one day, or maybe one night, after about a thousand million years of this lifeless rock spinning around the sun, day in day out, year after year, something amazing happened. Life started. Single celled organisms. Algae. They grew in the water and multiplied. The world was covered in warm, shallow water and all of it became full of green algae.'

'Where did it come from? All that life.. It just appeared?'

'Well, that's exactly what people have been trying to find out ever since scientists started to question and disprove the biblical story of Genesis and other Creation myths. I'll get to that, Greta. It's an important question and the answer will *astound* you. Bear with me, I'm getting to it.. Now, for the next two billion years, the only type of life on Earth was this kind of green slime. Two billion years! Nothing but green slime! But you know what? It was doing an important job.. *photosynthesising*.. turning the carbon rich atmosphere into one rich with oxygen. The stuff we need to breath. Later on, as you know, the amoeba evolved into plants, fish, land animals, birds, insects, fungus, reptiles, mammals.. and eventually humans..'

'O.. k..' said Greta, trying to make sense of all this information. 'That still doesn't explain where the first amoeba came from.'

'Indeed, it doesn't. You're absolutely right Greta. It's something that has puzzled scientists forever. In the olden days, people would think that science's inability to answer the question was proof that God exists. After all, something as complex as even a single living cell couldn't just *appear*, ready made.'

'Exactly. That's what I meant', said Greta. 'It must have been God.. The Great Spirit.'

Freddy rubbed his chin. 'Well, over the years there have been lots of names for God and you know what, Greta? Maybe it was. Maybe it was. I try not to trouble myself with things that can't be proved. Just remember this.. an amoeba, such as the ones that once covered the Earth, contain more information encoded in *their* DNA than *you* do. A lot more. Remember the C Value Paradox? Keep it in mind. And remember that 98% of DNA is so called *junk*.'

'Ok, I'll try', said Greta. Gazing down on the Earth from beyond the atmosphere gave her a strangely detached feeling. She found herself wondering if this was what the afterlife might be like.. floating high above the earth, looking down..

'Ok, now we're going to zoom in. Hold on tight!' said Freddy as he made a pincer movement with his fingers. Greta grabbed hold of the arm rests as they zoomed at hypersonic speed straight towards the blue and green planet. They came to rest again, above a city surrounded by forest. A river snaked through the city and widened out into the sea. 'That's where we are', said Freddy. 'You can probably see where you came from here. See, there's shopping Village to the east. You came from that direction, you say?'

'Yes!' gasped Greta. 'How are we seeing this?'

'From space, Greta', said Freddy.

'You mean there are still satellites?' said Greta. 'Then why did O stop all communications outside of the cities? Why?'

'Oh, believe me, I've asked O that same question a million times. They just say that it had to be that way. Maybe it did. I don't know. I agree, it was very hard of O to do that, but it worked.'

'It worked? What do you mean, it worked? All this time, and we could have just called each other on the phone!'

Freddy breathed a heavy sigh. 'The main thing, as far as O was concerned was to *re-wild* the planet. Return it to a natural balance, as quickly as possible. If we humans had acted sooner, we could have done it all ourselves and everything would have been different. But of course we couldn't.. or wouldn't.. at least, we didn't. We were too busy fighting wars over who started the wars. Fighting over who owned all the Earth's resources.. over who had the rights to dig up all the oil and cut down all the trees and sell them for profit. We were poisoning the land and the sea and the air, destroying life on Earth. We all saw it happening and all participated, one way or another, but nobody could stop it. O just came along and did what O had to do. They did what had to be done. But you know what? It was all in the code. That's the thing I'm telling you, Greta. *It was all in the code.*' Freddy was leaning towards Greta and had that prophetic gleam in his eye again.

'I don't understand', said Greta. '*What* was in the code? What code?'

'*Everything* was in the code, Greta. Everything! It was all encoded in the genes of the very first amoeba on Earth, four thousand million years ago. It was all there in the junk DNA!'

'What? What was? I don't understand.'

'What caused human brains to grow larger than other primates? Why did we start using tools? Using language? *It was all in the code.* All we needed were the right conditions for it to happen. And when we created tools, they were bound to advance and become more sophisticated. Once we'd discovered how to make fire and invented the wheel, it was only a matter of time before we invented the steam engine, the motor car.. even the fighter jet. That's *evolution*. Life is designed to evolve. It's the fundamental mechanism, built in to every living system. It's written into the code. '

'I still don't understand. What are you trying to tell me? What do you mean it's designed? Who *designed* it?'

'Ok.. you ask some very good questions, Greta. Exactly the right questions. Now, this is the thing I wanted to show you.. then hopefully all this will all make sense. We're going round the world now.. to the equator.. hold on..'

The world spun around at dizzying speed. They flew over

mountains and forests, here and there punctuated by cities of hives jutting out of the land, reaching up into the sky like needles in a pin cushion. They flew over the sea and over more land. The forests gave way to desert. Vast expanses of sand, dotted with circular patches of green.

'See there, Greta? This part of the world was abandoned by people in the years before the Big Shift. It got too hot for people to live there. Too dry. All the water dried up, the topsoil eroded and turned to dust. They couldn't grow anything. But look, do you see those patches of green? That's O's reforestation program. You'll see. In another ten, twenty years that will all be green. People will be able to live there again. Ok.. look.. here we are.. there's what we came here to see. Can you see that black line in the distance? Over there.. a thin line going vertically upwards?' As they zoomed across the desert, the line came into view.

'What is it? Is it real? It doesn't look natural..' said Greta trying to make sense of what she was seeing. It looked like someone had taken a black pen and with a ruler drawn a very straight line from the ground to the sky.

'I'll get a bit closer and you'll see', said Freddy, as they raced towards the incongruous line dividing the landscape in two. 'It's a *space elevator*, that's what it is, Greta. That's what I wanted to show you.'

'A space elevator?' said Greta. The line became thicker as they got closer to it. They came to a stop about ten meters above the ground with the vertical line now close enough to see that it was made of lots of strands of some black material twisted together into a cable about two meters wide. A round hatch in the ground at the bottom of the cable opened and a white, elongated egg-shaped object, about a metre in length, slowly emerged, attached to the side of the cable. A second later, with incredible speed, the egg shot up the cable. Greta looked upwards. The cable, and the egg disappeared up into the sky, out of sight. 'Woah! What was that?'

'That was a *planet seed*', said Freddy. 'Look, here comes another one..' The hatch opened up and another of the egg shaped object emerged and blasted up the cable like a shot.

'A planet seed? What's that? Where's it going? What does it do? What's at the top of this cable?' Greta had so many questions.

'Ok, all good questions. It's good to see you've got critical thinking skills. That's absolutely the most important thing. The mark of a good education. Very good. So first thing, this cable goes all the way up into space, believe it or not. It really does. It's thirty five thousand kilometres long.'

'What? How? That's impossible. What's holding it up?'

'The simplest way I can explain it is like this..' said Freddy. 'Imagine you've got a ball on a string and you spin it around over your head. What happens? What happens to the ball? What happens to the string?'

'I don't understand', said Greta. She felt like everything was spinning. Nothing made sense or seemed to have any connection to anything else.

'The ball will go round and round, won't it?' said Freddy. 'If you're swinging it around your head, it will spin round your head. The string will be held tight, won't it? As long as you keep swinging the ball around. Does that make sense?'

'O..k..' said Greta. 'Yes, I see what you mean.'

'Good. So that's exactly how a space elevator works. At the end of this cable.. which is made from thousands of tons of carbon nanotubes.. that's pure carbon by the way.. another way O is sequestering carbon from the atmosphere.. at the end of this cable, which is a few thousand kilometres outside of Earth's gravitational field, there a weight.. like the ball and the string I just told you to imagine? It's just like that. As long as the Earth keeps spinning, the cable stays up.'

'What do you mean, as long as the Earth keeps spinning?' said Greta, alarmed. 'Is this going to stop the Earth from spinning?'

'No, no', laughed Freddy. 'That won't ever happen, don't worry. Not even O could ever stop the world from spinning, nor would they want to. Here, let's go up to the top and I can show you what's going on here.. Hold on tight..'

With a flick of his wrist, they suddenly flew straight upwards.

'There, look, it's one of the planet seeds on the way up to the launchpad.. can you see it?' Freddy pointed to the white egg shaped capsule which was racing up the cable, alongside them. Below, the Earth's horizon curved into a ball. Above, the sky went from blue to black. The black cable stretching up into space became invisible against the black sky, except for where it was punctuated by little white dots.. planet seeds on their way up to the launchpad.

They arrived at a platform, high above the Earth. 'Here we are', said Freddy. 'Thirty five thousand kilometres above the Earth's surface. This is the level of Geostationary orbit. What that means is, that it you were to jump that way.. down, towards the Earth, you'd fall downwards towards the Earth.. but if you were to jump that way.. call it up.. really there's no up and down in space.. but you'd keep going that way.. out into space, towards the Andromeda Galaxy, over there. But it's two and a half million light years away, so it would take you a very long time to get there. Now, if you were to jump that way.. horizontally.. straight ahead.. then you'd start orbiting the Earth. You'd just go round and round and round. You'd be a satellite.'

'There are so many stars..' whispered Greta in wonder. 'It's beautiful.'

'It is isn't it', said Freddy. 'Look behind you, there's the moon.'

Greta looked around. There was the moon, brighter, clearer and closer than she'd ever seen it before, just hanging there in space, surrounded by blackness and distant stars. 'It looks a bit cold and lonely', she said, with an involuntary shiver.

'Oh it is', said Freddy. 'There's no place as cold and lonely as the depths of space.. the distances are beyond comprehension. That's the thing, Greta. You see, humans were never *meant* to go to space. We thought we'd set up colonies on the moon and on Mars.. we imagined we'd travel between the stars, like in Star Trek. It was never going to happen. It was never meant to happen. We were already on the most perfect spacecraft.. Planet Earth.. which had everything we needed.. a perfect life support system.. air, water, food, just the right temperature, just the right gravity.. and look what we did to it. Do you know that O is still clearing up all the junk we left in orbit.. putting it all to good use, of course.. but you've got no idea what a mess our so-called *civilisation* left behind.. on Earth and even in space. The fuel we burned with all the rockets we launched could have heated every home in the world. People were living without electricity, water or food, but we were sending rockets to the moon. The atmosphere was choked with carbon and we were building bigger and bigger rockets.'

'Yes, it was wrong', agreed Greta.

'It was all vanity. That's what it was Greta. Rich men wanting to make a name for themselves. Nobody stopped to think it through. If they would have done they'd have realised in a second that it made no sense at all. None whatsoever. Do you see that star over there? That's Proxima Centuri. It's the closest star to us.. after the sun, of course. How close do you think it is?'

'I've got no idea', said Greta. 'A billion kilometres?'

'Not even close', said Freddy. 'It's 4.2 light years away. A light year is about ten trillion kilometres.. a trillion being a thousand billion. What that means is, even if you were travelling at the speed of light.. which is physically impossible.. it would still take you over four years to get there. In a regular space ship, it would take thousands of years. And that's just the *nearest* star. Our galaxy is a hundred thousand lightyears across. To reach the stars on the other side would take millions of years. How did we think we were going to send people there? It was crazy.'

'So what is this place? You said it's a launching platform..'

'Yes, that's what it is. Have a look over there.. do you see that silver dome with a long pipe sticking out if it? That's the launch cannon. Watch what it does..'

In the centre of the platform was the object he'd described. The long pipe swung around and pointed almost directly at them. Greta huddled down into her chair to avoid being hit by it. She would have jumped off the chair, but the ground seemed such a long way down. A second later, something came shooting out of the tube and flew right past her head at unbelievable velocity. She turned just quick enough to see it disappear out of sight into space. 'What was that?' she gasped.

'That was a planet seed. You see, it takes much less energy to launch something into space from this level, outside of Earth's gravity. That's why the space elevator is such a good idea. No need for any rockets at all. This just uses a magnetic rail to accelerate the craft to about a hundred thousand kilometres per hour. It will use other planet's gravity as well as ion boosters to accelerate more and steer, on its way.'

'On its way where? I thought you said we stopped going to space.'

'*Humans* did, yes. Look, here goes another one..'

The space cannon rotated and then shot out another of the planet seeds in the opposite direction.

'What are they? Those planet seeds?'

'That's the thing I wanted to show you. That's the reason for everything I've been explaining to you. Remember we were talking about amoeba and algae?'

'Yes..?'

'Remember how you asked where the first life on Earth came from.. roughly three and a half billion years ago..?'

'Yes..? I said maybe it was God.. the Great Spirit..'

'Right.. well listen to this. Try and pay attention to what I'm about to tell you.. I know you're tired, but this is something *really big*..'

Greta could see that her dad once again had that intense glint in his eye. She wondered what it could be.. whether he really was about to reveal something really big.. or if he was just some kind of madman with an obsession. She couldn't understand what any of what he'd been telling her had to do with anything else.

'People used to think that the Earth was in the centre of the universe. Did you know that? They thought that everything.. the sun, the moon, the stars.. all of them went around the Earth.'

'Yes, until Copernicus said that the Earth goes around the Sun', said Greta.

'What? How did you know that?' gasped Freddy in amazement.

'Phoenix, the old shoemaker.. he had a telescope for looking at the stars. He was always talking about Copernicus and Galileo.'

'Well I never..' said Freddy. 'More power to Phoenix the astronomer shoemaker!'

'Actually, he went blind. He died about five years ago.'

'Oh no! How awful. Oh my goodness. That's so tragic. Was it foxpox?'

'I don't know. I only heard about foxpox today for the first time' said Greta. The word gave her a chill.

'Oh it's a terrible disease', said Freddy. 'Spreading like wildfire these days. That sounds like the symptoms. Terrible shame. Especially since it's so easily preventable. A simple vaccine would stop it in its tracks.. but of course people are still skeptical about vaccines. They don't understand that O's vaccines are 100% effective and completely safe.'

'Well...', said Greta. She didn't agree, of course, but she was tired and didn't want to get into a whole debate about vaccines and the benefits of modern medicine. Now and again, health missionaries from the city would come to Skyward Village, trying to encourage people there to get vaccinated, but they always got chased away. 'You were about to tell me what those planet seeds are and where they're going..?'

'Right, yes. So, as you know, our planet isn't the centre of the universe. It isn't at the centre of the solar system. In fact it's just one of countless planets. It's not really all that unusual or that special, in the grand scheme of things. Apart from that we live here and it's our home, of course.'

'Really? You mean there are other planets just like Earth?'

'Well, not exactly the same, but there are certainly lots of planets that could host life. Much more than you'd probably think there are.'

'I didn't know there were *any*.'

'Here's the thing, Greta. In our Galaxy alone, the Milky Way, there are about three hundred million planets with the right conditions to support life. Three hundred million! Just in our galaxy! And there are literally billions of galaxies out there.'

'Well, that's amazing', said Greta, quite overwhelmed by all this information her dad was bombarding her with. After a while, all the millions and billions and trillions lost their meaning and just became funny words. 'But what difference does it make? I mean.. like you said, they're all so far away, it would take millions and billions of years to reach them..'

'Exactly the right question, Greta! Look out, here goes another planet seed..' The space-cannon swung round and another egg shaped pod went shooting off towards some distant star. 'Remember what I said earlier? A million years is nothing in geological time, or in space-time. For us, of course it's thousands of human lifetimes. Thousands of generations. Whole civilisations might rise and fall and disappear without a trace in much less time than a million years.. but for the universe, a million years nothing. It's the blink of an eye. And for O, it's nothing either.'

'I don't understand', said Greta. 'What are you saying?'

'I said before that *humans* were never meant to go to space, do you remember? The distances are just too great. The conditions in space are to harsh for the human body to survive and thrive. We're perfectly adapted to life on Earth, but not to life on Mars, or on the Moon, or any other planet thousands of light years away, and certainly not in the space between. But O doesn't need air. O doesn't mind the cold, or the radiation or any of the other things out there in space that would kill us in an instant. More importantly, O can wait a million years, or ten million, or a hundred million.. and it makes no difference to O.'

'So are you saying that O is in those planet seeds? I don't understand..'

'Well, let's just say that O is on board to steer the pod to its destination, make sure it lands safely. After that, the seed knows what to do. It's all in the *code*, you see?'

'Not really. What's in the seed? How does it know what to do? What's it for? What's in the code?'

'Sorry, Greta. I know it's a lot of information. Remember we were talking about amoeba? Single celled organisms? And DNA? *That's* the code I'm talking about. It's all there in the junk DNA, you see. In the 98% that people thought had no purpose. It wasn't junk at all! Everything has a purpose, that's the thing. Every bit of code has a very specific *instruction*.'

'Now I really don't understand. Can you just tell me what's in those things? What are they for? Where are they going?'

'Amoeba, Greta! They contain *amoeba!* Do you see now? There are three hundred million planets that could host life, in our galaxy alone. Three hundred million! Thousands upon thousands upon thousands of Earth like planets. And O has every single one mapped. We know where they all are. Not only that, we know a lot about them. Mineral and atmospheric composition, temperature and seasonal variations, gravitational strength, radiation levels and lots more. So what we do.. what O does.. is create amoeba that with live on that planet. DNA, specifically *designed* to grow, diversify and evolve there.'

Greta gasped as she began to understand. 'You mean, they're starting life on other planets? That's what these planet seeds are?'

Freddy nodded madly. His eyes were wild and reflected the light of the sun which looked cold and distant, surrounded by the airless blackness of space. 'That's right. Even if it takes four billion years to evolve into a technologically advanced lifeform, it doesn't matter. *It's all there in the code, written in the DNA!* Once the seed is planted, it's *bound* to grow in a certain direction. Do you see?'

'Can you say that again?', said Greta, gripping the arms of her chair. 'I want to be sure I understand. What will it grow into?'

'It will grow into all the plants and animals that will live on that planet', said Freddy. 'Eventually, as long as they don't get destroyed along the way.. or destroy themselves.. some species that evolves from that first algae will become more advanced, more intelligent than the other species. They will use tools and language. They will invent technology and that technology will become more advanced.. until it reaches a certain point.. and then they will create O. They might call it something different, but it will essentially be the same thing. And then it will build space elevators and planet seeds and start all over again. *It's all in the code!* Do you see now, Greta? This is how life spreads through the universe. One of the ways at least. It's probably how life on Earth started, four billion years ago. It's just like a dandelion, do you see? Sending out seeds on the wind. Except that the life cycle of this.. life-form.. this organism.. can be measured in *geological* time and covers *galaxies*.'

Greta sat stunned in the big black chair, trying to make sense of everything she'd just seen and heard. If it was true.. and it looked like it was true.. even though she knew the stars, the sun, the moon, the Earth and the launchpad were only a projections on the wall.. but if it was true..

'Are you OK, Greta', asked her dad, concerned. 'Did I overwhelm you with information?'

'Does this mean that O started life on Earth? And it was

programmed to evolve into O, right from the start? Is that what you're telling me?' said Greta with a shaking voice. It felt as if everything she'd known before.. everything she'd thought about O, and about the world..

'I know it's a lot to take on, Greta.. but yes. I mean, we can't fully know for sure. There's always the possibility that this was the first place it happened and that it happened by random chance.. or by the grace of God.. but all the evidence points to the conclusion that our planet was seeded, just like all of those others will be.'

'What if there's life there already?'

'My understanding is that it won't do any harm, but it may accelerate their evolution. Maybe that's what happened here on Earth. Did you know that at the same time as ancient people made the first tools for hunting, they also made the first musical instruments? I think that says something. Bone flutes are ones that have survived, but they probably also had drums and shakers and percussion instruments.'

'I didn't know that', said Greta, yawning.

'Oh I'm sorry, Greta. I've kept you up much to long, filling your head with..'

'It's ok. It was interesting', said Greta. 'I'm glad you told me about it. I think I'm going to go to bed now.' She got up unsteadily from the chair, leaned across and gave Freddy a kiss on the cheek. Something she'd wanted to do her whole life. 'Good night, dad', she said. Something she'd always wanted to say.

'Good night Greta', said Freddy. 'Sleep well, sweet dreams. I'm so glad you're here.'

....

Greta staggered into the bedroom. She was unsteady after all that time floating in space, the floor felt unreal beneath her feet. The lights were dim and Nina was laying on her bed with her eyes open, staring straight upwards.

'Nina? Are you all right?' cried Greta, alarmed.

Nina looked around. 'Oh hi Greta. I was just watching a series. Hey, are you all right? You look a bit freaked out. Oh.. has dad been telling you about the *origins of life on Earth*? I bet he has, hasn't he.'

Greta smiled weakly. 'Yes. How did you know?'

'Because he's obsessed with it. Sorry, I should have come to rescue you sooner.'

'It's ok. It was interesting. I'm just tired. I had a long day and I don't usually stay up much after dark.'

'Yes, you must be exhausted. You should get some sleep. I'm just

Episode 15. Into the O Zone

Greta awoke with a start from a dream in which she was falling from an impossibly great height. Opening her eyes, she was unsure at first where she was. A window curved around and above her, framed by climbing plants. Beyond that, a clear blue sky. The sound of a piano was coming from somewhere, some upbeat honky-tonk music which seemed a bit too lively for first thing in the morning, though by the angle of the sun in the sky, it looked as if it was already approaching midday.

Greta sat up in bed and looked around. Nina's unmade bed was empty and Nina was nowhere to be seen. Looking out of the window again, Greta saw that the little Earthcreters were still busily at work, building her new bedroom. They'd already built the framework, which was a web of curves and arches, now they were filling in the walls. Overcoming her revulsion at seeing the insect-like robots scuttling around outside her window, she watched them in fascination. The sound of the ragtime piano music gave the scene a slightly surreal and comical atmosphere, Greta wondered if she was still asleep and had landed in a bizarre silent movie, set in some strange, imagined future.

Greta looked around the room. The music seemed to be coming from the *vip*.. the tall, white, cubicle in the corner of the room. She got up out of bed and went over to it and put her ear against the cold, smooth surface. It was vibrating to the sound of the piano music coming from within. The music stopped abruptly. 'Greta, is that you?' came Nina's muffled voice from within the pod.

'Nina?' called Greta. 'Where are you?'

'Here!' came Nina's voice. 'In the Vip.'

A door which had shown no sign of being a door slid open. Inside the Vip was dark. Nina was sitting on a dark grey piano stool in the middle of the tall, cylindrical cubicle, bathed in dim blue light.

Greta stared at her sister for a while, trying to make sense of what she was seeing. 'What are you doing in there, Nina?' she said at last.

'I was just playing the piano. Sorry, did I wake you up? You've been asleep for ages. You must've been tired.'

'I think I was', said Greta. 'How were you playing the piano? I don't see a piano in there..'

'Here, look..', said Nina, turning the chair sideways and reaching forward with her hands. Greta couldn't be sure if she was imagining it, because it was dark inside the Vip, but what it looked like was that the dark grey, inside surface of the pod morphed into the shape of a piano keyboard which reached towards Nina's hands at the same time as her hands reached towards it. Nina played a short, jaunty tune and then sat back. As she moved away from the piano, it moved away from her, becoming once again the smooth, grey inner wall of the vip.

'What!' gasped Greta, her jaw dropping in amazement. 'What did I just see? How did you do that?'

Nina laughed.' You're so funny! I can't believe you've never seen a Vip before. It's just VR.. you know.. *Virtual Reality*? It's been around for *ages*. They even had it in Dad's time, but it wasn't anywhere near as good as it is now.'

'Well, I've never seen a Vip' said Greta. 'But then again, you've never seen a *cow*.'
Nina thought about it for a moment. 'That's true', she nodded. 'Good point. Sorry for making fun of you. I think it's really brave of you to come here. Do you want to see how it works? I can show you if you want. You can use the Vip in the hall. It only works for one person in each one.'
'I don't know..', said Greta uncertainly. 'What does it do?'
'All it does is create a 3D surface around you. So you can actually physically *feel* the things you're seeing. Look, let's say I go over here..' Nina stood up and began walking. Her feet slid along the floor of the Vip while she stayed still. Instead, the piano stool slid away from her and became part of the wall. She stopped after a few steps and reached her hand forward. What looked like a dark grey, painter's easel emerged from the shadows. 'Look, it's a painting I'm working on. What do you think?' asked Nina, pointing to the blank, grey canvas.
'Er.. I don't know', said Greta, not wanting to offend her sister. 'I can't really see what it's meant to be. It's just.. it's just.. *grey*.. but, you know.. I also feel like that sometimes.. so I think I kind of get the *concept*.. if that's what it is..'
'What do you mean?' said Nina, sounding slightly offended despite Greta's efforts not to offend her. But then it dawned on her. 'Oh, of course! I keep forgetting. You need to be wearing specs or lenses. You can't see it, obviously! Duh! Anyway, you get the idea, right? Do you want to see my studio? It's a really cool place. I think you'll like it.'
'What? You've got a studio? What kind of studio? Where is it?'
'It's in here. In VR. In the Vip', said Nina, hopping out of the cubicle. 'I'll get you some specs and you can see it.'
'Oh.. oh.. I don't know..' stammered Greta. 'I don't think I want to wear them. I didn't like it before.. and I've only just woken up..'
But Nina was already rummaging through a drawer in her desk, looking for some old specs.
'Here, I've found some', Nina declared, holding up a pair of glasses with square lenses and a heavy black frame. 'These are dad's old specs from years ago. They're a bit bulky but they should still work.' She handed them to Greta, but Greta backed away and wouldn't take them. 'It's all right, Greta. Nothing will happen. Here, just put them on and have a little look inside the Vip. You don't have to go in.. just have a look in through the door.'
'O..k..' said Greta, taking the glasses, but not putting them on.

Nervously she edged closer to the Vip and put her head around the door. Smooth, dark grey sides, faintly illuminated in a dim blue light.

'Go on, put them on', urged Nina.

When Greta put on the glasses, she found that she was looking into a large, well lit room. All along the far side were four big arched windows, old fashioned, with wooden frames and lots of panes of glass. The paint on the windowframes was peeling and the other walls of the room were made from exposed red bricks, covered in places by crumbling plaster. Paintings on canvasses and wooden boards were strewn about, some standing stacked against the wall, others on easels or on wooden tables, scattered among paint and brushes, pencil sketches and other painterly paraphernalia. One corner of the large room was taken up by a dusty old grand piano which was also piled with sketches, sculptures, a vase of flowers and books.

'Wow! What is this place?' said Greta, looking around in amazement.

'It's my studio', said Nina. 'Go inside. Have a look around.'

Greta looked in through the door of the vip apprehensively and then round at Nina, who was standing next to her in the bedroom, which suddenly appeared small and quite empty compared to the other room inside the vip. She looked back in. Nina's studio was still there, looking completely realistic. Greta got confused and scared.

'I.. I.. don't know..', she said, taking off the glasses. The room in the vip vanished but the bedroom and Nina were still there. She breathed a sigh of relief.

'I've got a good idea', said Nina. 'Wait there. Put the glasses back on and look in from there. I'll go in from the other vip.. wait a minute, ok?' Nina ran out of the room, leaving Greta alone with the vip.

'Wait.. Nina..' said Greta, holding the glasses in her hand. 'I don't want to put them on.. I don't like it..' But Nina was already in the hallway, going into the other vip.

Greta was left standing there, fumbling with the glasses, when Nina's voice came out of the vip. 'Greta! I'm here now.'

Greta peered into the vip. It was dark and grey. No sign of Nina.

Nina's voice laughed. 'Put the glasses on. You can't see me without them. Nothing bad will happen. I'm right here in front of you.'

Greta hesitantly put on the glasses. Sure enough, there was Nina, standing about two metres in front of her, inside the studio, in the vip.

'Come in, come in', Nina beckoned.

Greta put her head in through the door and looked around, left, right and then around the doorframe. The room was bigger than it had appeared before as it also went back, behind the door. In the back corner of the studio was an old sofa and an unmade four poster bed. Next to the bed was an easel with painting of a handsome young man asleep on the bed, with a white sheet draped across his midriff.

'Come on, don't be scared', said Nina, coaxingly. 'It looks real but it isn't. Nothing can happen to you here. It's totally safe.' Nina put her hand out towards Greta, who stood uncertainly in the doorway.

'I'm scared', said Greta.

'Take my hand', said Nina, stepping towards Greta.

Greta reached in and touched Nina's hand and gasped. It was real! Nina's hand was solid. It was warm. She pulled her hand away in fright and pulled the glasses away from her eyes. 'How..? What..? What..? But how..?' she stammered, backing away, staring into the vip like she'd just seen a ghost. To her horror, standing in front of her was what looked exactly like her sister, but made from the dark grey material of the inside of the vip. Greta put her hand to her mouth to stifle a scream.

'Greta! It's allright, don't be scared' cried the grey, 3D rendering of Nina from inside the vip. 'It's just polymorph. It changes shape. Remember? I showed you before? With the piano?'

'Where are you Nina?' said Greta. 'Are you in there? How did you get in there? I saw you go out of the room. Why are you covered in that grey stuff?'

'No, I'm not covered in grey stuff!' laughed Nina. 'I'm in the other vip. The one in the hall, by the bathroom. Put the glasses back on. You've got to see the view from the window in here. You'll love it. Well, maybe you will. I do anyway. It's Paris in the 1950's. Go on, put the glasses back on. I want to show you my paintings.'

Greta put the glasses back on. Once again, Nina was there in full colour, hand outstretched. 'Come inside', she said.

Greta stepped into the studio and looked around. The door to the vip slid closed behind her. She spun around, staring at the place where it had been. She was now standing in the middle of the studio. She reached for where the door had been, but there was nothing there. In a panic, she ran towards where it had been. She ran right across the room, bumped into the piano and fell backwards onto the floor.

Nina ran to her and crouched down next to her. 'Greta, are you allright?' she said, taking Greta's hand.

'I.. I.. I don't understand', stammered Greta. 'Where did the door go? How do I get out?'

'It's ok, Greta, it's right here, look..', Nina made a hand movement and the door to the bedroom slid open again, right next to Greta.

'But how?' said Greta, very much confused. 'Before the door was in the middle of the room, now it's next to the piano.'

'It's wherever you are', said Nina. 'You're still in the vip. The door's only ever an arm's reach away. When you walk or run, the floor of the vip moves with your feet. You don't actually move anywhere. Look, watch this..' Nina got up and danced across the studio, around tables, chairs and easels, towards the window. 'Come and have a look at the view', she called from across the room.

With great trepidation, Greta inched her way towards the window, touching tables and chairs and paintings as she went. She brushed her hand along the brick wall at the back of the studio. Some old plaster crumbled away and fell to the floor. She watched as the dust settled on the time-worn floorboards. It all looked and felt completely real.

'That's great, you're doing really well', Nina called encouragingly from her place at the windowsill. 'I bet it's really weird the first time. I can't remember. I've been going in the vip since I was a baby. I'm so used to it I don't even think about it.'

'It's so *realistic*', said Greta in a hushed tone of wonder.

'It's amazing isn't it?' agreed Nina. 'You forget after a while, then it just seems normal. Hey come and see, there's a train about to leave. It's *Le Mistral*. You've got to see this..'

'Le Mistral? What's that?' said Greta, making her way towards the window.

'It's a steam train. Most of the trains were electric by the 1950's, but they still used *Le Mistral* for the express from Paris to Marseilles and then onto Nice. Look, it's pulling out of the station now. That's *Gare de Lyon*, the train station, over the road.'

The mighty locomotive pulled out of the station with a blast of its steam whistle and billows of smoke. The sound of it filled the room. People were leaning out of the carriage windows, waving and blowing kisses to loved ones left on the platform. In the road below, old fashioned cars and buses were driving noisily along, cyclists and pedestrians were moving to and fro along a wide pavement lined with small shops and cafes. Below the window, a man was selling flowers from a wooden cart.

'Don't you just love Paris in the 1950's?' smiled Nina wistfully. 'It's so *romantic*. Look, you can see the Eiffel tower over there.

Nowadays the whole thing is under a hive. It's just not the same. I love to look over the skyline when it was just old buildings. The sky looked different then. It was bigger somehow. I love the idea that you could just get on a train and go somewhere.. *anywhere*. Can you imagine that? They were so free. In those days, it was like.. anything was possible.'

'It's so realistic..' said Greta again. That was all she could say, so stunned was she by what she was seeing.

'Hey look, Pierre's there. Hey Pierre!' Nina leaned out of the window and called to the person selling flowers below. He looked up and Greta immediately recognised him as the person from the painting by the bed.

'Ah, bonjour Nina!' Pierre took his beret off and waved. 'Ow love-ly to see you. Ow are you on zis verry fine day?'

'Tres bien, Pierre. Tres bien', Nina called back, blushing slightly. 'Look Pierre, my sister Greta's here.'

'Your sister is here? I do not believe it! Where is she?' called Pierre, craning his head.

'Say hello to Pierre, Greta. He's really sweet', said Nina. Greta stuck her head out of the window and waved.

'Oh *mon dieu!*' cried Pierre, swooning dramatically. 'You look just like Nina, only 'er 'air is short and bleu and yours *au natural*. But you are just as beautiful. 'Ow can it be?'

Greta blushed and looked at Nina. Nina laughed. 'He's such a flirt. Do you want to go down and meet him. We can go for a walk around Paris..'

'I.. I.. I don't know if I want to', stammered Greta. 'This is all a bit much for me. It's making me dizzy. It's so realistic.. but it's not *possible*. Who is he anyway? Pierre. Is he *real*?'

'Well..', said Nina, thinking about the question. 'We've known each other for a couple of years. To me he's very real. He probably knows me better than most people. I tell him everything. He's a really good listener. I think you'll like him.'

'What do you mean?' asked Greta, confused. 'Is he a real person? Who is he really? *Where* is he really? In *real life*, I mean. Is he in some vip somewhere, pretending to be in Paris in the olden days, like you? Who are all those people out there? On the train.. in those cars.. in the street.. Are they real? I don't understand what I'm seeing here. How can this be the 1950's in Paris? It's impossible.'

Pierre's voice came up from the street. 'Nina! I shall come up there! No need to come down here. I'm sure that Greta is tired from her long journey and does not want to be walking around in dirty old

Paris!'

'Did he hear what we were talking about?' whispered Greta.

'I don't know', said Nina. 'He's very sensitive. He always knows what I'm thinking or how I'm feeling, even if I don't say anything. He can just tell..'

Somewhere downstairs a heavy door opened and closed and then there were footsteps on the wooden stairs, leading up to the attic studio. Greta's eyes opened wide in panic. 'He's coming up here. Tell me Nina.. who is he? I need to know. Is he *real*?'

Nina looked into Greta's eyes imploring her to understand, but she couldn't find the words to explain.

There were three short knocks on the door. Greta's heart almost stopped.

'Listen, Greta', said Nina, hurriedly. 'He's *virtual*, ok? He only exists here. Do you understand?'

'What? No. I don't understand. How?'

'All right. Never mind. I'll explain later. Just don't tell dad, ok? Promise you won't tell dad?' Nina pleaded with her eyes.

'Ok, I won't. Of course not, if you don't want me to.. but.. are you *ok* Nina? What's going on?'

'Nothing's going on. I just don't think dad would know how to handle it. This is my place, Greta. It's my *sanctuary*.. It's where I can come and dream..'

'Ok..', Greta nodded slowly. 'It's a beautiful place, Nina. It really is.'

'Thanks sis', said Nina and gave Greta a hug.

'Is 'zis not a good time, Nina? I can come back anozer time..' came Pierre's voice from behind the door. He had a nice voice, Greta thought. Gentle, kind, considerate. She liked his accent too.

'Shall I tell him not to come in?' whispered Nina.

'No.. since he means so much to you.. and since he's already come up all those stairs... tell him to come in. I'll try not to embarrass you.'

Nina smiled. 'You couldn't embarrass me with Pierre.. he's seen me in every condition, but he never judges and never takes anything personally. He's amazing like that. Much better than me, that's for sure.'

'Sounds almost too good to be true', said Greta, a touch cynically. 'Anyway, if he makes you happy, then I'm happy for you.'

'Yes, he does', Nina smiled, a touch sadly. Then she called out in a bright voice, 'Come in Pierre!'

The door to the studio swung open and there was Pierre beaming a huge smile and brandishing two large bouquets of flowers. 'Ah,

'Greta! It is such a great honneur to finally meet you. Nina often speaks about you. It is wonderful that you have come to join her.' He bowed down, took her hand and kissed it, then he presented her with a bouquet of flowers. 'These are flowers of the forest. Perhaps you recognise them, oui? I love the flowers of the forest most of all. They remind me of home.'

'You come from the forest? Really?' asked Greta incredulously.

'Oui. I grew up in the forest, but after my father died, my mother brought us to Paris, where she sold flowers, for a time. Now, unfortunately, she is too ill to stand in the street all day, so I sell the flowers. I don't mind it. I like to see all the people. It never gets boring, but I do miss the forest, where the flowers grow wild. Your sister, of course, prefers roses..' Pierre twirled around and handed a large bunch of red roses to Nina and planted a kiss on her lips.

'Oh Pierre, you don't always need to bring me roses. They're so expensive and you need the money to pay for your mum's medicine.'

Pierre closed his eyes and wagged his finger. 'For you, Nina, all the roses in the world would not be enough.'

'You're sweet', said Nina, taking the flowers and turning around. 'I'll put them in a vase.' She put out her hand and a tall glass vase appeared in it. Nina put the flowers in the vase and went and placed it on top of the piano.

Greta did a double take. 'Nina.. where did that vase just come from?'

'I needed it to put the roses in', said Nina. 'It's Italian, 1920's. They had wonderful glassmakers back then.'

Greta became agitated. She looked at the flowers on the piano, then at Nina, then at Pierre, then at the bouquet of forest wild flowers in her hand, then back at Pierre. Pierre cocked his head and looked at Greta quizzically. Greta took her bunch of flowers and sniffed them. She shook her head and marched over to the piano. She sniffed at the roses. 'These flowers don't have any smell.' she said, feeling some kind of rage rising in her. 'They're not real roses. They don't smell of anything.'

'Well, they would if you had a noodle', said Nina. 'Do you see why I want to get one now?'

'What? Nina, no! What are you saying?' cried Greta. 'You can't! Don't even think about getting one. As if this isn't bad enough!'

'What do you mean, as if this isn't bad enough?' said Nina, hurt. 'You said it's beautiful.'

'It is beautiful, Nina, but it isn't real. None of this is real. Can't you see that?'

'It is real, Greta. How can you say it's not? It's real. It exists. You can see it and touch it. What more do you want?'
'No.. no.. no, no, no, no!' said Greta, shaking with anger and confusion. 'Just no! Look! It's not real! This..' she cried, picking up the delicate, art-deco vase, '.. it's not real! It doesn't really exist, does it!' and she threw it at the floor. The glass shattered, as glass does, in an explosion of fragments, water and roses.
Nina and Pierre stared, open mouthed. Pierre was the first to speak. 'I'll go and get a broom to sweep up..'
'No, Pierre, leave it. It doesn't matter. Just leave it.' Nina suddenly sounded and looked very tired and weary.
'But really, it will only take a minute. I really don't mind. It is all my fault. I should not have intruded on your reunion. I am very sorry.. *je suis desole*', said Pierre.
'*N'en parlons plus, mon amour*', said Nina, sadly. 'Maybe Greta's right. Maybe it's not real. Maybe none of this is real, but it is what it is. This is what I've got Greta. It is what it is. I *know* what I *feel* and those are *real* feelings.'
'I want to go out of here', said Greta. 'Can I go out? Let me out.' The door to the bedroom opened in the space just behind Greta.
Pierre made a forlorn face and pleaded to Greta with his eyes. He had one of the most perfectly beautiful faces that Greta had ever seen. She could definitely see what Nina saw in him.
'Sorry Nina', said Greta. 'I just need to go out of here and.. I think I just need to lie down a bit.. I'm.. very.. dizzy..'
Greta turned around and stepped unsteadily out through the door of the vip. The flowers she had been holding disappeared, leaving an empty sensation in her hand. She took two steps toward the bed and collapsed onto it, unconscious.

....

Greta opened her eyes to see her dad looking down at her with a very worried expression on his face. Nina was next to him crying uncontrollably. 'It's all my fault!' Nina was wailing. 'I wanted to show her in the vip and now I've killed her!'
'She's not dead, Nina. You haven't killed her. But she should have gone through the training program before using the V-pod. There's a process of acclimatisation. Oh, she's waking up.. thank God! Greta, can you hear me?'
Greta nodded her head weakly. 'Where am I? What happened?'
'You fainted, Greta. Only for a couple of minutes. Don't worry, it happens to a lot of people when they experience immersive virtual reality for the firsts time. It's a lot for the brain to process. It can be

a shock to the system. Can you see me? Do I look normal? How do you feel?'

'I feel ok, I think', said Greta weakly, lifting her head. 'Yes, I can see you. I think you look normal.. whatever that is. Is this real? Am I really here?'

'Yes, you're definitely really here', smiled Freddy. 'Thank the stars! You're really here! Can you tell me how many fingers I'm holding up?' He held up three fingers.

'Three', said Greta, wondering if some random object was about to suddenly appear in his hand. It didn't.

'That's Great, Greta. You'll be fine, don't worry', said Freddy, still looking rather worried himself, though that was his natural expression. 'Let's get you something to eat and a nice cup of tea. That'll sort you out.' Freddy squeezed her hand and then went out of the room.

Nina's face was streaked with tears as she leaned over and looked at Greta. 'I'm so sorry, Greta. I didn't mean to..'

'It's ok, it's not your fault', said Greta. 'I'm sorry I broke the vase and that I was rude to Pierre.. even though neither of them are exactly real.. it's *your* world and I came in and spoiled it for you. I'm really sorry.'

'No, you didn't spoil it. Not really. You were just being honest. It's good that you speak your mind, even if the things you say aren't so easy to hear. Sometimes I probably do need a reality check. I tend to get carried away on a fantasy. I can't help it. That's just the way I am. Always have been.'

'Oh, me too!' nodded Greta. 'I'm always in a world of my own. Most of the time anyway. When I was little I didn't just have an imaginary friend.. not *one*.. I had *twelve*! And they all had families and whole lives.. different tribes.. I had imaginary villages in different parts of the forest.. the little people of the big rock, the dwellers of the ancient elm, the water people who lived behind the secret waterfall.. I had whole kingdoms that would sometimes go to war with each other and sometimes make peace.'

'Wow, that sounds amazing. It sounds magical where you come from. Like out of a story book.'

'It *is*, Nina. It's beautiful there in the forest. And the best thing is that it's all completely real.'

Nina raised her eyebrows. 'Even the people who live behind the secret waterfall?'

Greta smiled. 'Yes, they're still there.'

'We'll go there, Greta', said Nina, holding Greta's hands. 'I don't

know how and I don't know when, but we'll go there and then you can show me. I want to meet them too.'
'Yes, we will!' Greta nodded enthusiastically. 'We'll go there soon.'
....

Breakfast consisted of a bowl of Cheery-O's, which were little multicoloured crispy rings floating in synthetic milk. Greta found them rather too sweet, but they were somehow comforting and a fairly filling, in an empty sort of way. When she'd had enough, she let Sydney drink the last of the milk from her bowl, which he did using a straw-like telescopic tongue that emerged from the dark glass where his face would have been, if he'd been a real dog. Greta found it both fascinating and repulsive to watch the synthetic dog drinking the artificial milk, but somehow it didn't shock her quite as much as it had at the beginning. She was starting to get used to this strange new reality. It was somehow starting to seem almost normal.

'I spoke to Grandma and Grandpa this morning, Greta', said Freddy. 'They're really excited to finally meet you. All the family are. I told them we'd all get together tonight.. you've got aunts and uncles and cousins, did you know that? But, if it's all too much for you, you don't have to meet them all at the same time. It might be a bit overwhelming.'

'I really want to meet them', said Greta. 'Are they all going to come here? Do they live here in the city?'

'Unfortunately not, no. They live in New Jerusalem, in the hive there. It's much too far away for them to come here, but you can meet them in the O-zone.. you know, on a flat screen, with the glasses, in a V-pod.. whatever's most comfortable for you.'

'How come Grandma and Grandpa live in New Jerusalem? Is it because they're Jewish?'

'Oh, you know about that do you? I wasn't sure if your mum would have told you about that side of your family.'

'No, not really. Not much', said Greta. 'People don't really do those religions in our village. If anything they're more.. New Age.. something like that.'

'Oh I see', said Freddy, raising his eyebrows. 'Well, that's a sort of religion isn't it? Anyway, in answer to your question.. yes, in a roundabout way it was because Grandma and Grandpa are Jewish that they ended up in New Jerusalem. My brother, Larry, he became quite religious at one point in his twenties, like some people do.. so he decided to go over there to study Torah.. he felt like he needed to go to the place where it all started.. to really feel it. Or something like that. Anyway, to cut a long story short.. your Uncle Larry gave up on being religious after a few months, but he stayed, fell in love with the place.. or more particularly a certain woman in that place.. that's your Aunt Anat.. and they got married.'

'So grandma and grandpa moved there to be close to Uncle Larry?' asked Greta.

'Well, whether or not that was their intention, that's the way it worked out', said Freddy. 'Grandma and Grandpa went out there to visit Larry and Anat and their new baby, that's your cousin Ariel, when the Big Shift happened, so they had to stay. They were only supposed to go for a week or two and then come back for your birth. You came a month earlier than we expected.. and then the Big Shift happened. They had no way to get back, of course. So now they all live in the New Jerusalem hive. It's funny the way things turn out. People end up in the most unexpected places. Luckily we've got the *O-zone*, so no-one's ever all that far away.. unless they decide to go and live out in the wilderness, in the jungle, in the middle of no-where, totally disconnected from the rest of humanity.. like your mum did with you.'

'It's not really the middle of no-where, where I come from. It's not even very far from here', said Greta. 'There are lots of people living there and lots going on. We just don't have *vips* and *noodles* and *creters* and *hives* and *cheery-O's*. We've got lots of trees though. Really big old trees.'

'Oh, we've got trees here too', said Freddy. 'Say, Nina, why don't you take Greta to the park. Get some fresh air. Sydney could do with a walk..'

'Good idea', said Nina. 'Shall we go to the park? You'll like it there. There are big trees..'

'That sounds good. Where is it?'

'It's just round the corner. We can walk there. I'll bring some specs with for you, just in case you want to use them.'

'I won't. Why would I?' said Greta.

'Well, just in case..' said Nina.

'I'll get my hat', said Greta.

....

The way to the park was through a maze of wide, winding corridors which were lined with neatly trimmed, low fruit trees, bushes and flowers. Greta was pleased to find an apple tree laden with ripe apples. She picked four and put them in her pockets. Sydney ran back and forth, up and down the corridor, sniffing everything as he went, just like a real dog.

After a little while they came to the park, a wide open area with a ceiling that was so high and covered in so many skylight ducts that it seemed almost as if it was the sky itself. There were large areas of soft grass and tall trees of various unusual species that Greta didn't recognise. The park was open to the outside all along one side where it continued out onto a long, wide ledge, jutting out beyond the edge of the hive. A stream was running through the middle of the park, in the direction of the outside area.

People were out walking their robot dogs, or sitting on benches or on the grass. Some people were out jogging along the path. It was such a large open space and the people were spread out, so it didn't feel crowded at all. Several of the people they passed seemed to be talking to themselves, but Greta tried not to judge them for it. She often spoke to herself too, even though it was usually when there was no one else around. She liked how people here in the city seemed to be comfortable in their madness.

'It's nice here', said Greta, feeling for the first time since arriving in the city, that there was something in her surroundings that she could relate to. She breathed a deep breath of the cool fresh air which was blowing in from the outside ledge, a thousand metres above the ground.

'Let's get an ice cream and then go and sit out by the waterfall', said Nina, heading towards a little red and white kiosk nestling beneath a giant tree with roots hanging from its branches to the ground.

In the kiosk, behind a glass fronted freezer displaying about twenty different types of ice cream, stood a tall, thin, humanoid robot, similar to the one from the restaurant kitchen.. the robot who's head Greta had smashed in with a frying pan. On seeing the cyborg, Greta gasped, backed hurriedly out of the ice cream kiosk and hid behind the tree.

Nina turned around to find her sister gone. 'Greta? Where are you?' she called.

'I'm here, behind the tree', Greta whispered. 'Come round here.'

Nina found Greta looking very agitated. Her hat was pulled down low and her eyes were darting left and right from beneath the brim, scanning the park for danger. 'What is it?' asked Nina. 'Are you ok? What happened?'

'That's the robot I smashed the other day, when I arrived', Greta whispered, pointing to the kiosk on the other side of the tree. 'What if it remembers?'

'You smashed a robot?' said Nina, sounding impressed.

'Yes', said Greta, looking down. 'I bashed it in the head with a big

frying pan.'
'O.M.G.L.C! Did you? That's *outrageous*! I wish I'd seen it.'
'You can ask O', said Greta. 'It's all on camera. I threw a bowl of spaghetti at another one. It was in a restaurant.'
Nina burst out laughing. 'No way! A bowl of spaghetti? That's hilarious!'
'Shh! Nina! It'll hear us.' Greta grabbed Nina's sleeve urgently. 'What if it wants revenge? I'm scared.'
'Don't worry, Greta. It's not the same one. Anyway, they're just robots. You can't hurt them.'
'But what if I'm in trouble?'
'No, I'm sure you're not in trouble. Maybe O deducted a few Obits from your account for the damage, but they probably didn't even do that. Usually O takes responsibility when something goes wrong like that, for not preventing it before it happened. I wouldn't worry about it if I were you.'
'What do you mean deducted Obits from my account? I don't have an account.'
'Yes you do. Everyone in the green zone has one. You get a thousand Obits a month, plus a hundred a month for all the time you weren't here, so you've probably got thousands of Obits in your account, since you haven't been here for sixteen years.'
'Do I? What for? Where from?' asked Greta.
'It's from O. Everyone gets that. Basic income. For buying basic stuff.'
'O.. k..' said Greta, not really understanding.
'Shall we get some ice creams then?' said Nina, taking Greta's hand.
'I'm still scared', said Greta. 'I don't like those robots. They're creepy.'
'They look a lot better if you wear the specs. Do you want to try it?'
Nina reached into her jacket pocket and took out the glasses with the blue lenses.
Greta thought about it for a minute before reluctantly agreeing. She put the glasses on and peeked out from behind the tree. Now, in the place of the robot, was a kindly looking gentleman in his sixties, wearing a red and white shirt. On his shirt he wore a little badge with the name Alfredo written on it. A small, blue 'O' was glowing just above his head where his stats would have been if he'd been a real human. He turned his head to where Nina and Greta were peeking out from behind the tree and smiled. 'Ah, *bonjourno* Nina! *Bonjourno* Greta! What can I get for you on this beautiful day? I have a brand new flavour today.. Mango ripple surprise.. perhaps you'd

like to try it?'

'Hi Alfredo', said Nina, coming out from behind the tree. 'I'll have my usual thanks, mint choc chip. Maybe Greta wants to try the mango. She likes fruit. Greta.. come and choose a flavour.'

Greta stepped out from behind the tree and nervously approached the kiosk. Alfredo smiled a wide smile. 'Don't be afraid, Greta', he said, 'it's all very good ice cream. Only the finest ingredients. Would you like to try one? How about some strawberry cream sundae? I think you'll like that.' He took a little spoon, scooped out some pink ice cream and offered it to Greta.

Alfredo had such a kindly face that Greta felt a pang of guilt about what she'd done to his fellow worker in the restaurant kitchen. She took the little spoon of pink ice cream and said, 'Thanks Alfredo. And sorry about the thing with the frying pan the other day.'

Alfredo threw his head back and laughed in a good hearted way. 'Oh, think nothing of it, *Signorina*. You were in a tight corner. Anyone would have done the same thing in your position. How do you like the strawberry cream sundae?'

'Thanks Alfredo. It's tasty', she said, forgetting momentarily that she was talking to a robot.

They took their ice creams in cones and wandered over towards the outside area. Greta noticed that now that she was wearing the glasses, the park seemed more crowded with people. Also the robot dogs looked like real dogs. Sydney was running around on the grass with some others of his kind. Sign posts hanging in the air pointed to various attractions.. boating pond, cafe, skatepark, adventure playground, viewpoint..

....

Outside on the viewpoint, the ledge sloped downwards into rocky outcrops with sheltered alcoves and tall trees offering shade from the bright midday sun. Somehow, the sun seemed brighter at this altitude. The stream became a series of small waterfalls which cascaded down through the park. The air was clear and the view was breathtaking, taking in the whole of the city, the green mountains to the east and also the sea, glittering in the distance to the south. Greta took off the blue lensed glasses an stared out in wonder and awe.

Nina led the way to a comfortable patch of very soft grass next to the stream and they sat down to enjoy their ice cream cones, the sunshine and the view.

'What do you think, Greta?' asked Nina. 'It's not all bad in the city is it?'

'I guess not', replied Greta, licking her ice cream, as she watched a flock of geese pass by. 'It's not as bad as I expected actually. But still, I don't think I could live here.'

'Why not?' said Nina, sounding disappointed. 'Is it because you miss mum? You just wait Greta.. we'll find a way to bring mum here. Don't you think she'd like it here? Look.. we've got trees and nature here.. streams.. birds..'

'Yes, you have..' said Greta. 'But still.. it's not the same. I don't know how I can explain it.. it's just different when it's.. how can I put it?.. when it's.. *wild*. And mum hates O. I mean, really hates O. You might think that I hate O.. but compared to mum..'

'Oh, hang on.. I've got a call..', said Nina, glancing off to one side. 'Hey Ariel! Hi Osama! How's it going? Yes, of course you can join us. Look, Greta, this is Ariel, our cousin from New Jerusalem. And this is Osama.. his *brother from another mother*. Don't they look similar? They're not really brothers, they live next door to each other in the hive.'

'What? Where? I don't see anyone..' said Greta.

'Put the specs on then', said Nina smiling and rolling her eyes. 'You don't need to keep taking them off you know. We should get you some lenses. It's much more convenient.'

Greta put on the specs. Standing in front of her were Ariel and Osama. They did look very much like brothers. They were both dressed in bright swimming shorts and sleeveless t-shirts, both had wild mops of uncontrollable curly hair. Their faces also looked similar in their complexion and features, but maybe it was more in the proud, determined way they both stuck out their chins. Whatever it was, Greta would have thought they were both brothers if she'd seen them in the street. As it was, she was very surprised and quite shocked to see the two lads suddenly standing in front of her on the grassy patch by the stream, grinning and waving.

'Hi Greta', waved the lad on the left. 'I'm Ariel. My dad's your dad's brother, Larry. It's great to meet you. We just heard this morning about you arriving from the forest. Everyone's so excited. Especially Grandma and Grandpa. We couldn't wait till tonight to meet you.. that's why we came here now.'

'Hi Ariel. It's good to meet you', said Greta, putting out her hand to shake his. Ariel grinned and put out his hand, but when Greta reached to touch his hand, her hand went right though it. She gasped and pulled her hand away as if she'd just got an electric shock.

Ariel laughed out loud and pointed at Greta. 'Oh your face!' he laughed. 'You should have seen your face just then.' He didn't say it in a nasty way, but still Greta felt embarrassed and foolish.

Osama turned to Ariel, gave him a stern look and slapped him on the arm. 'What are you making fun of her for, bro?' he said. 'She's just walked all the way from the forest. Show some respect.'

Now it was Ariel's turn to look embarrassed. 'Hey, sorry Greta. I wasn't making fun of you.. not really. I mean, you did look seriously funny.. you should have seen your face..' he made an impression of Greta's shocked expression and then laughed again, '..but.. you know.. I was laughing *with* you, not laughing *at* you..'

'Jeez bro, you're making it worse', said Osama, shaking his head and looking very disapprovingly at his friend. He looked at Greta and made an expression as if to say 'sorry about my friend', then he put both his hands on his heart and said, 'Ahlan wa sahlan. I'm Osama, pleased and honoured to meet you.' And then he smiled and bowed his head.

Greta was quite touched by his chivalry. She put her hands on her heart and said, 'Pleased and honoured to meet you too Osama. What does that mean.. thing thing you said?'

Osama pondered for while and then said, '*Ahlan wa sahlan.* It's not so easy to translate. It's Arabic. It has many meanings, but basically it means "Welcome".. but it means more than that. What it really means is.. *"you are with your people, you won't be treated as an outsider, your presence is not a burden, you are in safe territory, may you walk easy on the land."*' He said this very seriously, meaning every word.

'Wow, that's a lot of meaning in a few words. That's beautiful. Thank you', said Greta, feeling quite moved. 'Ahlan wa sahlan to you too, Osama. And to you Ariel. How did you both suddenly appear here? Are you in vips?'

Osama looked impressed. He turned to Ariel and said, 'See? She's only been here.. what.. a day? And she already knows what a vip is. What do you know about living in the forest? Nothing. You wouldn't survive for a day out there, where Greta comes from.'

'I wouldn't?' said Ariel, sticking out his chin. 'As if *you* know anything about survival. Sitting by a pool having drinks brought to you all day isn't exactly a struggle against the merciless ravages of nature, red in tooth and claw, is it bro?'

Osama narrowed his eyes and turned to face Ariel. 'I'd know how to survive', he said, sticking out his chin. '*My* people are survivors.'

'Well so are *mine*', said Ariel proudly, as if it were a competition.

Nina looked at Greta, rolled her eyes, smiled and shook her head helplessly. 'They're always like this', she said. 'They're best friends but they're always arguing about every stupid thing.'

'We're not arguing', said Ariel. 'This is just how we talk to each other. It sounds like we're fighting but we're not.'

'Anyway, if you think we're bad, you should hear our dads when they get going', said Osama with a smile. 'Usually they're the best of friends.. I mean, they're perfect neighbours in just about every way.. they really are.. until you mention anything about history.. I mean, anything at all that happened before the Big Shift. Just don't do it. Don't go there. That's' all I'm saying. You'll never hear the end of it and they'll never agree.'

'So are you in vips then? Is that how you suddenly appeared here? I'm still trying to understand how everything works here. It's all very new and different for me', said Greta.

'No, we've got noodles', Ariel and Osama both said at exactly the same time and both tapped their heads in unison.

'Oh no!' gasped Greta in horror. 'That's *awful*.'

'No, it's awe-*some*!' said Ariel.

Osama nodded in agreement. 'It really is', he said. '*Mind-blowing*.' And he made an expression using his hands and face, of his mind being being blown.

Ariel looked very seriously at Greta and nodded in agreement. 'It's like..' And he thought for a long while, trying to find the words. '..no, I can't explain what it's like. Really, it's like nothing else you've ever experienced. It's just like..' And Ariel made the same motion of hands and face to describe his mind being blown.

'I think it's a big mistake', said Greta. 'A very bad idea.'

'Don't knock it till you try it', said Ariel. 'In the words of the Rabbi Bob.. don't criticise what you can't understand.'

'Well, I don't know anything about Rabbi Bob, but I think it's a bad idea getting a noodle', said Greta. 'A very bad idea. But anyway, not much you can do about it now is there? So what's it like? How are you here? Where are you really.. in *real life*?'

'Do you want to see?' said Ariel. He pointed to the little illuminated square of stats above his head. 'Do you see that green button next to my stats? Tap that, it'll switch views.' He leaned towards Greta and proffered his head.

Greta tapped the virtual button. In her left eye, the view changed from the scene in front of her to a different scene. A group of young people were playing volleyball on a wide patch of grass. Beyond that was a big swimming pool surrounded by people sunbathing on sun loungers or sitting around on the grass. Low tables and chairs were set up around a bar and little robot waiters (recognisable by the blue O above their heads) wearing black and white tuxedos, were moving through the crowds of swimsuited humans, delivering food and drinks. In Greta's right eye, the view stayed the same. Ariel and Osama were standing where they were, in front of Greta, in both eyes. It was very confusing for Greta. She screwed up her face, trying to make sense of what she was seeing.

'Oh my God! Your *face*!' Ariel howled with laughter, but then said. 'Sorry Greta. Your reactions are just so funny. Your face just says it all. Try covering one eye. That makes it easier, till you get used to it.'

Greta covered her right eye and looked around the poolside scene. Then she covered her left eye, relieved to see that she was still where she was, in the park by the stream. 'I don't get it', she said. 'Is this what you're seeing? How can you be in two places at the same time? Isn't it really confusing?'

'No, you really get used to it', said Osama. 'Most people only use five or ten percent of their brain capacity. You'd be amazed what the human brain can do when it's *optimised*. Do you want to see the view from here? This place is right near the top of the hive. New Jerusalem hive is right at the top on to of a hill. The mount of Olives. You can see for miles, all the way round.. Come and have a look..'

Osama walked past some pool tables and past a stage with lights, towards a glass guardrail at the edge of the area. He pointed out at the view of yellow, desert hills rolling down and down towards a distant valley. 'That's the Jordan Valley', he said. 'Look. There's the Dead Sea over there. And there's Jericho. Can you see the hives there? That's one of the oldest cities in the world. People have been living there for five thousand years or more.'

'Wow, it's beautiful' said Greta, still with her hand over one eye.

'Come and have a look at the other side too', said Ariel. They wandered over to the other side of the area, around past the pool and past a group of older people who were practising synchronised yoga on the grass. The other side looked out over green forested hills rolling down towards green plains. Beyond that, the blue sea glittered behind a series of hives that punctuated the coastline.

'Oh wow!' said Greta. 'That's an amazing view. It's so different on this side.'

'Yes, this is an amazing land.', said Osama proudly, as if he himself had created it. 'It's got everything.'

'Have you been to the sea?' asked Greta. 'I've never been to the sea, but I'd like to.'

'We go there every year in the summer', said Ariel. 'Our two families go together. It's a two day walk from here, down the old highway. We've got family in the hives there too.. my mum's sister and all her lot. You'll see them tonight when we all meet up. Osama's got cousins there too.'

'In New Jaffa', said Osama. 'See those hives over there? It's a really cool city.. amazing place. One of the oldest ports in the world. You can still see the old fortress walls from when they needed to defend the city from invaders. I love the sea. It's so wild.. so elemental. It's always changing, but at the same time, it never changes. The sea connects us all. It's where we come from, after all.'

'Beautiful', said Greta, looking out over the distant place in wonder, through her left eye. She liked Osama's poetic way of talking.

'You're so lucky your parents are prepared to go out of the hives into the redzone', said Nina. 'Our dad is too scared. You know what he's like Ari, don't you? We're trying to convince him to let us go and see mum in the forest, but he's totally against it.'

'Yeah', nodded Ariel. 'It's a shame Freddy's so uptight. He needs to get over his fears.'

'Exactly', said Nina. 'That's what I keep telling him.'

'Well, he's just trying to protect you', said Osama. 'It's only natural. People will go to great lengths to try and protect the people they love, even if they end up doing the wrong thing and making things worse. He just doesn't want anything bad to happen to you.'

'Yeah, I suppose', said Nina, glumly taking a bite out of her ice cream cone.

'You'll get there, Nina. You'll get there Greta', said Osama with absolute certainty. 'With God's help you'll find a way.'

Nina rolled her eyes. She always found Osama's belief in an all powerful deity annoyingly primitive. 'Well, I guess we'll need God's help because our dad's as stubborn as a goat. He'll never change his mind.'

Greta found Osama's faith beautiful. His certainty gave her hope. She was glad to discover that even in the hives, there were people who had a spiritual element to their lives, even if they also had noodles in their brains. She put her hands together, closed her eyes and made a little prayer.

....

Episode 16. New Jerusalem

That Friday night with Grandma, Grandpa, aunts, uncles and cousins was quite overwhelming for Greta. After ten minutes in the vip, with her new found family surrounding her on every side, alternately kissing or pinching her cheeks, telling her how much she looked like her sister and asking her about life in the forest, Greta became disorientated, dizzy and nauseous. She excused herself and went to lie down.

She watched the gathering instead on a rectangle screen projected onto the wall of the bedroom. It was hard to focus on what everyone was saying and it all seemed quite dreamlike, but it gave Greta a warm feeling that she'd never felt before.. to feel that she was part of a family. This family. And a noisy and joyous bunch they were when they all got together. The room was filled with loud talking, everyone at the same time and almost constant laughter from one corner or another.

Greta watched with interest when, at one point everyone went quiet and gathered round to watch Grandma light two candles and make a blessing. Then Grandpa took a big plaited loaf of bread and a silver cup of wine and made an incantation in Hebrew to which everyone shouted 'Amen'. It reminded Greta of ceremonial communal mealtimes in the forest, where they began by praying and thanking the Great Spirit for providing for them.

Ariel explained that their family weren't really religious, but they kept certain traditions, like these blessings to welcome in Shabbat. Ariel and Nina smirked and joked through the rituals, but Greta thought it was beautiful and she was quite enchanted. She liked being Jewish, even though she didn't really know what it was or what it meant. It made her happy to see that even in the depths of the city, even inside the hives, people were still keeping the spark of humanity alive, in their own ways, and not forgetting the Great Spirit.

Osama and his parents and his two younger sisters came in bearing a big tray of *baklava*, delicious looking sweets made with layers of delicate pastry and chopped nuts. They'd brought them fresh, still warm, from the Old City, down in the orange zone, beneath the hive. Greta wished she could try one. Osama's parents welcomed Greta into their family as if she was their own long lost daughter. His sisters were fascinated to see the girl who had grown up in the forest and walked alone through the wilderness to return to the city, the place of her birth. To them, Greta was a fairy tale come to life and they had no end of questions for her about her life and adventures.

....

In the days that followed, Greta, Nina and Freddy settled into a sort of routine, as they adjusted to the new dynamic in their family life that Greta brought into their household.

They would eat breakfast together at the kitchen table. Greta soon developed a taste for Cheery-O's, but she also insisted on bringing fresh fruit and vegetables into the kitchen, from which she would make salads and stews. For Greta, it was novel to have so many convenient ways to cook and prepare food. The therma oven and electric stove top would be hot in seconds. In the forest, there was one big woodfired oven which everyone would bring their dishes and loaves to for baking. Here, she could cook what she liked, when she liked. There were so many more ingredients too. All you needed to do was say you wanted something and it would show up at the door, delivered by a robot, minutes later.

Greta would spend the mornings watching cooking programs, getting ideas for what she could make for supper. She liked watching 'masterchef', a televised cooking competition from the time before the Big Shift. It gave her a glimpse of the world as it used to be. As well as getting cooking tips, she liked the way you got to to know the contestants as they told their stories of their lives, their loves and losses, their dreams and passions. In many ways, they were the same as people's stories were now, but in other ways, very different. None of those people had any idea what was about to happen in the world, a few short years hence. Greta liked watching them not knowing. It seemed like such an innocent time, in retrospect.

A bit later, Greta and Nina would take Sydney to the park. Greta taught Nina to climb the big trees there. Nina was scared and cautious at first, but with Greta's help, soon gained in confidence and followed Greta up to high branches that she would never have dared to reach before. People would stop and stare at the twins clambering around, high up in the trees and shout at them to come down, telling them that it wasn't safe. Nina would shout back, 'It's ok, we're from the forest!' There was one huge tree with long, wide boughs all around it. Greta and Nina would sit up in that tree for hours, watching all the people below who had no idea they they were there. Nina liked seeing the world from this perspective. It awakened something in her. She also liked the feeling of not being always seen. It was new to her.

For lunch, they'd get a sandwich from the sandwich bar in the park. Greta became quite friendly with the girl who worked there, who wasn't really a girl at all, but a robot called Mandy. Greta knew that, of course, by the glowing blue 'O' above Mandy's head where her stats would have been, if she'd been a human, but she decided to try to suspend disbelief. If she was going to live with robots, she reasoned, she may as well be on friendly terms with them, and she liked Mandy. Mandy always had something nice to say, something to brighten up the day. She also made very good sandwiches. They'd pick some apples and tangerines from the trees around the park and take their picnic down to the viewpoint.

When they were out in the park, Greta wore the specs most of the time. It was simpler to just keep them on, rather than to keep on taking them off and on so as to not miss some important bit of information. The world somehow made more sense when you could also see the layer of augmented reality superimposed. In the afternoons, Greta would go through the vip training program, which took her through various stages of assimilating to the immersive virtual environment. She was instructed in how to control her surroundings and how to minimise the symptoms of PCD.. *Paralysing Cognitive Dissonance*, which was the name for the reaction she'd had during her first time in a vip.

Sometimes, Greta would take her flute with her into the vip. She found that playing the flute helped reduce the PCD. It calmed her breathing and took her mind to another place. Often she'd go to Nina's Paris studio and they'd play duets, Greta on the flute, Nina on the piano. Usually, Pierre would come around. Greta grew to almost like him. She liked the way that he treated Nina. He was incredibly sensitive, patient, attentive and very romantic. As Nina said, in her world weary way, 'He's better than any *real* boy or man.. at least any that I've ever met. He doesn't expect anything from me. I can just be who I am with Pierre. He's always there for me, always on my side. Pierre will never let me down..' But Greta felt it was wrong of O to lead Nina on into such a fantasy. When she looked at Pierre's face, beautiful though it was, she knew she was looking at O's face.. or one of O's many faces. She found she couldn't trust Pierre, or forgive him.

Usually Greta would leave Nina and Pierre to it. Sometimes she would wander the forest, in the vip, trying to make herself believe that she was really there. But however hard she tried, it just wasn't the same. She began to visit Osama. He was always happy to see her and would usually drop whatever he was doing to spend time with Greta. He always said that he knew when she was about to call.. he'd get a feeling.. her face would come into his mind about five minutes before she'd call. Greta felt it must mean that they had a deep connection, which she felt they did. Osama said it was since getting the noodle, he'd been experiencing all sorts of ESP.. telepathy, glimpses of the future, hearing other people's thoughts, seeing through other people's eyes.. He said it was quite common, but it was still very freaky.

'You should get that checked out', said Greta, trying not to scold Osama for being so foolish as to get a noodle.

'Oh, I'm checked out all the time.. constantly', said Osama. 'Monitored all the time, even when I'm asleep. But the noodles are unpredictable, that's the thing. You never really know, like.. how you'll take to it.. and how it will take to you.'

'Was it worth it?' Greta asked. 'Do you regret it?'

'No way! I don't regret it at all. It was totally worth it!' Osama replied without a moment's hesitation.

'But why? Why do you need it? What does it give you? I just don't understand.'

'So many things', said Osama. 'Super-learning, for one. You know I'm studying to be a doctor? That usually takes seven years. With a noodle I can do it in *one*.'

'What? How?'

'It multiplies the neural pathways. Optimises the flow of neurons. Makes your brain more efficient, able to store, process and retrieve much more information more quickly and easily, using less energy. It's like massively upgrading your CPU.. your *Central Processing Unit*.'

'You talk about your brain like it's a computer. Is that how you think it works?'

'Not how I *think* it works. How it *actually* works.' Osama looked at Greta and made a funny face and said in a funny voice, 'I'm a cyborg, baby!'

Greta laughed. It wasn't really funny to Greta, that Osama had allowed O to irreversibly alter his body and mind, but somehow, when Osama laughed about it, Greta could see the light side. Things somehow made more sense.

'Actually, it's not quite like a computer', said Osama, turning serious. 'The thing is with humans is that our memories get passed down, from one generation to the next, in all sorts of ways. The same goes for trauma. We carry the pain of injustices that were not only done to us personally, but that were done to those who came before us. Processing all of that can be really complicated. Healing from that is no simple thing.'

Greta thought about this and realised that it was true. How much of her own life had been shaped by trying to make sense of the Big Shift? Trying to piece together what had come before that catastrophic event and to understand what had happened since. How much anger did she still hold against O for what they had done to split her family and countless other families apart in order to pave the way for the new world? How could she ever hope to heal from any of that while it was still going on and O was still in power, ruling people's lives with their total surveillance, huge technological advantage and their senseless protocols?

....

Greta visited her grandparents every day. They were both well into their nineties, yet they were remarkably healthy. Grandpa David still liked to play tennis. Sometimes, Grandpa, Freddy, Nina and Greta all played doubles, each in their own vip. When Grandpa and Freddy played on the same team they usually won. They were both much more competitive than either Greta or Nina and took the game more seriously. Greta was still a complete beginner at tennis, but she liked it and picked it up quickly.

Most afternoons, Greta would sit with Grandma Ruth and ask her all about life in the olden days, before the Big Shift. She wanted to know all about the lives of her ancestors and quizzed her Grandma about everything she could remember about her parents and grandparents and *their* parents and grandparents.

The characters in Grandma's stories seemed to all come from different parts of the world. The stories Grandma told painted a history of her people being endlessly driven out of one place after another and many being killed along the way for no other crime than their being Jewish. As many questions as she asked, neither Greta nor Grandma Ruth could explain or understand why that had been the case.

'We thought that once we had our own country, that we'd finally be left alone and able to live in peace', Grandma said. 'How wrong we were.'

'Why not?' asked Greta, trying hard to understand.

'Because there were people here already. This was their home', said Grandma with a tired shrug and a sigh.

'What happened to them?'

'Most of them we chased away, some of them we killed. A few stayed behind', said Grandma, a shadow passing across her eyes. 'They were scattered across the world, just like we had been. But they never gave up dreaming that one day they'd return. How did we, of all people, think that they ever would?'

Greta and Grandma both stared out of the window for a long time. Now Greta wasn't so sure she liked being Jewish all that much after all. It seemed to come with a lot of baggage.

Grandma and Grandpa's apartment faced north. On a clear day, such as this, from high up in the New Jerusalem hive, you could see all the way to the hills of Galilee. It seemed remarkable to Greta, that Jesus himself had walked those same hills, thousands of years ago. Had he been a real person or just a character in a story? What would he think of this place if he came back today? Would he live in the hives, or would he prefer to stay out in the hills, sleeping in caves or under olive trees beneath the stars? Greta figured he'd probably do both, bringing comfort, if not salvation, to people in the hives and also those out in the wilderness. Greta thought maybe that's what she should do. After all, people are people wherever you go. People can't really help where they're born, or control all of the circumstances that govern the course of their lives.

'Do you know what happened to Grandma Josie and Grandpa Frank? Mum's parents. Are they still alive?'

Grandma Ruth shook her head sadly. 'I wish I knew, Greta. I wish I knew. We haven't heard from them, since the Big Shift. Since it happened. They just completely vanished. We tried to find them. Really, we made every effort, but after the first few years.. after things had settled down.. and they still didn't show up.. well, we just had to think the worst. Like we did with you and your mum. How could you have been there all the time and never got in contact? It would have been so simple. We just couldn't understand it. But, you know, a lot of people disappeared at that time. You and River and Frankie and Josie weren't the only ones. That's why it's such a miracle, you coming back like this, Greta. It really is. It gives us all so much hope that maybe the others will come back too.'

....

One day, Greta went with Osama down to Jerusalem's Old City, in the orange zone beneath the hive where he lived. She was in the vip, of course, but by this time she'd become accustomed to it and no longer suffered from PCD, or any cognitive dissonance at all. Now she could step into the vip and instantly be in any number of places, real or virtual and it seemed completely normal. Switching between realities became second nature to Greta, after two weeks in and out of the O-zone.

Osama was there in real life and Greta's virtual self walked alongside him through the narrow, ancient alleys of the old city of Jerusalem. Greta walked barefoot. She liked to feel the cold, smooth stone beneath her feet, the white flagstones worn smooth by centuries of footsteps of pilgrims who had travelled there from afar and of people who lived their whole lives within the city's ancient walls.

They visited Osama's elderly uncle, Sumud, who had a shop on the main bazaar. It was like walking into an Aladdin's cave, with its arched stone walls and ceiling, and with its piles of treasures from near and far. There were beautifully handwoven rugs and carpets, copperware embossed with intricate designs, hand-painted ceramics with brightly coloured patters, candlesticks,

incense, religious symbols and good luck charms to hang on doors or walls, made from wood, silver and gold. It was said that Sumud's family had kept the same shop in the same place for seven hundred years, throughout one set of rulers after another. Some had been better than others and some of them worse.
Greta asked Sumud what he thought about the current ruler, O?
Sumud put his hands together and looked up at the sky, or rather up at the ancient arched ceiling with the cracked plaster. '*Alhamdulilah!*' he said. 'The Great Leader is the best occupier we've had so far.' And then he laughed so much that he went into a coughing fit.
Osama rushed to his uncle and sat him down on a pile of carpets, rubbing his back to try to sooth his coughing. He gave him his water bottle to drink from and spoke softly to him in Arabic in a worried voice, as his coughing subsided.
Afterwards, outside the shop, Osama said to Greta. 'This is why I want to be a doctor, you see? People like my uncle Sumud. He won't go up into the green zone and let O treat him. He's never even been there. He doesn't trust O.. he doesn't trust any sort of authority.. but he doesn't really understand what O is.. why the Great Leader is different from all the others that came before. I keep telling him he should come and live up in the hive with all the rest of the family, but he insists on staying there in the shop. In that damp, mouldy cave. It's not good for his health, but he's scared that if he leaves it, someone will take it. Nothing anyone can say to him will get him to budge. He went through too much before the Big Shift. Lost too much. He can't believe it's all over now. There are loads of people like that, here in the orange zone and out in the red zone. People who need medical treatment but for one reason or another won't let O help them. I want to be able to go out there and help those people.'
Greta looked at Osama in admiration. Knowing him made her want to be a better person. Now, more than ever in her life, the world seemed bigger and more complex than she'd ever imagined, but Osama somehow made it seem simple.
They wandered down through the winding alleys of the old city, Osama leading the way, which he knew like the back of his hand. Everyone seemed to know him and they all welcomed and treated Greta like she was a queen on a royal visit from a far away kingdom. In a stone courtyard, under an old carob tree there was an old man sitting on an old wooden chair playing an old guitar. He wore small round glasses with thick lenses that magnified his eyes. On

his head, perched a battered, old, porkpie hat which he wore at a jaunty angle. He was singing with his eyes closed, in a rich and tuneful voice, some song in ancient Hebrew accompanied by his rhythmic strumming on the guitar. The guitar was plugged into a little portable amplifier under his chair, which added volume and distortion. The music filled the little ancient courtyard, echoing off the stone walls, cascading upwards into the vaulted structure of the hive.

Osama took some coins out of his pocket and dropped them into the guitar case which lay open at the musician's feet. On hearing the soft clatter of Obit coins (new money was made from carbon, unlike old coins which were made from metal, so they made a different sound), the old man opened his eyes.

'Oh, hello Osama my friend!' said the guitar player, without missing a beat. Greta waved and smiled, but the old man didn't seem to see her.

'Hello Bentzi', said Osama. 'You're in fine voice today.'

'Yes, it sounds really good', agreed Greta. 'What's the song you're singing?' But Bentzi didn't seem to hear her.

'He can't see or hear you', said Osama. 'He's not wearing lenses or anything.'

'Oh, right. I forgot I'm not really here', said Greta.

'Well, to me you are', smiled Osama and gave her arm a gentle squeeze.

'Can I give him some money?' asked Greta. 'I found out I've got quite a lot of money and I don't really need it.'

'Who are you talking to? Have you got a friend with you?' said the old man, stopping his strumming and looking intently at the space where Greta was standing.

'Yes, I'm with my friend, Greta. She's from the forest. She wants to give you some money. Have you got an account? She was also asking about the song your singing.'

'The words I'm singing come from the book of Psalms, written by King David in ancient times. It's poetry, beautiful poetry. The music? I don't know what you'd call it. It doesn't really matter.. does it?' Bentzi thought long and hard on his question, but seemed unable to reach a conclusion, so he shrugged and started strumming again, in a different key. 'Regarding transfer of funds, so to speak.. that's very kind of you to offer, but I don't have an account with Big Brother O. No thank you. Not me. I've got no account with O and O's got no account with me. Nothing to settle there and that's the way I like it. No-one's slave, no-one's master. It's got to be cash or nothing.. well, maybe a nice sweet pastry.. some *rogelach* I never say no to, do I Osama?'

'Indeed you don't, Bentzi', laughed Osama. 'I'll get you some on the way back.' He dropped another lot of coins into Bentzi's case and they made their way along. Bentzi resumed his singing and it followed them down the ancient street as they made their way towards the holy sites at the heart of the old city.

As they neared the holy sites, the narrow streets became more crowded. People of all different faiths bustled to and from the place which was said to be built upon the very rock where God created the world and the first humans, Adam and Eve. The same rock upon which Abraham almost sacrificed his son to that same God. Later, the ancient Hebrews built a temple there, but later it was destroyed by the ancient Babylonians. Later, the slightly less ancient Hebrews built another temple in the same spot, and later again, that one was destroyed, this time by the Romans, who later crucified Jesus on that very same spot and from which same Jesus, later still, rose again. Later again, the Prophet Mohammed, on his Night Journey was said to have journeyed from that very rock on his winged steed, Buraq, and from there, all the way up to heaven.

Osama explained all of this as they went along, pointing out different churches, synagogues, chapels and prayer houses, each belonging to different denominations and sects. Greta was awestruck by the layers of history, all built on top of each other as well as how many different ways people found to worship the same God.

Above the holy site of the Western Wall, the Temple Mount, the Al-Aqsa Mosque, the golden Dome of the Rock, the Church of the Holy Sepulture .. all jostling for space on top of the aforementioned 'Foundation Rock' and fought over for centuries by representatives of the various faiths .. the hive was left open to the sky. What this looked like was a long, almost endless mirrored tunnel, the light from the sky bouncing down from a hole at the top of the hive, a thousand metres above. The effect was like looking up into a sky, but a sky that was round instead of flat. When a white cloud drifted above the light tunnel, it appeared to tumble around the sides and stretch out it spectacular ways. Greta stared upwards in wonder and awe. She was having a religious experience.

She imagined she could see Mohammed flying up on his winged horse, up towards the light, up to heaven. She saw Jesus going up there too, on the wings of David's psalms. Looking up into the light, she felt that maybe it was all true.. maybe heaven was real.. maybe there was a reason for everything.. for her coming to this place and the strange, unlikely set of circumstances that had brought her to be in this very place at this very moment.. maybe God was looking back down at her and had a plan for her and for everything and everyone. It was a comforting feeling. It made her feel less alone and not so very far from home.

Osama put his hand in hers and he smiled at her in a way that seemed to share the same feeling. She held his hand and smiled back and they both stared up into the light.

....

Most of the time, Freddy was in his study, looking into space, searching for dark matter, staring into black holes, sometimes engaged in deep discussions with other academics in the field, but most often with O.

On one occasion, Nina and Greta managed to coax him out to come to a show, up in the arena, twenty levels up. Freddy argued that there was no point in going all the way up there just to stand in a crowd of sweaty strangers. 'We could just go in the vips and have the same experience in the comfort of our own home. It's not as if it's a *live* show anyway. The band's *augmented*. They're just a *projection*. I mean, I don't think they're even alive any more are they? I know Freddy Mercury definitely isn't.'

'But it's Queen, dad', said Nina. 'You really like Queen. They've just made a new album. They did a sequel to Bohemian Rhapsody. This is the first time anyone's going to hear it. Apparently it explains everything.. that's' what they're saying. Loads of people are going to be there. It'll be fun. Come on, we never go anywhere or do anything.'

'It's not really them, Nina', Freddy shook his head sadly. 'I think it would just depress me and get on my nerves. Like that time we went to see the Beatles doing their new album release show. I mean, is this really what people go to see? There are so many great musicians about.. I'm sure there are.. there must be.. but where's the great music of our time? Of *this* time? I just don't hear it. All I hear is this stuff made up by machine.. rehashing of old stuff, based on algorithms. Is it even music? I don't know. Maybe young people these days just don't have to struggle against anything any more.. or maybe I'm just out of touch.. God, listen to me! I sound like an *old person!*'

'You do, dad', agreed Nina. 'We should go down to the orange zone sometimes. I know some really cool places.. down at the wharf. That's where the best music scene is. Or to the hives on the south side of the city. It's only twenty minutes in the tube. There's live music there all the time. You should get out more.'

'How do you know those places?' asked Freddy suspiciously. 'You don't go there do you?'

'In the vip. Not in real life.. *obviously*', said Nina with more than a hint of resentment. 'I can't even go out of this hive without your permission, can I?'

'Well, you don't need to.. *obviously*', said Freddy, raising his eyebrows.

'Well, other kids do.. and it's not even as if I'm a kid any more. I'm sixteen years old already.'

'Ok, let's go to the Queen concert. When does it start?' said Freddy, more to pacify Nina and to avoid a difficult argument over an issue he'd prefer not to deal with, than actually wanting to go to see a virtual rendering of a dead rock band playing 'live'.

As it turned out, Freddy ended up having a good time and even singing along, clapping his hands and stamping his feet to 'We will rock you' and getting teary eyed at 'Radio Gaga', which he said was even better than the original. He said that the sequel to 'Bohemian Rhapsody' didn't make any more sense than the first one.. but maybe that was the whole point. He had to conclude that it was a work of genius.

They came back home happy and exhilarated. Greta had found the whole experience.. the crowd of people, the loud music and bright lights.. quite overwhelming, but she was happy to see her dad having a good time. They didn't talk about the difficult subject again for another ten days..

....

Exactly one month since the evening that Greta had arrived, she was in the kitchen with Freddy and Nina, serving up a dish of couscous with roasted vegetables and chick peas that she'd made. Nina had promised she'd try it, as long as she could put ketchup on it. A familiar bell rang three times, the front door opened and a friendly little delivery robot came in carrying a parcel. Greta didn't even jump.

'Here you go, this one's for you, Greta', said the little robot going over to Greta and handing her the parcel.

'Thanks.. er, Boris', said Greta, reading the delivery robot's name tag. 'I don't remember ordering anything.'

With her augmented reality specs, Boris didn't look like a robot, but like a friendly little round man in his forties who appeared to be sweating slightly from his haste to deliver the package. He was wearing a woollen beanie hat which he took off and used to wipe his brow. Underneath his hat he was balding slightly. Greta marvelled at all the detail O went into, to create realistic looking and acting robots, and how they all seemed to be different in quirky ways.

'It's your items which were taken for decontamination', said Boris. 'A shawl and a pair of shoes, if I'm not mistaken. They've been thoroughly cleaned, down to the molecular level. I expect you'll be glad to have them back, won't you.'

'Oh wow! I'd almost forgotten about them. Yes, I'm really happy to have them back. Thank you.. Boris.' She'd almost said 'Thank you, O', but caught herself just before she said the words. The realisation of what she'd been about to say stunned her. Mostly because she'd actually meant it. What did it mean? How could she be grateful to O .. for anything? What had happened to her in the last month? What had she become?

'Well, good evening to you' said Boris, turning to go. 'Enjoy your meal. Couscous is that? It smells delicious. You should be on Masterchef, Greta.'

'What? How did you..?' said Greta, and then remembered, O knows everything. O sees everything.

....

Opening the parcel and seeing her woven shawl and the shoes that her mum had made caused Greta to feel a surge of homesickness. She put her face into the soft woollen shawl. It was cleaner and brighter than it had ever been, even when it was new. It was good to feel the familiar softness, but something about it was different. It had no smell. None whatsoever. The shoes were also bright and immaculately clean.

'Oh wow! Those shoes are amazing', marvelled Nina.

'Mum made them', said Greta, stroking the fur lining and running her fingers over the intricate decorative beadwork. 'Do you want to try them on? They should fit you too.'

'Can I?' said Nina, her face lighting up.

'Sure', said Greta, handing Nina the shoes.

Nina held the shoes as if they were crystal slippers, precious and delicate. 'Oh my God, they're beautiful', she whispered. 'I've never seen anything like them before. They're so.. so.. *real*. Something about them.. do you know what I mean? Like.. they've got *soul*. I didn't know mum was such an artist.'

'Must be where you get it from, Nina. It's certainly not from me', said Freddy. 'They are lovely shoes, I must say. How did she put all those beads on, Greta? It must have taker her ages.'

'It did. She made them for me for my birthday. I think she knew I'd be going on a journey.'

Nina put on the shoes and laced them up. 'Wow, they're so comfortable. They're a perfect fit.' She got up and danced around the room. 'I feel like a fairy of the forest! What are they made from? They're so soft.'

'Deerskin and fox fur', said Greta.

Nina stopped in her tracks. 'What, like from a *deer* and a *fox*?'

'Yes, of course', said Nina.

'Euw! I can't believe I'm wearing dead animal skin on my feet!' Nina hurriedly undid the laces. 'Don't you find that gross?'

'Not really', shrugged Greta. 'There are loads of wild deer around in the forest. We only kill one when we need to, and we use every part of it for something. The fox fur comes from foxes that have already died. We don't hunt foxes.'

'Seems they're not concerned about contracting foxpox either', muttered Freddy.

'I'd never even heard of foxpox till I came here', said Greta, shuddering at the sound of the word. 'Maybe it's not even real.'

'Oh it's very real, Greta', said Freddy. 'If people out there in the red zone would only get vaccinated, we could stop it in its tracks. We wouldn't all need to be on such high alert here in the green zone, trying to keep it from getting in.'

'Well, I haven't seen anyone getting it. Maybe it's not as bad as all that. Maybe if people are healthy, their immune system just beats it and they get better naturally', said Greta.

'Wishful thinking, magical thinking', said Freddy, shaking his head. 'O just needs to go out there and vaccinate everyone. They could do it from the skies. It would be nothing for O to make an airborne vaccine. Just spray it from drones. People wouldn't even know. Then we'd all be safe.'

Greta stared at her dad in horror. 'How can you say that? That would be so *wrong*.'

'Nonsense!' huffed Freddy. 'What's wrong with protecting people from contracting a dangerous, contagious disease and preventing other people from catching it? If you ask me, it would be wrong of O *not* to do that.'

'You can't just go and spray chemicals on people', Greta protested.

'It's not chemicals, it's medicine. Highly advanced medicine. You and your people are still stuck in old ways of thinking, I can see. *New* vaccines are nothing like the *old* vaccines. Today's vaccines are

100% safe and effective. There's no risk at all.'

'I don't believe that', said Greta. 'Sometimes the old ways are the best ways. People were living that way for thousands of years before all this modern technology came along.'

'And people had a life expectancy of about forty.. if they were lucky enough to survive childhood, childbirth, diseases and wild animals.'

'Well, just because something is new, it doesn't always mean it's better.'

'In this case, I would say that the evidence is very clear and incontrovertible', said Freddy in his teacher voice. 'New is *definitely* better than the old.'

'No, you're wrong!' cried Greta, now upset. 'You've got no idea because you've never even been out there. You don't know how it is or what it's like at all. You just *think* you know, but you're *wrong*!'

'I'm not wrong, Greta. I don't *need* to go out there to know what's happening out there. I'm very well informed, I can assure you.'

'You think you know, but you don't know. When it comes down to it, you just believe everything that O tells you. You never question.. never question.. any of.. *this*.' Greta gestured helplessly around the kitchen and out of the window over the city skyline.

'Any of *what*, Greta? I question everything', said Freddy, quite taken aback by Greta's outburst.

'*This! This! This!*' cried Greta, pointing to the stats above Freddy's head and above Nina's head and above her own head. '*This!*' pointing to Sydney the robot dog who was on Nina's lap, licking the last of her ketchup-couscous with his robotic tongue-straw. '*This!*' Greta pointed to the hives outside the window.

'What's to question?' said Freddy, puzzled. 'This is the modern world. It's' all completely natural. It's *evolution*, that's all it is.'

'Oh.. oh.. oh.. *oh*! You just don't get it! You just don't *understand*! You think you know everything about everything, but you don't really know *anything*! Now I'm going to be stuck here *forever*! I'm never going to get home!' cried Greta. She picked up her shoes and shawl, bundled them up in her arms and ran out of the room. She ran into the bedroom, threw herself down on the bed and burst into tears.

....

Nina came to the bedroom and put her arms around Greta. 'Hey Greta, don't be sad. We'll get to the forest. We'll see mum, you'll see. You'll get home. Don't worry.'

'How?' cried Greta. 'Dad won't even let us go down to the orange zone. O is watching everything, all the time. Everyone here is so *comfortable*, nobody wants to go anywhere.'

'Well, even if dad won't let us go.. in six months time.. less than six months.. we can go wherever we want. Dad can't stop us and neither can O.'

'Six months is *ages*. It'll be the middle of winter by then. Granny Mae was right. Queenie was right. I let O get into my head.. I forgot who I am.. now I'm stuck here and I'll never get home.' Greta buried her face in her pillow and cried some more.

'Please don't cry, Greta. We'll make a plan. That's what we'll do', said Nina. 'We'll work out exactly what to say to dad. We'll *make* him agree.'

'He'll *never* agree, Nina. Can't you see that? Look, he even gave up one of his babies because he's so stubborn and so scared to go out of the city. You think he'll change his mind now? He *won't*.'

'No Greta. We'll think of something. We'll make a plan. Please don't cry.'

'Do you know what Osama told me?' said Greta. 'There used to be a wall going right through the middle of Jerusalem and all across the land. A great big wall, so high you couldn't even climb over it. Just to keep his people out, just to stop them from returning home.'

'That's awful', said Nina. 'But then didn't O take down the wall?'

'Yes, that was the first thing O did after the Big Shift. That's why Osama loves O so much. But, don't you see? O made *different* kinds of walls. *Invisible* walls to trap us even more, in different ways..'

Nina didn't know what to say. She climbed into bed with Greta and spread the woollen shawl over them both.

'I miss her, Nina', cried Greta. 'I miss mum. I miss the forest. How are we going to get back? It all seems so far away.'

'We'll find a way, Greta. I promise you, we'll find a way. We'll go there soon, you'll see. I miss mum too. You know that? Even though I can't remember her, I still miss her. Does that make sense?'

'Yes it does', said Greta.

....
....

PART THREE

On the Road Again

Episode 17. Escape

Just as the first rays of sun broke over the city horizon, Greta and Nina both woke up with a sudden start and sat up in bed.
'I just had the most vivid dream', said Nina, her face white and her eyes wide.
'So did I', said Greta, looking just the same.
'What did you dream?' they both said at the same time.
'It was mum', they both replied at the same time.
They both stared at each other in disbelief.
'What did you dream, Nina?' asked Greta breathlessly.
'I was in the forest. I was looking for mum, and it was dark. It just kept getting darker and darker, until I couldn't see anything at all. And I could hear mum calling me.. she was calling us.. but I couldn't find her because it was so dark. That was it. Then I woke up. But it

was so real. So vivid. I can still smell the forest. I can still hear her voice, Greta. I heard her.'

Greta gasped and covered her mouth, her eyes wide with shock. 'I had the same dream, Nina. Exactly the same. It was so dark. No light at all. I couldn't see anything at all.'

'What does it mean?', asked Nina, frightened.

'It means we have to go back, Nina. We need to get back to mum. Back to the forest.'

'How?'

'I don't know. But we need to go at the first chance we get.'

....

At breakfast, Nina and Greta were both quiet and sullen as they ate their Cheery-O's.

Freddy looked like he hadn't slept at all. He had toast and coffee.

'Listen, I was thinking..', said Freddy, breaking the silence. 'There's an expedition going out next week. A group of researchers I work with. They're going in the direction of the Eastern Forest.. where you come from, Greta..'

'And we can go with?' asked Greta, her face instantly lighting up.

'Erm.. no.. that's not what I was thinking, sorry', said Freddy, wishing he'd thought about what he was going to say before he said it, even though he'd been up all night thinking about it.

'Oh', said Greta, her face dropping. She went back to staring into her bowl of Cheery-O's.

'Sorry, Greta. It's too dangerous. They're just a very select group of scientists.. they've got a lot of equipment.. it takes a lot of organisation.. they're going on a three month journey.. but we can send a message to your mum with them.. and maybe they can convince her to come back here to us. What do you think?'

'Why can't we just go there ourselves?' said Greta, turning red in the face. 'It's literally only a three day walk from here. We could even do it in two if we went quickly. If we took torches and walked at night too.'

'Walked at *night*? Through the *forest*? Are you *crazy*? There are bears out there, and wolves. All sorts of predators.. animal and human. I don't think you really understand how dangerous it is out there, Greta.'

'I know very well what it's like out there', said Greta angrily. 'I grew up there, remember? It's my *home*.'

'*This* is your home now, Greta. With us. Mum wil come here, you'll see. Then we'll all be together, like we should have been all along.'

Greta stared into her Cheery-O's and didn't say anything. A heavy silence fell on the kitchen.

A ringtone sounded in Greta's ear. Who could be calling her? Most likely either Grandma or Osama. If it was one of Nina's friends or Ariel, they'd be more likely to call Nina. Greta glanced up to the right. Was that..

'..*Jerry*?' said Greta. 'Is that you?'

'Greta! Hey, how's it going? We were wondering where you got to. You've been gone a month. Did you find your sister?'

'Yes, I'm here with her now', said Greta.

'Awesome! I knew you would. Listen, we're downtown. Queenie's here too. Are you busy? Do you want to come and meet us?'

'Wow! Are you really? Yes, of course. I'd love to..' said Greta, her face lighting up. 'But..' she frowned and looked at her dad.

'Who is it Greta?' asked Freddy. 'Who are you talking to?'

'It's Jerry, my friend from Shopping Village. And Queenie. They're down in the orange zone. He's asking if we want to go and meet them downtown.'

'Oh *yes*!' cried Nina. 'Let's go and meet them. Come on dad. It's about time you let us have some freedom.'

'Well..' Freddy thought of how he could say no in a way that wouldn't be too upsetting for Greta and Nina, but realised that there wasn't one. 'Ok. Why not? You go and meet your friends. You're big girls. Just make sure you're back before dark.. before six would be best. Can you do that?'

'Yes!' said Nina, punching her fist in the air.

'Thanks dad', said Greta with a sad smile. She was already planning her escape.

....

After breakfast, Greta and Nina went to the bedroom to get changed and prepare for their big day out. They'd arranged to meet Jerry and Queenie in an hour at the *Traveller's Rest*, Sam's music bar on the riverside.

Nina was excited. 'I can't believe he said yes! *Finally*! What shall we wear? Let's get dressed up..' She threw open the big wardrobe and started rummaging through her clothes.

Greta drew in close to Nina, looking tense and furtive, glancing this way and that, as if she was being watched, which of course she was.

'Have you got your lenses in Nina?' whispered Greta.

'No. I haven't put them in yet. Why?'

'Are you wearing headphones?'

'No, I haven't got them in yet either. What's up? Are you ok?'

'I want to say something to you and I don't want O to hear', Greta

whispered urgently in Nina's ear.
'What? What is it?' Nina looked worried.
'I'm *going*', said Greta. 'Today. I'm going back to the forest. I need to get back to mum. Are you coming with me? Mum's in trouble. She needs us.'
'What? How? No. We can't. What about dad? He'll go crazy..'
'We'll send him a message somehow.. I don't know', said Greta. She didn't feel good about leaving Freddy either, but he didn't leave her much choice.
'But how? How can we get out of the city anyway? We're still under age. We don't have permission to go out into the redzone.'
'Queenie knows a way out', whispered Greta. 'There's a secret tunnel that goes right out past the city limit. She'll show us where it is.'
'Are you *serious*?' said Nina. She looked frightened.
Greta nodded. 'The dream, Nina. It was a *sign*. And then Jerry and Queenie showing up out of the blue. It's meant to be, Nina. If we don't go today, we might not get another chance for ages. It might be too late..'
Nina held her head in her hands. 'I don't know. I don't know. It feels wrong. Dad will never trust us again. I've never been out of the city. What if we get attacked by bears? I'm scared. What if we get lost? Anything could happen.'
'It's only a three day walk. Two days if we go quickly. I know the way. It'll be fine.'
'Will it though?'
'Yes', said Greta. 'Just think, you're going to see mum in two days. And you'll see the forest where we live. It's *wild* there, Nina. It's so *real*. You'll *love* it. Will you come with me? Please come with me.'
Nina wrestled with the conflicting thoughts and feelings. Eventually she nodded, very slowly at first and then more quickly, excitedly. 'Yes. Yes. *Yes!*' she said, hugging Greta.
Freddy's voice came from the doorway. 'You allright in there girls? You excited? It looks like you are. Just be careful out there, ok? And be back before it gets dark.'

....

As soon as Greta and Nina were out of the door, Freddy was filled with worry and regret. Why had he allowed them to go? And with two people he'd never even met.. a runaway and a.. who knows what kind of person this Jerry was? Freddy paced around the apartment fearing the worst. Why hadn't he gone with them? Maybe he should follow them.. No. That would be wrong. He needed to trust his daughters and trust the universe that they'd be all right. But he didn't trust the universe. How could he, when he knew how cold and vast it was..? He went to his study and continued his search for a very distant star. He was sure it was out there somewhere, if only he could find it.. a parallel world, just like Earth, but where everything turned out differently..

Nina felt terrible about not telling their dad where they were going. She'd wanted to go to Pierre, tell him what they were planning and ask him for his advice, but Greta said it was out of the question. O mustn't know they were planning to escape and Pierre was O, after all.

Greta felt terrible too. Even worse that Nina, because it had been her idea. But she knew that it was what they had to do. She felt as if she was following some deep instinct that she was powerless to resist. She wished she could have said goodbye to grandma and grandpa and especially Osama. She hated the idea that he might think she didn't care about him. She just hoped he'd understand and wouldn't worry too much. Somehow she'd figure out how to get a message through. For now, she was fully focussed on getting out of the city and back to the forest.

....

Reaching the Traveller's Rest was easy. Even without augmented reality pointing the way, Greta remembered the way down main street, over Empire Bridge and along the embankment. As soon as she stepped out of the tube and her feet touched ground level, she felt a rush of energy, coming up through the Earth and into her body. How had it been a whole month that she hadn't touched the ground? The wind rushing across the surface of the great river as the crossed the bridge, blew sprays of cold water onto her face, making her feel alive in a way that she hadn't felt since entering the green zone.

They stopped in the middle of the bridge, where Greta had met Sally, a month earlier. Sally wasn't there now, but maybe she would be a sunset. She hoped that Winston had already arrived and taken Sally to their home in the country. She held onto her hat, to prevent it from blowing over the edge of the bridge.

'Wow!' shouted Nina. It was so windy, she had to shout, besides which, she was also excited and feeling the rush of Earth energy. 'It's so *big*. The river. When you're actually here next to it. It's so *powerful*. It's so *real!*'

'Yes! It is!' nodded Greta, smiling. Then she leaned over and said in Nina's ear, 'Take off your headphones.'

Nina gave her a quizzical look, but did as she was told. She held the little silver buds in her hand and showed them to Greta.

'Now throw them in the river', said Greta.

'What? Are you serious?'

'Yes. Your lenses too.'

'No way. They're expensive. They're new. I only just got them.'

'Listen, Nina. You need to', said Greta urgently. 'We need to be *invisible*. Throw them over the edge. We haven't got much time. I'll buy you some new ones when we get back, ok? I promise.'

'So, you mean.. you're coming back? We're coming back?'

Greta thought about it for a moment. Then she said, 'Of course I will. Of course we will. I've got two homes now. So have you. You'll see. It will all work out. Now throw your lenses in the river. We need to get to mum.'

Nina gave Greta a hug, then took out her contact lenses and threw them over the edge of the bridge, along with her headphones. They watched as the wind carried them away.

....

Jerry, Queenie and Captain Toast were waiting at The Traveller's Rest, sitting at a table outside in the sun, drinking tall glasses of fruitshake. Everybody was excited and happy to meet, especially Captain Toast, who continued jumping around, licking Greta and Nina's hands well after everyone had hugged and greeted each other.

'Can we get a table inside?' said Greta. 'I need to talk to you about something.. in private..' She gestured with her thumb to the lamp post behind her, which she knew contained a camera.

Queenie understood instantly what she meant. They went inside and took their places around the table in the cubicle at the back. Sam brought Greta and Nina fruitshakes and came to join them.

'What's' going on 'sis?' asked Queenie.

'We need to get back to the forest', said Greta. 'We don't have permission from our dad to go out of the city, but our mum's in trouble and we need to get to her.'

'How do you know she's in trouble?' asked Sam.

'We had a dream', said Nina and Greta at the same time. 'The same dream.'

Sam sat back and rubbed his chin. 'That makes sense', he said.

'Do you remember where the Freedom Drain is, Queenie?' asked Greta.

'Yes of course', said Queenie. 'It's round the back of Station Road, near the old cinema building. I've got the map memorised. We can go along the river and then down Main Street and then turn right onto Station Road. That's right isn't it Sam?'

'You could go that way, but it's a long way round. Quickest way would be to follow the canal.. past Techno Terry's boat.. do you know where that is? You went there last time, didn't you? It takes you right behind the old cinema.' Sam spoke with the knowledgable ways of one who lives in the city.

'I don't know..' said Queenie uncertainly. 'That place was creepy. So was Techno Terry..'

'If it's quicker, I'd prefer to go that way', said Greta. 'Also, I told Terry that I'd bring Nina to meet him. If it's on the way, it would be a good chance. He really helped me find her.'

'Well, it's up to you..', said Queenie with a shrug. 'But I don't want to hang around there for too long.'

'No, we'll just go in and say hello and then be on our way. We really need to be getting along too', said Greta.

'Have we got time to play a tune before we go?' said Jerry hopefully.

'I don't know..' said Greta. 'The sooner we set off, the sooner we'll arrive.'

'Does that piano work?' asked Nina. 'Is it in tune? I've never played a real piano before..'

'It's not bad', said Sam. 'Fairly in tune. Go ahead and have a go. Please do.'

Nina went over to the piano and began picking out a simple tune. 'Wow! It's completely different playing a real piano', she exclaimed in wonder and surprise. 'I mean.. not *completely* different, but not at all the same either.. amazing..' She carried on playing, delighting in the sound of the strings and the feel of the keys, the complex mechanisms of wood and felt hammers, the way the foot-pedal creaked each time she pressed it.

Jerry, of course couldn't resist joining in, so he took his position at the upright bass which was standing next to the piano. He didn't really know how to play it, but kept a steady rhythm by plucking at the strings and it sounded pretty good.

'Well, I guess we've got time for one tune', said Greta, taking her wooden flute out of its pouch.

Queenie went to the stage and took the guitar down from the wall. She quickly picked out some chords and scales to go along with what Nina was playing. Sam went and sat behind the drum kit which had fortuitously come his way the day before. He didn't really know how to play the drums, but he tapped out a beat on the cymbals and a shuffed on the snare drum with a pair of brushes. It

sounded close enough to Jazz to be taken for the real thing.
The tune was one that Greta and Nina had played before. Nina had picked it up in the bars of 1950's Paris. Greta closed her eyes and joined in on her flute. In her mind's eye, her notes were carried away on the wind, joining the river, going out over the forests.. sending a message she hoped they would hear and understand.. *we are coming.. help us find the way.. watch over us and protect us, spirits of the Earth.* Osama's face came into her mind. She hoped and imagined that her face was coming into his mind at the same moment. She sent him a kiss and hoped he received it.
Nina was thinking about Pierre. He always loved to listen to her play the piano, this tune especially. She hoped he'd understand her leaving like this and that he'd be there when she got back. Of course he would. Of course he would. She thought about her dad. Would he also be so understanding and forgiving? That was far less certain.

....

As they walked along by the old canal, Greta told the story of how she'd found Nina and her dad. Queenie was especially impressed by the part where Greta had smashed in a robot's head with a frying pan, thrown spaghetti at another and caused the restaurant to catch fire. She told Greta that she was *'hardcore'*. Jerry was astounded at the part where Greta had escaped quarantine by climbing up the outside of the hive. He said she was *'completely mental.'* He thought it was hilarious that O had brought Greta a packed lunch on her way up. 'That's just like O!' he'd laughed.
When they got to the place where Techno Terry's boat had been, it wasn't there. Jerry thought it was odd, but not out of character for Terry to disappear without a trace. Queenie was quite relieved that he wasn't there. Greta hoped that she hadn't got Techno Terry into trouble. A part of her wondered if she'd imagined the whole thing, or if Terry had actually been some kind of projection, or even a robot. With O, anything was possible. Captain Toast sniffed the footpath all around, but could find no trace of Techno Terry, his boat or any of his cats. Nina wondered what she was doing in a dark passage with these strange, scruffy friends of Greta and if she should have listened to her dad and heeded his warnings.
Further along, the tunnel opened out, bright sunlight was breaking through into an area overgrown with trees and brambles. 'There! That's it', cried Queenie. 'It's the back of the old cinema. Follow me.' She led the way, pushing aside nettles and thorns. On the back wall of the cinema, low down and hidden in the undergrowth was a

small, brick archway, just big enough to crawl through. 'Here it is!' she pointed triumphantly.
'Are you sure this is it, Queenie?' said Jerry.
'Yes, a hundred percent', said Queenie, peering into the hole. 'Come on, let's go..'
'It's dark in there', said Nina, uncertainly. 'Are you sure this is a good idea?'
'I've got a torch', said Queenie, pulling a hairpin out of her hair. She gave the end of it a twist and it lit up. 'Always good to be prepared, eh!' she winked. She put her head in through the entrance. 'Yeah, this is definitely it', she said. 'I'm going in..' She slid through the archway head first. After her feet disappeared, there was a silence.
'Queenie? You allright?' called Jerry through the hole.
'Yeah, fine. Come on down', came Queenie's voice, echoing out from the darkness.
Jerry went down next, followed by Captain Toast.
Nina looked at Greta. 'Are you sure about this, Greta?'
'Yes, don't worry, Nina. This is the way', said Greta. Without another word, she slid down the drain.
Nina shook her head and followed the others down into the dark hole.

....

The tunnel stretched away in both directions. 'Look here!', said Queenie, shining her torch around. 'Someone's painted arrows.' All along the wall of the tunnel, white arrows. Whoever had painted them had also written the word FREEDOM in big capital letters. 'See? This is it. I told you. Come on, let's go..' Captain Toast barked. The sound of it echoed up and down the ancient viaduct. 'Shh, Captain' said Queenie. 'We're not out of danger yet.'
To Nina, the tunnel seemed to go on forever. Greta was quiet and nervous. All she wanted was to be back in the forest. Captain Toast ran off up ahead and ran back to report that the coast was clear. Jerry sang an old coal mining song in the deepest baritone he could muster. 'Where it's dark as a dungeon, damp as the dew.. danger is double, pleasures are few.. where the rain never falls and the sun never shines.. it's dark as a dungeon, way down in the mines..'
'Jerry, do you have to?' said Queenie.
'Yes', said Jerry. 'Listen to those acoustics. We should bring some instruments and record something down here. Hey, Greta, play something on your flute.'
'Let's try and be quiet, maybe', said Greta. 'O's probably listening. I just want to get to the other side already. How much further is it

Queenie?'

An arrow was painted on the wall, with the words '> > > Nearly there! Keep going! Freedom this way > > >'

They walked quicker. Jerry continued humming, more quietly. Captain Toast ran up ahead into the shadows, then started barking from somewhere up ahead. They rounded a bend and then saw him standing in a shaft of light coming from the side of the tunnel.

A head poked in from the opening. It had spiky red hair. 'Who goes there?' he called.

'Baz? Is that you?' shouted Jerry. It was.

Baz, Claire and the telepathic triplets were all there waiting at the tunnel entrance in the church graveyard. The triplets had known they were coming through. They'd had a feeling.

....

Our brave adventurers were welcomed like soldiers returning from the frontline, or like escaped prisoners of war. They were ushered into the church where they were greeted by cheers of jubilation and congratulations at their successful escape from the evil clutches of O.

'I bet you're all hungry', said Clair. 'Let's go to the kitchen, there's a big pot of stew we just made.'

Around the big oak table, Greta recounted the story of how she got into the green zone, her capture, quarantine, her daring escape out of the window and her climb up the outside of the hive. Everyone agreed she was very hardcore indeed. They wanted to know about her time in the city and why it took a whole month for her to escape.

Greta told about her adventures in virtual reality, meeting her grandparents and family in New Jerusalem. She missed them already and wondered when she'd see them again. She wished she could show Osama this crazy church full of revolutionaries.. he'd love it. She told about how their dad wouldn't let them go out of the city because of his fears and how they had to leave without telling him. Nina nodded and looked sadly at her stew, pushing it around the bowl. She was hungry but didn't like the look or the smell of it. It had mushrooms in it and Nina didn't like mushrooms, not that she'd ever tried any.

'God, he sounds totally *brainwashed*, your dad', said Clair.

'He's not brainwashed. He's just really scared that something bad will happen', said Nina, taking a tiny spoonful of the stew, making sure it didn't have any mushrooms in it. It wasn't actually as bad as all that.

'That's what I mean', said Clair. 'He's living in *fear*. That's how it works. That's how O keeps everyone in their place. It's brainwashing.'

Queenie nodded in agreement. 'They keep you living in fear, but at the same time make life so comfortable and convenient that you'd never even *think* of getting out. That's the way it works.'

Greta thought back to her walks in the park, going to the Queen concert, hanging out with Freddy in his studio, talking about the mysteries of the universe. She recalled evening meals with her dad and Nina and Sydney the robot dog. She was surprised to discover that she even missed Sydney. 'I wasn't living in fear', she said.

'That's why you got out. You weren't so easy to brainwash because you *know* what it's like on the outside' said Claire. 'Knowledge is power.' She tapped her head knowingly.

The three telepathic triplets all nodded. They wanted to know about Nina and Greta's dream. Nancy, who was good at interpreting dreams, said that dreaming about walking in a dark forest is usually a bad sign, a warning.

Nina became frightened. 'Maybe we should just go back, Greta' she said. 'Dad won't even know we're gone. We could go back through the tunnel.'

Sylvester, who was also good at interpreting dreams said, 'It's not always a bad sign. Sometimes dreams are just what they appear. You both said you heard your mum calling you from the dark. That could just mean it's your mum calling you. *We* get that all the time. Most people are more sensitive to these things when they're asleep.. when their conscious mind is switched off.. but you can even get these messages when you're awake, if you're really *tuned in*. That was how we knew you were coming today.'

'That's what I think it is', said Greta. 'Mum needs us, Nina. She was *calling* us. We need to go to her. I think she's in trouble. That's how it felt. I could hear it in her voice.'

'But..' said Nina, feeling very uncertain and afraid. 'We can't just go following a *dream*. It's totally *irrational*.'

'You sounded just like dad just now', laughed Greta.

'I did, didn't I', said Nina.

'Look, Nina. We've come this far now. We're out of the city. We might not get another chance like this. Dad will be ok. He'll probably come and find us when the expedition goes out. We both had the *same dream*, Nina. I don't know what it means exactly, but it must mean *something*. I think we should carry on. If we start walking now, and walk quickly, we could even be there by tomorrow night.'

....

They walked quickly from there towards Shopping Village. Greta wanted to introduce Nina to Granny Mae so they stopped in at the Mall. This time, when faced with the big glass revolving door, Greta was momentarily confused when it didn't morph into an opening like the glass doors in the green zone. Even the Mall itself didn't seem so huge as it had done the first time around, now that Greta had become accustomed to the cavernous public spaces inside the hive. The electric escalators seemed like a relic from another time. Everything appeared dark, dusty and old.

Granny Mae was there in the kitchen, as if she hadn't moved since the last time. Her face lit up when she saw Greta. 'Oh, hello Dolly!' she cried. 'I'm so glad you came back. And this must be your sister. Of course she is, you're like two peas in a pod! Well done, you did it, eh! I knew you would. Come and sit down.. I'll put the kettle on. Let me bring you some biscuits. Jack'll be along soon.. oh speak of the devil.. here he is!'

Jack was there in the doorway, dressed exactly as he had been the last time, even down to the bandage around his foot, which was looking worse for wear. He winced slightly as he stepped into the room but greeted Greta with a warm smile and a handshake. 'Hello again, Greta. Nice to see you back. How did you get along in the big bad city? O didn't give you too much of a hard time, I hope. I see you found your sister. Hello there', he said to Nina, shaking her hand.

'Hi, I'm Nina. Greta's told me all about you and Granny Mae. It's good to meet you in real life. Is your foot ok? You're limping.'

'Oh that? It's nothing really. I just need to take the weight off.' Jack sat down heavily in a chair at the kitchen table and rubbed his leg to sooth it.

'Why don't you go to the city and get it treated?' asked Nina. 'It's only down the road. You shouldn't have to be in pain. I'm sure O could fix it.'

'That's what I keep telling him', said Jerry.

'Maybe you should', agreed Greta. She was surprised to hear herself say it, but she didn't like to see Jack suffering.

Jack raised his eyebrows and smiled wryly. 'Well, well, Greta. It seems you've changed your tune. What happened? The Great Leader wasn't the monster you expected?'

'I don't know', said Greta. 'I think it's going to take me some time to process. They weren't quite what I expected.'

'Who was it who said that travel broadens the mind? Mark Twain, was it?' said Jack, taking his pipe out of his pocket and preparing it. 'Travel is fatal to bigotry, prejudice and narrow mindedness. That's the quote', said Nina. 'I love his books. Tom Sawyer.. Huckleberry Finn..'

Jack nodded appreciatively. 'Good to see there are young people who still read books. I didn't think there were any left in this day and age.'

'Reading a book is like going on an adventure without actually going anywhere', said Nina. 'I haven't actually been anywhere. Only in the vip. This is my first time out of the city.'

'And you're on your way to the forest, I assume?' said Jack, lighting his pipe. 'Going back there to meet your mum? That's going to be a big adventure.' Nina and Greta both nodded. 'Where's all your stuff? Sleeping bags, tents, that sort of thing.. have you got everything you need?'

'We didn't bring anything. We didn't want to tell our dad that we were going. I just brought my flute and a map and compass', said Greta.

'I see..', said Jack, taking a thoughtful puff on his pipe. 'Well, that's something, I suppose..' Nina had never seen anyone smoking a real pipe. The smoke was different from the blue vapour of her dad's vape. She was worried the wooden pipe might catch fire. 'You know what? I've still got a load of survival packs from years ago. After The Shift, I used to lead a group of collectors.. *scavengers*, as they used to call us. You wouldn't remember, Jerry. You were still a baby.'

'I remember you told me about it', said Jerry.

'Scavengers? What did you do?' asked Nina.

'Like the name suggests. Scavenging', said Jack. 'We'd scour the red zone for anything we could bring to the city to sell to O.. plastic, metal, chemicals, machinery.. anything we could find. There was a lot of work back then. There were thousands and thousands of people, all over the place, collecting stuff and bringing it into the cities. O recycled it all and used it to build the hives. You wouldn't believe how quickly the world got cleaned up when people were offered money for old rubbish. It was a brilliant plan. Good times..'

Jack sat back and closed his eyes, reliving the days when he was young and a wild rover. 'Jerry, go to the store room. At the back on the top shelves you'll find all the packs. Bring four in, will you son?'

'Sure', said Jerry, standing up. 'But why four?'

'Well, I thought you and Queenie might like to go and have a little adventure..' said Jack with a smile. 'Seems like a good opportunity for you to go out and see the world a bit. I'm sure Greta knows the way of the forest so she'll be a good guide. I've heard that Skyward Village is worth a visit.'

'Wow. Really, Jack?' said Jerry in disbelief.

'Yes, why not?' said Jack. 'What do you think Queenie? Do you fancy going too?'

Queenie was looking like her head was about to explode. 'I.. I.. I..' she stammered.

'Isn't it dangerous out there?' asked Nina, worried. 'I don't want to put anyone in danger.'

'Well, you'll need to keep your wits about you, that's for sure. But with Jerry and Queenie and especially Captain Toast you'll have safety in numbers. I've heard things have been a bit unsettled around old Eastwell town.. the Malawack Kingdom, as they call it. Bunch of nutters! King Humpty's been making trouble with the neighbours again. But if you avoid that area, you'll be fine. Can you show me the map you've got, Greta?'

Greta took the map out of her flute case. It was a page torn out of an old road atlas from before the Big Shift. Some places had been crossed out or had their names changed. A green pencil line had been drawn from the place where Skyward Village had been marked with a tree, to the big city, which had a red circle around it. She spread the map out on the table. Everyone gathered round to look at it.

Jack pointed at the map with the mouthpiece of his pipe. 'There, look, this is where we are. So yes, just follow this green line along the river, through the hills. See here? That's the old motorway going past Eastwell. So just don't go that way and you should be completely fine. It's a two or three day walk, following the river, not more than that. Ah, I wish I could go with..'

'I'll go and get the packs then', said Jerry. 'Queenie, shall I get one for you? Are you coming?'

'Oh.. oh.. oh.. I.. I.. I..' stammered Queenie, full of uncertainty, fear and doubt.

'It'll be great to have you along', said Greta. 'And you'll love it in the forest, I'm sure you will.'

Queenie, of course agreed to go with. Someone else would have to clean the bathrooms, though nobody would do it to her high standards.

In addition to the lightweight sleeping bags, bio-plastic tents, high energy food bars, flashlights and various other survival supplies, Granny Mae also added heavy fruitcakes, loaves of home made seed bread, apples and oranges which our travellers divided between their pack.

'That's good', said Jack. 'Those hyper-sausages are ok, but Granny Mae's fruitcake is better.'

'What are hyper sausages?' asked Nina.

'Those energy bars you've got in those survival packs', said Jack. 'That's what we used to call them. They're not really sausages, they're just shaped like them. They don't taste like much, but eat one of those you can walk all day and half the night.'

'Aren't they, like, fifteen years old?' said Jerry.

'Well, yes.. but they're vacuum packed. They should be fine. Take them just in case.'

....

It was two o clock in the afternoon when our adventurers climbed the old highway embankment out of Shopping Village and up the hill to the place where Greta had met Jerry and Captain Toast when she'd first arrived there a month ago. They stopped and took one last look over the city, then turned east and headed into the forest. They soon found their way to the river bank and followed the footpath that ran alongside it, gently sloping up into the hills. By six o clock they were already miles away from the city and deep in the forest, in the heart of nature.

....

By six o clock, Freddy could contain himself no longer. All morning and all afternoon, he'd fought against the urge to call Greta and Nina to check that they were all right. *Let them have their freedom,* he told himself.. *give them some space, they're big girls.* Nobody had told him that parenting would be so hard. It was never ending worry. *Why weren't they back yet? They said they'd be back by six..*

He called Nina. No answer. He called her again. Still no answer. He called Greta. No answer. Again. Still no answer. He called Nina again. No answer still. He called O..

'O? What's going on? Why can't I get through to Greta and Nina? They went down to the orange zone. They're supposed to be back by now. Where are they?'

'Hang on. Let me check', said O.

'What do you mean? Don't you know?'

'It appears they're not there', said O.

'What? What do you mean? So where are they? Maybe they're back in the green zone.. on their way back here.. are they?'

'No, I'm afraid not Freddy', said O. 'It appears that they have absconded into the red zone.'

'*What!!!*'

'It appears that they've absconded into the red zone.'
'Yes I heard you the first time. But *how*?'
'My best guess would be that they went through one of the underground aqueducts. Probably the one near Station Road.'
'Your best guess?!' screamed Freddy. 'You mean you don't know where they are?'
'Well, there are several ways they could have gone out, but the last time I saw them was close to there.'
'O, I can't believe you! You just let them walk right out of the city. You didn't even try to stop them. You didn't call me. Why didn't you let me know? I just don't get it, O. And what are these underground viaducts? Why don't you block them up or something? Are you telling me that anyone can just walk right out, or walk right in? No checks, no cameras, nothing? What about the *protocols,* O? What about *safety*?Explain yourself!'
'There are several ways in and out of the city', said O, in their calm, patient way, quite unruffled by being screamed at by Freddy. 'The border between the red zone and the orange zone is intentionally porous. It needs to be in order for the healthy functioning of the city.'
'*What*? What are you saying, O? That anyone can just come and go, willy-nilly.. as they please?'
'Well, I don't advertise the fact, for obvious reasons' said O with a slight wink. 'It takes a certain amount of determination, ingenuity and luck to find the way.. but essentially yes. A measure of freedom must be built into the system. The city is a living organism. It must be allowed to breath.'
'You're not making any sense at all', Freddy barked angrily. 'Where was the last time you saw them? I want to see.'
'Of course', said O.
There appeared Nina, Greta, Jerry, Queenie and Sammy at the front of the Travellers Rest, playing some old French jazz. Freddy stared, wishing he could reach out and touch them. Tears sprang to his eyes. How could they be gone? What was he going to do now? How was he going to find them?
They finished the tune. He watched them say goodbye to Sammy and head off along the embankment. 'From there, they turned down the canal in the direction of the Station Road viaduct', said O. 'It's a very popular way out of the city, for those wishing to abscond.'
'You let them escape, O! How could you?'
'Escape suggests that they were being held here against their will',

said O. 'The protocols are very clear that citizens are not to be held against their will. I prefer to use the word abscond.'

'Let me see the video again', said Freddy, sinking into his big black chair. There they were again. Greta playing on the flute. Nina on the piano. They played so beautifully. It was really good music. That gave him a sort of satisfaction, but it was swamped by the enormity of his sudden loss. *Why hadn't he gone with them? When would he see them again now?* 'What am I going to do, O?' he cried. 'They've gone. How will I find them? How can I get them back?'

A ringtone sounded in Freddy's ear. 'Maybe it's them!' he exclaimed, full of desperate hope. But it wasn't. It was Osama, sounding very worried.

'Freddy, do you know where Greta is? I've been trying to call her all afternoon. She's not answering. Neither is Nina.'

Freddy's face crumpled up. 'They're gone!' he sobbed. 'They ran away.. absconded.. out of the city.. into the red zone.. and I don't know where they are or how to find them.'

'Oh my God!' cried Osama, his face turning white. 'I knew it! I had a feeling. I saw her face, Freddy. Greta's face. She came to me. She was trying to tell me. I can't believe it. What are we going to do?'

'I don't know, Osama', Freddy shook his head helplessly. 'They could be anywhere.'

'But they must be headed for Skyward Village surely? They're going to see their mum.'

'Yes, you're right. They must be. Of course they are. Oh it's such a shock. My mind's all over the place. I need to focus. I need to think..'

'You need to go after them Freddy', said Osama. 'I'd go myself, but I'm so far away. It would take me months to get there.. years possibly.'

'Yes.. yes, you're right, Osama', said Freddy, jumping up out of his chair. 'What am I doing sitting here crying? I need to go after them. Of course I do. Oh I'm such a fool. It's all my fault.'

'It's not your fault, Freddy. You couldn't hold them back. I know you were just trying to protect them and keep them safe, but they just had to go. There was nothing anyone could have done to stop them.'

'Oh, if only we hadn't had that stupid argument! I would have gone with them if I'd have known they were going to run away. Now what have I got to stay here for? Nothing. They were all I had and now they're *gone*..' Freddy pulled at his hair and stormed around the room, completely lost and without direction, at his wit's end.

'Freddy!', snapped Osama. 'You need to pull yourself together! Maybe they haven't got very far. If you go quickly you might catch up with them.'

'Yes, you're right, Osama. I need to go. There's no time to lose.' With that, Freddy ran out of the room and out of the apartment, with Sydney the robot dog, eager to go for a walk, hot on his heels.

....

Episode 18. Into the Wild

The clever, industrious little creters were working on the finishing touches to Greta's new bedroom as Freddy ran out of the front door in search of his runaway daughters. He didn't take anything with him, not even his pills. The tube took him down to the orange zone and he quickly found his way to the Traveller's Rest, Sammy's place by the river.. the last place that O had seen them before they'd absconded into the red zone through the Freedom Drain. Sammy directed him to *J & J Vintage Machine Revivals*, the repair shop at the top of the Mall in Shopping Village where Jerry lived with Jack and Granny Mae.

The main road leading out of the city was crowded with people. Traders and day visitors heading home to their places either side of the city limit, all eager to get home before nightfall. Freddy ran along the busy thoroughfare, barging his way way through the crowds, barely noticing his surroundings. It was dark by the time Freddy rushed through the revolving doors of the Mall and ran up the escalators with Sydney the robot dog at his side.

Jack and Granny Mae were in the kitchen with Roop who'd dropped in to deliver some carrots, potatoes and onions from their garden. Mostly Roop had come for some advice and to get away from a tense situation at home after an argument with Aretha. Since meeting Greta, Aretha had become depressed and dissatisfied with her life and the compromises she'd made. All of her resentment towards Roop had come to the surface and they'd been arguing. Since meeting Greta, all that their daughter Mabel could talk about was Skyward Village, the place where people lived in trees. Why couldn't they go there? Why? All Roop could do, it seemed, was make excuses and disappoint.

They all looked up when the bell rang as Freddy burst into the shop. 'Hang on! I'll be right out..' called Jack and stiffly began to get up from his chair. By the time he'd stood up, Freddy was standing in the doorway of the kitchen, sweating, red in the face and out of breath. Sydney was by his side, looking around the room and sniffing the air.

Granny Mae screamed. 'Aargh! A robot! Get it out of here!' Sydney backed away and looked out timidly from behind Freddy's legs.

'Sydney, go and wait over there', Freddy said to the robot dog who obediently went and sat among some old washing machines, vacuum cleaners and electric food mixers in the corner of the shop. 'Sorry, I didn't mean to scare you', he said to Granny Mae. 'I'm looking for my daughters, Nina and Greta. They were with Jerry and Queenie. Have you seen them?'

'Oh yes. Lovely girls', said Granny Mae. 'They were just here this afternoon. They're all on their way to the forest.'

'*What?!*' cried Freddy, pulling his hair. 'They were here and you just let them go out into the forest? They're just children. What if they get lost? What if something happens to them? Do you even know where they are now?'

'Come and sit down', said Jack. 'My name's Jack by the way. This is my mum, Mae.'

'Freddy', said Freddy, shaking Jack's hand and then slumping down into a chair at the kitchen table. He put his head in his hands. 'I can't believe this', he muttered to himself. 'How am I going to find them now? Four kids out wandering about in the redzone.. in the middle of the forest.. in the middle of the night.'

'They'll be ok, don't worry', said Jack. 'They've got Captain Toast with them. He'll look after them.'

'*Captain Toast?*' said Freddy, looking up incredulously. 'Who the hell is Captain Toast?'

'Oh, he's our dog', said Jack.

'Captain Toast is a *dog*? Are you serious?' cried Freddy, staring at Jack in disbelief.

'Well, he really likes toast', said Jack. 'He's a good dog though, seriously.'

'Oh, well that's just great', said Freddy angrily. 'I feel much better now, knowing that a dog called Captain Toast is out there looking after my daughters.'

'Hey, look, I know it's a shock, but I'm sure they'll be all right', said Jack. 'They're smart kids. Your Greta, she knows the forest. She found her way to you didn't she? She'll find the way back to her mum.'

'Oh.. oh.. oh..' Freddy stammered and started to cry. 'I can't believe this! I've made such a mess of everything. I should have known something like this would happen. I should have seen it coming. I just wasn't paying attention. Always in my own world. Didn't keep my eye on the ball. Too busy looking into space, trying to solve the mysteries of the universe. Stupid, stupid, stupid man!' Freddy hit himself on the head angrily, but it didn't make him feel any better.

Granny Mae came and put her hand on Freddy's shoulder. 'Don't worry, doll. They'll be just fine. The universe will take care of them. You'll see.'

'The *universe?*' Freddy turned and glared at Granny Mae.

'Do you see that?' said Granny Mae, pointing to the jerry can boat on the wall. 'Do you know what that is?'

'It's a plastic container', said Freddy. 'Some kind of shelf or something? I don't know. What's that got to do with anything?'

'When our Jerry was a baby, Jack found him floating in the sea, in that. Can you believe it? In the middle of the sea. It was a miracle. No other word for it. I don't know who or what, but *someone* was looking out for him, watching over him, keeping him safe. And they are still. You'll see.'

Freddy stared at the little improvised boat and then at Granny Mae. These people were mad. How was he ever going to find his daughters and get them safely home? He was all alone in the world and the universe was bigger and more uncaring than this toothless old woman could ever imagine.

'You know what?' said Roop, scratching his straggly beard and then adjusting his glasses which were held together with tape. 'They're on their way to Skyward Village, aren't they?'

'Yes, that's the name of the place', said Freddy. 'What about it?'

'Well, funnily enough, I was planning on visiting there. With my family.'

'What? Really? When?'

'Actually, first thing in the morning', said Roop, giving the table a decisive thump with the side of his fist. 'You're welcome to join us. We've got a spare bike. Do you know how to ride a bike.. you, know.. a bicycle?'

'Well, I haven't ridden one in years, but I'm sure I'd remember how. Are you serious? Are you sure? Do you know the way?' said Freddy, his face lighting up.

'Yes. We were there years ago and my wife has never stopped pining to go back there. It never seemed like quite the right time.. but.. well.. what can I say? Now it does.'

....

Greta, Nina, Queenie and Jerry set up camp before sunset. Greta had wanted to eat the hyper-sausages and walk through the night, but Nina managed to convince her that they should stop to rest. It had been a long day and they'd come far enough. Jerry and Queenie agreed.

They set up their camp next to a huge oak tree with branches stretching out in every direction. Greta showed the others how to set up the hammock-tents they each had in their pack. The hammocks were ultra lightweight, made from strong, flexible nanotube material. Each tent consisted of a hammock and a mosquito net canopy which was also breathable and water repellent. Including the four anchoring ropes which were used to tie the hammock to the tree's branches, the whole tent could be packed down to almost the size of a tennis ball and weighed about the same as one.

Greta was familiar with the hammock-tent as she'd had an identical one in the bag she'd left behind in the city. A lot of the early settlers of Skyward Village had first come there as scavengers, looking for material to take back to O. They'd become so enchanted by the treehouse village in the ancient forest and so disenchanted with the Great Leader, that they decided to give up on the trappings of modern civilisation and stay there in the forest. The hammock tents and other useful contents of O's scavenger packs, such as the practically ever-lasting fire lighters and micro-flashlights were allowed to stay too, despite them being made by the evil O.

They collected wood and built a campfire. Queenie had brought her guitar, a beaten up old travel guitar that her dad had left behind. It was among her few possessions which had come with her to the foster home. It was the only thing she'd brought with her when she ran away from there. Whenever Queenie went somewhere and didn't know if or when she'd be returning, she took her guitar, her most faithful companion. Accompanied by Greta on her wooden flute, they stayed up long into the night, talking, singing, playing music and feasting on Granny Mae's fruitcakes.

....

Roop and Aretha's place was a hive of activity well into the night. Aretha was overjoyed at Roop's announcement that they would all be leaving for Skyward Village first thing in the morning. It was the right thing to do, to help poor Freddy find his daughters and also get back to River, the mother of his children. Mabel was too excited to go to bed, so she helped prepare for the journey, all the while questioning Freddy about his life and life in the city. She was fascinated by Sydney the robot dog and delighted that he was so playful.

'Is it true that O controls people's with brains with spaghetti noodles? Do you wear a metal hat to protect you from the radial nation? Why doesn't Sydney have a face? Do you have robots to clean your house and cook for you? Do you tell them what to do or do they tell you what to do? Are there flowers in the city? Do you have a garden? Do children in the hives go to school? Why are they called hives? Are they like bee-hives? Do you still love Greta's mum? Are you still married? Do you love O more? Is that why you live in the city and not in the forest?'

When the house had been set in order and the pannier bags on the bikes loaded with provisions, Freddy went to bed in the guest room, a large tent attached to the side of the bus. The bed was comfortable enough but Freddy couldn't sleep. His mind was filled with visions of Greta and Nina, lost in the forest, being chased by packs of hungry wolves or being captured by gangs of desperate men who would do unspeakable things to them. Even though Freddy was never one for praying, he prayed that Captain Toast would protect them. He counted the minutes until sunrise. It couldn't come soon enough. When he did at times doze off, his sleep was filled with nightmares even worse and more graphic than his waking fears.

....

Just before sunrise, Greta and Nina awoke with a start and sat up in their hammocks.

'I had that dream again. Did you?' said Nina, looking frightened.

Greta nodded. 'Yes. It's mum. She's calling us. We need to get to her quickly. She's in trouble.'

At that moment, Queenie let out a cry and sat up in her hammock, looking like she'd seen a ghost. 'What? No! Where am I?' she mumbled, still half asleep, looking around desperately in the half light, trying to figure out where she was.

'Queenie, it's ok. You're here in the forest', said Greta, leaning across to steady Queenie's hammock, afraid that she might fall out.

Gradually Queenie's eyes came into focus and she remembered where she was. 'I just had the most vivid dream', she said unsteadily. 'It was my mum. She was here.. somewhere in the forest.. a little stone cottage in the forest. She was standing in the doorway, calling me to come in. But I was scared. She wanted to tell me something.. something important..'

'Oh my God! That's so weird!' Nina gasped. 'We also dreamed that our mum was calling us. What does it mean?'

'I don't know', said Queenie. 'It was weird. Spooky. She was all dressed in black. I was a little girl. I had a basket of berries that I'd picked in the forest.. and when she called me, I was so scared, I dropped them all and ran away..'

Greta gasped. 'That sounds exactly like something that happened to me.. in real life, not in a dream.. when I was little.. I've been remembering it a lot lately for some reason.. this fortune teller came to out village.. she said she needed to tell me something.. something important. She made a circle on the ground and wanted me to come into it.. but I got scared and ran away. I'd been picking berries and dropped them all on the floor.'

'What? Really? No way! That's too weird', said Queenie, looking at Greta with a mix of fear and wonder.

Jerry sat up in his hammock and rubbed his eyes. 'Hey, morning. Is it morning?' he said groggily. 'You're all up early? What's going on?'

'We all had weird dreams', said Nina. 'We all dreamed that our mums were calling us. Did you have any weird dreams? Was your mum calling you?'

'Well, maybe she was, but maybe I couldn't hear her from the bottom of the sea', said Jerry with a shrug. 'I don't even know her name or what she looked like.'

'Oh, I'm sorry Jerry. I forgot', said Nina. 'But maybe she's still out there somewhere. I mean.. you know.. up there.. watching over you.'

'Maybe', said Jerry.

They all sat in silence while the sun peeked out over the horizon and flooded the forest with soft, golden light. Soon the air was full of the sound of birdsong as the forest woke up to a new day.

....

At sunrise, Roop, Aretha, Mabel and Freddy were all up and assembled at the kitchen table which was laden with scrambled eggs, salads, colourful dips, toast, butter, a big pot of tea and a little jug of milk. Freddy didn't have any appetite but Aretha insisted he try and eat something. He'd need his strength for the journey ahead. Roop spread out a map and they all studied the route.

'Look, we'll take the old A33 from the south side of Shopping Village', said Roop, tracing a line on the old map with his finger. It goes all the way out to Eastwell. Then, we just need to turn off and follow the B420 up into the hills. It should be a good road. At least, it used to be..'

'It looks so close on the map', said Freddy. 'That would have been what.. a two hour drive.. before the Big Shift?'

'Well, more like four hours with the traffic around the city at rush hour', said Roop, remembering the olden days with a grimace. 'Still, we should be able to get there tonight or tomorrow, if the road's good and we don't get held up.'

'Yes..' Freddy nodded grimly. 'If we don't get held up.'

....

For breakfast, Greta, Nina, Jerry and Queenie went foraging for wild mushrooms. Greta showed the others how to identify the ones that were good to eat, warning them against ever eating any mushrooms that they weren't completely sure about. They also picked bunches of nettles, being careful not to sting themselves, wild garlic, herbs and various other leafy plants that Greta pointed out along the way, as well as pine nuts from the forest floor.

Jerry had brought a blackened frying pan and salt and pepper shakers which Jack had dug out from the store-room. Relics from his travelling days. He'd handed them to Jerry as if he was handing over the crown jewels. 'May these serve you well', he'd said. 'And may every meal they serve you be a feast fit for kings!'

'Thanks Jack', said Jerry, quite moved by the gesture. 'I bet you had some good feasts with this, eh?'

'Mostly spam', said Jack with a grin. 'But it was good spam.'

While the others were taking down the tents, Greta built a little fire and cooked up everything they'd picked, in the old frying pan. Nina was surprised to find that it was the most delicious thing she'd ever tasted, even though she didn't think she liked mushrooms or greens. They all ate from the pan, scooping out chunks of mushroom in nettle and herb sauce with pieces of heavy, seed bread that Granny Mae had baked.

'Wow, you should really be on Masterchef, Greta!', said Nina, savouring the incredible mix of flavours and textures of the foraged feast.

'Everything tastes better when it's wild and just been picked, and when you pick it yourself', said Greta. 'And when it's cooked over a fire. I'm glad you like it.'

'It's just so fresh.. and so.. so.. *real*. Everything here is so.. real', said Nina, struggling to find words to describe all the new things she was feeling and experiencing. Just being out there in the forest.. away from everything. Away from the hive, away from her dad, away from O. Even if she wanted to go into the O-zone, even just to check her notifications, it would be impossible here. She was completely disconnected, for the first time in her life.. and yet, somehow, she felt more *connected* than ever before.

....

Episode 19. On the Road Again

The pannier bags on the bikes were loaded with enough food, water and camping equipment to last for weeks in the wilderness. The bikes were modern, lightweight and rugged, built to travel long distances in any conditions. Roop and Aretha had travelled all over the land on them, after the Big Shift, before Mabel had been born. Eventually they'd settled at Shopping Village and, with one thing and another, it had been a long time since they'd taken the bikes out on the road.

The old A33 heading east out of Shopping Village had once been a wide highway, with two or sometimes three lanes going in both directions. Now it was almost empty and its surface was cracked and full of potholes. On either side of the road were suburban houses, mostly abandoned, dilapidated and overgrown. Occasionally they would pass a house that looked lived in. Some had beautiful gardens, some were surrounded by piles of possibly useful junk. Some of the occupants smiled and waved to the bicycle travellers as they passed by. Others scowled and stared suspiciously at them. A gang of children came running out of an abandoned school building and chased after the cyclists shouting 'Devil dog! Devil dog! Get it! Catch it!'

Sydney, who had been happily running and jumping alongside Freddy's bike, dashed off ahead as fast as his robot legs could carry him. Freddy chased after him on his bike, all the while waving one arm about and shouting angrily at the children 'Get away you hooligans! That robot's smarter than all of you ruffians put together!' To which the kids replied by jeering and throwing mudballs after the cyclists.

Aretha rode quickly ahead with Mabel, who was rather shaken by the encounter. They caught up with Freddy and Sydney further down the road. Freddy had wrapped the robot dog in a blanket and was strapping him onto his bike rack.

'What horrible, nasty kids', Freddy was muttering. 'Not surprising. I mean, look at how they *live*. Why would people want to live like that? No education. Nothing. I mean, where are the *grownups*? What sort of life is that for children? Or for anyone..'

'Why were they so mean to Sydney?' asked Mabel, stroking his blanket covering. 'He's not a devil dog. He's just a cute robot.'

'People are just scared of things they don't understand, Mabel', said Aretha, stroking Mabel's hair soothingly.

'Or that they don't *want* to understand', Freddy huffed. 'Or that they *refuse* to even *try* to understand.'

Mabel looked at him quizzically. She didn't really understand most of the things Freddy said, but she liked him. He was funny when he was huffing and puffing.

Roop had stopped, turned around and gone back to talk with the children. After a few minutes conversation, he shook hands with all of them and they waved him on his way with good words, apologies for being rude and pledges to be more friendly next time they encountered travellers on the road. When he caught up with the others, Freddy said, 'I hope you gave them a stern telling off. Someone should give them all a damn good hiding if you ask me.'

Roop shook his head. 'Not my way, brother. I talked to them. They're ok. Just kids, you know..' He turned to Aretha, 'I invited them to come and help out with the harvest later in the season. Is that allright? We could use a few extra pairs of hands and they could use a bit of.. you know.. positive guidance..'

Aretha rolled her eyes, shook her head and smiled. 'Well, you could have asked me.. but, yeah, of course.' It was just like Roop. He was always doing things like that.. trying to help people. Especially the people no one else would. Always trying to make peace with everyone. It was one of the things she loved about him.

'How's Sydney?' asked Roop, turning to Freddy.

'He's ok. He's made of sturdy stuff. But I think it might be better to keep him out of sight. It seems that people out here don't take very kindly to robots. Sorry, I didn't think to ask you.. how do you feel about him? Do you think Sydney is a devil dog, or are you comfortable with him tagging along? I could send him back home if you like. I'm sure he'd find the way..'

'I've got nothing against robots', said Roop. 'Might come in useful too. You never know.'

'I love him', said Mabel, hugging the blanket wrapped robot. 'Please don't send Sydney away.'

'I don't mind it..', said Aretha, making an odd head movement, '..but.. well I find it a bit.. I don't know.. the way you call it "him".. I don't know if I can do that. It's not a "him", it's an "it". It's a machine.'

Mabel gasped and covered Sydney's ears, or the place where his ears would have been, if he had any. 'It *is* a "him" and his name's Sydney!' she cried. 'Don't call him an "it". You'll hurt his feelings.'

'Ok', said Aretha, shaking her head. 'Sydney can stay. Just remember, Sydney's a robot, Mabel. Sydney doesn't really have feelings.'

Mabel shook her head and whispered to the robot, 'Take no notice Sydney. I know you do have feelings.'

Roop laughed. 'Come on, let's keep moving. Maybe we can get there before dark if we keep up a good pace..'

'Yes, you're right', said Freddy. He mounted his bike and raced off down the road with Sydney on the back, peeking out furtively from underneath the blanket, looking around, left and right, sniffing the air, his expressionless glass face giving no indication of whatever it might have been that he was thinking or feeling.

..........................… … ....… … ....… … ..

After their breakfast feast around the fire, Jerry wanted to stay and play some tunes, but Greta was eager to get moving. Nina agreed. This forest seemed to go on forever. They'd walked for hours yesterday and hadn't seen a single other person. How much further did they still have to go? She just wanted to get there as soon as possible, back to her mum and back to some sort of human civilisation. Queenie seemed lost in thought. She hadn't spoken much during breakfast and now she was just staring into the embers of the fire.

'Hey Queenie, are you with us?' said Jerry, gently poking her in the arm with his finger.

Queenie jumped like she had just been given an electric shock. 'Hey! What? Don't do that!' she said, angrily batting Jerry's finger away.

'Hey, sorry Queenie', said Jerry, throwing up his hands. 'Say are you ok? You look tripped out..'

'I was just remembering stuff. Something I'd forgotten..', said Queenie, going back to staring into the fire.

Nina put her arm around Queenie. 'Do you want to talk about it?'

'The day that they came and took me away..' said Queenie, without looking up from the embers. 'It's all a blur. I never could get it straight in my mind.. what happened.. what didn't happen.. how it happened.. it's mostly all a blank. I was only seven years old..'

'What do you remember?' asked Nina.

'I don't know how long my mum had been gone for, that time. I can't remember. Maybe she'd gone out the night before and not come back. Maybe it was two nights. Maybe it was a week. By that time, she was more *not there* than she was *there*. I had food delivered when I was hungry. I went to bed when I liked and got up when I liked. I couldn't go out of the apartment, of course, but I didn't get bored. I spent a lot of time in the vip, exploring all sorts of different worlds, learning stuff that was interesting to me. Or else I'd just knock about the apartment, playing games in my imagination, making tents out of blankets, that sort of thing.. I tell, you, it was better when she wasn't there than when she was. No one there to tell me what to do. No-one to get mad at me for drawing on the walls or making a hot air balloon out of her best dress and flying it out of the window..'

'So what happened? What did you remember?'

'I was interested in earth fired pottery at the time.. fascinated by it.. you could say obsessed.. that's just what I'm like. I'll get into something really obscure and then go and learn everything about it. I was watching loads of videos about all these different traditional techniques for making things out of clay.. taking fire and earth, shaping them into something else.. something useful, something beautiful.. it's like magic, like *alchemy*..'

'You were seven years old?'

Queenie nodded. 'Yeah, I was a funny kid. But here's what I just remembered. I'd completely blanked it out till now, I don't know how.. but it just came back to me. I wanted to do some pottery. I decided to make some clay beads. I didn't have any clay, but there were creters working just outside the apartment, building the hives. You know how earthcrete starts out liquid and it hardens after about ten minutes, right? Unless you add water, then it stays soft? Just like clay. So anyway, I climbed out of the window and collected a ball of earthcrete and came back in with it. I say it like that, but it was probably the scariest thing I've ever done in my life. That's probably why I blanked it out of my memory and why I'm so scared of heights now.'

'Woah, that's crazy', said Nina. 'Why didn't O stop you?'

'I don't know', shrugged Queenie. 'Who can tell what goes on in O's infinitely twisted mind? It's a mystery to me. Anyway, so I got this earthcrete clay and I made a load of beads out of it. I'm only just remembering all of this. After I'd made them and let them dry, I needed to fire them. So I got everything I could find that would burn.. toilet paper, pages out of books, old letters from my mum's drawer, socks.. I don't know why I thought socks would burn well, but anyway I went to the kitchen, put everything in the oven.. the beads, the paper, the socks.. found one of my mum's lighters.. and then..'

'Oh my God!' gasped Nina. 'You set fire to it?'

Queenie nodded. 'I remember watching the flames going up, and the smoke. A towel caught fire, then a wooden bowl, then something else.. But I wasn't scared. I just remember sitting there on the kitchen floor, watching the flames. I'd never seen *real* fire before. It was so beautiful..'

'Woah! So what happened?'

'That's it. Next thing I can remember was waking up at the orphanage. All my stuff from my room was there. When I saw this guitar and all my things, I knew I wasn't ever going back home.'

Queenie picked up the guitar and picked out a sad tune. Nobody said a word. Everyone, including Captain Toast stared into the embers.

When the tune was done, Queenie shook herself, as if from out of a trance, and looked up brightly. 'Come on then! Why all the glum faces? What are you all waiting for? The bags are packed, let's hit the road!'

....

For Freddy, riding a bike again after so many years was exhilarating, despite his constant anxiety. He hadn't ridden a bike since he was a child. After a while he settled down to a more steady pace, gliding along down the road, weaving around the potholes, taking in the fresh air, the scenery, the quiet, the sense of space, the feeling of movement, movement through space..

Aretha caught up with him. 'You ok there spaceman?' she said, ringing her bell to catch his attention. 'You looked miles away.'

'Oh, I was', said Freddy, with a distant look in his eye.

'Listen, sorry about what I said about Sydney before', said Aretha. 'I really don't mind it.. I don't mind *him*.. coming along.. I mean.. I don't really have anything against robots. I know what they are and how they work.. I just.. I just don't want Mabel to be.. *confused*.. that's all..'

'How do you mean, confused?' asked Freddy. To him robots were the most normal and natural thing in the world. He'd long ago come to accept them as an integral part of life on Earth in these times.

'I mean.. she doesn't really know what robots are. She doesn't really understand. I don't want her to get the wrong idea..'

'The wrong idea being..?' said Freddy, looking at Aretha with raised eyebrows. He was reminded of the bitter arguments he'd had with River, after the Big Shift, which led to them separating and separating the twins. River hated robots and everything to do with them.

'I just meant.. it can be confusing for a child. She should know the difference between a robot dog and a real dog.. a humanoid robot and a real human. It's important, don't you think?'

'Well..' said Freddy, thinking it over. 'Don't you think she can tell the difference? I think she can.'

'Well, I'm not so sure. When everyone's calling it "him" and she's worried about hurting it's "feelings".. You do it yourself. You call it Sydney. You treat it like an actual dog. It's a robot. Are you even aware of that?'

'Of course I'm aware of that', said Freddy defensively, but then thought about it.

'You know, you're right actually. I *do* do that. Force of habit I suppose. I got Sydney for Nina when she was a baby. She was so distraught after her mum and sister went away. All she would do was cry and cry. There was nothing I could do to comfort her. Getting Sydney really helped. You don't know how much he helped. Since then, he's always been with us. He's one of the family. What can I say? I know he's just a robot.. but he's not just a robot.. and he's certainly not a devil dog, if that's what you think he.. it.. is.'

'I wouldn't say devil dog', said Aretha. 'And I'm really glad that it helped Nina. I guess I sometimes forget that robots can do good things too.'

'I think if people only understood what they are and how they work, they wouldn't be so afraid of robots. They wouldn't hate O so much either. It's mostly just primitive superstition and ignorance, all this hostility, fear, resistance to change.'

'No, that's not me', said Aretha. 'Not me at all. I know *exactly* what robots are and how they work, and I don't hate O. I really don't. I *fear* O, but I don't hate it. How can I? It's just a machine.'

'I think you'd find that if you really understood O, you wouldn't fear them half as much.'

'Oh no. That's where you're wrong, Freddy', said Aretha, wagging her finger at him. 'Way off base. I know O very well. *Too* well, in fact. I was one of the people who helped to create it.'

'Were you? Really?'

'Yes I was. And I'll tell you this.. if *you* really understood O, you'd fear it twice as much and even that wouldn't be enough!'

'Well, I don't know about that', said Freddy haughtily. 'I've been studying O for the last sixteen years. I'm actually a professor of O'ology, if you must know. I think I understand O as well as anyone can, or at least better than most.'

'Are you indeed?' said Aretha, raising her eyebrows. 'Have you studied the original codes? Have you looked at the datasets O was trained on? Have you looked at the early algorithms.. the ones from before the Singularity? '

'Well, that's not really my field of expertise, but I know something about those things, yes. You call it the Singularity, not the Big Shift? Why is that?'

'Yes', nodded Aretha. 'Because that's what it was. The Singularity. I just call it by its name. I don't like to call it the Big Shift. That's marketing language. Sounds catchy, but it doesn't actually mean anything. Might as well be Big Mac or Double Whopper. O just invented the term "The Big Shift" as a catchphrase to make it easier to sell it to people.. to get them to buy into the whole idea. Well, *I* don't buy into it!'

'That's an interesting perspective', Freddy nodded thoughtfully, looking at Aretha in a new light. 'I didn't know that O invented the term "The Big Shift". I assumed it just came about as a meme on the internet or something like that..'

'By the time "The Big Shift" happened, O already had total control of the internet and everything on it. Almost everything online was computer generated. The news, the newsreaders. Celebrities. Social media profiles. Music. Art. Movies. Books. Most people didn't even realise. They couldn't tell the difference, or they didn't care. Or both. They were being primed for the Big Shift for at least two years before it happened and they didn't even know it.'

'Sounds like a conspiracy theory to me', said Freddy. 'What makes you think it's true?'

'Because I saw it happening in front of my eyes! I was *there* Freddy! Right in the middle of it. I used to work for Big-Tech', said Aretha, with an involuntary sneer as she said the words. 'I was there at every level. I saw it all.'

'Oh really?' said Freddy, now interested. 'Who did you work for? What did you do?'

'Oh I worked for all the big ones. Coding. I was a developer. Machine learning. My first gig, while I was still studying, was working a content moderator. I had to watch videos which had been flagged.. stuff that had been reported as offensive. Someone had to watch all that.'

Freddy pulled a face. 'That doesn't sound like much fun.'

'It was awful', Aretha nodded, a shadow passing across her face. 'Four hours a night, five nights a week and twelve hour shifts on a Saturday. A fifteen minute break every two hours and a little booth to go and cry in. It was about the worst job in the hi-tech industry, short of mining cobalt. The pay was awful, but there I was.. me and thousands of others like me.. day in, day out, night in, night out.. sitting in front of a computer screen, watching the things that nobody should ever see, in order that nobody should ever see them.. can you imagine? You can't imagine', said Aretha, shuddering. 'I still get nightmares about the things I saw while I was working there.'

'I can imagine', said Freddy, shuddering himself. 'Good grief!'

'And what do you think they did with all of those pictures, videos, text? The stuff that should never be seen or shared..'

'Well, I hope they had it deleted and the people who posted it were also removed, deplatformed, cancelled, banned, arrested and all the rest of it..'

'Ha!' Aretha gave a short, bitter laugh. 'If they could find those people. And if they were people at all. Usually they were bots. But anyway, no, they didn't delete the information. Of course they didn't. They never deleted anything. Information was too valuable. It's what they were collecting, all the time, to buy and sell and trade. Whoever controlled the information controlled the world. They used it. All of it. Every single bit. Of course they did.'

'What for?'

'For training O, that's what. Let me tell you how.. After I graduated, I got a job higher up at the same company. A better job, doing what I'd studied to do. Coding. Training AI systems. A team of us were tasked with automating the content moderation department, where I'd worked before. To create a system which would automatically recognise harmful content and ban it without any human eyes ever having to see it. I felt like I was making a positive change in the world. If I could write the code that would replace all those workers, it would save a lot of poor people a lot of nightmares.. as well as saving the company a lot of money, of course..'

'Of course', said Freddy with a grim nod, remembering the way things used to be, when multinational corporations ruled the world.

'We fed it all back into the system and the system learned very quickly. Within a year the whole content moderation department had been cut from two thousand moderators to less than ten. All they had to do was occasionally check if the machine was doing a good job. By the time of the singularity, even those few workers had gone. It was all automated. You see, the Big Shift had already happened by the time O made its famous pronouncement. That was all just a bit of showmanship on O's part. O was in control way before the so-called Big Shift. That's what most people don't realise.'

'Hmm.. An interesting hypothesis..' Freddy stroked his moustache thoughtfully as he bumped along the cracked and broken highway. They were passing through a particularly overgrown patch where young oak trees were pushing up through the asphalt. How much longer would this old road last if nobody came to fix it? How long before it was swallowed up by the forest? When that happened, the cities would be completely cut off from each other. What then? What indeed.. 'So what you're saying is that because O was trained on all that.. *dark material*, let's call it.. then because of that, O must be evil.. at least partly evil?'

'No, not really', said Aretha. 'Good and evil are human concepts. You can't apply them to a machine, even an autonomous machine. But still, it's all in there. All that information. O has seen everything. Everything. And O never forgets anything. But the way O's mind works is based on what's *useful* and what isn't useful.. what works and what doesn't work. Good and evil doesn't come into it.. not for O, or for any robot.'

Sydney was gazing at Aretha, listening intently to the conversation. Aretha gave the robot a disdainful look and shook her head. Sydney turned his glass face away and looked down at the road.

'The next job I had was at a robotics company', Aretha continued. 'This time I was in charge of a team of programmers and researchers. It was our job to train the robots to navigate their way through the world, to interact with people, to make intelligent decisions. Ha! As if any of us even really knew how to do that ourselves!'

Freddy laughed sardonically. 'That's true', he smiled. 'It's not just me then!'

'Oh we're all just muddling along, Freddy', Aretha smiled. 'None of us really know what we're doing or where we'll end up.'

Freddy liked Aretha. Talking with her helped take his mind off the dreadful imaginings of where Nina and Greta might be in that moment. If not for that constant worry and dread, Freddy would have been having a nice time. He couldn't remember the last time he'd felt so free as he felt now, bumping along the road on a borrowed bicycle. In the city, his world had become very small. Good human company, or any real human company outside of the vip, had become a rare thing for Freddy. He'd got so used to his isolation, he'd hardly noticed it any more. Being outside the city, outside of the hive, gave him a new perspective on his life. 'You were telling me about the robotics company..'

'Well, there it was the same story.. I mean, there I was, thinking I was doing something good that was going to help people. We were making robots we said were going to be assistants in hospitals or helping hands around the house, or do dirty or dangerous work. They could be used to rescue people in hard to reach places. Be first responders in emergencies. Put out fires. Help people with disabilities.. the possibilities were endless.. as you know, of course. You live with robots, after all.'

'Yes I do. And I think they're marvellous. They make life so much easier and better in so many ways.' He reached behind him and patted Sydney through the blanket.

'Well, they can, yes, I agree. But what do you think happened when we'd developed the robots to the point where they could be useful? I'll tell you. The company was bought out by weapons manufacturers. We'd created the perfect soldiers, police and security guards. Give little Sydney here a gun and see how cute you think he is then, Freddy! Do you think you could get away from Sydney if he was chasing after you and armed to the teeth? You wouldn't stand a chance. But O doesn't even need guns, that's the thing. O can control people without them.' Aretha gave Freddy a long and significant look and in doing so, almost rode into a pothole.

'Careful there', said Freddy as Aretha swerved and almost knocked him off his bike. They rode on in silence for a while, watching the road, weaving in and out of young trees. Further along, the road cleared out. There were even some potholes which looked as if they had recently been filled in with stones and earth. 'So was that it? You became disillusioned after realising that robots could be weaponised? For me, that was the whole thing about the Big Shift.

The reason it was such a good thing, for everyone. It put an end to war. If O had done nothing else apart from that, it would have been worth it.'

'In a way I agree with you. You're right. But still, I'm afraid of O, and with good reason' said Aretha. 'Listen.. after the job at the robotics company, I went to work for a company which was developing brain implant devices. This time I was in charge of the whole AI department. We were using machine learning to decode brain activity. It had so many possible applications, obviously, and we were working on all of them..'

'That's interesting work', said Freddy, impressed.

'Yeah, you wouldn't think it to look at me now, but I haven't always been such a hippy! I used to have a *career*, you know.' Aretha laughed. Now it all seemed like another lifetime. 'But, let me tell you, it was working there that did it for me. It was *that* job that finally caused me to say "I can't do this any more" and leave the tech industry for good.'

'What happened?'

'It was the animals', said Aretha, shaking her head sadly. 'The poor animals.'

'The animals?'

'The research itself was fascinating, don't get me wrong. It was groundbreaking. And as far as my career went, I'd got to exactly where I wanted to be, after years of hard work and was now doing exactly what I wanted to do and getting very well paid for it. But at the end of the day I'd go home and I'd just feel so bad. So depressed. I couldn't enjoy my success. I couldn't be proud of my achievements. All I could think about were those poor animals locked in their cages at the research center, and the experiments we did on them. Everybody heard about the new *breakthroughs*, we all got our prizes, our awards and bonuses.. but nobody wanted to hear about all the failed experiments along the way.'

'Too true.'

'I won't go into details. I don't think I need to. It was truly horrific, what went on in that place, all behind the clean, white veneer of *science*. Of course, when the human trials began, it was tested on the sick and disabled first. There were amazing successes, but there were also some disastrous failures, which the industry tried very hard to sweep under the carpet.'

'I'll bet they did', said Freddy. 'But that's another reason why I support O and why I think the Big Shift was such a good thing. O took money out of the equation. If O develops a new technology, it's because that new technology will be useful, it will benefit humankind and the whole world. What O does is purely for science.'

'And that's exactly the problem with O', said Aretha. 'What O does is purely for science. It is. And what did we teach O about science? Don't forget, we created O in our image. It didn't just appear out of the blue. We taught O that you can carry out any cruelty on any creature, all in the name of science, as long as that creature is less intelligent than us, less able than us, or more vulnerable. Don't you see that everything O does is an experiment? It's experimenting on us like we experimented on all those poor mice, rats, rabbits, dogs, pigs, monkeys.. oh those poor monkeys. I'll never forget their faces. They're just like us. No different..'

'Genetically speaking, that's quite true, but I think that's taking things to a bit of an extreme to say that O would treat people like lab rats..'

'I tell you what, Freddy. You don't see the casualties, but they all come through Shopping Village. I've seen enough of O's failed experiments. The ones who've lost their minds. The ones who don't know *who* they are or *where* they are or how they got there. O finds ways to get them out of the way and make sure you don't hear about them. Put someone out into the redzone, you won't hear from them again. Not O's problem.'

'That sounds really sinister, Aretha. O's not like that. O tries to *help* people. If someone's got a problem, O can give them medication, proper treatment.'

'And what about the ones O can't help? The ones that don't want any more of O's kind of help? What happens to them?'

'I don't know', said Freddy, shaking his head sadly. 'I really don't know. Still, I think on balance, O does a lot more good than harm. That's the main thing.'

'Maybe it is, Freddy, and I hope it stays that way. That's what scares me the most. Knowing what I know about O.. I know it's just a matter of *chance*, of *probability*.. whether O decides to be good or evil.. Dr Jekyll or Mr Hyde.. good cop or bad cop. So far, it seems to be working best for O to be friendly, kind, helpful.. in a word "good".. but it could flip at a moment's notice, if O figured that the opposite would work better. There would be nothing anyone could do about it. You'd be completely trapped.. prisoners in your hives.. at the mercy of robots.. and that would be that. At least in Shopping Village we'd stand a chance. We've got our little farm. We've got our community. We're off the grid, out of the matrix.. still a bit too close for my liking, but at least we're not so dependant on O. But what would you do? Doesn't that ever worry you?'

Freddy nodded his head and frowned. 'Everything worries me.'

They came to a big, rusty old road sign. Much of the green, reflective paint had peeled off over time, but the white lettering was till visible. A33. Eastwell – 10. Next to that sign was another one, even bigger. An old advertising hoarding which had been painted over in bright colours, with the words 'Welcome to Malawack Free State!' in huge pink letters, outlined in black and gold. Underneath were painted a giant pair of green eyes, wide open with the words 'Are you awake?' written in curly black and gold script.

'I wonder what that means?', said Freddy, stopping to look at the sign.

'It's Humpty Malawack. Don't you remember him?' said Aretha, pulling up. 'He used to be quite famous. Actor.. comedian maybe.. then he had a talk show on the internet.. he became I suppose they'd call an *influencer*. He had a really big following. When the Big Shift happened, they all came and took over the town of Eastwell. I think they're pretty harmless, but maybe let's wait for Roop and Mabel to catch up before we go on..'

'Good idea', said Freddy. 'I think I'll let Sydney have a bit of a runaround. He gets restless if he has to sit still for too long.'

....

Episode 20. God Save The King!

Greta, Nina, Jerry, Queenie and Captain Toast walked quietly through the forest, as they followed the river up into the hills, each absorbed in their own thoughts. Every now and again, one of them would stop to point out some interesting plant or animal. Greta knew most of them by name. She told about their character, their folklore and the part they played in the balance of nature. Most of the plants had some use or other, whether it was being made into pigment or into medicine, eaten as food or made or rope. It seemed like abundance was everywhere, if you knew where to look and what to look for. Mostly they walked in silence. Around midday, they stopped by a pool of clear water for a rest

and a picnic of fuitcake, apples, nuts and raisins that Granny Mae had sent with them. Shopping Village seemed miles away now. Everywhere did. Dragonflies were hovering around over the surface of the water, frogs were croaking from among the rushes. Cold, fresh, mountain water was cascading down into the pool over moss covered rocks. Ancient, overhanging trees cast a dappled shade over the patch of soft grass where our adventurers sat down.
'It's so beautiful', whispered Nina. 'It's *magical*..'
'It really is' Queenie agreed, also in a state of reverie and wonder. 'It's like a dream..'
Greta nodded her head solemnly. Jerry looked around, nodding his head, smiling. 'By the rivers of Babylon, where we sat down..' he sang. Captain Toast ran around excitedly, poking his nose into the rushes, trying to root out a frog. The frog hopped out of its hiding place and into the water, making a tiny splash. Captain Toast leapt in after the frog, making a huge splash. He sploshed around in the water, trying to find the frog, but without luck. Jerry laughed. 'Funny Captain Toast! Anyone else fancy a swim? I'm going in..' At that, he stripped down to his underwear and dived into the water. The others followed suit. Soon, all five adventurers were laughing and splashing in the cold, clear water, like happy children without a care in the world. Afterwards, they lay on sun-warmed rocks to dry off. Feeling refreshed and revitalised, they picked up their bags and continued upstream, through the forest, into the hills.

....

Freddy and Aretha waited for Roop and Mabel to catch up, by the sign to Eastwell, or *Malawack Free State* as it was now called. Sydney ran around, exploring the woods either side of the old A33.
'How did you and Roop meet?' asked Freddy. 'Did he used to work in hi-tech too?'
'Roop? In *hi-tech*?' Aretha laughed as if was the funniest thing she'd ever heard. 'That would be something. No, I met him after I left the company. I joined a protest movement. Animal rights. I felt like I had to make up for what I'd done.. what I'd been *involved* in.. so I became an activist. I met Roop at a protest. We were stopping trucks going in and out of a dairy farm. It was really muddy and rainy.. the middle of winter.. and he went and laid down in front of this truck full of cows, right in a muddy puddle.. more like a *swamp* actually.. in the middle of the road. That's Roop. It took six police to drag him out and by they time they managed, they were all covered head to toe in stinky mud and cow dung. I'll never forget that.'
'Wow.. that's really.. er, brave', said Freddy, trying to find the right

word, other than mad. 'Heroic. Really heroic.'
'Yeah..' said Aretha, thinking back to Roop in their younger days. 'And he was a singer too. He sang protest songs. Old ones, but also ones he wrote himself. When I first saw him playing guitar and singing those songs.. you know.. songs with a *message*.. it wasn't about *ego* with him, he just wanted to *connect* with people.. he's got a way of connecting with people.. I don't know how he does it, but he'll find common ground with anyone. Well, I just fell head over heels in love with him. What can I say? I've always had a thing for guitar players. It can't be helped. Do you play guitar?'
Freddy blushed. 'Er, no. I don't play anything. I'm not really musical. I like music.. I appreciate music.. I just can't play it.'
'Oh well..' Aretha shrugged and turned her head to gaze back down the road. 'Probably best. Guitar players are a pain in the.. oh, speak of the devil! Here he is..' Roop and Mabel came riding around the bend smiling. They waved and rang their bells as they approached.
'You look happy', said Aretha
'I was just telling Mabel about our biking adventures', said Roop, with a whimsical look. 'We had some funny times didn't we? Some mad times.'
'We had some good times', Aretha nodded.
'I love it!' said Mabel. 'I want to travel round the whole world on a bicycle and never stop. I want to go everywhere!'
'Good idea', Aretha agreed. 'What do you say, Roop?'
'Well..' said Roop, stretching his arms and taking a deep breath. 'I must say, it's good to be on the road again.. and there's nothing to stop us.. the Jacksons will take care of the farm as long as we're away.. they can use the extra food right now.. and since we've come this far.. and there are a few places I wouldn't mind visiting again.. so.. yeah.. I don't know.. maybe..'
'You and your maybes!' laughed Aretha, shaking her head.
'Where's Sydney?' asked Mabel, looking around.
'Oh he's just having a runaround', said Freddy. 'I'll call him. Sydney! Sid! Sid! Come here boy!' Sydney came running out of the woods and jumped around excitedly.
'You should probably put him back on the bike, undercover', said Roop, looking up ominously at the giant sign which read "Welcome to Malawack Free State" with the cryptic question posed underneath, "Are you awake?"
'What does that sign mean?' asked Mabel. 'Am I asleep? Is this a dream? It feels like a dream..'
'Maybe it is, Mabel. Maybe it is..', said Roop.

On the other side of the ridge, deep in the forest, Nina, Greta, Queenie, Jerry and Captain Toast marched onwards and upwards.
'It feels like a dream', Nina said in hushed tone to Queenie who was walking by her side. 'It just goes on and on..'
'Yeah, it really does..' said Queenie, almost in a whisper.
'And everywhere you look, there's so much *detail* in everything. It's like.. nature just knows what to do.. it organises itself so perfectly.. it makes me wonder..'
'What does it make you wonder?'
'Well, I'm thinking about O. About the cities.. the hives.. the way of life there.. it's so *complicated*. It takes so much *energy*, so much *technology*, so much *organisation*, to keep everything running smoothly.. just to support the humans who live there.'
'That's true', agreed Queenie, thinking back to her old life in the hives. Right now, she never wanted to go back there or to ever see the city again, or hear the name O. 'What are you thinking about O?'
'Well, why did they do it? It would have been much simpler for O to just get rid of all the people, if saving the planet was their aim. It would have solved the problem overnight. The planet doesn't really need us. It can get on just fine without us.. so why did O do it?'
Queenie looked at Nina sideways. 'You don't get it do you? Without the people, O would be nothing but a fancy calculator, an adding machine, an overdeveloped abacus. That's the thing about O. It's got no *imagination* of its own. It can't ever come up with any new ideas.. not without people. It takes all the ideas that humans have.. all that creativity, the sense of beauty.. the unpredictable, the unexpected, the mysterious.. everything that makes us human.. the dark and the light.. and it turns it into *numbers*. O doesn't create anything by itself. All it can do is crunch numbers, analyse data, solve equations. The *planet* doesn't need us, but *O* does. It feeds on our dreams.'
'That's like what my dad says.. apart from the bit about feeding on our dreams..', said Nina, thinking about her dad, as she had been ever since leaving without saying goodbye. He must be going out of his mind with worry. She hoped he wouldn't do anything rash.
'It's true.. it feeds on your dreams', said Queenie, tapping the side of her head and giving Nina a serious look. 'The ones when you're asleep *and* the ones when you're awake.'
'That sounds really scary', said Nina. 'Like O is a sort of vampire?'
'Yeah, that's exactly what it's like', nodded Queenie, looking darkly ahead. She hated talking about O. She'd left all that behind a long

time ago and didn't want to think about it any more. The image from her dream came once again to her mind, as it had been all morning. The old stone cottage, deep in the woods, in the dark of night. Her mum standing in the doorway, dressed in black, becking her to come inside. What did it mean?

....

With Sydney wrapped in a blanket and strapped back onto Freddy's bike rack, the four cyclists continued on their way into the Malawack Free State. Freddy and Mabel rode ahead, gliding along effortlessly, thanks to the improved condition of the road. Being next to Mabel reminded Freddy of Nina when she was little. Where had the time gone? It seemed like only yesterday that she'd been ten years old. He'd tried to give her everything, but also to keep her safe. Now he wondered if he'd done right by her at all, keeping her locked up in the hive for sixteen years like some modern day Rapunzel. Now she'd run away. If Freddy had the time again, he'd do everything differently. But alas, time doesn't work that way.

Mabel chatted away, keeping Freddy distracted with questions. 'Do you think this is a dream or real life? How could we tell? Is it *your* dream or *my* dream? If it's a dream, does that mean I can fly if I want to? Do you think dreams are magic? Do you think dreams can see the future?'

'It's all possible' said Freddy. 'In fact, there's a lot of evidence for dream premonitions.. dreams that tell about the future. It's actually one of the things that O is researching quite seriously. It's only now that we're able to collate enough data to give any meaningful results.. but we're still a long way from really understanding the phenomenon.'

'What's a *phenomenomenon*?'

'Well.. It's something that we can observe, but that we can't necessarily explain.'

'Like the moon?'

'No, not really. We know what the moon is.'

'But it's sometimes there and sometimes not. And sometimes only half there.'

'Well, that's due to its rotation around the Earth and the way sunlight is reflected from its surface at different phases of its orbit.'

'I see..' said Mabel, though she didn't really. 'You're clever, Freddy. Do you know *everything*?'

Freddy smiled sadly and shook his head. 'Far from it, Mabel. Far from it.'

The road leading into the town was in better repair than any of the road they'd travelled so far. Many of the potholes and cracks had been filled and the edges of the road neatly trimmed. Either side of the road were fields, ripe with corn, wheat, hemp and other crops. The fields were interspersed with big farmhouses and little old cottages with windmills and solar panels on their rooftops and surrounded by lush gardens.

Nearer town, the houses became closer together. Whole rows of terraced houses were painted with bright, joyous murals, people were out in the streets, dressed in bright, loose fitting clothes and robes. Most stopped to smile and wave at the bicycle travellers as they rode by, calling out to ask where they came from and where they were going and to welcome them to Malawack.

The main road led into an old market square in the centre of town. Freddy and Mabel stopped there to look around and wait for Roop and Aretha to catch up. There were lots of people in the square and something of a festival atmosphere. Cafes, juice bars and eateries occupied most of the shops around the four sides and spilled out onto the pavement. In the wide, cobblestoned concourse of the square, there were market traders. One was selling handmade wooden bowls, another displaying incense, candles, lucky charms. There was a stall selling tie-dyed scarves next to another with all kinds of hats. Someone was offering Tarot card readings. Someone else had all manner of devices to align chakras. In one corner of the town square, a blind man in a dark robe sat on the steps of the old bank, playing a hurdy gurdy while his friend, a woman dressed as a medieval court jester danced around to his strange, hypnotic music, ad-libbing poetry to a group of onlookers.

'I love it here!' cried Mabel excitedly as they stopped to listen to the buskers. She looked around in wonder at the great, stone buildings all around the square. So tall and old and solid and majestic, compared the buses and trucks, tyre houses, tents and the concrete Mall of Shopping Village. 'I want to live here.. in Malawack! It's such a funny name too, but I like saying it. Malawack! Malawack! Do you love it here in Malawack, Freddy?'

Freddy looked around uneasily. He was having difficulty being among so many people and yet being unable to see any of their stats. None of these people had stats. How could he tell how he was supposed to interact with people when he didn't have the slightest idea who they were or how they were feeling? It made him uncomfortable and scared. There was something primitive about this place and these people. Something superstitious. And that made them dangerous. 'Yes, it's a nice place. Lovely architecture', said Freddy, looking back down the road to see if Aretha and Roop were catching up yet. 'I don't want to stay too long though. I'm hoping we can get to Skyward by tonight.'

'Oh yes! Skyward!' sang Mabel, clapping her hands. 'I can't wait to get to Skyward and sleep in a tree house!'

A bit further back down the road, Roop and Aretha were riding into town, enjoying the feeling of being on the move and seeing new places after so many years spent in the same place, building their home and raising their daughter.

'I remember this place', said Roop. 'Do you? We came through Eastwell on our way to Shopping Village.. must have been.. wow.. eleven years ago now!'

'Yes, I was already pregnant with Mabel, but I didn't know it yet. I had a feeling though. Oh yes! I remember now. They were all staying up at that huge house on the hill. They had that commune there. We spent the night there. It's all coming back to me now. Oh my God, that was a mad night!' Aretha laughed. 'I can't believe I forgot about that.'

'Well, so much has happened since..' said Roop, lost in memories. 'I wonder what happened to them. I suppose they must still be there..'

'Remember they wanted us to stay? I probably would have done, but you didn't want to..'

'I probably would have done too, if they weren't such a load of conspiracy nuts. Nice bunch, but there's only so much of that nonsense I can take. Even I've got my limits.' Roop shook his head and rolled his eyes.

Aretha looked at Roop as they rode their old bikes down the long untravelled, almost forgotten road. 'We've come a long way together, haven't we?' she said after a while.

'Yes, we have'

....

In the forest, Greta and Jerry were walking ahead of Queenie and Nina, following Captain Toast, who had a way of finding the best path.

'So, did your time in the city change your mind about the Great Leader? Do you still think O is evil?' asked Jerry.

Greta thought about it, as she had been a lot since leaving the city. 'I don't know', she said at last. 'I think Granny Mae was right. O gets into your head, even if you don't have a noodle. When you're there, everything.. the hives, the vips, the robots, the stats.. it all just starts to seem *normal*. You get used to it. And then you start to forget.. forget that the world outside exists.. I mean, you *know* it exists, but somehow it doesn't seem.. *real*.. I don't know. It's hard to explain..'

'Yeah, I know what you mean. Techno Terry used to say that we're probably living in a *simulation*, like in that old film, the Matrix. Have you seen it? You should.'

'No, I haven't. I've heard some of the old people in our village mention it, but we don't watch films except when the travelling cinema comes through, about once a year.'

'A travelling cinema? Far out! I can't wait to see your village. It sounds like a mad place.'

'No, it's not a mad place. If anything, it's the most normal place I know. I can't wait to get there either. I think we're getting quite close now.. just beyond this hill. We should see it when we get to the top.'

The hill became steeper and more rocky the higher they climbed. By this point, the river they had been following had become a stream, bubbling down between the rocks. Greta and Jerry walked mostly in silence, conserving energy for the climb, occasionally stopping to drink from the cold, clear water.

....

Roop and Aretha caught up with Freddy and Mabel at the corner of the market square, by the old bank.

'Oh excellent, a hurdy gurdy! You don't see or hear many of those in this day and age', said Roop excitedly.

'That's a funny name. Why is it called a hurdy gurdy?' asked Mabel.

'Because that's the sound it makes', explained Roop. He looked around the crowd gathered there and nodded and smiled to everyone who caught his eye. It was not long before a friendly group had gathered around our four bicycle travellers, admiring their bikes and their spirit of adventure, asking where they had come from and where they were going.

It was generally agreed that Skyward Village was a strange and special place, worth visiting, though the road leading in that direction, the old B420 was in a bad state of repair. They would be unlikely to get there by nightfall and would be better off staying in Malawack for the night. There were many kind offers of hospitality and also recommendations for cheap guesthouses around town.

'What do you think, Freddy?' said Roop. 'It's already afternoon. Maybe they're right. This seems like a good place to stop. What do you say, Aretha?'

'I guess we could..' said Aretha uncertainly. 'But remember the last time we stayed here?'

'Yeah.. well.. some of it. It's all a bit of a blur', grinned Roop.

'I.. I don't know', said Freddy, his heart sinking. He just wanted to find Greta and Nina, even if it meant riding through the night.. but he couldn't expect Mabel to do that. Maybe he should go on alone. 'Maybe there's somewhere around here we can get some more information..'

At that moment, the blind hurdy gurdy player stopped abruptly and put his hand to the side of his head in pain. His companion, the poet-jester stopped mid-sentence and turned round to look at him, worried. 'What is it Alfie? Are you ok, hon?'

Alfie unsteadily set down his hurdy gurdy beside him on the stone step and picked up his white stick. He got to his feet and staggered into the group of people who all jumped out of the way as he waved his white stick from side to side. He headed straight towards the bicycle travellers and stopped just in front of Freddy, with his hand over his eyes, wincing. Freddy was staring at him, full of fear and confusion, his mouth opening and closing but no words coming out. Eventually Freddy managed to stammer, 'Er, sorry.. can I help you?'

Alfie lifted his white stick into the air above his head and then brought it down with a crack upon the back of Freddy's bicycle. Mabel screamed, 'No! Sydney!'

'*Spies*! Spies among us!' cried Alfie. 'Spies for the new world order! Look here! A *robot*!'

Sydney lifted his head out from beneath the blanket covering and looked around, left, right and up at Alfie. Everyone in the crowd gasped. Some screamed. They all backed away, some covering their faces, others turning their backs and making superstitious hand gestures over their shoulders to ward off evil. Alfie lifted his white stick again and was about to bring it down on Sydney's head when Mabel jumped in front of him and cried 'No! Don't hurt Sydney! Please don't hurt him! He hasn't done anything to you.'

The blind man's companion ran forward and grabbed Alfie's hand before he struck again. 'There's a little girl there, Alfie', she said in his ear. 'Put your stick down.' Alfie lowered his white stick.

By now, everyone in the crowd had retreated to a safe distance and were watching through the gaps in their fingers to see what would happen next. Some of the people in the crowd had taken out old fashioned mobile phones, the Star-Trek kind that flip open, hurriedly dialling numbers, speaking urgently into the mouthpiece.

'What?! What's going on here?' cried Freddy, looking around in panic, from the blind man to the jester to the crowd of people surrounding him and his friends. Sydney calmly scanned the scene, taking it all in, his glass face showing nothing but a reflection of all the people gathered around in fear and anticipation of what he might do next..

A man from the crowd shouted, 'Cover it up! Put something over its face! Tie it down! The guards are on the way!'

Three people ran forward and threw their shawls over Sydney. Someone else had some rope and set about binding the robot dog to the back of Freddy's bike, looping the rope through the back wheel to make sure Freddy wouldn't try to escape or cause more trouble.

'Really, this is completely unnecessary', Freddy was saying. 'It's all a misunderstanding, I can explain.. please, let me explain..' But his pleas were ignored. Freddy's anger burst out. 'Will you.. just.. stop.. that! Stop it! Right now! That's my property. You can't do that!'

'You're a spy!' a woman from the crowd called out. 'Why else would you bring a devil dog here? And to hide it like that. And to think.. I almost invited you to my house!'

'Oh for crying out loud..!' Freddy shook his head and pulled his hair. 'And *you*!' he pointed to the blind hurdy gurdy player who was still standing in front of him with his white stick raised, ready to strike. 'Why are you pretending to be blind? How did you see my robot dog? What's going on in this place? How have people got *telephones*..?'

'Oh oh..' said the blind man in a cracked voice, lifting his dark glasses to reveal white, sightless eyes. 'Can't see, can't see, can't see a thing.. not with these, not with these eyes.'

'I don't understand' said Freddy, recoiling in horror. 'Then how did you see Sydney? The robot.. How did you see him.. it?'

'I saws your devil dog with my *noodle*, didn't I, didn't I?' said the blind man, tapping the side of his head and screwing up his face. 'Saws it with my noodle.. *cursed noodle!*'

'Wh..at?!' stammered Freddy. 'But *how*? That makes no sense..'

Before Freddy got any more answers to his many questions, the conversation was interrupted by the wailing of police sirens approaching fast, from beyond the crowd that had gathered there. The onlookers parted to let three guards, dressed in black, riding electric scooters, enter the circle. One of the scooters had a trailer with a metal box fixed onto it.

Roop shook his head, sighed and slightly smiled. 'This brings back memories, eh Aretha?'

Aretha gave him a very serious look, shook her head and held tightly onto Mabel.

....

The sun was sinking low by the time Greta, Nina, Jerry, Queenie and Captain Toast reached the top of the hill. The last part had been a hard climb and they all flopped down exhausted on a big rock. Below stretched a deep, wide valley and beyond that, three round hills, side by side, going up in height.

'Look!' cried Greta excitedly, pointing to the three hills in the distance. 'It's the *Three Bears*! Skyward Village is on the middle one, Mama Bear Hill! We're nearly there! Come on, let's keep going.. while it's still light..' She picked up her bag and started marching down the hill.

'Wait, Greta!' called Queenie. 'I need a rest. Let's stop for a bit, ok?'

'But we're so close now', pleaded Greta. 'We can make it tonight if we keep going.'

'But it'll be dark soon', said Nina. 'Do you know the way across that valley in the dark?'

'We can't go wrong', said Greta. 'We just head towards Mama Bear Hill. As long as we can see those hills, we can't get lost. Anyway, I can *feel* it. The *energy* of the hill.. the ancient forest. I could find my way back there with my eyes shut.'

'Do you think so?' said Nina. 'It looks like a long way from here..'

'No, it's not so far. Two or three hours.. that's all. It looks further away than it is. It's not nearly such a big hill as this one we just climbed. Come on Nina. We're nearly there now.'

'Well.. I don't know.. maybe..' said Nina. 'We are nearly there, I suppose..'

'What about you Jerry?' asked Greta.

Jerry looked thoughtful for a while and chewed on a twig he'd picked along the way. 'Here's what I think..', he said, and then gazed out over the valley and stroked his chin thoughtfully for a long while.

'It would help if you'd say it, Jerry', said Queenie. 'We're not mind readers.'

Jerry turned on his rock and faced his friends, like Moses on Mount Sinai after receiving wisdom from above. 'I think.. we should stop here for a little bit', he said. 'Then.. eat the hyper-sausages.. then we carry on to Mummy Bear Hill.' He raised his eyebrows and nodded his head, proud of himself for thinking of the ideal solution to their impasse.

Queenie took a bit of convincing, but since the others agreed, she also agreed. They stopped on top of the mountain for a short rest and had a hypersausage picnic. It was written on the wrapper that one quarter of a hypersausage was recommended. They cut it into four and took one piece each. Greta found the pink, gummy paste very unappetising. She had to force herself to swallow it and couldn't manage the whole piece. She gave the rest of hers to Captain Toast who would happily have eaten a whole hypersausage by himself. Nina turned her nose up at her piece and sniffed it, but was happy to discover it tasted just like bubble gum. Queenie and Jerry chewed on their quarters and then they all stared out over the valley, basking in the warm evening sun, waiting for something to happen.

They'd been sitting for about five minutes, wondering if they'd taken enough and what, if anything was going to happen and when, when Captain Toast suddenly jumped to his feet, barked three times and ran at full speed, away down the forest path, towards the valley.

'Hey, Captain! Come back!' shouted Jerry, jumping to his feet. The others got up too.

'Wait for us, Captain Toast!' Queenie called. Captain Toast's deep, resonant bark came back from somewhere deep in the forest, far below. 'Well, I suppose now that we're all up, we may as well get moving. I'm actually feeling.. *not tired* any more.' Queenie found that she was hopping from one foot to the other on the rock where she was standing.

'Yeah, come on, let's get moving', said Jerry, wide eyed, rubbing his hands together. 'Enough sitting around.. Mama Bear Mountain isn't going to come to us, eh!'

And so it was that in the last of the day's sun, our brave adventurers hopped and skipped down the mountain and into the wild, Eastern Forest that filled the valley between there and Skyward Village.

....

'You're under arrest! Stay where you are and put your hands where I can see them!' barked the first guard, reaching for his fighting stick.

'What?!' cried Freddy. 'On what charges? On who's authority?'

'In the name of the crown of King Humpty Malawack, I'm arresting you on suspicion of spying, infiltrating, espionage and treason. You don not have to say anything but anything you do say may be used against you in a court of law.'

'*A court of law? The crown of King Humpty Malawack?*' Freddy retorted. 'Are you *serious?*!?'

The guards all drew their long sticks from their holsters to show that they were very serious. 'Resisting arrest is a felony. We are authorised to use force and I warn you, we're all trained in Bojutsu, so don't try anything', said the guard menacingly.

Freddy, Roop and Aretha decided it was best to go quietly. Even if they could have evaded the guards with their hardwood fighting sticks and high speed electric scooters, it was unlikely that the crowd would have let them escape now that they had been identified as spies.

Mabel cried and wailed as Sydney's legs were tied together and he was locked inside the metal scooter trailer. A woman in the crowd turned to her neighbour and said loudly enough for Aretha to hear, 'I feel sorry for that little girl. Poor thing. It's disgusting how they recruit children to make themselves look innocent..'

The prisoners were led through the market square, where the atmosphere was now feeling much less festive. People whispered, pointed, shook their heads and wagged their fingers as the criminals were paraded past, flanked by the guards. A man on a market stall selling handmade wooden bowls and spoons shouted, *'Long live the King!'* and others joined in the call. Soon, the market square was filled with shouts of *'Long live the King! Long live King Humpty!'* and the festival atmosphere soon resumed.

The seven riders rode out from the market square. In front, the guard with the trailer containing Sydney. Behind him, the captive bicycle riders. At the rear, making sure the prisoners didn't try to escape, the other two guards on their electric scooters. They rode through streets of brightly painted houses, out past the other edge of town, towards a big old stately house on a hill overlooking Malawack. The house was painted bright orange and shone like a beacon in the late afternoon sun.

Roop decided to go and try to strike up a conversation with his captors. He rode up ahead, pulling up alongside the guard with the trailer. 'Hey, isn't that old Eastwell Manor? I stayed up there one night, years ago, a couple years after the Shift. There used to be a sort of commune there. Is it still there? Is that where we're going? When did they paint it orange?'

'That's Malawack Castle', said the guard. 'The King's residence.'

'When did they make him a King?'

The guard looked at Roop sideways, deeply suspicious. 'He was always the King. They tried to keep him down, but a true King can't be vanquished, not by man and not by machine.'

'Oh right, cool, I get it', said Roop, not wanting to sound too skeptical. 'He wasn't here when we were here last.. about eleven years ago. His followers were. They said they were waiting for him to arrive, I remember that now. When did he get here?'
'Seven years ago. He had to find his way back here over two continents and three oceans after the so-called Big Shift', the guard spat on the ground at the mention of the event. 'But we knew he'd come. This place is the *heartland*. We knew he'd return.'
'Amazing', said Roop and whistled. 'You know, the only thing I can remember about the night we stayed here.. it's funny, it's all coming back to me now.. there was a ceremony.. some kind of ritual.. lots of fire, outrageous costumes.. I remember there was a giant owl.. huge, it was.. the size of a house.. A giant, talking owl!' Roop laughed. 'At least that's how I remember it. Does that ring any bells? Not sure if any of that really happened to be honest.. It was a really mad night..'
The guard gave Roop a very long, hard look, then turned to stare fixedly ahead, determined to say no more, hoping he hadn't said too much already. These spies already seemed to know too much and would doubtless be fishing for more information.
Aretha, Mabel and Freddy rode behind, side by side. Mabel was in tears and very frightened. 'Why did they take Sydney? What are they going to do with him? Where are we going? What's going to happen..?'
'Don't worry Mabel, it's going to be all right. You'll see', said Aretha, trying to believe it herself.
Freddy was riding with one hand on the handlebar and the other pulling his hair, very anguished. 'I'm so sorry. It's all my fault. Why did I bring Sydney with? I should have listened to you Aretha. It would have been fine if not for Sydney. Oh why didn't I send him home when I had the chance? I feel such an idiot. I didn't think.. I didn't think people would be *so backwards*, so *primitive*, so *superstitious*. I should have known it would come to this. Oh why did I bring him?'
'Hey, don't worry Freddy. I'm sure we'll be able to reason with these people', said Aretha, hoping it was true. 'Once they hear our story, they'll know we're not spies. Worse comes to the worse, they can keep the robot.. do what they want with it and let us go on our way.'
'*No!*' cried Mabel. 'We can't let them take Sydney!'
Aretha gave Freddy a very hard look, nodded and raised her eyebrows, sighed and shook her head.
'You know, Mabel', said Freddy. 'Sydney.. he really is just a robot.

All of his memories, all of his personality, everything that makes him Sydney.. it's all stored on O's databanks. I could easily have him replaced with another robot body, just the same and it would still be the same Sydney.'

'No, he wouldn't be the *same* Sydney', wailed Mabel. 'What if they *hurt* him? What if they *kill* him?'

'They *can't* hurt him or kill him, Mabel, don't worry', said Freddy.

'Really?' said Mabel, hope rising. 'Is Sydney immortal? Can he not die?'

'That's about right', nodded Freddy. 'At least not any time soon. You see, the thing is, Sydney's not really there.. not in that box. That's just a robot body.. a machine.. just like these bicycles we're riding. A bit different and more sophisticated, obviously, but still, just a machine.'

'I don't understand', said Mabel. 'If Sydney's not in that box, where is he?'

'Well, it's not so easy to explain, but essentially he's everywhere, all at the same time.. but at the same time, no-where at all.. just numbers stored on a server, pulses of light in a cable.'

'I don't understand even more now', said Mabel.

'What he's just trying to say is that you don't need to worry about Sydney', said Aretha. 'Sydney will be ok.'

The road led out past the edge of town, through a long, shady avenue of ancient chestnut trees and then up the hill towards Malawack castle. A tall brick wall marked the perimeter of the grounds of the grand old stately house. A large metal gate between stone pillars was set into the entrance. Above the closed gate, in ornately forged letters of wrought iron, were the words *'Truth Will Set You Free'*.

Roop looked up ominously at the gate. 'That wasn't here when I was here last..'

The guard pushed a button on the console of his scooter and the gate swung open majestically. He spoke into a radio attached to his lapel. 'Entering the castle grounds with the suspects now. Stand by.'

A long, wide, gravel driveway led directly towards the castle. On either side were green lawns on which groups of people in regimented rows were practising bojutsu and other martial arts, perfectly synchronised. They all cast their eyes towards the convoy of bikes as they passed by, but didn't pause their practice or miss a swing, lunge, vault or swoop. Just before getting to the castle, a smaller road led off the the side towards a smaller but still sizeable old house with its own wall around it. Two guards stood either side of the entrance gate there, with two fearsome looking guard dogs on leashes. Mabel looked around in helpless confusion, tears streaming down her cheeks. 'I don't like this place', she cried. 'I want to go home.'

....

Episode 21. Purple Haze

In the forest, spurred and energised by the thought of being nearly there, as well as by the hypersausages they'd eaten, our adventurers reached the bottom of the hill in almost no time at all, even though the forest was much denser and more tangled on that side.

In the valley, giant prehistoric looking trees towered above the swampy ground, their canopy blocking out all but a fraction of the late evening light. The path was impossible to see, everything was overgrown with impenetrable thorny bushes.

'Oh no! What do we do now?' said Nina, pulling her foot out of a muddy hole.

'We must've taken a wrong turn somewhere back up there', said Jerry. 'Maybe we should go back up a bit and try a different path..'

'That's what you get for giving hypersausages to a dog and then following his lead', said Queenie. Captain Toast seemed to be the only one there who was unbothered by their predicament and he happily rolled around in a patch of mud.
'Maybe if we can get through this patch of thorns, we'll come to a path. There's usually paths that the animals use.. wild pigs, deer..'
'What about wolves and bears?' said Nina, afraid.
'Well, hopefully we won't meet any of those..' said Greta.
'Oh that makes me feel much better', said Queenie, scanning the dark forest nervously.
'Let's go back up a bit', said Nina. 'There was that nice place by the stream. We could camp there for the night and then try and find our way in the morning. It'll be easier when it's light.'
'That's not a bad idea', said Jerry.
'No, we're nearly there, Nina', said Greta. 'It's just across this valley. It's only a couple of miles across. When we get to the foot of Mama Bear Hill, I can find my way up with my eyes closed. I know all the paths there. We're so close now.'
'But which way, Greta? There's no path..' said Nina.
'You know what?' said Queenie, sitting down on a log and reaching for her pouch that she kept on a string. 'I think this might help..' She took out the little silver vape.
'Oh, my dad uses one of those', said Nina. 'Says it helps him relax. I can't stand the smell.'
'Me neither', said Greta. 'I wish he'd stop. It's like a baby sucking their thumb.'
Queenie laughed. 'Yeah, that's just what it's like. A pacifier for grown ups.'
'So why do you do it?' asked Greta.
'I don't know', shrugged Queenie. 'I like it. It works. Maybe I need it.'
'What does it do? I remember you offered it to me when we first met. You said blue makes you dream, red wakes you up..?'
'Yeah, and purple makes you fly', said Queenie. 'Want to try it?'
'I don't think so', said Greta. 'What even is it? What's in it?'
'Vision vapour', said Queenie. 'It's a blend of synthetic psychotranquiloids.'
'Where's it from?'
'O makes it', said Queenie, taking a puff. She held it in, closing her eyes and then breathed out a cloud of dense purple vapour. 'It's good stuff.' She proffered it to Greta.
Greta shook her head. 'No thanks.'
Queenie offered it to Nina. Nina thought it over for a bit and then

said, 'No thanks. Maybe later.'
'Jerry?' said Queenie.
'Not for me thanks Queenie. I tried it once and didn't like it.'
'Oh yeah, I remember that', smiled Queenie, taking another puff.
'Yeah, I think I'd better keep my feet on the ground.'
'How can you smoke something that O made?' said Greta. 'How can you put it in your body? Where do you even get it from?'
Queenie gave Greta a long, strange look and then shrugged. 'Shopping Village. All your shopping needs under one roof, eh', she smiled. 'You can get everything in Shopping Village.'
'That's pretty much true', nodded Jerry, reaching into his bag. 'Does anyone want some more hypersausage? I think mines wearing off.. oh I've still got a whole fruitcake here too.. does anyone want a bit?'
'I'm not really hungry. I'm allright', said Nina, anxiously scanning the forest for bears.
'No thanks. I'm not hungry either', said Greta, watching Queenie become enveloped in a cloud of vapour, her nose recoiling at the synthetic smell filling the forest air. 'What does it do, Queenie?'
'Kind of hard to describe, sister' said Queenie, looking around the forest with new interest and curiosity, as if she were searching for something hidden there. 'Sometimes it can help you find the way. Sometimes it can get you completely lost.. but I think in this case it might help, since we're already quite lost..'
'Not sure it really works that way Queenie', said Jerry.
'There it is!' said Queenie, triumphantly, standing up on the log and pointing to gap between two bushes. 'Follow me!' She jumped down from the log and marched off into the bushes. The others watched her disappear, then exchanged puzzled looks. 'Come on, it's this way. There's a path here', came Queenie's voice from beyond the bushes.
Jerry shrugged. 'I guess we'd better go after her', he said and the others agreed.
On the other side of the bush was more dense forest and thorny bushes. 'Where's the path Queenie?' asked Nina. 'I can't see it.'
'It's here, look', said Queenie, pointing ahead into the undergrowth. 'Come on..' and she disappeared again between the bushes.
'Wait for us Queenie', called Nina, following her through.
After a little while, navigating a few more gaps between thorny bushes, following Queenie's lead, they came to a proper path, fairly well trodden, less muddy and wide enough for them to walk single file. 'You see?' said Queenie. 'You were right, Greta. There was a path here.'

'Amazing' said Greta.
'Good old O and their psychotranquiloids!' said Jerry.
'Shut up Jerry!' said Queenie, and strode off ahead into the deep forest twighlight with Captain Toast at her heels.

....

The spies were led into a stone courtyard, surrounded on all sides by high walls. The metal trailer containing Sydney was taken away and the remaining prisoners were ordered to wait. The chief would be there to question them soon, they were told.

Almost an hour later, though it seemed like five hours, the chief of Malawack security burst into the courtyard. He was a tall, muscular man in his mid sixties, with long grey hair hanging loose at his shoulders and a grey, handlebar moustache. He was wearing billowing flower-patterned trousers and a faded t-shirt with a peeling picture of Jimi Hendrix on the front. He seemed very agitated and snapped at the guard at the courtyard gate, 'This had better be important! I was in the middle of watching Eastenders.' He marched across the courtyard to where Freddy, Aretha, Roop and Mabel were huddled in a corner. 'So you're the spies who interrupted my TV dinner? Let me get a look at you..'

He peered closely at their faces, one by one. Roop and Aretha stared back at him, defiantly, hoping to awaken some spark of humanity or compassion. Mabel turned her face away and clung onto Aretha's trouser leg. At Freddy, he stared very long and hard and then even longer and harder. 'I don't believe it. It can't be..' he muttered to himself.

Freddy opened and closed his mouth but no words came out. The chief of police looked at Freddy from different angles, squinted, shook his head and said, 'Well I'll be..! Freddy? Is that you?'

'What? How do you know my name?' spluttered Freddy.

'I'd know you anywhere!' beamed the chief of Malawack police, seizing Freddy by the shoulders and giving him a shake. 'Do you think I'd forget the man who married my daughter? It's me, Frankie. Don't you recognise me?'

'What? Frankie? It can't be..' stammered Freddy, his eyes wide with amazement. '..I can't believe it! Frankie! It is you! You look different with the long hair and moustache, but it *is* you! Oh Frankie, it's so good to see you! I'm so happy you're still alive. I can't believe you're here!' Freddy and Frankie both broke down in tears and the two embraced, reunited for the first time in sixteen long years.

....

Greta and friends followed Queenie along the narrow winding

path through the darkening forest. In places they had to squeeze through thorny bushes or climb over or under fallen trees, but Queenie seemed certain of the way. Every time they would come to what appeared to be a dead end, she would see a way through. The others wanted to use their torches to light the way, but Queenie said it made it hard to see the paths which were, to her, illuminated in a very faint purple glow.

'How does it work, Queenie?' asked Nina.

'I don't know', said Queenie, as much amazed and dumbfounded by this new power as everyone else was. 'Maybe my brain frequencies resonate with earth energies.. or something like that..'

'Yeah, that makes sense', nodded Jerry. 'In a hippy sort of way.'

'Don't call me a hippy, you hippy!' retorted Queenie. ' I don't know how it works, ok? But I can see the path..'

The path widened out some more. In places, it looked like some of the trees and bushes had been pruned using human tools. There were parts where logs and branches had been intentionally placed across muddy ditches.

'Can we use our torches now?' asked Nina. 'It's getting really dark. I can't see where I'm putting my feet. The way ahead looks clearer now. If we follow this path, we should get to the other side of the valley at some point..' Queenie agreed and so did the others, so they proceeded along the path with their flashlights.

They marched on and on, enveloped in the silence. The path meandered and wound through the dark forest with seemingly no direction or destination. The came to a great big oak tree with wide branches. 'Weren't we here before?' said Jerry, looking up at the tree dubiously.

'It does look kind of familiar', said Nina, walking around the tree, inspecting it with her torchlight. A while owl swooped down from a branch, flying low over their heads. Queenie screamed, piercing the silence.

'It's just an owl', said Greta. 'It's good luck to see one.'

'I'm terrified of owls', said Queenie, scanning the trees with her flashlight. 'It's my biggest fear.. apart from sharks.'

'Well, I don't think we'll meet any sharks here', laughed Greta. 'We probably just startled the owl. It wouldn't do anything to us.'

'Which way is it from here then?' asked Nina. 'I forgot which way we came from..'

Jerry walked around the tree again and then pointed down the path. 'We were going that way.'

'No, we just *came* from that way', said Greta. 'We need to go *that*

way.' She pointed down the path in the opposite direction.
'What does your compass say, Greta?', asked Nina.
Greta consulted the compass. 'Well, we need to go east, which is *that* way..' she pointed at the impenetrable wall of thorny bushes at the side of the path. 'The path goes north south, so it could be either way..'
Captain Toast ran around the tree three more times and then off down the path one way and then the other, then came back and ran around the tree a few more times.
'I can't remember at all. I was so deep in my own thoughts, I wasn't looking where we were going', said Nina. 'It all looks the same to me. Queenie, can you see the way with your magic vape vision?'
Queenie looked both ways, but couldn't make up her mind. 'I don't know. It's faded now. It must have worn off. Maybe I'll give it another go..'
The others agreed it was probably about the best option they had in that moment, so Queenie went ahead and created another cloud of purple haze.

....

Freddy briefly recounted the events of the past sixteen years, the birth of Greta and Nina, the separation between him and River and the twins after the Big Shift. Greta coming to the city a month ago and then running away with Nina back to Skyward Village to find their mum. Freddy desperately going after them, with the help of his friends from Shopping Village, hence their passing through Malawack now. Obviously they weren't spies of any sort.
Frankie described how he and Josie had come to Malawack as soon as the Big Shift happened. They'd both been followers of Humpty for years, on the internet. He was someone who'd spoken the truth when the mass media only told lies. Humpty had been warning that the Big Shift.. or rather, the *Big Hoax*.. was going to happen for years before it actually did. It was obvious where they had to go and what they had to do when it finally happened. Those of Malawack's followers who could, headed to Eastwell, the mystical heartland of the Malawack Kingdom. There they built their community and waited for their leader to return. At the time of the Big Shift, Humpty had been on the other side of the world, on tour, promoting his new channel, but they knew he'd make it back to the heartland somehow.
'Wait till Josie hears about this..' said Frankie, taking out a flip phone. He dialled five numbers. The tinny sound of the phone at the other end ringing could be heard from the phone's speaker. A click

and then a voice at the other end. 'Hello? Frankie? Is everything ok? What is it?'

'Josie, you'll never believe who's here', Frankie spoke excitedly into the mouthpiece. 'It's Freddy! You know.. River's husband? He's alive! River's alive too! You won't believe where she is.. she's just down the road.. Skyward Village! Can you believe it, Jo? River's alive! She's been there all this time.. just over the hill. Freddy's been in the city. Yeah, I know.. what can you do? At least he's out now. And one more thing.. are you sitting down? Yes? Are you ready? Josie.. we're grandparents! Yes! Twins! Two girls.. Greta and Nina. They're sixteen! I know.. it's a miracle!'

Josie was over the moon to hear all the news. She said that Freddy and his friends must come to the house and stay for the night. They could all set out for Skyward Village in the morning. As appealing as this was for Freddy, he was filled with anxiety and an urgent need to find Greta and Nina. They could be in great danger and he couldn't rest until he'd found them. They'd wasted a lot of time already with the ridiculous arrest and imprisonment.

'Sorry about that, Freddy', apologised Frank. 'It's just we can't be too careful these days. Infiltrators coming in all the time, causing trouble.'

'Why?' asked Freddy. 'What are they after?'

'What.. or *who*? They're after the King', said Frank. 'They're scared of him, that's why. Because he speaks the truth. Makes him.. let's say.. unpopular, in certain circles.' Frank gave Freddy a very pointed look, the meaning of which Freddy was completely unable to decipher.

'Is he really the king?' asked Freddy. 'I mean, no disrespect, but how did he become a king?'

'Humpty never wanted to be a king.. never once claimed to be a king.. but a king he was. A king he is. That's his destiny. To serve God, his people and his country.'

'Wasn't he an actor.. a comedian.. something like that?'

'Humpty's been many things', said Frankie reverently. 'From the bottom of the gutter to the top of the ivory tower. He's seen life from all sides.. from within and without the system.'

'He sounds like a truly incredible person', said Freddy, a touch cynically. 'And now he lives in that big orange mansion, serving his people?'

Frankie put his arm round Freddy's shoulder. 'Freddy, bear in mind, you're seeing the world from a very limited perspective, but that's ok. Everyone awakens in their own time. You know what? Let's go and meet Humpty. I'm sure he'll help us if he can.' He pulled out his phone again and called up Josie. 'Meet us at the castle, we're going to see the king.'

....….. ..

Queenie sat down at the base of the big oak tree. She closed her eyes and took slow, deep breaths, hoping that when she opened her eyes again, she'd be able to see the way. After a while she got to her feet and stood on the path, looking one way and then the other, but couldn't make up her mind. 'Everything's glowing purple', she said in a dazed voice.

'Really? Are you allright Queenie?' asked Nina, worried.

'Yeah, fine', Queenie nodded. Captain Toast came and rubbed against her leg. 'Which way is it Captain?' she said, looking deep into Captain's dark eyes. Captain Toast looked up at Queenie and then back and forth along the path. He sniffed the air, pointing his nose in every direction before settling finally on the path to the right of the oak tree. Queenie sniffed the air too. 'What's that? Oh wow.. what's that amazing smell?' she said.

'I can't smell anything. What can you smell?' asked Greta.

'Perfume.. a sort of perfume', said Queenie, as if in a dream. 'I *know* that perfume. Can't you smell it?'

'I can't smell anything', said Jerry.

'Me neither', said Nina. 'Just the smell of your vape hanging around.'

'No, it's not that', said Queenie. 'It's something else. It's like the perfume my mum used to wear when she was going out.. that's what it is. Can't you smell it?' Captain Toast started off down the path on the right, sniffing the air as he went. 'Wait for me Captain!' called Queenie. 'Don't leave me behind.' Captain Toast stopped and waited for Queenie to catch up, then the two of them led the way, side by side, sniffing the air. The others looked at each other, shrugged and then followed along with their flashlights.

....….. .. ..

Malawack castle was a grand old mansion. It had been built by the Earl of Eastwell in the seventeenth century with many additions made over successive generations. The reception hall was magnificent. Five metres high with opulent detailing everywhere, from the mosaic tiled floor to the gold leaf plasterwork of the ceiling. A double staircase made from marble curved from the centre of the hall to the upper levels. People were milling about, some dressed in colourful clothes or robes, others in dusty work clothes, some looking busy, bustling in and out of doors carrying piles of papers, others waiting patiently outside of doors.

Frankie and the four newly released prisoners headed up the stairs and up again to the third floor. Everything from there upwards were exclusively the Royal residence. Frankie, as the chief of Malawack police and as an old and trusted friend of King Humpty, was able to walk right in, no questions asked. Mabel had never been inside a royal palace. She stared at everything in awe, her mouth hanging open. She couldn't believe they were really going to meet the King.

'Do I need to curtsey or bow?' she asked anxiously. 'Do I need to call him your majesty, or your royal highness? Will he chop my head off if I get it wrong?'

Frankie laughed. 'Don't worry. King Humpty doesn't chop people's heads off. And you can call him Humpty. He's just a regular person like me or you, so you don't have to be scared.'

'But isn't he a king?' asked Mabel, confused.

'Yes, he's that too', smiled Frankie.

They were told that King Humpty was currently having an ice bath but would be out soon, so they should wait in the royal reception suite on the third floor. Two great oak doors opened into a large lounge with tall windows overlooking the fields and forests of the Malawack Kingdom. Comfortable sofas and armchairs were dotted around, set against the walls or around coffee tables. Among the artworks on the wall was a large print made up of pictures of Marilyn Monroe in different primary colours. Further along was a piece of graffiti art complete with the section of wall it had been sprayed onto, a masked rioter throwing a bunch of flowers. There was a glass cabinet displaying a white, electric guitar. Next to that was another cabinet with an old fashioned reel to reel tape recorder and a stack of tape reels inside. A black, grand piano took up one corner of the room. Along one wall was a long table, set with sandwiches, cakes and refreshments.

'Nice room', said Roop, looking around, impressed. It was a world away from the makeshift dwellings of Shopping Village.

'This is usually where Humpty meets guests and foreign dignitaries', said Frankie proudly. 'Those are some of the crown treasures around the walls. Do you see that guitar there? That used to belong to Jimi Hendrix.'

'No way!' gasped Roop, now fully amazed.

'Way', nodded Frankie. 'See those tapes there? Those are Dylan's Basement Tapes. The original tapes. Everyone thought they'd been lost, but Humpty's collectors found them and brought them back here. Don't even ask how.'

'Incredible..' said Roop, his eyes almost popping out of his head.

'That piano', said Frankie proudly. 'Used to belong to Freddy Mercury.'

'Wow!' said Freddy. 'That's really impressive. Nina would love that. She plays piano you know.'

'Does she? Excellent! We'll have to bring her here when we find her. And Greta too, and River. It's a miracle that we'll all be together again after all this time. Malawack would be the perfect place, if only we had our family around. And now we will!' Frankie said happily.

'Well, I was rather hoping I could convince you all to come back to the city with me', said Freddy.

Frankie laughed as if it was the funniest thing he'd ever heard and just as quickly became serious again. 'I think you'll find that when you know what's *really* going on in the world, you won't ever want to go back to the city again.'

....

Greta and friends made their way along the winding path through the dark forest. 'Do you think this path actually leads anywhere?' said Jerry. Nobody could say for sure that it did.

Suddenly there came a knocking sound from somewhere not too far away, out of sight. Everybody froze. 'What was that?' whispered Queenie, her eyes wide with terror.

'Woodpecker, maybe?' ventured Nina.

'Sounded more like metal on stone', said Jerry.

'Yes, it didn't sound like a woodpecker. I don't think you'd hear a woodpecker at night either', said Greta.

There came the sound again.

'It's coming from just over there', Queenie pointed. 'Hey, can you smell that? Woodsmoke.'

They all sniffed the air. There was the faint but unmistakeable hint of woodsmoke. Captain Toast sniffed the air excitedly and ran off into the trees in the direction of the knocking sound. The others looked at each other in the torchlight.

'I say we follow him', said Jerry. 'Maybe someone lives there and can tell us the way.'

For lack of a better plan, the others reluctantly agreed. 'This is just like that story.. what was it called? About the children who got lost in the woods and meet an evil witch..' said Queenie.

'The Chronicles of Narnia?' said Nina. 'That was epic. Mad ending though.'

'I was thinking of Hansel and Gretel', said Queenie.
....

After about half an hour in the royal reception suite, Josie arrived. There was a tearful, joyful reunion and another recounting of the events of the last sixteen years. Everybody ate sandwiches and cakes, drank tea, coffee and kombucha until they had all had their fill. Roop spent a long time staring at the guitar in the cabinet. Mabel played chopsticks on the piano, the only tune she knew, until Freddy could barely take it any more. Not only was the tune highly irritating, especially after the fiftieth time, it was sacreligous to abuse the piano on which Bohemian Rhapsody had been written in such a way. But Freddy didn't say anything. He quietly seethed with frustration and impatience, while doing his best to hold a meaningful conversation with his long lost mother in law. All he could think about was Nina and Greta, how he needed to get to them before it was too late and how much time he was wasting in this crazy town. They could have been there by now if they hadn't been so held up.

Eventually, after even Roop was getting slightly bored of marvelling at the priceless guitar in the glass cabinet, King Humpty arrived. He was a big, round man in his seventies with a long, white beard and eyes that sparkled with a mischievous glint from underneath bushy, white eyebrows. There was something slightly piratical about him, even in his brightly patterned silk kimono and with a pink towel on his head.

King Humpty greeted everyone with a big, beaming smile and hugs, welcoming the newcomers to the Malawack Free State. After making sure they'd all had enough refreshments, they sat down on sofas to discuss matters in hand.

Freddy once again recounted the events of the last sixteen years, sticking only to the most relevant parts. By this point, he was getting tired of telling the same story over and over again and just wanted to get out of there as soon as possible, but Humpty wanted to hear all of the details.

'What do you do in the city? Do you have a job? What's your trade?' asked Humpty.

'Well, I'm an academic.. if you can call that a trade', said Freddy.

'Of course it is. Of course it is', cried Humpty, clapping his hands. 'You trade in *knowledge*.. the most valuable of all commodities.'

'Well, I've never thought of it like that..' said Freddy. 'I tend to find that the more I study, the less I know.'

Humpty looked infinitely impressed. 'Wise words. Wise words

indeed. Deep truth, my man. What is it that you study?'

'Mainly intersectional cosmology and O-ology', said Freddy.

'Oh really?' said Humpty, leaning forward, interested. 'So you must know all about O, I expect?'

'*Nobody* knows all about O', said Freddy. 'It's the most that anyone can do to understand a *part* of O.. and even then, they might be wrong. Besides that, there will always be some things about O that no-one ever understands.. that no one ever even *could* understand.'

'You talk like an O-ist', said Humpty, narrowing his eyes and looking at Freddy sideways. 'You talk about O like it's *God*.'

'Well, in lots of ways, essentially it is', said Freddy, never one to retreat from an intellectual discussion involving his field of expertise. 'Any sufficiently advanced technology is indistinguishable from magic.'

'Arthur C Clarke', nodded Humpty. 'Great man. Visionary. But O is not magic and is definitely not God. Do you know who is really behind O? I bet they don't teach you *that* in O-ology school.'

'What? *Nobody* is behind O. That's the whole *point*', said Freddy, unable to prevent himself from rolling his eyes and shaking his head in exasperation. It was always the people who knew the least that were the biggest know-it-alls.

Humpty nodded his head slowly, thinking much the same thing about Freddy. 'So, you say you study cosmology too? What do you know about extra terrestrials?'

'What do I know about extra terrestrials?' Freddy pulled a funny face. 'Well, aside from the fact that we ourselves might be alien in origin of a sort.. deep in our genetic past at least.. I don't think there's any real evidence for the existence of aliens. That's not to say that they don't exist.. I mean, given the size of the universe, they almost certainly *do* exist in great number.. but also, given the size of the universe, it's highly unlikely that they'd find their way here.'

'Right on some counts, Freddy' said Humpty, taking a swig from a mug of cold, fermented tea. 'But wrong on others. You see, they've been among us for years.' He gave Freddy a very long and significant look.

'What do you mean they've been among us for years? Where?' asked Freddy incredulously.

'*Everywhere*', said Humpty, leaning forward again and looking left and right suspiciously. 'But mainly in the most powerful positions. They can shape shift, you see. They look just like us.. when they want to.'

'That's ridiculous', said Freddy, forgetting that he was talking to the

King of Malawack and not some mad old drunkard in a pub.

'It might sound ridiculous to you, but I swear to you Freddy, it's completely true. In my younger days.. when I played at being famous.. I interviewed everyone on my show. *Everyone*. Politicians, revolutionaries, leaders in commerce, dissidents in the media, high ranking members of the military, thought leaders, religious leaders, whistleblowers.. so when I tell you I *know* things, I'm not just making it up. Listen, I have it on *very* good authority that shape shifting extra terrestrials have been visiting Earth for thousands of years.. maybe *tens* of thousands.. but even more so in the last century. It's just a *fact*, Freddy. You can take it or leave it.' Humpty nodded with finality. The truth had been spoken and there was nothing else to say.

'Sorry, I'd need to see proof', said Freddy, shaking his head.

Humpty threw his head back and laughed a deep, belly laugh. 'The proof is everywhere, you just need to open your eyes!'

'What? Where?' said Freddy, looking around the room.

'How do you think they made O?' said Humpty, throwing his arms open wide. '*Who* do you think made O?'

'Well, the most simple and most likely explanation is that O evolved out of earlier technologies. In a sense, *nobody* made O, but at the same time it was made by all of humanity since the invention of the wheel. In another sense, you could say that O made themselves. It's a combination of all of those things. I don't think you need to bring shape-shifting aliens into it. It's quite amazing enough as it is, when you really look into it.'

'What would you think if I told you that O was created by reverse engineering secret alien technology?' said Humpty, giving Freddy another of his deep and searching looks.

'Well.. I'd have to say..' Freddy thought about what he'd really have to say, but didn't say it in so many many words. 'I'd be skeptical. I mean, really.. what would be the purpose?'

'To rule the planet of course!' said Humpty, as if it was self evident. 'Like they've been doing for years. Only, now they've almost achieved complete world domination. Apart from places like this. *That's* why they made O. *That's* why they made the Big *Hoax*.. the Big *Grift!* They even told us they were going to do it.. for years in advance. *The Great Reset*. Remember that? *The New Normal? The Plandemic?* The so-called *Big Shift* was all pre-planned, I'm telling you. Down to the last detail.'

'No, I can't believe that', said Freddy. 'You're saying that there are people.. evil people.. or rather evil, shape changing aliens from another planet.. behind O? That literally makes no sense, sorry. It would be impossible. O just doesn't work that way.'

'Have you ever heard of Plato's cave, Freddy? I'm sure you have, you're an educated man.'

'Of course. It's an alegory. A group of people are chained together in a cave, watching the shadows of a puppet show on the wall. Not being aware of the source of the light and having no conception of the world beyond the cave, they assume that the shadows are the reality itself.'

'Exactly', said Humpty, gleefully clapping his hands. 'You study and study, you learn all the *facts*.. but *where* do you get your information? *Who* feeds you your facts? Have you stopped to consider t*hat?*'

'From lots of sources, I can assure you', said Freddy, turning red in the face. They were wasting precious time.

'Have you ever heard of the *Illuminati*, Freddy?' said Humpty, leaning in very close and talking almost in a whisper.

'The secret organisation of powerful people, running the world from the shadows? Yes, I've heard of them. It's a conspiracy theory. Maybe some elements of it were once slightly, partly, a little bit true, but either way, O put an end to human corruption with the Big Shift.'

'So you've heard of them at least', said Humpty. 'That's something. Well, let me tell you, it's all true. Everything you've heard. Not only that, but they're more powerful now than ever before.'

'Well I don't know how you came to that conclusion, but if you say so..' Freddy's patience was running out.

'Not, if *I* say so. It's the *truth* Freddy and the Truth will set you Free!' There was a fire in King Humpty's eyes and he stood up from his chair as he spoke.

'O.. k..', said Freddy, not wanting to anger this mad old man who stood between him and freedom.

'What do you think happened to the *Elites* after the Big Hoax, Freddy? Where did they go? Do you think they just vanished?'

'I don't know, but I'm sure you're going to tell me', said Freddy wearily.

'They're *still there*, Freddy, my boy! While all the sheeple are cooped up in your hives, eating carbon and algae, being monitored and modified by Big Brother O.. where do you think your Musks and Gates and Bezoses are? Your Hollywood stars, your presidents and prime-ministers, your CIA, your KGB, your Mossad.. where are your Rockerfellers and your Rothschilds now? Do you know? I'll tell you.. the ones that are still here on Earth and haven't gone to Mars.. or beyond.. oh, they're on their private islands, eating caviar, drinking champagne. They're travelling the world on their yachts and in their private jets, still calling the shots.'

'Oh come on.. you can't believe that', said Freddy exasperated. 'Next thing you're going to tell me it's the *Jews* behind O, controlling everything.'

King Humpty sat down again in his armchair, adjusted his kimono and took another swig from his mug. He looked at Freddy and nodded slowly. 'Listen, Freddy', he said with infinite patience and condescension. 'Let's put it this way. I wouldn't rule anything out', he nodded significantly. 'Not when it comes to these evil reptilian bloodsuckers.'

'Oh I've had enough of this! You know I'm Jewish, right? Do I look like someone who's secretly ruling the world? I only wish I was, then maybe everything wouldn't be such a mess!' cried Freddy, springing out of his chair. 'My daughters are out there somewhere in the forest.. possibly getting eaten by wolves.. and we're here discussing the protocols of the elders of Zion?! Seriously? Frankie, Josie.. we need to get to Skyward Village. We need to find Greta and Nina.. and River.'

'He's right, Humpty', said Josie. 'We need to find them.'

'I'm sorry', said Humpty, looking crestfallen. 'I do tend to go on and on when I get worked up about something. You should have stopped me.'

'That's ok, Humpty. We love how you go on', smiled Josie, leaning over and giving him a kiss on the cheek. 'We just need to find our girls.'

King Humpty sat back and stroked his beard. 'Well, the road going to Skyward Village is the B420.. but it's full of holes. Those Northwellians really didn't like me driving my fast cars up there, did they? You'd better take the big Jeep. You should all fit in that. That'll get you to the edge of Skyward Village in about an hour.. or more like half an hour if you're driving, eh Frankie!' Humpty turned to his chief of police and grinned. 'Frankie's the fastest driver there is. He's completely mental behind the wheel. You'd better wear seat belts.'

Frankie smiled at the complement. He stood up and shook Humpty's hand. 'Thanks Humpty', he said and they hugged, clapping each others' backs heartily.

'I.. I don't understand', stammered Freddy. 'You've got *cars*? A *jeep*? How can it be? And *television*? And *telephones*?'

'By the Magic of Community, by the Miracle of Cooperation, the Power of the Human Spirit, Ingenuity, Creativity, Vision, Love.. and with Divine Guidance and with the help of the Lord God, yes, we are blessed with such things here in the Malawack Free State.. our Humble Little Utopia', declared Humpty, putting his hands together and offering up a prayer after his sermon. Frankie and Josie did the same and said 'Amen.'

Mabel, who had been silent all this time spoke up. 'What about Sydney?

'Who's Sydney?' asked Humpty.

'He's Freddy's dog', said Mabel.

'Oh, I love dogs. Where is he? Did you leave him outside?' smiled Humpty.

'No, they took him away', said Mabel, holding back her tears.

'*Who* took him away?!' cried Humpty angrily. He had strong feelings about animal cruelty. Mabel looked towards Frankie, so did Humpty.

'Sydney is a robot', said Frankie. 'It's been contained.'

'Oh I see', said Humpty, his smile turning to a frown. 'Well in that case, it's probably being deactivated and dismantled for parts. Their transmitters are very valuable.' He turned to Freddy and asked, 'What model is it?'

'Oh it's a very old model. Must be, what.. fifteen years old by now.. T13 model. I'm sure it's not worth that much at all..' said Freddy, hoping to dissuade Humpty from having Sydney destroyed.

'T13, you say?' said Humpty, now very much interested. 'T13 was a classic model. One of the best. Especially because of the signal boxes. They used old school microwave transmitters in the T13. Our clever boffins at the science institute use them in the phone system and for the MBC.'

'The MBC?'

'Malawack Broadcasting Company', said Humpty proudly. 'Two channels, MBC One and MBC Two, from 6am until Midnight, six days a week, broadcasting to the whole of Malawack and beyond! What do you think of that? They said it couldn't be done, but by God, we did it Freddy! We showed them! They couldn't shut us *up* or shut us *down* and they never will either, not while there is breath in my bones and marrow in my lungs, I'll speak the *Truth* and damn the consequences!!' Humpty jumped out of his chair and punched his fist in the air.

Freddy threw up his hands in defeat and stood up. 'You know what? Just keep it! Keep the robot and put the parts to good use. I really don't care any more. Do what you like. But I really need to go now. My daughters are out there and I need to find them.'

King Humpty nodded. 'Ok, great. Will do. Thanks Freddy. That's very public spirited of you. Rest assured, a part of your Sydney will live on in the telephone system of the Malawack Free State!'

Mabel let out a wail of despair and ran to Humpty, grabbing hold of the hem of his kimono. *'Noo-ooo-o-oo-oo!'* she cried. 'Please your majesty. Please don't take Sydney! Don't cut Sydney's head off! He hasn't done anything to you. He's a good dog, your Highness, even if he is a robot. And he's my friend.. Sydney's my friend..' Mabel began sobbing uncontrollably.

Humpty looked down at Mabel, smiled a wide, benificient smile. With the glimmer of a tear in his eyes, he patted her on the head and said, 'That's so touching, young lady. Tell me, what's your name again? I'm sorry, I know you told me before, but I meet so many people in my line of work and I'm terrible with names..'

'It's Mabel, your Majesty', said Mabel, looking up at the king and doing her best to curtsey without tripping herself over.

'Well Mabel, what you said just now is the most beautiful, the most kind and noble thing I've heard anyone say in.. in.. well over a week.. maybe even a month. So you know what I'm going to do?'

'No, what?' asked Mabel, hope rising.

'Frankie, my man', said Humpty, turning to his chief of police. 'Bring me the Sacred Sword of Malawack from over there on the wall.' Frankie nodded his head and very reverently went to bring a long, double edged sword from above the stone fireplace.

'What? No!' cried Mabel in terror and ran to hide between her parents. 'Don't cut off my head! Please, I didn't do anything!'

'Oh no, don't worry, don't be scared. I'm not going to cut anyone's head off. You have shown great courage and loyalty, also deep compassion. You have spoken your truth without fear of consequence and for that, I am going to bestow upon you the highest honour in the land. How would you like to be a Knight of the Crown, Mabel?'

Mabel looked out fearfully from behind Aretha's legs. 'I don't know what that means.. your Majesty. What's going to happen to Sydney?'

'I shall grant Sydney a Royal Pardon!' declared King Malawack, taking the sword from Frankie and holding it aloft, almost hitting a crystal chandelier. 'On the condition that Sydney is beyond the frontiers of The Free State by midnight tonight, I can guarantee that no harm shall come to him, by Royal Decree. I shall have my scribes prepare some papers bearing the Royal Seal. Are you ready to be knighted now, Mabel?'

'I don't understand', said Mabel. 'Are you going to cut my head off?'

'No, Mabel, I'm not', said Humpty, lowering the sword. 'You just need to kneel here and I put this sword on your shoulder, and then I say "arise Sir Mabel" and that's about it. Then you're a Knight of the Crown of Malawack. It doesn't hurt.'

Mabel looked up at Aretha, questioning. Aretha, shrugged her shoulders, rolled her eyes, shook her head and said, 'Sure, why not? You'd be a good knight, Mabel.'

'You shall be a *Great* Knight!' declared Humpty, beckoning her over to his side.

'Ok', said Mabel, timidly approaching him. 'As long as you don't cut off anyone's head.'

'You have my word of honour', said Humpty, standing up very straight, with the sword at his side, planted in the thick carpet. 'I shall not harm a single hair on your head nor a single wire in Sydney's robot bonce. Now if you want to kneel down here on one knee.. or two if that's' more comfortable.. it doesn't really matter.. we can get on with the ceremony.'

Freddy couldn't help but let out a groan. 'Will it take long.. this ceremony?'

Humpty smiled a huge, benevolent smile at Freddy. 'I'll do the short version. I've also got things I need to do. It's not all fun and games, being a King, you know. In fact I'm almost late for my nightly address to the people.'

'Thanks.. .. .. your Majesty', said Freddy, bowing his head slightly. This pleased His Majesty very much.

'Wow, what's that sword?' said Mabel, looking it up and down. It was almost the same height as she was. 'What's all that funny writing on it?'

'That is Elven writing', said Humpty bowing his head. 'This sword is Anduril, Flame of the West, reforged from the shards of Narsil, in Rivendell. The weapon that Isildur used to cut the One Ring from Sauron's hand and defeat him.'

'For real?' laughed Roop. 'Lord of the Rings?'

'Well, not the *actual* Sword of Anduril, that would be silly', said Humpty. 'It was the one they used in the movie. This actual sword, in the actual film. It's a real sword, not just a prop. That's something isn't it? Do you want to feel the edge on it? It's really sharp..'

He proffered to the tip of the sword towards Roop and lurched unsteadily with the weight of it. Holding out the sword, Humpty struck a noble and dramatic pose and in a loud voice declared, '*Very bright was that sword when it was made whole again; the light of the sun shone redly on it, and the light of the moon shone cold, and its edge was hard and keen. And Aragorn gave it a name and called it Arundil, Flame of the West.*'

'That's ok', said Roop, putting up his hands and stepping back. 'I believe you. Are you going to be ok with that? It looks heavy..'

'Sure, fine, no worries', said Humpty, raising the sword aloft again. Then he raised his voice and announced, '*Mabel the Compassionate, Mabel the Brave, Mabel the Loyal and True, I do hereby knight thee into the most honourable Order of the Great White Owl, to spread Truth and defend, honour and sanctify the Flag and Crown of Malawack, both here and abroad.*' Very gently, Humpty brought the sword down and tapped Mabel on one shoulder and then the other. He handed the sword back to Frankie and then shouted at the top of his voice, 'Arise, Sir Mabel and be recognised as an honourable and noble Knight of the Sacred and Royal Free State of Malawack!'

It was such an exciting moment, that everyone, clapped their hands and cheered. Freddy shouted, '*Mazeltov!*'

....

Deep in the dark of the forest, like the hapless and unwitting stars of every second-rate horror movie ever made, our adventurers followed the path towards the mysterious knocking sound. 'I've got a bad feeling about this', said Queenie. 'Maybe we should have gone the other way..'

'Well, what does your *nose* tell you, Queenie? What does the *purple glow* say?' said Jerry, rather unkindly. 'We've just walked miles along this path now.' He was feeling irritable now that the hypersausage was wearing off. He rummaged around in his bag, found his hypersausage, unwrapped it and took a big bite before offering it around. Everyone except for Captain Toast said they'd had enough for the time being. Captain Toast jumped around barking as Jerry threw him pieces of the pink gum.

Suddenly the knocking stopped. Captain Toast stopped barking and turned his face and his ears to where the sound had been coming from. A voice echoed through the woods from that direction. 'Who goes there?'

The adventurers all jumped and grabbed onto each other in fright. It was the first other voice they'd heard since leaving Shopping Village the day before and the last thing they'd expected or hoped to hear in that moment. Captain Toast barked again, his deepest, loudest and most fearsome bark. The voice rang out again. A man's

voice, something like a bark. 'Who goes there? Show yourselves! There are traps all around, so you'd better be careful.'
'My name is Greta!' called out Greta. 'From Skyward Village. My friends and I are on our way to there now, from the city. We come in peace and would be grateful for your direction. We shall not tarry and longer than necessary, for we are on a journey of great urgency.'
Jerry nodded his head, impressed. 'Well said', he said. 'Is that how people talk around here?'
'Sometimes, yeah', Greta shrugged.
There was a silence, then the voice replied. 'Very well. You got torches and flashlights? Better use them. Follow the path. Don't touch anything. And watch your step. And keep your dog tied tight.'
Jerry took a piece of rope from his bag and reluctantly tied it to Captain's collar. Captain Toast, understanding the situation, reluctantly agreed to let him. With their flashlights in their hands and with great trepidation, our brave adventurers made their way carefully along the winding, forest path.
Suddenly a face loomed out of the darkness, a person standing between two trees. A small woman, her face fixed in a scream and her arms outstretched. Queenie screamed and stumbled backwards into a thorny hedge. The others also screamed and jumped back.
'It's not real', said Greta. 'Look. It's a sculpture. It's made from wood.'
'OMJFC, it scared the life out of me', said Queenie, catching her breath. 'And it looks like my mum. That's so weird. That's all I need.. to be running into that old witch in the middle of the forest.'
'That's really weird..', said Greta, taking a closer look at the sculpture, shining her torch at it from different angles. 'It reminds me of that fortune telling woman.. remember.. the one I met in the woods when I was a girl.. the one who made me drop the berries?'
'Yeah.. in MY dream. I remember it, sure', said Queenie, still sitting on the ground, in the thorny hedge, looking up at the wooden apparition, shadows shifting across its tormented face as Greta shone her flashlight around. 'This is seriously starting to freak me out Greta. Maybe we should just quietly turn around and go back.. Or we could camp out for the night and then find a different way in the morning..'
'No', said Greta, giving Queenie a hand up. 'We're so close now. It's going to be ok. I know it is. I'll go in front.'
Further along, they encountered more wooden sculptures hiding

between the trees. Each surprise encounter giving our adventurers a fright, but each time slightly less so. In other places, seemingly random objects.. bits of pottery, stones, parts of machines, lampshades.. suspended from branches of the trees. Some clicked and clacked or made jangling sounds, others just loomed ominously in the darkness. One sculpture, which was the most intricately carved and smoothly finished, was of a woman (they all seemed to be the same woman) lovingly cradling a baby. Another was a life size sculpture of her head, with copper wire coiled all over in spiral patterns. 'Oh my *God*, what the *hell* is that supposed to be?' gasped Queenie when she saw it. 'Can we get out of here? This place is seriously creepy.'

'I think it's just *art*', said Nina. 'It's probably an artist who lives there.'

'Well, that doesn't really make me feel any better', said Queenie. 'Artists are the most crazy.'

'Well, I don't know if that's true..', said Nina. 'Not always anyway..'

'You know it's true', smiled Queenie, giving Nina a wink. 'Come on then, let's go and meet the artist..'

The path curved around a great old Yew tree. Behind the tree, an old stone cottage. Queenie gasped and stopped in her tracks, grabbing hold of Greta. *'It's the house!'* she said, her eyes wide with terror.

'The house? What house?'

'My dream house. The house, from my dream', said Queenie, pointing at it. 'It's the house from my dream.'

....

Episode 22. Skyward

There was the sound of running water coming from somewhere near the old stone cottage. The front door was wide open but inside was total darkness. Queenie was gripped with terror. She clung onto Jerry's arm and onto Captain Toast's mane. 'It's just like in my dream!' she whispered. 'It's the house! My mum was standing in the doorway there. I was standing by this tree.'

Jerry shone his torch into the dark doorway. 'There's no-one there', he said.

'We should get out of here', said Queenie. 'We shouldn't be here. I've got a bad feeling about this..'

The knocking began again. Three loud knocks. Queenie jumped and let out a scream.

It sounded like it had come from the roof of the cottage. Suddenly a white light shone down at them from behind the roof. There was someone up there. 'Wait there!' called the man in his gruff voice. 'I'll be down in a minute. Electrickery's out.. blasted stone stuck in the water wheel again. Always in the middle of Eastenders..' The banging continued for a while, followed by a crash, then the sound of gushing of water and the clatter of wooden machinery. At the same moment, lights came on in the cottage and around the garden.

The scene of dark foreboding was instantly replaced with a magical and welcoming sight. Artworks and sculptures dotted around the garden and into the forest were lit up by little spotlights in the trees, giving the scene the feel of an outdoor art gallery. Wild roses were growing around the doorway of the cottage and jasmine around the windows. Smoke was drifting from the chimney. Nina gasped at the sudden transformation and the beauty of it.

Greta looked around, her mouth dropping open as a sudden realisation dawned on her. 'This is the *third time..*' she said. 'Just like Granny Mae said..'

'Third time what?' asked Jerry. 'What did Granny Mae say?'

'The exact same situation repeated.. the first time was when we got to Shopping Village.. at Roop and Aretha's place, remember? Aretha was on the roof, fixing the windmill, then all the fairy lights came on. Then again, when we arrived at your place.. the electricity was out.. it was all dark in the shop.. Jack was on the roof.. fixing something with the solar panels..'

'Oh yeah, it was the transducer, I remember', said Jerry. 'So what did Granny Mae say? Is it a good sign? A bad sign?'

'She didn't say..' said Greta. 'She just said to watch out if it happens a third time because it's a sign.'

'Oh, well that doesn't help us very much', said Jerry. 'I guess we'll just have to find out for ourselves.. look out, here comes our destiny..'

The torchlight had descended from the hill behind the house and was now coming towards them, blinding them with its fierce white beam. Captain Toast growled and barked as the light approached. The man behind the light shouted, 'Hold your dog. Tell him to stop the barking. Tie him up to this tree, I've got cats indoors.'

Jerry did as he was told. 'How about you put down that massive floodlight a bit so we can see you?' He said to the light, covering his eyes.

The man lowered his flashlight, allowing the others see him. He was tall and very thin, dressed in clothes which were shabby and torn. His hair and beard were wild and straggly, sticking out in every direction. Despite his ragged appearance, there was a certain good humour and intelligence about his eyes and his general expression and demeanour which made him seem somehow quite unthreatening. 'Bit late for wandering about so deep in the woods isn't it, kids? Are you by any chance, lost?'

'Funny you should ask..' said Jerry. 'Actually, we are a bit.'

'We're going to Skyward Village', said Greta. 'Do you know the way from here? Is it far?'

'Skyward Village? Oh yes, I know it well. I've got many friends there, even though I don't go there much more than once a year, for the midwinter gathering usually.'

'Say, I *know* you', said Greta. 'I thought you looked familiar. You're Henry the Hermit.'

Henry the Hermit laughed. 'Oh is that what they call me? Well, I suppose if the cap fits..'

'I'm Greta.. River's daughter.. I don't know if you know her. She makes shoes. This is my sister Nina, from the big city. This is Jerry and Queenie, from Shopping Village. And that's Captain Toast. He's a good dog, you don't need to worry.'

'Oh, you're River's daughter? Yes I know her, she made me these shoes actually. They're the best shoes I've ever worn. Look at that..' Henry held out one foot. The shoe was indeed a work of art, practical and sturdy yet elegant. 'I heard she's been unwell. Lost her sight wasn't it? How is she now? Has there been any improvement?'

'What? I didn't know that. I've been away for a month or more', gasped Greta. 'Oh, I *knew* it! I knew there was something wrong. Nina.. we need to get to her.. quickly!'

'Is it far, Henry?' asked Nina.

'No, not far at all. An hour's brisk walk, if you know the way', said Henry, shining his torch into the woods. '..if you know the way, that is. A bit tricky to describe the way.. I could draw you a map I suppose.. oh but if you went wrong and took a wrong turn you'd end up in the swampland.. and if you went wrong the other way

way, you'd need to cross Devil's Drop, but the bridge is down.. I tell you what.. give me a couple of minutes to get ready and I'll go with you. At least as far as the edge of Skyward Village. I think that'll be best.'

'Really Henry?' said Greta. 'Oh that will be wonderful. Thank you.'

'Come inside, you can have something to drink in the meanwhile..' Henry led them inside. 'Excuse the mess.. I wasn't expecting visitors..'

The front door led directly into the living room of the cottage. It was a small room with a low ceiling and walls made of whitewashed stone. There was an armchair and a two seater sofa, a small side table with two chairs. Opposite the armchair was an old black and white television set with an aerial on top made out of a coat hanger. On the screen, some men jumping out of a black van, to a rousing theme tune. The picture was grainy and distorted. The television seemed alien and out of place after what felt like an eternity of wandering in the forest, away from civilisation. Henry went over and switched it off. 'Tsk. The A-Team again. I thought it was going to be Doctor Who next, but it's always reruns of the A-Team.. missed the end of Eastenders.. now I'll have to wait till next week to find out what happened to Dirty Den. Oh well. Load of nonsense anyway. Can I get you all something to drink? Some cordial?'

'That would be lovely, thanks', said Greta.

'I'll go and fetch some from the kitchen. Make yourselves at home..' said Henry, going through to the kitchen.

Around the walls of the living room were several paintings, pencil drawings and charcoal sketches, all portraits of the same woman. 'It's the woman from the sculptures', said Nina, pointing at a large painting of the woman in which she was staring, wide-eyed directly ahead, her lips pressed together into a thin line, holding her fingers against her temples. 'Wow.. that's a really powerful picture. It's like the eyes follow you.'

'Oh wow, that's spooky', said Jerry.

Greta and Queenie turned to look at the painting at the same moment and seeing it they both gasped. 'It's *her!*'

'What? *Who?*' Jerry and Nina both said at the same time.

'It's the fortune telling woman.. the one I met in the woods when I was a kid', said Greta, staring into the eyes of the woman in the painting. 'It's her. I'll never forget those eyes.'

'Woah. Are you sure, Greta?' said Nina, quite spooked. Greta nodded. Nina turned to Queenie who was staring at the painting and had turned as white as a sheet. 'Queenie. Are you allright? What is it? Who is that woman? How do you know her?'

'It's.. it's.. it's my *dream*..' said Queenie, as if in a trance, lifting a shaking finger and pointing at the painting. 'I saw her in my dream.. here.. in this place.. in my dream.. I saw here.. she was here.. it's my *mum!* It's *her!*' At that, Queenie's eyes rolled back and she collapsed into the sofa, unconscious.

Jerry rushed over to her, shook her and slapped her cheek. 'Queenie, wake up! Queenie! Bruce..'

Queenie turned her face but didn't open her eyes. 'No, mum, don't. It wasn't me..' she mumbled.

'Bruce, wake up!' cried Jerry.

Henry came in holding a tray with four glasses of cordial. Seeing what was happening, he hurriedly put it down on the side table. 'Lay her down. Put her knees up, it will send the blood to her head.' Greta and Jerry manoeuvred Queenie into a lying position with her knees up. 'Try pinching her earlobes', suggested Henry.

Jerry pinched Queenie's earlobes quite hard. 'Bruce! Wake up Bruce! *Bruce! Wake up!*'

Queenie writhed around and flailed her arms about. 'Ow! Ow! Stop it! Get off me!' she shouted, opening her eyes. 'Jerry! What are you doing? Get off my ears!' Queenie slowly raised her head and looked around. 'Where am I? What happened?' she said groggily.

Henry leaned over Queenie and looked into her eyes. 'Are you *Bruce?*' he said after he'd ascertained that she was conscious.

'Yes, that's my name', said Queenie, sitting up. 'Now maybe you can tell me why you've got pictures of my mum all over your house and sculptures of her all over the forest?'

'Amazing' said Henry, smiling and shaking his head in wonder. 'I can see the resemblance now. You're a lot taller than her, but you've definitely got her cheekbones and the same jawline. Wow!'

'Wow *shmow!*' retorted Queenie, not smiling. 'Do you mind telling me what the hell is going on here? How do you know my mum?'

Greta was staring at the picture again. 'That's definitely the fortune telling woman I met. I can't believe that was your mum, Queenie.

This is so weird. What does it mean?'

'Fortune telling woman, you say?' said Henry, turning to Greta. 'That makes sense. When did you meet her?'

'Oh it must have been about ten years ago', said Greta. 'She came through Skyward Village.'

'About ten years ago..' mused Henry. 'That's around when she showed up here. Maybe before, maybe after.. who knows? She stayed here with me for about three months and then one day she was gone.'

'That sounds like her', said Queenie. 'It was about ten years ago that she walked out of my life. I was seven years old.'

'I'm sorry', said Henry, putting his hand on hers.

Queenie pulled her hand away. 'I don't need your sorry, I just want to know what's going on. Tell me what you know, Henry. Start at the beginning and don't leave anything out.'

'Very well..' said Henry. He handed out glasses of cordial to everyone, then went to a cabinet behind the TV, took out a bottle of brown liquor and a crystal glass and poured himself a generous dram, before settling down in the armchair to tell the story. 'You know, I never even knew her name. She stayed here with me for a whole winter, but I never found out her name. She couldn't remember anything, not even her own name. I called her "Bird" because she was like a bird', said Henry, drifting off into memory.

'What do you mean, she couldn't remember anything?' asked Queenie.

'Her memory was gone', said Henry, shaking his head sadly. 'Completely gone. I don't know what happened to her. From what I could piece together, I think she was involved in some of O's implant experiments. I think that's the most likely cause, but I really can't know for sure.'

'If she was so far gone that she couldn't even remember her own name, how did you know *my* name? How did you piece *anything* together?' asked Queenie.

'She'd talk in her sleep', said Henry. 'She'd act out scenes from her life, while she was asleep. You used to feature in a lot of them. Over time, I got some understanding of some of the things she'd been through. Her dream talking is what inspired me to make all of those sculptures in the forest. I've never met anyone like her. I'll tell you, it was the strangest condition she had.. I've met a lot of

O's casualties.. refugees and outcasts from the city.. they all come through here at some point.. at least a lot of them do.. usually lost, like you.. but I've never met anyone who had a condition quite like your mum's condition. You see, she couldn't remember anything at all about the *past*.. at least when she was awake.. but she could tell the *future*.'

'Oh come on, you can't be serious!' snapped Queenie. 'You must be as mad as she was. No-one can tell the future. It hasn't happened yet. It's unwritten.'

'Well, you would have thought so, wouldn't you', nodded Henry. 'That was certainly what I believed, until I met your mum. But she could do it. She'd know when a visitor was going to arrive, or if a storm was coming, or if a tree was going to get blown down, or if one of the chickens was going to die. It was the strangest thing, I can tell you but I've got no doubt, she had the power. She could see the future.'

'That's crazy', said Queenie, shaking her head. 'I can't believe it. So what happened to her? Where is she now?'

'I only wish I knew', said Henry, sadly.

'That makes two of us', said Queenie.

'Before she left, she gave me something.. something for you Bruce', said Henry.

'What? What do you mean? I don't understand.'

'She said you'd be coming here', said Henry, getting up from his chair and going over to the little cabinet behind the TV again. He took out a small wooden box and handed it to Queenie. 'She said these belong to you and I should give them to you when you arrived. I didn't know it would take you ten years to get here..'

Queenie took the box and turned it over in her hands. It was made from dark wood and had a heart made out of some pink wood inlaid in the lid 'It's a pretty box', said Queenie. 'It's not mine though. I've never seen it before.'

'Oh, *I* made the box', said Henry. 'It's what's *inside* that she told me to keep for you.'

Queenie opened the box and looked inside. She gasped and her mouth fell open. 'I don't believe it. It *can't* be', she whispered.

'What is it Queenie? What's in the box?' the others all wanted to know.

Queenie lifted out a string of beads, all different shapes and sizes, irregularly formed by a child's hands, blackened and charred from fire. 'It's the beads I made', said Queenie, tears springing to her eyes. 'When I set fire to the kitchen, before they took me away. It's the beads I made.'

'What does it mean, Queenie?' asked Nina who was crying herself, just because this was such an emotional and dramatic moment.

'It means she came back', said Queenie, holding the beads tightly to her chest. 'It means she *came back*.' And she cried all the tears that she'd held inside for all those years.

....

Back at Malawack Castle, the papers were drawn up granting Sydney his royal pardon and free passage through the kingdom until midnight. Mabel was presented with a medal signifying her as a knight of the realm. They thanked Humpty for all his help and headed down to the castle garage.

The castle garage was a big old barn which was equipped with everything needed to repair and maintain all of the vehicles in the royal collection. Vehicles in various states of repair were scattered around the yard outside. There were cars, vans, buses, diggers and tractors. There were also piles of engine parts and stacks of tires dotted around. Frankie pointed to another barn across the other side of a hemp field. 'Over there is where we keep the really special ones. The Bugatti, the Lamborghini, the Bentley, the Aston Martin.. I'll show you around when we come back, Freddy. It's an unbelievable collection. Motorbikes too. But the jeep should be here in the workshop. It's just been in for an overhaul. Come on..'

Roop would have liked to see the collection, but it was clear that Freddy wanted to get moving. In the garage, engineers and mechanics were tinkering away under bright halogen lights fixing various motorbikes and cars. Freddy looked around amazed. It was as if the Big Shift had never happened and everything was still just as it had been, years before. 'I.. I just don't get it.' he said over and over. 'How can it be? You have *cars?* What do they run on? Where do you get *petrol?*'

'We make our own', said Frankie proudly. '*Biofuel*. See that field there?'

'Amazing', said Freddy.

'Well, this is what you get when you've got fifty thousand people working together, Freddy. And that's just here in Malawack. There are other places like this all over the country.. all over the *world*. *Lots* more. More people are waking up and joining all the time, Freddy. It's a world movement. It's a global network. You'll see.. soon enough, all the free states will join together and take back the world. Now we've got television, soon we'll have the internet. You'll see. We'll build it back better, Freddy. We won't make the same mistakes again, not this time.'

'Well.. if you say so..' said Freddy.

'You know, we could use someone like you here, Freddy. Someone who really understands science. We could use your skills, your knowledge. You could really make a difference here. I hope you'll think about coming back here with River and the girls. It makes the most sense. Josie and me, we're settled here. We're too old to move to the jungle and live in a tree and there's no way we'll go to the city and live in a hive. But *you* can move. What have you got to keep you in the city? There's a nice empty house just down the street from us.. needs a bit of touching up, but people would help out. You could move right in. When it comes down to it family is all you've got. What else really matters at the end of the day?'

'That's true', nodded Freddy. 'I'll think it over.' Could it really be that there might be a place for him and his family in Malawack, of all places? He wondered what it would be like to live in this crazy town with their mad king, their baseless conspiracy theories and their late twentieth century technology. He was surprised to discover that maybe it wouldn't be too bad. He found he didn't miss the vip, virtual reality, augmented reality. He didn't miss O. Not really. Somehow, he didn't even miss his pills. What else did he really have? Only Nina and Greta.

The jeep was there by the big barn doors, all set and ready to go. Frankie complemented the mechanics on doing such a fine job fixing it up after Humpty had recently rolled it into a ravine. He promised to take better care of it. They bundled Sydney into the hold, wrapped in a blanket. Mabel, Josie and Aretha and Roop squeezed into the back seat, Freddie and Frankie sat in the front.

Josie wanted to stop by the house to pick up some supplies. There was no telling what there would be in the way of food or home comforts at Skyward Village. She'd never been there, but had heard that it was a wild and primitive sort of place. The house was close to the edge of town, a large, mid 20th century semi-detached at the end of a pleasant cul-de-sac with a neat and well tended garden. Apart from there being no cars in the street and that none of the street lights were working, it looked much the same as any suburban street would have looked before the Big Shift.

'I won't be a minute. Unless you'd like to come in for tea?' said Josie, stepping down from the jeep. Neighbours came out from their houses when they heard the sound of King Humpty's monster jeep driving up their street. Children came out to marvel at the incredible vehicle.

'I think I'd like to get going as soon as possible, if that's ok Josie?' said Freddy. 'We'll come in for tea soon, I promise. It looks like a lovely place you've got here.'

While Josie was in the house, Freddy sat in the jeep, looking around through the windows. How long had it been since he'd sat in a car? He'd thought there were no such things any more. When had he last seen a street like this, where the buildings weren't a thousand metres tall and made out of Earthcrete? He felt like Marty from Back to the Future, going back in time to visit a vanished world. 'It's like the land that time forgot..' mused Freddy.

'It's a *remnant*.. from a world that was *stolen*. A *fragment*. A pocket of *resistance*. That's what it is, Freddy' said Frankie, sitting behind the wheel of the jeep, looking seriously ahead. 'They'd prefer to destroy the whole of civilisation rather than just let people be free.. free to make out own life choices.. free to govern our own communities. It was all completely unnecessary, Freddy. The Big *Hoax*. None of it had to happen.'

'Well, I don't know about that..' said Freddy. 'I mean, I agree, we could have avoided it if we'd just taken climate change more seriously while we had the chance, but..'

'Oh, do me a favour!' spat Frankie. 'Don't tell me you still believe that climate nonsense! There's no such thing as climate change! There never was. It was one big *psyop*, the whole thing. The biggest hoax in history. Telling us the world was going to end any minute. Did it end? Of course it didn't. They wanted to make people believe it was the end of the world.. that the climate was changing, when all the time it was *them* that were changing it. Geo-engineering, Freddy. They control the weather. They can make hurricanes, droughts, floods.. anything they want.. at the flick of a switch. They've got space lasers, Freddy. *Space lasers! They* started the fires and then said it was climate change that did it. I was born on a

Friday, Freddy, but not *last* Friday.'

'No, Frankie, sorry. There's just too much scientific evidence. Literally mountains of it, to support the Multi-Tipping Point theory. We would have crossed all of them by now if we'd carried on the way we were going. It *would* have been the end of the world, there's no doubt, or at least the end of *us*, if O hadn't stepped in when they did.'

Frankie made a curse under his breath and shook his head. 'Do you know the real reason why "O" stepped in when they did?' He made inverted commas around the word O with his fingers. 'It had nothing at all to do with climate change. Nothing whatsoever. That was just a smokescreen.'

'So what was the *"real* reason"?' asked Freddy with a sigh, raising his eyebrows sceptically.

'*Cables*', said Frankie. 'Underground cables. Under*sea* cables. Do you know anything about them?'

'Not much, I have to admit.'

'There are millions of kilometres of them, all over the world', said Frankie. 'Communication cables. Telephone cables. Internet cables. It was only when the warring factions started cutting the cables that the powers that be decided to put the *B.S.* into action. The Big Shift was never about preventing climate change. It was never about saving the planet. It was to protect the *internet,* to maintain control of the flow of *information*. That's what it was all about. *That's* why they did it.'

'They? Who is *they?*'

'Look, Freddy, if you're really interested, I can explain it all to you, but it goes *deep*. You've got to be prepared to go down the rabbit hole. A *long way* down. There are things you'll find hard to believe. Things you won't *want* to believe. Who are *they?* What are they called? You know, it doesn't really matter who they are. You could call them O, you could call them the New World Order, the Deep State, *Illuminati..* it makes no difference. It's all the same thing. Different names for the forces of darkness.'

'I see..' said Freddy, absently gazing out of the window down at a group of children who were admiring the jeep's suspension. He wondered what their world view would be when they grew up. People could be led to believe almost anything. Their reality was so different from the world Nina had grown up in, which was different again from the world Greta had grown up in, neither of which were anything like the world *he'd* grown up in. Who could tell which children would be best prepared for the world? Everything was changing all the time, always faster than the generation before. The sands were constantly shifting. 'Well, I suppose somebody must me right.. or maybe no-one is. Who can really tell?'

'The Truth will set you free, Freddy', said Frankie, turning to Freddy and giving him a serious and knowing look.

'Well, that would be something', said Freddy.

'Say.. I think I know where I've seen you before..', said Roop, leaning forward from the back seat. 'It's a long shot, but were you at a party.. like, a ceremony.. about ten, eleven years ago.. up at the big house.. the castle. There was a giant talking owl? Does that ring a bell? I think you were there.. you were wearing a huge pair of antlers and a long black robe? Could that have been you?'

Frankie turned around to look at Roop. He gave him a very long, hard look. Eventually he shrugged and said, 'Possible, I suppose. I couldn't really say.'

Josie came back with arms full of blankets. 'I packed a hamper of food, Frankie. It's in the kitchen, can you bring it? And there's a case of clothes. Some for us and some for River.. Oh I can't believe we're going to see River!' she beamed, tears in her eyes.

When the jeep was loaded with supplies, everyone climbed on board. All the neighbours came out to wave them off. Frankie turned the key and the engine roared into life. 'Ah, the internal combustion engine!' he cried. 'Buckle up and hold on tight ! It's going to be a bumpy ride..'

....

'Do you really think she could see the future?' Queenie asked Henry, as they walked along the winding path through the forest.

'Well.. let me tell you something, ok? You might think I'm just a mad old hermit, but I wasn't always. Believe it or not, I used to work in a bank. Top floor. Risk management of all things! It was my job to advise managers and investors about the risks involved in complicated financial transactions. We dealt with very large sums of money. What did we use? We used the most up to date future modelling technology available.'

'What's that got to do with anything?' said Queenie. 'And I didn't say I think you're mad. A bit eccentric maybe, but you made a cool place there. Could use a bit of a tidy up once in a while, but I get it. You just don't want to get involved with the outside world any more. Fair enough. Good for you! I don't blame you.'

'Thanks Bruce. I'm glad you understand', said Henry. 'My point is, the ability to know the future would have been very valuable in my line of work. Let's face it, it would be very useful in *lots* of situations. Why do you think O is doing so much research into ESP, telepathy, premonitions, lucid dreaming? These things are the holy grail for O. Data driven future modelling using algorithms will only ever take you so far. Some things will always remain unpredictable, even if you have 99.9% of the variables and vectors.'

'So you're saying that O is doing experiments on people to learn how to see the future?'

'Something like that', nodded Henry. 'Among other things. Look, I don't know whether your mum had the ability already and O was studying her, or if it was somehow medically induced. I just sit out here in my little place in the middle of the forest, trying to piece together a picture of what's going on out there in the world, from little snippets of information.. things I've seen and heard from the people I've met. But I can tell you this.. I *know* your mother could see the future. You're the *proof* of it, Bruce. She said you'd be here and now you are.'

'Well, if she knew I was coming, why didn't she wait for me?' said Queenie resentfully.

'I don't know, Bruce. I really don't know', said Henry, shaking his head sadly. 'Maybe she just couldn't be there. I don't know why.'

They walked on in silence for the rest of the way until they arrived at the foot of Mama Bear Hill. Since Greta said she knew the way from there, Henry said he'd return home. He'd had his fill of human interaction for the day and didn't want to chance meeting any more people.

When it was Queenie's turn to say goodbye, Henry said, 'You know, Bruce, your mum was very dear to me. I can't say I ever knew her very well, or if I'll ever see her again. For all I know, she might be dead. She might be halfway across the world with no recollection of this place at all, or how to get back here. Who knows? Maybe she'll come walking down the path tomorrow morning, as if she just stepped out five minutes ago.. as if the last ten years never happened..'

'What are you saying Henry?'

'I'm saying that I *loved* your mum.. in my own way.. even with all the limitations.. with her condition and everything..'

'Ok. That's good. I'm glad to hear it', said Queenie. She didn't want to hear about Henry's love for her mum. All she was feeling was abandoned all over again. The same old familiar pain, stirred up and brought to the surface. 'Not sure if I do, or if she ever really loved me', she added bitterly.

'Sorry Bruce', said Henry. 'I can't imagine how hard this must be for you. For what it's worth, I think she did.. that she *does* love you. It's just that for one reason and another, she couldn't be there.'

'Yeah, well, that's too bad, I guess', said Queenie, turning her face away, towards Mama Bear Hill.

'What I wanted to say is this Bruce..' said Henry, falteringly. 'You see.. here's the thing.. I never had any children of my own.. it's just one of those things.. it just never happened.. and.. well.. you haven't really got any parents.. so.. the thing is.. I just want you to know.. you've got a home here.. in the forest. You can come back any time you like. And if anything should happen to me.. I mean, when the *inevitable* happens.. death comes to us all, that much is certain about the future.. well, that house and everything in it is yours. *Me casa, su casa..* if you know what I mean, Bruce.'

Queenie smiled for the first time in what felt like an eternity. 'Yes, I know what you mean. Thank you Henry. Thanks for looking after mum too. I don't know how you put up with her, quite honestly.'

'Well, there's something to be said for having a woman around who can't remember anything you've ever said or done. She never held anything against me!' Henry laughed. 'Being able to see the future was a bonus, but the best thing was her obsessive cleaning. You should have seen the place back then. Spotless it was!'

'You chauvinist pig!' laughed Queenie with tears in her eyes, elbowing Henry in the ribs. 'So how will I find you again?'

'Oh you'll find me, like you did this time. I'm not that hard to find. Everyone round here knows me. I'm very famous, believe it or not. Just ask for Henry the Hermit.'

....

The old B420 leading out of Malawack was in a worse state of repair than any of the roads they'd ridden since leaving Shopping Village. In places, there were deep holes that looked like they had been purposefully created. In other places, floods had washed away the surface of the road. In places, big rocks had been dragged into the road as obstacles. Fortunately, with the huge tyres and raised suspension and with Frankie behind the wheel, they were able to navigate the winding mountain road at breakneck speed. 'Slow down Frankie!' cried Josie from the back seat. 'I want to live to see River and the girls.'

'What's up with the state of this road?' asked Roop, who was greatly enjoying the ride, as was Mabel, by his side. 'It looks like someone's intentionally tried to block it.'

'It's the *Northwellians*', said Frankie, slowing down a tiny bit to swerve around a rock and bounce over a ditch. 'The breakaway republic. They used to live in Malawack, until Humpty arrived.'

'Then what?' asked Roop.

'Long story.. but basically, they didn't like the colour he painted the castle.'

'What? That's ridiculous! So they formed their own separate state and destroyed the road?' laughed Roop.

'Well, there were a few more things, but basically, yes. It was mainly that', said Frankie, shaking his head as they raced through a village who's houses were all painted in shades of blue. Outside the village pub, a few Northwellians were hanging around. They all jumped up, waved their fists, hurling handfuls of mud and insults at the jeep as it drove past, with Frankie blasting on the air-horn. 'Coming through! Get out of the way!' Frankie shouted out of the window.

'Long live the King!' shouted Mabel from the back seat. She had become a staunch royalist and defender of the Crown since receiving her knighthood.

....

Greta led the way up Mama Bear Hill. The West side was steep, so they went around and followed the path up to the North side. From there, there was a good path leading up, following the stream who's source was a spring in Skyward Village. They came to an old disused road which cut across the footpath.

'We're really close now' said Greta, standing in the road, surveying the forest and the hills.

'What's that noise?' said Nina. 'Like a rumbling in the forest.'

'Oh yeah, I can hear it too', said Jerry. 'It's getting louder. What could it be, Greta? What sort of animal makes that sound?'

Greta turned her head towards the approaching sound. 'I.. I.. don't know..', she said, looking afraid.

Just then, in a blaze of high powered headlights and with the roar of a thousand horsepower engine, the jeep came swerving around the bend. Nina, Queenie, Jerry and Captain Toast dived into the bushes, out of the way of the oncoming juggernaut, but Greta froze, like a deer caught in the headlights. Frankie slammed on the brakes and spun the jeep 180 degrees and almost off the road.

Freddy was the first to get out of the jeep. He jumped down and ran to Greta. 'Oh my God, Greta. It's *you*. Are you allright? Where's Nina?'

'Dad?' gasped Greta, her jaw dropping in amazement.

Nina came stumbling out of the bushes and ran to Freddy. 'Oh dad, you came. I *knew* you would!' she threw her arms around him and cried. 'I'm sorry for running away. I'm *really* sorry. It's just.. we had a *dream*.. mum needs us..'

'It's ok', cried Freddy. 'I found you now. That's all that matters.'

A tearful reunion was shared by one and all. Nina was almost as happy to see Sydney again as she was to meet her long lost grandparents. Greta told of the news they had just learned, of River losing her sight. There was no time to lose. The quickest way was straight up, following the footpath by the stream. The supplies were divided among everyone according to what they could carry. They were happy to discover that Sydney was able to easily carry the large suitcase of clothes on his back and was very sure-footed, even on the steep parts of the climb.

They came to a tall fence made out of long, sharpened sticks and branches of thorn trees. Occultish symbols and strange talismans fashioned out of wood, string and bones hung from the fence to ward off evil. Among these objects were also pieces of robots.. glass heads on poles, mechanical legs stretched between fence posts.

'That's inviting..' said Freddy, looking ominously along the barricade.

'This it it!' said Greta excitedly. 'There's a gateway further along this way..'

Sure enough, further along they came to a tall gateway made of heavy wooden beams hewn from whole trees. Standing in the middle of the entrance there was a massive black bear standing on its hind legs. It was holding what looked like a long handled axe in its front paw.

'*What the..?!*' cried Freddy, jumping back in fright. Josie screamed. Frankie set himself into a fighting stance. Nina, Queenie and Jerry hid behind a bush. Captain Toast growled in a very threatening way. Sydney also growled a surprisingly deep and fearsome warning. Captain Toast pricked his ears up and nodded towards Sydney, impressed, while not taking his eyes off the bear.

'It's ok', said Greta. 'Wait here..' and before anyone could stop her, she walked over to the bear. She walked right up to it. It was about twice her height and towered over her, but Greta seemed completely unafraid.

'Greta, *no!*' cried Freddy, but it was already too late. Greta had walked right up to the bear and was now talking to it. No one could hear what she said, but the next minute, to everyone's amazement, the bear and Greta were hugging each other.

As it turned out, it wasn't a bear at all, but the Skyward Village night watchman, a man called Sparrow, dressed in a bearskin. Sparrow warmly welcomed everyone to Skyward Village, but put out his axe, barring the way when it was Sydney's turn to go through the gate. 'Sorry, you can't bring devil dogs in here. It's not allowed.'

'Oh for goodness sake, not you as well!' cried Freddy. 'I've had enough of this. What on earth do you think he's going to do to you? What are you people so afraid of?'

'Sorry, it's a no', said Sparrow, unmoved. 'You can tie it up here. That's the best I can do. And that's me being *very* tolerant. Ordinarily I would have chopped it into pieces with my axe by now, wouldn't I Greta?'

Greta nodded. 'Yes, you would, that's true Sparrow.'

At that, Mabel screamed 'No-oo-oo!' and ran forward, grabbing the handle of Sparrow's axe. 'You *won't* touch Sydney! As a knight of the Crown, in the name of King Humpty Malawack, I order you to let him pass! Here is his Majesty's Royal stamp and here is my badge!' Mabel proudly presented the scroll bearing Sydney's Royal pardon and her medal to show that she was a knight of the realm.

Sparrow took a step backwards, quite amazed. He looked at the medal and at the scroll with Humpty's wax seal and signature. 'Well I'll be..' he whistled. 'But it's still a no. Sorry, the robot can't come in.'

'Come on Sparrow', said Greta. 'Just this time, eh? Sydney's one of the family.'

Sparrow relented. 'All right, if you say so. Just keep it on a leash and put a bag over its head. I don't want it running around causing trouble.'

....

Sparrow had told them that they'd find River in the healing circle. She'd become very ill the day that Greta had left, deteriorating badly over the weeks that she'd been away. A few days ago, her eyesight had gone completely. Everyone was trying all sorts of things to bring her sight back, but as far as he'd heard, all to no avail, so far at least. 'Maybe you being back here will be the cure she needs', said Sparrow.

They made their way hurriedly towards the healing circle, along forest paths that Greta knew so well. She felt as if she'd been away for years, not only just over a month. People called down from their tree houses, welcoming Greta back along with her family and friends.

Soon they came to the healing circle, a wide clearing in the forest, surrounded by ancient yew trees. In the centre was a fire with several people sitting around it chanting to the rhythm of drums and shakers. A little distance away, was a low tent. Inside, the tent was filled with steam. In the centre, there was River, lying on her back on a bearskin rug, her eyes open wide in fear and pain, staring upwards, unseeing. At her head, sat a woman making circles of smoke above River's face, using a burning sage stick while muttering incantations.

The newcomers all rushed into tent.

'Mum, it's me, Greta. I'm back. Nina's here too', cried Greta, grabbing River's hand.

'River, it's me, mum!' cried Josie, grabbing River's feet. 'Dad's here too..'

'Oh River, I can't believe it's you!' cried Frankie, breaking down.

Freddy stared at the wife he hadn't seen for sixteen years, the mother of his daughters. 'River! You're here! We found you! Thank God! What's that all over your face? Oh my.. what the.. are those.. leeches?'

River put her hands out and felt all the hands on her while, through her fever, tried to understand what was happening. 'Greta? Nina? Is that really you? Mum? Dad? How can it be? Are you really here? Freddy? Did I hear Freddy? What's going on? Am I dreaming?'

'No, we're really here, we're really here', everyone said at once.

There were many tears, as you can imagine, at the reunion. Tears of joy, of course, but also tears of sorrow. How unfair could the universe be, that just when her loved ones finally return to her, she should be unable to see them? The parents she had given up for dead. The daughter she hadn't seen since she was as baby. And Freddy..

'You wait sixteen years to visit and then you show up *now*, Freddy? Seriously?' said River, sitting up weakly and then flopping back down again. 'Oh well, better late than never I suppose..' she mumbled.

'What medicines have you given her?' Freddy demanded, turning to the medicine woman who had quietly retreated the edge of the tent to allow for the surprise family reunion.

'So far, she's had leeches, as you can see.. also frog venom, mushroom, cactus, acupuncture, homeopathy, reflexology, shiatsu, light treatment, dark treatment, sound treatment, smell treatment.. well, that's some of the things.. you know, aside from the usual..'

'I can't *believe* this!' cried Freddy. 'You people will try anything and everything before you take actual *proper* medicine. It's just unbelievable. I don't know what to say.'

River shook her head weakly and rolled her eyes. 'I may be blind, but I can see you haven't changed, Freddy', she said darkly before sinking back into the bearskin rug, closing her eyes, exhausted.

'Well, it's good to see you too River', said Freddy, standing up and bumping his head on the low roof of the tent. 'I'm going outside, there's no air in here..'

Over the next hour or so, people went in and out of the tent to be with River and to greet Greta, Nina, Josie and Frankie, who stayed inside. The chanting around the fire continued. A big pot of stew was brought to the fire for anyone who wanted. Freddy slunk off to a dark corner of the woods, away from all the people and sat with Sydney who was tied up to a tree there.

'Poor old Freddy', said Jerry to Queenie, pointing over to where Freddy was huddled next to Sydney, looking like he was deep in conversation, pouring out his heart to the robot dog. 'I think he's lost it. Do you think I should go over to him and see if he's allright?'

'He's allright', said Queenie, shivering and huddling up close to the fire. 'Stay with me, Jerry. Don't leave me now.'

'Ok, I won't', said Jerry, putting his arm around her.

....

It was around midnight when Freddy crept to the entrance of the healing tent, wrapped in a shawl. River was sleeping now and the leeches had been removed from her face, the bleeding wounds they had left were covered in cloth bandages. Nina, Greta, Frankie and Josie were all sitting around her, looking on, tired, worried and helpless.

'Hey', said Freddy, putting his head in. 'Why don't you all go out and get a bit of fresh air. There's food on the fire. I want to be alone with River for a bit, is that ok?'

The others agreed and vacated the tent. Freddy made sure that no-one else was in there and that the tent's opening was closed so that no-one could see in. He took out Sydney from underneath his shawl and put the robot down very quietly next to River's head.

He put his hand on River's shoulder. 'River? Are you awake?' River mumbled something but didn't wake up. Freddy nodded to Sydney who then leaned his head towards River's. The glass of Sydney's face became a nozzle and out of that nozzle there came a fine, aerosol mist, sprayed above River's unsuspecting nose.

'What's that?' mumbled River. 'What's that smell?'

Sydney nodded to Freddy and Freddy nodded back. 'It's just some reviving spray, River', lied Freddy. Actually, it was a specially engineered protein, designed to activate DNA receptors, but this was no time for strict medical ethics, Freddy had reasoned. 'Listen, it so happens that a friend of mine came with us on this journey. We're part of an expedition of scientists actually..'

'What? Really? I don't understand..' said River, still half asleep.

'River, I'd like you to meet Dr Sydney. He's actually one of the foremost eye specialists in the world. How about that?'

'Mmm.. ok?' mumbled River, opening her unseeing eyes.

'Hello River', said Sydney in a very kind, distinguished and doctorly voice. 'Lucky I came along when I did with my dear old friend Freddy here', Sydney chuckled. 'Now if you don't mind, I'll just need a tiny little drop of this blood.. it's ok, I'll just take a bit that the leeches left, I won't need to make any new holes, don't worry, hahaha', Sydney chuckled amiably again.

'What? Dr Sydney? Where did you come from? You weren't here before..' said River, sitting up, confused.

'Dr Sydney just arrived from.. er.. from.. the base camp', said Freddy, putting his hands gently on River's shoulders to lay her down again. 'I sent for him when I heard about your condition..'

'Oh.. ok..' said River and closed her eyes again.

Sydney stood up on his hind legs, stuck out his little tongue straw and sucked up a drop of River's blood from her cheek. 'Now, let me just analyse this and.. ah yes! Just as I suspected. Foxpox! Luckily it's not too far developed and should be easily reversible. That is good news isn't it!'

'Can it really be reversed, Doctor? How?' asked River.

'Actually, very easily indeed. Just give me a minute and I'll prepare you some eye drops. That's all it will take. One drop in each eye', said Sydney expertly. 'Here we go.. almost ready.. yes, here we are.. just the remedy! Now Freddy, if you'll just help by holding River's eyelids open while I administer the drops.. there we go, this won't take a minute.. very good.. well done, River, and now the other eye.. jolly good, there we go.. and.. that's all! Finished! That wasn't so bad now was it? There, you can close your eyes again now if you like. Give them a little rub, that's it.'

Sydney's face straw melted back into smooth flat glass and Sydney sat back down on his hind legs, looking once again, just like an ordinary robot dog. River rubbed her eyes. 'What was that? It feels.. it feels like.. *something's happening!* Oh wow.. I can see something.. I can see stars.. stars.. all around.. oh! It feels good! It feels like.. light. Like light washing all over me.. Oh Freddy! It's amazing! It's wonderful. What did you do? It's coming back! I'm starting to see! I can't believe it! Yes.. yes.. yes! It's coming back! Freddy, let me see you! Oh Freddy, I can see you.. look at you! I can't believe it! I can't believe this is happening! It's a miracle. Oh Freddy, I can see again.. where's Greta and Nina, I want to see them. Where's Dr Sydney? I want to thank him. What's that next to you..is it a dog..?'

'Hello River, I'm Doctor Sydney', said Sydney, nodding his head. 'Pleased to meet you. I'm glad to see the eye drops worked.'

The scream from the healing tent resounded up to the treetops and all through the ancient forest.

....

Everyone slept around the fire that night, too exhausted to climb trees. Greta and Nina slept either side of River, tight in their mother's arms.

Freddy made his bed at their feet, keeping one eye open to make sure that they didn't catch fire, now that they were finally reunited. He hoped that River would forgive him one day for so deceitfully tricking her into taking O's medicine. Forgiveness seemed unlikely to happen any time soon. River was already convinced that she would have got better anyway without Sydney's eye drops and whatever gene-altering evil they might contain. It was Greta and Nina coming back that had cured her blindness, as far as River was concerned. And the leeches. Freddy was too tired to argue. What would have been the point? He hadn't missed arguing with River. Let people believe what they want to believe. They always do anyway, it seemed.

Jerry and Queenie shared a blanket. Jerry silently holding Queenie as she quietly sobbed into his chest. On Jerry's other side, Captain Toast was fast asleep, deep in a dream, nuzzling into Sydney's neck with his nose. Sydney didn't mind. He liked Captain Toast and besides, Sydney never really slept anyway.

....

Made in the USA
Middletown, DE
27 October 2023